THE SIXTH EVENT

J. P. Carol

ISBN: 1497596319
ISBN 13: 9781497596313

Prologue

In the year 14 B. C., deep in the Judean Desert and built into the Southern mountain cliffs that faced the Kidron Creek, was the Mar Saba Monastery. It was a sacred place where hundreds of Priests came from all over to seek isolation and seclusion to heighten their personal and religious experience. The Monastery sat North of the Dead Sea and Southeast of Bethlehem and was considered a place of religious sanctuary.

The Priests of the Monastery, or 'Hermits' as they came to be known as, would stay to themselves in complete solitude, and never interacted with each other except during the weekly prayer sessions. But one Priest who had come to the Monastery three years before to seek enlightenment, found that in many ways he was different from the other 'Hermits'.

His name was Assad.

And Assad found that at certain times, despite the isolation that the Monastery offered, he enjoyed the company of others.

And he especially enjoyed visiting the tribes that had settled in the desert to the East of the Monastery. He had established ties with them, and in turn, they considered him as their Priest, and the one that they would turn to for comfort and encouragement in times of need.

And during those times when he would visit them, he looked forward to sitting around the fire listening to the tribesmen as they spoke about their families and children, and discussing other things of interest. It was what he felt made him more well-rounded not only as a Priest, but as the humble Man that he was.

But for the last couple of weeks he had been having dreams that would cause him to awaken in the middle of the night. And for the life of him, he could never recount the dreams, but they left him with the feeling as if he was meant to do something of importance. It was a feeling that he could remember experiencing only once before, and that was when he had decided to come to the Monastery for enlightenment and growth three years before.

But this time the feeling was stronger. Much stronger.

It was a feeling that he couldn't explain, nor cast aside. But somehow he knew that he had to make the trek into the desert for the truth to be revealed to him.

So he prepared for the long journey.

In the early hours of the morning, he set out from the Monastery and headed East, crossing the Kidron Creek and out into the desert. During his days of travel, he prayed that the reason for this journey would be revealed to him so he could understand what it was that he was meant to do.

After traveling for many days, he finally arrived at the tribe settlement.

And as usual, the tribesmen were delighted to see him, and welcomed him into their tents with open arms and to share their evening meal with them around the fire. All that evening the tribesmen spoke with the Priest about many things, but still Assad had the feeling that he was to complete something.

The next morning when Assad awoke, he left out of the tribe leader's tent and walked through the settlement, acknowledging those that he passed.

"It was good to be back among his friends," he thought to himself.

As he continued to walk, he found himself leaving the confines of the settlement as he ventured out into the desert. As he kept walking, Assad felt as if there was someplace he had to be.

He didn't know how long he had been walking or how far he had traveled out into the desert. But when he stopped, he saw that the Sun had traveled across the sky and was now sitting low in the West. And he could feel the cold night wind as it began to blow across the desert sand.

It was then that Assad realized just how far he had ventured.

Assad decided to rest for a while and then he would make his way back to the village before anyone worried about his absence. He knew that spending the night in the desert without fire, proper shelter and water could mean a most certain death. As he sat down in the sand to rest, he looked around himself perplexed as to what had possessed him to wander so far from the tribe's encampment.

While he rested, Assad thought that he heard a voice calling to him off in the distance.

"Assad! Assad!" called out the disembodied voice.

Turning from one side to the other, the Priest saw no one. The desert before him as empty. Then he heard the voice as it called to him again.

"Assad!"

"Who is speaking to me?" asked Assad out loud.

Then he looked behind himself still seeing no one who could have been calling to him.

And then as he turned back around he was startled as he saw a woman walking toward him across the sand. She was smiling as she approached him, and was dressed in flowing white robes that billowed about her as the desert winds began to pick up and cast the swirling sand around her. She had shoulder length blond hair that was tucked within her hood, and her eyes were the most beautiful blue color that Assad had ever seen.

Wondering why a woman would be out in the desert alone, Assad started to rise to his feet to inquire. But before he could get to his feet, the woman suddenly appeared before him. And as she spoke to him, she gently placed one hand onto his shoulder.

And as she spoke, he noticed that she had a most unusual accent he had ever heard. Her accent sounded almost musical as her words rolled over each other, and then lightly landed onto his ear. He quickly realized that she was not from any of the surrounding lands that he was familiar with.

"Assad," she said. "It is time for you see that which is to be revealed to you."

"Have you been sent to show me?" he asked.

Simply nodding her head, the woman knelt beside him and gently eased him back onto the sand until he was lying on his back. As she knelt next to him, she gently placed two of her fingers onto his forehead.

"Sleep, Assad," she said as she leaned over him and continued to smile. "Sleep."

The Priest found that he couldn't keep his eyes opened no matter how hard he tried. Finally, giving in, he closed his eyes and slept. And as he slept, he dreamed as a full, yellow moon settled high in the blue, black sky overhead as it cast its soothing yellow light over him.

And then as the winds began to blow, the sand began to dance and weave around the two figures, creating intricate patterns as if to cocoon them within a protective shelter against the night cold.

And then as mysteriously as when she had first appeared, the woman was gone.

And Assad dreamed as he slept under the light of the full Moon.

Many hours had passed until the Sun had crept high in the sky. And as Assad sat straight up from where he had been lying in the sand, he looked around not knowing how long he had been asleep. But he could tell from the position of the Sun that it was now at least midday.

But his thoughts were not of what time of day it was.

His thoughts were of the vision he had just had while he slept.

"Such a strange place to dream of," he thought to himself. "Never have I seen such buildings as what I saw in my vision. They were so tall and massive that they looked as if they filled up the sky as far as the eye could see. And the chariots!" he exclaimed to himself. "They seemed to move themselves about without the benefit of Man or animal pulling them."

And some of the chariots Assad saw in his vision were so large that they carried multitudes of people at one time as they moved along roads that were as black as the night and seamless as they extended to the horizon and beyond. And then when he looked up, he saw other chariots as they sailed across the sky, and he thought he would fall to his knees for fear that what he was seeing was sacrilege. And the people and the manner of clothing that they wore were equally as strange to him. He could not begin to understand all of the sights that he had seen in his vision.

And then before his very eyes, he was witness to five of the most miraculous events he could have ever imagined as they occurred in places he was sure could only exist in his dreams. And then as he looked upon the sixth event, he wept uncontrollably as his heart filled with unbridled joy and he was redeemed. Yet something deep in his heart was telling him that these places were not of his time, and that they existed far beyond the borders of any land that he or anyone else had ever visited.

And it was then that he knew that all that he had seen was yet to come.

"Why is it that 'I' would have been given such a strange vision?" thought the Priest to himself as he got to his knees and stood up.

Just as Assad stood, a piece of parchment fell from his garments and tumbled into the sand.

"What is this?" he asked as he bent down and picked up the parchment.

As he looked at the parchment, he noticed that the writing scrawled across its surface was in his own hand.

"When did I write this?" he asked himself.

But before he could ponder it further, he heard voices calling out to him.

"Father!" "Father, there you are!" "Where have you been?" they called out.

As he looked up, he saw four men from the tribe settlement as they came towards him, their robes whipping about them as the wind came up from across the desert from the North.

"Here, here I am!" called out Assad as he made his way across the sand toward the men as they spotted him.

"We have been looking for you, Father," exclaimed one of the men as they approached, relieved that they had found him safe after a night alone in the desert without any food, water or shelter. "Truly, it is a miracle that we have found you," he said as he bowed to the Priest.

"I have been well watched over, my children," said the Priest as he greeted them.

"You have been gone all night, Father. We were worried," said another.

"All night you say?" asked the Priest dumbfounded as to why he wasn't thirsty and shaking with cold after spending the night in the desert without shelter. "I am sorry to have worried you," he said as he thanked them for coming for him.

As the tribesmen led the Priest back across the sand dunes toward the village, he pondered the images that he had seen in his vision, but did not understand. Amid the questions of 'why' he had ventured out into the desert alone, and 'how' he had survived the night, the Priest's thoughts were elsewhere.

He wondered where the woman that he had encountered had gone to. But as he looked around, he knew she would not be found. But he had been shown what it was that he had been seeking. And although he didn't understand it all, he knew that it was important enough for him to write it down, and that it was to be shared with all who would listen.

"Perhaps in time it will all be made clear one day," he thought to himself as he walked with the tribesmen.

After reaching the village, several of the men retired to their tents, tired but thankful to have found their Priest alive and well. But a few stayed with Assad as he sat before the fading fire as he read from the parchment that he had written upon.

As they sat by the fire and listened, Assad read aloud what was written, and when he had finished, he looked up.

"How strange!" the other men thought. "How can this be?" they asked.

But the Priest could not answer their questions because he himself did not understand it.

What he had read foretold that during the time of Modern Man, there were to be six events that were going to come to pass. Five of them would be miracles of such magnitude that they would not questioned by any Man.

The first would be the foretelling of the future by a child.

The second would be a 'taking' that would not be fulfilled.

The third would be one of self sacrifice by a common Man.

The fourth would be one of extreme heroism by a soldier.

The fifth would be one where a Man would rise from the death of disease and live again.

And the sixth was not a miracle as were the first five events.

The sixth event would be one that would cause Man to fall to his knees and reaffirm his faith, and from this, the world would be changed forever. Because true to his word, the Son will return.

"The Son?" "Whose Son?" "And where is it that this 'Son' will return from?" asked the tribesmen.

"That I do not know," answered Assad truthfully. "That I do not know."

Then Assad realized that the visions he had seen while he slept in the desert were of these six events as described on the parchment.

And then Assad noticed that there were numbers that were also written in his own hand, scrawled along the sides and across the top of the parchment. But no matter how hard he tried to understand their meaning, he found it was to no avail.

"Will wonders ever cease," he murmured to himself as he felt that his prayers had indeed been answered even though he didn't understand. "But the visions must be of some importance for them to have been shown to me," thought Assad to himself. "And I will pass it on to those willing to listen," he said as he retired to his tent.

When he awoke, it was already mid-morning, and the village was busy with activity.

As he stepped out of the tent, he left the parchment behind as he went to the edge of the village where he set about to wash himself at the well. Just as he was about to return, he paused as he once again thought that he heard someone call out his name.

"Assad! Assad!"

"Strange," he thought to himself as he looked around. "It sounded like the same voice of the woman who had called to him the other night when he was in the desert.

"Assad!" said the voice. "It is time."

"Time for what?" asked Assad as he spun around, trying to put eyes on who was speaking to him.

And then as he looked beyond the well out into the desert, there he saw the same woman who had come to him the other night as she slowly walked toward him.

"It is time, Assad," she said as she approached. "It is time to go."

"Go!" he exclaimed quickly. "I cannot leave now!" he said.

And then he thought for a moment, and then replied back to the woman.

"Yes, you are right," he said. "Perhaps I should go back to the Monastery and share with my Brothers the wonders that I have seen in my vision," he said, thinking that was what the woman was speaking of.

"No, Assad," said the woman. "Your vision will be shared through the parchment you have left. It is time for us to leave," she said. "It is time to go home."

"But....." protested the Priest as he looked back toward the village. "What about them?" he asked. "There is still much I have yet to do," he said. "They need me!"

"They will find their way, Father," she said as she gently took his arm.

"You are sure of this," he asked.

"Come," said the woman as she led Assad away from the well and out into the desert. "There are many wonders that await you, Father," she said. "Many wonders!"

And as Assad and the woman walked away from the well, he listened closely as her words sang to him, and she told him of what rewards awaited him for his steadfast faith. And as they walked toward the dunes in the East, the sands of the desert began to swirl about them as their images slowly faded away and then disappeared into the horizon.

Many years would pass, and the tribesmen would continue to tell stories of what their Priest had seen in his vision and what they thought had happened to him that day. The stories would be passed down to their children and to their children's children for years to come.

And the parchment that the Priest had brought back from the desert that night was passed on to those of his order at the Monastery. Some believed in his vision, and although they thought it was strange, they felt it should be passed on. Many others thought that he had gone mad from being in the desert for so long that night. But after much debate, the

Priests at the Monastery soon dismissed what their Brother had written upon the parchment. And over time they deemed the parchment as the ravings of a mad man and claimed it to be blasphemy.

And in that regard, they hid it from the rest of the world, with the intent that it was never to be seen by Man again.

CHAPTER ONE
Seattle, Washington

Thursday, 9:30pm

The downtown residential area of First Hill is one of the twelve districts that make up Seattle proper and is considered one of the cities' most desirable areas to live in. It was one of the first neighborhoods that had been settled in the area and is full of classic homes, amazing gardens and a plethora of churches representing the populace that resides there.

But for a Friday night in May, the streets were uncommonly deserted.

It was colder than usual in Seattle as a bitter wind blew down from the North chasing even the hardcore residents of First Hill off the streets and into their warm, comfortable homes for the evening. The skies above had already darkened as a light rain began to fall onto the deserted streets, casting an eerie, reflective glare from the moon above.

On the surface, First Hill was just as it seemed.

A quiet, idyllic neighborhood where families went about their everyday lives, going to work and to church, but not knowing that a battle between good and evil had just been fought in the shadows of their quiet city. A battle that was about to set the stage for the ushering in of the oldest prophecy known to Mankind.

Set in the middle of First Hill was St. Augustine's Cathedral, one of the Diocese's most acclaimed churches in the area. It was an iconic landmark known throughout First Hill and Seattle as its' brick steeples towered high above the cluster of trees in the area as it watched over all that it surveyed.

As the stone steps of the cathedral fanned out in front of its' stately entrance, it welcomed all who would enter the premises for prayer and blessings. But near the top of the stairs just to the right, hidden in the shadows, something was waiting. And it wasn't looking for prayers or blessings from the church.

Far from it.

It was waiting for someone it had spied who was making their way down the rain covered sidewalk in front of the church. As the lone figure of a man lightly jogged down the street and approached, the waiting figure moved itself further into the shadows to avoid detection until the moment was just right.

As a man dressed in a trench coat and no hat approached the church, he cautiously looked down the deserted streets praying he could make it before he was discovered. Even before he had attempted to make his way to the cathedral, he had to be fairly certain that he had disposed of his attackers. One thing he didn't want was to lead them to his contact at the church. But he knew that time was of the essence since he had been injured, and needed to seek help before he lost consciousness.

But just as he reached the steps in front of the cathedral, he stopped.

He felt something.

It was the same feeling he and the other Holy Warriors for the Vatican would get whenever they were in close proximity to the 'L'arginatos', or Demons that had been spawned from Hell to stop him and his Brothers and Sisters from completing their tasks. But he couldn't let on that he knew one of them was waiting for him. He had to let it think that it hadn't been detected forcing it to make the first move.

He may have been injured, but he was far from being out of the fight.

As he jogged up the steps that led to the front doors of the cathedral, he kept an eye out for any kind of movement in the shadows. The closer he got to the front doors of the church, the stronger the feeling in his gut got. It was as if someone had literally reached into his stomach and thrashed his insides about until he thought he was going to be physically ill. But along with that feeling was a sense of utter revulsion from whatever waited for him at the top of the stairs.

But he had been battling the 'L'arginatos' in the name of the Vatican for years now, and he knew how to mentally set aside the feelings he was experiencing and to move past them. It was something he knew had to be done again if he was going to survive this night.

Just as he reached the top of the stairs, the man paused and looked around. He had to make it look good.

And then from his far right, the figure of a young teenage girl slowly stepped out of the shadows.

She was dressed like a lot of the young kids dressed today in order to express their individuality. Her hair was dyed coal black and had bright, hot pink color highlighting the ends. She had several piercings including one through her nose, and was dressed in a mini skirt, a blouse and an oversized jacket, and wore combat boots with torn fishnet stockings.

As he watched her, she moved out of the shadows and moved closer to him.

"Hey, Man!" she said. "Have you got any extra change you can spare? I haven't eaten for a couple of days. Anything you got would help."

"No, I don't have any change," answered the man as he watched her intently, careful not to let her deceive him into letting his guard down. "But inside the church," he said as he nodded his head toward the front doors. "They can feed you, maybe give you a place to sleep for the night."

He had to make it think it had fooled him by appearing as a young teenage girl.

"Why don't you come inside with me," he said as he slowly continued to move toward the doors. "I'm sure they'll be able to help you."

As the girl watched him, her eyes glanced over toward the church for a moment and then came back to him.

"Naahh!!" she exclaimed. "They can't help me! But you on the other hand," she said as she slowly walked toward him. "You can do me a lot of good. Actually we can help each other."

"What do you mean?" asked the man as he watched her carefully.

"How long has it been since you've had a good 'fuck" Michael?" she asked brazenly as she smiled wickedly at him. "I bet it's been a long time,

3

hasn't it? I know the church keeps its' Warriors on a short, short leash. Com'on Michael!" she purred as she started to rub her hands over her breasts.

Right then and there he knew it was on to him when it called him by his given name.

"I'll let you take me right here on the steps in front of your precious church, Michael. Won't that be a kick?" she said. "I can give you something they could never give you."

As he continued to watch, she began to gyrate her body as if in the throes of lovemaking. Her hands had left her breasts and crept down between her legs as she lifted her skirt and started to moan.

"Michael!" she exclaimed as she lowered her head and moved toward him. "You can have me anyway you want," she said as her voice got lower and raspier.

And then he noticed that she no longer had pupils, and her eyes had turned a milky white color. Her true appearance as a Demon was coming forth as she continued to move toward him. He knew that since he was injured, his timing to attack had to be perfect, or he would be at a disadvantage that he might not be able to recover from.

"Michaaaell!!" she called out to him as she continued to move forward.

Before she could call out his name a third time, a dagger with a slightly curved blade and ancient markings on one side appeared in the man's right hand. And just as she made a quick move toward him with her arms outstretched and her mouth gaping wide, the man brought his right hand up and sliced through the air from the right to the left with his blade.

The first swing of the man's blade caught the left side of the girl's face and had neatly sliced a gash along her cheekbone from her ear to the corner of her mouth. And as expected there was no blood as the wound just hung open as if her mouth had become elongated and greatly deformed.

The impact of the hit had snapped the girl's head to the right. But before the man could readjust his stance, her head had jerked back and she was staring at him with blank, white eyes as she gave him a sinister smile.

4

"That's wasn't nice, Michael!" she rasped. "No matter what you and the others like you do, we'll possess the Prophets and keep the prophecy from coming to pass," she said as she attempted to lunge at him again.

Wasting no time as she moved toward him, the man dropped low to the ground and swept her legs out from under her. As the girl fell backwards, he swung at the girl again with his blade, but this time he found his mark. As his blade sliced across the base of the girl's neck from one ear to the other, her head seemed to simply fall backwards and then disappeared. And almost immediately, her body disintegrated right before his eyes.

And just as he stumbled and started to falter, to his left he thought heard the doors of the cathedral open and footsteps rushing toward him.

"Michael, are you alright?" called out the voice. "Are you hurt?"

Turning toward the voice, the man slowly nodded his head, and then felt himself fall to the ground as he lost consciousness.

Friday, 11am

As he woke with a start, Michael sat straight up as he tried to focus his eyes and shake the grogginess out of his head. Looking around, he realized that he wasn't familiar with his surroundings and that made him uncomfortable.

Disregarding the sharp pain on his left side, and the fact that it was accompanied by a wet, warm feeling, he frantically looked around trying to lay eyes on his weapon. A feeling of relief came over him as he saw the hilt of his blade protruding from under one of the pillows on the bed. Quickly grabbing his weapon, he placed it where he was comfortable he could get to it in a hurry, if needed.

And then he took an assessment of where he was.

It was a small room, probably nine by nine, and it had a single, square window on one wall that was covered with a curtain. Other than a small side table and a chair, there was no other furniture inside of the room.

He didn't know how he got there, but his memory of the fight he had been in the other night with several Demons was still as clear as day.

He had dealt with all of them quite handily. But at some point during the fight, he knew he had been injured.

Badly.

"Oh!" he exclaimed to himself as he looked down. "Well, that accounts for the pain on my left side," he said as he shifted his weight to his right side.

But the only thing he could piece together after the fight was that he had the gut instinct that he had to get to.....

"The cathedral!" he exclaimed to himself as his head started to clear. "St. Augustine's Cathedral!"

Now it was beginning to come back to him.

After his encounter with the Demons the other night, he knew that he had to get someplace safe. Somewhere he could find shelter and medical attention. And the only place in the area that was close enough for him to try and make it to was St. Augustine's Cathedral, in First Hill.

And then he remembered his encounter with the teenage girl on the front steps of the cathedral just before he lost consciousness. He closed his eyes and leaned back as he exhaled. No matter how long he did what he was assigned to do for the Vatican as a Holy Warrior, after every encounter it always seemed to weigh heavy on him.

He knew he was doing the right thing by eliminating the 'L'arginatos'.

"Hey, they were Demons spawned from Hell to reek havoc on Humans and to weaken their faith every chance that they could," thought Michael to himself. "They deserved to be sent back to where they came from. It was like sending a message that said their presence in our world would not be tolerated."

But it wasn't eliminating them that weighed heavy on him.

It was the fact that over the many years he had been a Holy Warrior for the Vatican, he wondered, 'Could he spend the rest of his life doing this? How long could he act like the fighting and the killing didn't affect him? Would he ever have the chance to find some kind of personal life for himself? Or was that what being a Holy Warrior for the Vatican meant?

As he pondered the multitude of questions he knew he had, it always came back to the one thing that he and the others like him had been told when they were initiated by the Vatican.

They were told, "This was a Holy war that would never end until the End of Days and the final judgment occurred. And as Holy Warriors, they were the defenders against all who would attempt to tear down Man's faith."

No matter how many times he had this discussion with himself or asked the same questions, he always came to the same answer.

Always.

Once taken, the commitment as a Holy Warrior for the Vatican was a lifetime commitment.

Just then as the door to the room swung open, a familiar face appeared in the doorway.

"Well, Michael! I see that you're awake!" said the somewhat portly man as he entered the room.

He was dressed in the garments of a priest of the church and was balancing a tray in one hand as he approached the bed.

"Father! It's good to see you," said Michael as he went to swing his legs out of the bed and attempted to stand to greet the priest.

"Oh no, my Son!" exclaimed the priest as he quickly put the tray down onto the table beside the bed and put one arm around his friend. "You are in no condition to even try and get up. If I had to guess, I'd say that you're going to be here for at least a couple of days, if not more. You were injured quite badly, my Son," said the priest as he helped Michael back onto the bed. "You need to rest."

"But I've got to report to the Vatican……," started Michael.

"I've already notified them that you're here are at St. Augustine's, and that you are safe. They agree that you need to recover before trying to leave," stated the priest. "But if you must contact them, it will have to be after you've eaten something. I insist!"

"You won't get an argument from me on that issue," said Michael as he leaned back in the bed. "I am kind of hungry."

"Good, good!" exclaimed the priest as he put the tray in front of Michael. "I know it's not anything fancy, but we have an excellent cook who, as you can see, keeps us well fed," said the priest as he playfully patted himself on the stomach.

As Michael dug into the food that had been provided, he forgot about the other evening and reveled in the calm and peacefulness being inside of the cathedral gave him. He had almost forgotten what it felt like living as a man of the cloth within the walls of the church.

No duty other than that to your God, the church and the parishioners that looked to you.

"It was a simple life then," he thought to himself as he ate his meal. "But I gave it up for a different calling. A calling where my other talents were much needed by the Vatican," he mused as he thought back to a different time in his life.

A time before he had become a priest and was a different kind of warrior. A time when he had served his country as a special opts soldier for the military. But that was a long time ago, and in a different lifetime. Now he was still in the fight, but this was a fight of a different kind. It was a fight to keep the 'L'arginatos', or Demons at bay, and he answered only to the Vatican.

As Michael cleaned his plate, the priest quietly sat in the chair on the other side of the bed and watched him finish.

"Would you like some more?" he asked.

"No, I'm good," answered Michael as he relaxed a little. "Thank you, Father."

"I'm sorry it took us so long to get to you on the front steps of the church, Michael," apologized the priest. "But by the time we realized that 'it' was somewhere outside of the church, we had to figure out exactly 'where' it was before we opened the doors. But I'm just glad that even though you were injured, you were able to handle 'it'."

"It's what I do, Father. I'm just glad I was able to get here," stated Michael.

And then as an afterthought he asked the Father a question.

"What about the others?" he asked anxiously. "Have you heard anything from the other teams?"

"As far as I know everyone has reported in here on the West coast," said the priest. "But Michael, we did lose someone last night," he said solemnly. "It was Thomas. He was caught off guard and somehow got surrounded by the 'L'arginatos' somewhere in Michigan. They found his body early this morning."

"Thomas?" exclaimed Michael as he tried to sit up. "What happened? How?"

"We don't know yet. We have a team that's gone in to recover his body. But as far as how it all went down, we don't have a clue as of yet."

"What's going on, Father?" asked Michael as he was forced to lean back to keep his own wound from breaking back open. "I can't remember when we've had so many attacks by the 'L'arginatos' before. It's like they're intentionally targeting the Holy Warriors with a vengeance."

"Like they're trying to eliminate as many of you as they can," offered the priest.

"Yeah, that's what it feels like," said Michael. "Is there something going on that you're not telling me, Father?" he asked.

"Only that I've never seen so many of them on the attack at the same time like they have been," said the priest. "It's like they've pulled out all of the stops and are coordinating their strikes with a purpose. Now what that purpose is, I haven't got a clue. But mark my words, Michael. Something is about to happen. Something…..big. And I think that the 'L'arginatos' are trying to stop it."

"Wait a minute!" exclaimed Michael as he remembered something. "The girl I fought out on the steps of the cathedral last night. She said something curious to me. At the time I wasn't in the frame of mind to think that it meant anything. But now, now I don't know."

"What exactly did she say, Michael?" asked the priest as he leaned in.

"She said something like, 'no matter what we do, they were going to possess the Prophets and keep the prophecy from coming to pass."

"Prophecy? What prophecy?" asked the priest as he leaned back trying to decipher what Michael had just said.

After a few moments of silence, Michael spoke.

"I only know of one prophecy that would cause that kind of fear in the 'L'arginatos'," said Michael as he looked at the priest.

"But no one knows when that will be, Michael. Not even the church," exclaimed the priest as he spread his hands out in front of him. "Besides, how would the 'L'arginatos' know anything that we don't?" asked the priest.

"I don't know, Father. It just doesn't make any sense," exclaimed Michael. "Do you suppose they could be referring to something that the Vatican is aware of and we're not?" he asked cautiously, knowing that there was a great deal of secrecy surrounding anything concerning prophecies that the Vatican was aware of, and didn't readily share with the public much less the people that worked for them.

"Anything is possible where the Vatican is concerned, Michael," said the priest. "I just don't know."

"Well, she was referring to something that's got them all riled up, that's for sure. And we're paying the price for it," commented Michael as he felt a sharp pain course through his body that caused him to stiffen.

Seeing that his friend and confidant was in pain, the priest stood up and reached for the tray.

"Get some rest, Michael. I'll check in on you a little later, alright? And then if you want, you can contact the Vatican."

"Thanks Father. It is good to see you," he said. "I think I might try and get a little more rest if you don't mind."

"You do that. Call if you need anything else," said the priest as he left the room quietly.

And although he wanted to ponder what the 'L'arginato' had said to him the other night, Michael found himself succumbing to the pain of his injury and decided to try and sleep. Laying his head down, he found it easier to relax than he thought it would be. And within minutes, he had fallen into a restless but welcomed sleep.

Friday, 2:28 pm

Michael didn't know how long he had been asleep, but for some reason he found himself being awakened by the oddest feeling. His head felt as if it was spinning, and all of the air in the room seemed as if it had been suddenly siphoned out. It was as if everything around him had simply… stopped. He found himself sitting straight up in the bed and frantically looking around himself for a second time in one day.

But this time it was different.

This time it wasn't about where he was as much as it was about what was happening. And although it felt as if there was no air in the room, he wasn't having any problems breathing. But for a moment, just a moment, it felt as if time itself had just stopped, and everything in existence was caught in a kind of time vacuum.

Moments later, the air in the room seemed to return to normal, and his head had stopped spinning. And for lack of a better way to describe it, it felt as if time had resumed. When he looked up, the door to his room had opened and the Father had stuck his head inside.

"Did you feel that, Michael?" he asked nervously.

"Yeah, I did, Father! What the hell happened?" asked Michael as he looked around. "It felt as if, I don't know! As if….."

But before Michael could finish his sentence, the Father completed it for him.

"It felt to me as if God himself had suddenly reached out, and for a moment, brought the entire world to a standstill."

And then the Father looked over at his friend with the oddest expression on his face.

"Michael!" he exclaimed softly as a trace of fear showed in his eyes. "I don't know why, but I feel as if something phenomenal is about to happen."

Feeling somewhat uncomfortable about what he had just experienced, but understanding what the Father meant, Michael answered.

"So do I, Father," he said quietly as he looked at his friend. "I got the same kind of feeling that something is about to happen. I don't know what it is but, I get the feeling that we may not be ready for it."

CHAPTER TWO
'The Foretelling of the Future by a Child'

(Friday, 2:30pm)

The 1st Miracle
Ciudad del Cano'n, Mexico (City of the Canyon)

As the old yellow school bus jostled and bounced its way down the old dirt road, it twisted and turned as it wound its way around the mountain. The driver, Carlos De Jesus Sanchez was looking forward to ending his long day and going home to his wife and a hot meal. But first he had to deliver the twenty some odd school children he had agreed to take up the mountain for a school outing, and then deliver them back to their village and their waiting parents.

Normally, his day involved going back and forth between the small towns and villages in the area, picking up and dropping off the locals in the area. But today he had promised his nieces and nephews who attended the local school in the village that he would take them and the rest of the students up into the mountains for a daytrip. And now that the day was almost over, he couldn't wait to drop his busload of students off and head home to his family.

As the students laughed and played among themselves, their teacher kept a close eye on them. She didn't want them to get too boisterous and unruly as to distract the driver. Going up into the mountains on the unpaved road made her somewhat uncomfortable, but now that they were heading home she felt that she could breathe a sigh of relief. All of the children were accounted for and there had been no unforeseen incidents.

It had been a good day for everyone.

As the bus continued its journey down the mountain, off in the distance the teacher could see the last turn that would bring them to the one and only bridge in their area. It crossed over the dry ravine to the other side of the valley where their town was. She hated crossing the bridge, but without it the locals would have to go further down the valley to lower ground and cross the ravine where it could take an additional two to three hours.

So she put her fear of heights aside and said a silent prayer, just thankful for the blessing of the bridge. For her people, it made the ability to travel and trade between other villages easier than it had been before the bridge had been built.

As ten year old Miguel Fernandez sat in his seat by the window, he swung his legs back and forth while he watched the trees along the side of the dirt road pass by as the bus made its downward journey. It had been a fun day for him up on the mountain with the rest of his friends, but he was anxious to get home to his family as well. For some reason, he felt he needed to be with them as soon as he could.

As he gazed at his image in the window, his small, round face stared back at him. He wasn't thinking of anything in particular, just happy to be going home. Suddenly, from behind him there was a quick flash of bright light. It had happened so quickly, that at first, Miguel thought that it had come from outside of the bus on the other side.

Turning quickly, Miguel swung himself around to see what it was that had flashed so brightly.

But as he turned, the other students on the bus were all still chatting away with each other as if nothing out of the ordinary had happened. None of the other students seemed to have noticed anything. Then he looked at the young boy sitting next to him.

"Vio usted esto?" "Did you see that?" asked Miguel quickly.

"Vio usted el destello brillante de la luz?" "Did you see the bright light?" he asked.

The young boy sitting in the seat next to Miguel just smiled and shook his head 'no'. He hadn't seen anything either.

"Pero vi un destello!!" "But I saw a flash!!" exclaimed Miguel as he quickly looked around the bus, certain he had seen something.

But no one else on the bus seemed to have noticed anything. Not even the teacher sitting at the front of the bus.

"Miguel," said the younger boy sitting next to him. "Puedo decirle algo? "Miguel, can I tell you something?" asked the boy sitting next to him.

Not waiting for an answer, the little boy leaned in and cupped his hand to Miguel's ear as he whispered something to him. After a moment the little boy leaned back.

"Ii usted tiene que decir al conductor del autobus, Ahom!!" "You need to tell the bus driver, now!" exclaimed the young boy under his breath.

Not believing what the little boy had just told him, Miguel looked toward the front of the bus.

"No puedo decir esto!" "I cannot say that!!" exclaimed Miguel as he looked back at the younger boy.

"Como sabe usted que este es verdadero?" "How do you know this is true?" Miguel quickly asked the little boy.

"Como es asi. Es asi y usted debe decirles." "Because it is so," answered the boy in a matter of fact tone. "It is so, and you must tell them."

And then the boy just smiled and said, "Bendito son los ninos que creen en el. Le aman. Relog para su vuelta. El viene." "Blessed are the children who believe in him. You are loved. Watch for his return. For he is coming."

Miguel frantically looked toward the front of the bus again, contemplating what he should do.

"Was this some sort of trick that was being played on him?" he thought to himself."

Because if it was, Miguel didn't think it was very funny.

Quickly looking back over to the young boy, Miguel was getting ready to tell him to go and tell the teacher himself when he gasped. The young boy with whom he had been speaking to only moments ago was no longer sitting in the seat next to him. Now sitting in the seat was a young girl he had recognized from his class who was about a year younger than he was.

Her hair was parted into two thick braids that rested on her shoulders and she had two red ribbons tied at the end of each braid. As she coyly smiled at Miguel, he quickly ignored her girly smile and began looking around for the boy who had just been sitting there.

Seeing that Miguel wasn't interested, the girl shrugged her shoulders and turned to join in the conversation of the other students.

"He couldn't have gotten up and moved away that fast," thought Miguel to himself as he strained to see where the boy could have gone to so quickly.

Frustrated by what he had just been told and not being able to find the boy who had whispered it to him in his ear, Miguel slumped back into his seat.

"But why would someone joke about something such as that?" he asked himself. "Truly, something such as what the young boy had told him was not something to joke about."

Then Miguel remembered the last thing that the boy had said to him. It was almost as if he had quoted a verse right out of the Bible. A verse, for some reason, Miguel felt he was supposed to repeat to the teacher.

The more he thought about it, the more he began to get the feeling that this was no joke.

Slowly rising up out of his seat, Miguel sidestepped the young girl sitting next to him and made his way toward the front of the bus.

Just as Miguel had reached the front of the bus, his teacher looked up.

"Que es ello, Miguel? Le embroman ellos otra vez?" "What is it Miguel?" she asked with concern. "Are they teasing you again?"

"No, no pienso tan. Pero el muchacho etras alli dijo que tengo que decirle algo" "No, I do not think so," said Miguel quickly. "But the boy back there said that I need to tell you something."

"Tell me what?" asked the teacher as she looked at Miguel intently.

Leaning over, Miguel quickly whispered to the teacher and the bus driver what the boy had told him. When he had finished, the teacher shot him a terrified look and without any warning jumped out of her seat.

"Que muchacho, Miguel?" "Which boy, Miguel?" asked the teacher as she looked toward the back of the bus, wondering who Miguel was speaking of.

She could not believe that any of her students would say such a thing.

"Quickly!!" she exclaimed to Miguel. "Show me who it was!!"

But as hard as Miguel tried, he could see no sign of the young boy who had spoken to him.

"But he was sitting right next to me, Senora!" exclaimed Miguel as he pointed to the seat he had just been sitting in.

Then his heart fell because he saw what the teacher also saw. Sitting in the seat next to where he had been was the young girl with her hair in pigtails

"Miguel!! What has gotten into you?" asked the teacher. "You do not joke about such things, do you hear me?" she said. "You will scare the other students!"

The teacher didn't need to mention how what he had said had already frightened her.

"Now go back to your seat."

"But Senora!" pleaded Miguel. "He was there! Truly he was! And he told me to tell you something else," said the boy. "He said to tell you, 'Blessed are those who believe in him. You are loved. Watch for his return, for he is coming.'"

The teacher gasped as her hand flew to her chest and her breathing became labored. As she stared down at Miguel, he was looking up at her with doleful eyes.

"Miguel!" she exclaimed. "You do not speak such blasphemy," she exclaimed quietly. "Now go back to your seat! Now!!"

Miguel felt he had always been an obedient child. He had always tried to respect adults and to always do as he was told. But something inside of him was telling him that this was different. For some reason he couldn't just dismiss what he had been told and act as if it never happened.

And there was something else.

Not only had Miguel never seen the young boy before, but he felt that there was something about him that was different. 'He' was different. For some reason it was as if 'he' didn't belong on the bus with the other students, but yet, there he was.

Miguel didn't understand why his teacher and the bus driver were having such a hard time understanding that they needed to stop the bus. Especially, since he had just glanced out of the front window of the bus and noticed that they were a short distance from the bridge that crossed over the ravine.

"Please!! Please!!" shouted Miguel at the top of his voice. "You must stop the bus!! You must stop the bus!!"

Hearing Miguel yell at teacher and the bus driver, all of the other students stopped what they were doing and turned toward the front of the bus where the commotion was coming from.

"What is happening, Senora?" " What is it?" "What is wrong with Miguel?"

As questions came from the students, the teacher realized this could get out of hand.

"Nothing! Nothing!" answered the teacher as she made her way past Miguel toward the other students in an attempt to calm them down. "It is nothing! Go back to your seats, now!" she said. "Miguel is not feeling himself. We need to be quiet for a moment so he can calm himself."

Then from out of nowhere, Miguel heard himself shout out as loud as he could.

"I AM CALM!! Why do you not believe me!!" he shouted. "The bridge is out!! The bridge is out!!"

Everyone on the bus froze where they were and just stared at him with shocked expressions.

Miguel's unexpected outburst had even startled him.

He didn't know where that had come from, but for some reason he had to make them understand. He could feel his face as it started to flush with heat and his breathing came faster and faster.

And then he said in a quiet, almost monotone voice, "Why do you not you believe me? The bridge is out and we will all die if you do not stop the bus."

The students panicked!

Pandemonium broke out on the bus after the students heard what Miguel had said.

The students began to scream and fall over each other as they tried to find a place on the bus they thought would be safe. And in the mist of the panic, Miguel felt himself waiver and then fall forward where he fainted right onto the floor of the bus, unable to hear the screams of the other students as his words sent them into a panic.

"Quiet!! Quiet!!" shouted the teacher as she tried to be heard over the din of the students' screams. "Children, please!! You must sit down! Sit down!!"

Then rushing to where Miguel had fallen, the teacher fell to her knees, and gently lifted his head and placed it in her lap. She was praying that he had only fainted and it was nothing more. Looking up from the floor of the bus, the teacher watched as the students' panic went into overdrive. She realized that there was no way she was going to be able to quiet the students now.

"Pedro, quickly! Pull over!" shouted the teacher to the bus driver. "Pull over, now!!"

Following her direction, Pedro put the brakes on and carefully guided the bus to the left side of the dirt road and onto the soft shoulder. As the bus rolled and then quickly halted its forward motion on the side of the road, its abrupt stop sent huge flumes of dirt and gravel into the air as it surrounded and covered the bus.

As the bus jerked to a stop on the side of the road, the teacher thought that would have quelled the students' panic. She was wrong. It hadn't. The students were still screaming, but now they were all pointing at something that was out of the window on the right side of the bus.

The teacher started to rise up and look in the direction that the students were pointing when she heard something. It was someone softly but frantically mumbling from her left side. When she turned her head to the left, she saw that it was Pedro the bus driver, and it was his voice that she was hearing.

The bus driver was sitting in his seat as he glared out of the front window of the bus. His eyes were staring directly in front of him and were as wide as saucers with the look of fear in them. A look of fear that sent cold shivers through the teacher's body. His eyes seemed to be fixed on whatever it was that the students were also looking at.

And then she noticed something else.

Pedro's left hand was tightly clutching the gold cross he always wore around his neck while he repeatedly crossed himself over and over again while he recited the Lords' Prayer under his breath.

Slowly rising up onto her knees, the teacher peered over the seats of the bus as she looked in the direction that the students were pointing. What she saw sent a shock of fear throughout her body that caused her to fall back and push herself as far away from the front of the bus as she could.

"No!! No!! No!! No!!" she wailed loudly as her fear overtook her. "This cannot be!! This cannot be!!"

But yet, there it was.

Jutting out from the other side of the valley and stretching across the wide ravine, was the bridge that had been used for years by her people. But what the teacher and the students on the bus were looking at wasn't a bridge connecting the two sides of the valley anymore. What they were seeing was the bridge as it extended out from the other side of the valley toward the side that they were on.

But then it just dropped off into nothingness.

It was as if someone had sliced the bridge in half and only left the far side intact. Everything else beyond that was just.....gone.

And very quickly it became clear to everyone on the bus that if the driver had taken the last turn in the road and had not stopped the bus when he did, there would not have been enough road for him to stop before reaching the area where the bridge used to be.

The school bus would have careened off of the road and into the ravine, taking all of the students with it.

Pedro, the bus driver paused briefly from citing his prayers and nervously turned toward Miguel who was now sitting upright on the floor at the front of the bus.

"How did you know, Miguel?" asked the bus driver in an incredulous tone as he just stared at the boy. "We all could have been killed. How did you know this was so?"

"The boy told me," answered Miguel simply. "The boy told me it was so."

And in the world today, there be Prophets among you.
Heed what they say.

The Vatican

Saturday, 6 am

As the Father approached the oversized mahogany doors, he quickly opened them and entered the office of the Eminence de Delmar.

He walked into a large opened aired space with several couches and tables set along the side, and one large, single desk sitting in the middle of the room. The room itself was decorated with various religious paintings on the ceilings and the walls and several statues precisely placed in the corners of the room. The collectable artifacts that the room contained were items that would surely be welcomed in any art collector's collection.

The Father made his way to the secretary's desk and announced himself.

"I am Father Domingo. The Eminence is expecting me," he said softly.

The slightly built man sitting behind the desk rose and bowed to the Father.

"One moment please, Father," said the young man in a quiet voice. "I will tell the Eminence that you are here."

"Thank you, my Son."

The young man turned and made his way to another double door directly behind his desk, knocked twice and then entered and closed the door behind him. A few moments later, he reappeared in the doorway and motioned for the Father to enter.

"The Eminence will see you now, Father," said the young man as he showed him into the connecting office.

Entering the quiet solitude of the Eminence's office, Father Domingo silently waited by the door until His Grace acknowledged him and told him to come forward. After a few moments had passed, the Eminence looked up from his desk and smiled at the Father motioning for him to come forward. He had his gold rimmed glasses on as he read, and as usual, they had slipped to the end of his nose where they were perched, waiting for him to gently slide them back up.

"Father Domingo. It is good to see you, my Son," said the Eminence softly. "Please sit, sit!" he said as he directed the Father to one of the chairs sitting in front of his desk.

"Thank you, Your Eminence," said the Father as he quickly moved forward and slid into one of the elaborately decorated chairs.

"I understand that you have some news for me," stated the Eminence as he looked directly at the Father.

"Yes, Your Eminence," he said. "We have a report of an event in Mexico that just happened. But this particular event is unlike the others that our Investigators have looked into. This event has one thing that separates it from the others."

"And what is that, Father?" asked the Eminence.

The Father swallowed hard before he spoke. He knew that what he was about to divulge was something that neither the Vatican nor the world was ready for.

But yet it was happening.

"Your Eminence, the child who was involved in the event that happened in Mexico, cited the phrase that is written at the bottom of the 'Manoscritto di se eventi', 'The Manuscript of the Six Events," he stated.

At first, the Father thought that the Eminence didn't hear him, and he was just about to repeat himself. And then before the Father could open his mouth to speak again, the Eminence's body slowly fell back into his chair as he simply stared forward.

And then after a few moments of silence, the Eminence spoke.

"Are your certain of this, Father?" he asked, with his voice just above a whisper. "There is no doubt? There can be no doubt!" he exclaimed.

"There is no doubt, Your Eminence," confirmed the Father. "It was witnessed by two people who were in the presence of the boy at the time," he said.

After a few more moments of silence, the Eminence spoke again.

"You know what must be done, Father," he said. "Dispatch the best Investigator we have, and they are to report back to me directly, is that understood? No one else! If this is in fact one of the events as predicted in the 'Manuscript of the Six Events', then we all must be diligent with what we do next," he said quietly.

"And Your Eminence," said the Father as he leaned forward. "If all of the other events in the Manuscript do come to pass as predicted, what then?" he asked.

"If it is so, then may God have mercy on us all, my Son!" he said. "May he have mercy on us all!"

CHAPTER THREE
'A Taking That Will Not Be Fulfilled'

Saturday, 10:30am

The 2nd Miracle
8th Arrondissement of Paris, Paris France.

L iving in the exclusive area of the Paris 8, Tilsitt district, at one of the highly sought after residences at the Hotel des Marechaux, was something that very few people would ever have the opportunity to experience. But for sixteen year old Josette Bastien, it was the way she had lived for all of her life. It was all that she knew.

It was the kind of life that only the extreme privileged would come to know.

Josette's Father, Adrien Bastien was a legend in France in his field of corporate business, making deals all over the world with other corporate leaders. And the fruits of his hard work was what had provided him and his family with only the best that money and power could buy. And that included their apartment at the Hotel des Marechaux that took up the entire top floor of the building.

The apartment had fourteen foot high ceilings with floor to ceiling windows, living and dining areas, a gourmet kitchen, and boasted of four bedrooms, each with their own bath. And along the Southern side of the building, there was a rooftop garden that only Adrien Bastien and his family had access to. The apartment looked out over at the Eiffel Tower and the Arch de Triomphe, two landmarks that were breathtaking any time of the year.

The Hotel des Marechaux residences sat off of a road that was restricted to only those who either lived inside of the exclusive area, or were invited by those who did. The restricted road was always manned twenty four hours and it's guidelines for entering the exclusive area were highly adhered to.

But none of that concerned Adrien Bastien's daughter, Josette. For her it was Saturday, and that meant that there was no school, no homework, no practicing the piano.

There was nothing that she 'had' to do.

It was her time and she was going to make the most of it.

"The weekend would only last so long," she thought to herself as she got up, quickly bathed, and then got dressed.

And for a sixteen year old girl, that meant spending the day with her girlfriends doing what they did best. And for her, that meant shopping with her Father's Black American Express card!

The maid had already set a tray of fresh fruits and warm buttered bread on her credenza while she was in the shower. When Josette came out of the bathroom, she quickly took a bite of the buttered bread, and licked her lips as the creamed confection continued to melt in her mouth.

"How wonderful it tasted," she exclaimed to herself as she reached over and then popped a ripe, deep red strawberry into her mouth and chewed it.

Yes, she knew that she lived the life of the very privileged. But she also appreciated the fact that not everyone had been afforded the luxuries of life that she had been born into. And that was something that her parents had made sure she understood. And in that regard, every year since she had turned thirteen, they made sure that she spent time volunteering during her summers with the less fortunate, whether it be through the private school she attended or through their church.

And of course, it was her Father's wish that after Josette graduated college, she would think of taking a job in his company when the time came. But for now, both he and his wife knew that as a teenage girl,

Josette had other interests on her mind that didn't include what she was going to do after college.

Her concerns mainly consisted of her friends, boys, shopping, and boys! Just like any other sixteen year old girl.

As Josette rushed out of her bedroom and down the hall she ran into her Mother.

"Josette, why are you in such a hurry?" She exclaimed as her daughter gave her a quick hug and a kiss on the cheek.

"I am late, Me're!" she exclaimed to her Mother as she headed for the front door. "I have to meet my friends! The car is waiting!"

"Josette! Do not forget!" called out her Mother. "You are to meet your Father and I at the restaurant at two thirty for lunch this afternoon. Do not forget, my dear!"

"I won't, Me're! I promise," called back Josette as she left out of the apartment and the door closed behind her.

After taking the elevator down to the basement where the secure, private parking garage was, Josette went to step out of the elevator with her earphones securely in place while enjoying one of her favorite songs. As she did, a man bumped into her as he quickly rushed into the elevator car.

"Hey Mister!" snapped Josette as she turned to give him a dirty look. "You are excused!"

But before she could even turn half way around, the man had quickly stepped in close to her and cupped his hand over her mouth and nose covering her face with a white cloth. Realizing what was happening, she had tried to fight him off but he had literally lifted her up off of the ground as she felt herself gradually begin to lose consciousness. She felt herself falling into a drugged stupor, but not before she saw a van with red writing on the side, shriek to a stop in front of where she and the man who was holding her were standing.

Within seconds, the man had lifted Josette up into the van as she felt another pair of hands reach for her and pull her into the back.

And then everything went dark as Josette lost her struggle to remain conscious.

As the side door slammed shut, the van slowly made its way through the expensive cars that were parked in the garage for safe keeping, and then proceeded to the garage entrance where the security guards were stationed.

"That was quick!" exclaimed one of the guards as he bent down to look at the driver.

"Ah, yes!" answered the driver back. "I only wish that all of our jobs were as uncomplicated, no!"

Nodding his head that he agreed, the guard pressed the exit button and waved the van through the gate and out onto the street.

⌒

Saturday 12 – noon

Inside of the residence of Adrien Bastien, the phone rang just on the hour of twelve noon.

After picking up the phone and inquiring who was calling, the maid listened intently. After a few moments of silence, she dropped the phone and quickly went in search of her employer.

Finding him in his office, the maid knocked rapidly on the door.

"Who is it, Maisene?" asked Mr. Bastien as he looked up from his desk.

"He would not say, Monsier!" she said frantically. "But he did say that it was about Josette!"

"Josette!" exclaimed the man quickly as he rose up from behind his desk. "What about Josette! What about my Daughter!"

"I do not know, Monsier! I do not know!" answered the maid.

Just as Mr. Bastien picked up the phone, his wife appeared in the door of the office and rushed to his side.

"What is it, Adrien?" she asked as a panic stricken look spread across her face. "What is happening with Josette?"

"Bon jour, this is Adrien Bastien. May I help you?"

As the man listened to the caller on the other end of the line, the look on his face went from concerned to terrified.

"What is it that you want?" he asked loudly as he looked at his wife.

"Whatever you want, I will get it for you! Please, do not hurt our Daughter! Please!" lamented the man as his head dropped onto his chest. "But I will need time to get that amount of money," he said to the caller.

After another few moments of listening, Adrien Bastien responded.

"I will do what I can! But please do not hurt her! Please!" he exclaimed.

The last thing he heard before the line went dead was where he was to deliver the money and there were to be no Police involved or they would kill his Daughter right in front of him.

As Adrien Bastien slowly hung up the phone, his wife stepped in front of him.

"Adrien! Adrien! What is it?" she exclaimed frantically as she grabbed his arm. "Please tell me they have not taken Josette! Please!"

But all that he could do was to nod his head.

Their Daughter had been kidnapped, and they were asking for a ransom for her safe return. And they made it clear that the Police were not to be involved or she would be killed.

But Adrien Bastien was not a foolish man. He had been making high powered deals with corporate people for years. And one thing that he knew was that you never go into any kind of deal without some kind of backup plan. You always cover all of your bases if possible.

So despite what the man on the phone had said, he called the Police. He told them what was happening and under what circumstances he would involve them, and that his conditions were to be met to the letter. Then he contacted his banker, and made arrangements for the money the kidnappers had asked for to be delivered to his home. And he let them know that he had been given only until Monday afternoon to get the money together.

Everything that Adrien Bastien did from this point forward was to one end. And that was to ensure the safe return of his Daughter, Josette.

Monday – 12 noon

The exchange was to take place at twelve noon, at one of the most popular tourist sites in Paris.

The Eiffel Tower on the second floor, on the walkway outside of one of the popular restaurants there.

After the Chief Inspector had agreed to Mr. Bastien's terms, it was understood that the Police could be present anywhere within the Tower, except on the walkway where the actual exchange was to take place. Mr. Bastien was to come with the money and leave it on one side of the walkway while the kidnapper stood further down on the other side with his Daughter. Once the money was verified by one of their own, Mr. Bastien was to walk the other way toward the elevator and his Daughter would be released.

Everything was going as planned.

Adrien Bastien exited the elevator and walked to the designated spot along the walkway on the right where a young man was standing. As he looked over to the left, he saw his Daughter standing between two other men by the railing along the other side. She looked disheveled and scared and had started to cry when she saw him walking toward her.

It took everything he had to control the urge to just rush over and beat the hell out of these men who dared to threaten his family. But he knew that he couldn't risk doing anything that would cause them to do harm to his Daughter. Because if everything went as he had planned, once the exchange was completed and his Daughter was safe, there was no way these men were going to get off of the Tower before being apprehended by the Police.

He had made sure of that.

Walking along the right had side of the walkway with the briefcase grasped firmly in his hand, Adrien Bastien approached the young man who was waiting for him.

Without any hesitancy the young man addressed him

"Is it all there?" he asked gruffly as he stared at the man. "Because if it is not, your Daughter is dead, do you hear me?"

Adrien Bastien simply nodded his head that he understood.

The young man then grabbed the briefcase and popped it open as he turned away from the tourists that were milling about on the walkway. As he flipped through the bundled stacks of money making a quick assessment of what was inside of the briefcase, he kept a close eye on Adrien Bastien.

Everything was going as planned until an off duty Police Officer who was also visiting the landmark with his family, happened to pass by the two men who were holding the young girl between them. He just happened to see one of the kidnapper's gun as he held it against their victim.

Not knowing what was happening, he escorted his family further down the walkway, and then returned to where the two men were standing. Once the off duty Police Officer approached the men who were holding the girl and announced himself as an Officer of the law, as far as the kidnappers were concerned, all bets were off.

"It is a trap! It is a trap!" called out one of the men holding the girl. "Run, Marciel! Run!"

Just as the man yelled, he kicked out one of the panels that was closest to him and grabbed the girl.

"No! No! Please don't!" screamed the girl as she tried to grab a hold of the side railing.

But it was too late.

To the horror of the tourists watching and the girl's Father, the man had grabbed the girl by her hair and had literally flung her off of the walkway ramp, screaming as she fell off of the Tower.

At first a deafening silence swept the walkway as the people watching couldn't believe what they had just seen. And then moments later when reality had sunk in, everyone on the platform began to run in all directions as they screamed at what they had just witnessed. Even the kidnappers took flight when they realized that something had gone terribly wrong with their plan.

Adrien Bastien could only stand there in shock as he saw his teenage Daughter being flung off of the walkway to her death. His mind had literally shut down as he fell to his knees and wept like a child.

Tourists were milling about on the ground level below the Tower, unaware of what had just transpired above on the second floor. All they heard was a loud crashing sound as they watched the body of the young girl bounce off of the roof of the first floor, and then smash into the ground at the base of the Tower.

The impact of Josette Bastien's body hitting the ground was so loud, it sounded like a water ball exploding as dirt and bits of concrete billowed upward.

People ran in all directions as they screamed.

"Oh, My God! What happened?" "What was it that fell?"

As the dust settled, people began to gather around the area of the impact, trying to see what they could as they continued to ask questions. Questions that were being asked that no one could answer until they saw what had fallen from above.

CHAPTER FOUR
'Self Sacrifice By a Common Man'

(Thursday, 6:00pm)

The 3rd Miracle
Los Angeles, California

As Benjamin Warren headed home, he guided his car onto the 101 freeway and headed North. It had been a long and tiring day and he wasn't looking forward to the drive home in LA traffic. And with traffic the way it was he figured that it would take him another thirty to forty minutes just to get to his turn off. But once he got off the freeway and out of the late rush hour traffic, he knew that he should have an almost straight shot home with very little traffic after that.

So for the time being, he focused on his family and spending time with them once he got home. And that above everything else helped to ease the long drive home. It was six forty by the time he got to his exit and turned the car toward the off ramp.

"Not too bad," he thought to himself as he glanced at the clock. "Not too bad at all."

Especially considering the two accidents he had passed earlier on the freeway. And because neither of the two 'fender benders' seemed to snarl up traffic any more than usual, he would take that as a good sign.

As he turned right off of the ramp, he headed for La Sienta Blvd, turned right and then two miles later, he turned left onto Calienta Drive. Now all he had to do was to take a straight shot down Calienta for about ten miles, and he would be at the housing development where five years ago, he and his wife purchased their dream home.

"Not bad for a salesman," he thought to himself as he drove through the upscale, middle class area of Los Angeles. "Not too bad at all."

And he wasn't just any salesman, either.

No.

He had made enough sales in the last quarter for his company to move him above and beyond all of the other salespeople he worked with. And that honor had gained him a very generous bonus, not to mention the tile of 'Salesperson of the Year'. He had a lot to be proud of and couldn't wait to share it with his family. And with that thought in mind, he picked up his speed, anxious to be among loved ones.

He was within five miles of his turn off of Calienta when he noticed that the fog was rolling in early as it crept lazily across the paved road. Of all the things, that was the only thing he didn't like about the area where they lived.

The fog.

Around this time of the year it would rise up and blanket the entire area without any warning, which made it difficult to navigate the turns. So he eased his foot up off the gas pedal and slowed the car down to a safe twenty five miles an hour.

He had just passed the sign showing that the development of Caliente Estates was three miles ahead on the right, when suddenly for no reason, he eased up on the gas pedal and pulled over to the right side of the road. As he stopped the car and turned it off, he just sat there for a minute.

"What the Hell?" he exclaimed as he sat behind the wheel of the car, stymied as to why he had pulled over to the side of the road. "Why did I do that?" he asked himself.

And then from out of nowhere a voice calmly answered him.

"Wait. Just wait."

"Wait??" Benjamin Warren asked himself as he looked around, not sure if he was answering himself or someone else he couldn't see. "Wait for what?"

Before he could ponder the question any further, he saw two head-lights off in the distance on the other side of the road as they slowly came toward him. It appeared that the car was having mechanical trouble as the driver of the other car carefully maneuvered their vehicle down the fog covered road, when the voice spoke to Benjamin again.

"Get out and go back to the sign, Benjamin. Now!"

Without hesitation, Benjamin Warren slowly opened his door and stepped out of the car onto the soft shoulder of the road. He closed his door, turned and walked back to where the sign he had seen only moments before was. As he walked, his shoes made a hollow, grinding sound in the gravel with each step that he took.

When asked later, why he followed the directions of the voice of someone he didn't know and couldn't see, he would respond simply, "Have you ever had the feeling that what you were about to do, was the right thing?" he would ask. "That's why I did it," he would say. "I just felt as if I was supposed to go back."

As Benjamin Warren walked along the soft shoulder of the road back toward the sign, he hadn't noticed that there was another pair of lights further off in the distance coming up fast behind the first car. If he had, he would have realized that not only was the vehicle moving too fast on the road for the foggy conditions, but that from the height and the size of the lights of the oncoming vehicle, it wasn't a car at all.

It was a semi-truck and it was coming fast.

As Benjamin Warren reached the sign, he turned just as the first car that was slowly maneuvering down the fog shrouded road passed. Just as it passed where he was standing, it continued to make odd noises as if the engine had now begun to stall. Then both the headlights and tail-lights went out and the car stopped.

"Now, Benjamin" said the disembodied voice calmly. "Now!"

Benjamin Warren picked up his right foot and stepped out onto the road, and then moved his left foot forward as he went toward the now stalled car sitting in the middle of the road.

The woman inside of the car was frantically trying to turn the engine over and restart it, but all the car did was to make a straining, high pitched sound as if someone had dragged a piece of metal across a piece of glass over and over again. When she looked up, she was startled by Benjamin Warren's sudden appearance at her side of the car. At first she let out a quick high pitched yelp, not knowing where he had come from, or what his intentions were.

But after that, everything happened almost instantaneously.

Both the woman in the car, and Benjamin Warren who was still standing at the side by the drivers' door, turned at the same time as they were suddenly bathed in the bright headlights of an eighteen wheeler as it barreled down the road and came up behind them.

The woman in the car emitted a loud high pitched scream, seeing only the silver grill of the semi-truck as it glinted from behind the bright lights as the truck was upon them.

A split second before, she hadn't noticed that the man who had appeared unexpectantly beside her car, had reached for the handle of the car door and had literally ripped it off of its' hinges sending it flying off in the darkness. And with his right hand, Benjamin Warren had reached in, ripped the seat belt off of the woman and pulled her out of the driver's seat.

As she felt herself being pulled out of the driver's seat by the unknown man, he pulled her to him as he turned his back toward the oncoming semi and knelt down onto the ground next to the car as he covered her body with his just as the truck was upon them.

As the truck driver looked ahead over the fog shrouded road, he thought he saw a shadow in the road just ahead of him beyond the headlights. But by the time the headlights' glare had bounced off of the stalled car in the road, it was too late.

"Oh God!!" screamed the truck driver as he slammed on his brakes as the image of the stalled car came into view.

He could only pray that there was no one inside. Then he saw two people as they turned and knelt next to the side of the car.

"Noooo!!!!!" his mind screamed as the realization of what was about to happen hit him. "Oh God, Nooo!!!"

As the woman felt herself fall onto the concrete road with the man on top of her, she heard it.

First it was the screeching sounds of the brakes of the semi as the driver tried to stop when the image of the stalled car sitting in the middle of the road with no lights came into view through the fog. And then the most horrific sound she had ever heard echoed through the night as the semi-truck slammed into her car demolishing it.

As the semi-truck's brakes locked, it skidded along the side of the road as its tires peeled off and the burnt smell of rubber filled the air. A little more than a half of mile from where the woman's car had first stalled, the eighteen wheel semi slid along the concrete road and then careened onto the soft shoulder, casting dirt and gravel into the air in huge clouds before it came to a stop. But not before its trailer had fish-tailed and swung itself around to the left, flipped over and then rolled as it disconnected from the truck.

Even with the brakes applied, the sound of the eighteen wheel semi hitting the car was deafening. The impact carried the debris of what was left of the car at least a half a mile down the road where the truck finally came to a stop. After the truck had come to a full stop, the driver just sat in his seat gripping the wheel until his knuckles hurt.

He couldn't believe what had just happened. He couldn't believe he had just hit a car.

"And Oh God!" his mind screamed. "Those people next to the car! Those people….." he cried.

His body heaved with emotion as the realization hit him. He couldn't see their faces because they were huddled on the ground, but he saw their bodies as the front of the truck rolled right through them.

Trying to compose himself, the driver opened his door and stepped down out of the truck. Parts of metal, glass and other debris were spread all over the road. What had been a car were now unrecognizable pieces of scrap metal and pieces of upholstery and nothing more. As he looked around, he realized that he himself had dodged a bullet. His trailer was now on its side as it blocked part of the road about a fourth of a mile down from where his truck had come to a stop. Right then and there he knew it could have been worse.

Much worse.

If the trailer hadn't become disconnected from the truck when it rolled, it could have dragged the truck and him with it. And if that had happened, he knew he probably wouldn't be standing where he was right now.

Then he thought of the two people he had seen crouched on the ground when his truck hit the car.

"Oh God! Oh God, forgive me!" he said out loud as he shakily ran back up the road to where the initial impact had occurred.

As he sidestepped pieces of metal and remnants of what had been parts of the interior of the car, he became frantic. He didn't know if he could do this, but he knew he had to see if perhaps, just perhaps he could see where the impact had thrown the two people he had hit.

As he walked he heard sirens off in the distance as fire trucks and ambulances made their way to the scene. It was obvious that the sound of his semi hitting the car were too loud and horrendous for the residents of the neighborhood to have mistaken it for anything else but a terrible, horrific accident.

When he came to where the initial impact had occurred, he paused. The smell of gasoline stung his nostrils and caused his eyes to water as he tried to make sense of everything. He couldn't believe that this was happening. Then he saw the shadow of the bodies of the two people he had hit. They were still in the middle of the road among the debris, tightly hunched together as they had been when he had first seen them.

He paused not sure he could do this. He wasn't sure he would be able to look at how his truck had maimed and tore apart the two people he had hit. But for some reason he had to look at what he had done.

He had to see.

Just as he got to where the bodies were, he could hear the ambulance and fire trucks as they pulled up. He could hear voices and could see the lights flashing behind him as they created weird dancing shadows in the darkness around him.

But he wasn't focusing on them. For some unknown, morbid reason, he had to see.

Then he heard a disembodied voice from behind him call out, almost bringing him out of his trance.

"Sir!! Sir, are you alright? Are you hurt?? Is anyone else hurt?"

"Was that someone talking to him?" he asked himself as he continued to move forward in a self-induced daze.

If it was, he paid them no mind.

He had to see.

As he slowly approached the two bodies, he stopped.

What he saw caused him to fall to his knees where he stood and he began to weep uncontrollably. He couldn't believe what he saw and knew that for as long as he lived, he would never forget it.

Never.

CHAPTER FIVE
Los Angeles, California

Saturday 11:45 am

As the Detective pulled into the first available space she saw, she quickly got out of her car and made a B-line for the front entrance of the Police Station. As she walked into the building she noticed that there seemed to be more activity going on around the precinct than usual for a Saturday morning.

Actually, it was getting closer to the noon hour, but the Lieutenant was going to have to excuse her being late. She had just got the call from the precinct less than an hour ago that the Lieutenant wanted to see her. And from the message her boss had left, it seemed like it was hella important.

So, here she was, with only a couple of hours of sleep and probably looking like it.

"But hey!" she thought to herself. "I'm here!"

She and the others on her team had pulled an all-nighter trying to follow up on some of the new leads they had just received from a 'source' on the street about the serial killer they had been tracking in the LA area. He had been appropriate nicknamed, the 'Penance Killer'. And she knew as well as the others did, that you jump on all leads while they were fresh or you were 'shit out of luck'.

And that's what she and her team did all night long. Not the way she would have liked to have spent her Friday evening, but it came with the job. And for now, she was okay with that.

She knew that being the only African American female Detective on the force in her precinct was a big deal. She always felt that she had something to prove to everyone. And with her being in her early thirties didn't help matters any. Not only did she have to fight the fight that all women have to deal with in a male dominated field like the Police force, but being African American and younger than most didn't help.

But Abbey was up for the challenge and whatever it took she was going to make it work. Even if it killed them and her in the process.

But thankfully it never came to that.

Not only did she work well with the other officers and detectives in the precinct, but she carried her own weight. And they grew to respect her for that and her good detective work that helped her to assist in solving one of LA's top profile serial cases a few years back. She not only impressed her fellow officers, but the top brass as well.

With that being said, she was now a lead detective with her own team of four officers who already had an impressive conviction record of the cases they had solved. The detectives that worked with Abbey all grew to respect her, and knew that their success was due not only to her leadership skills, but also to the fact that their team worked well together and had good instincts about the cases they were assigned.

Especially Abbey.

She would get gut feelings about the cases and the people they were investigating and would pick up on things that had escaped everyone else's scrutiny. And most times it would turn out to be the one thing that helped to solve the case. It baffled some of the officers on how nine out of ten times she was right about most things. Some thought it was just a woman's intuition that made all the difference, but whatever it was, they just went with it.

And in the process they had become a tight knit working unit that was more like a family than anything else, and would back up and protect each other at all costs.

"Not bad for a thirty something, Black woman in a male dominated field like the Police force," she thought to herself as she walked through the security station.

As she passed through the scanning machine, she overheard several of the officers talking about something that had happened last evening. She only got bits and pieces of the conversation as she was waved through, but it seemed to have had the whole force talking.

By the time she had taken the elevator to the 2nd floor, she had already heard bits and pieces of three to four separate conversations about the accident that had happened the other night in a residential area of LA.

"Do you believe that?" said one of the officers in the elevator to her companion. "And after such a horrific accident, too!"

"There has to be a logical explanation for it!" answered the other officer. "I mean, there has to be! Right?"

"What the hell did I sleep through?" Abbey asked herself as she exited the elevator and made her way down the hall to the 'Bull Pen'.

"Hey Abbey, how's it going?" called out an officer as he approached her in the hall. "Another long night, huh?" he asked as he stopped to chat.

"You know it," she answered as she stopped. "But it comes with the territory, right?"

"Yeah, I guess so," he said.

And then he asked, "Are you guys any closer to catching that bastard piece of shit you've have been looking for?" he asked.

She always did like Kurt.

He was a 'no' nonsense kind of guy who unfortunately, didn't have any kind of a filter when speaking about something that he truly felt strongly about. But in this case, Kurt was voicing what everyone else at the precinct and in the LA area was thinking about the high profile serial killer case that she and her team were currently working on.

"Actually, I think we may be getting closer than we've ever been," said Abbey as she lowered her voice.

"Well, when you do bring him down, I'd like a personal invite," he said as he leaned in toward her. "You know, maybe before the rest of the force shows up," he said with a wicked smile. "I'd like to show him a little piece of my kind of justice, if you know what I mean?"

"Now Kurt," she said with a little bit of humor in her voice. "You know as officers of the law we're supposed to uphold all rights of any suspect we catch and detain," she said. "They're innocent until proven guilty. Right?" she asked as she looked at him intently.

"Yeah, okay. If you say so," he replied as he moved away from Abbey and continued down the hall. "But you and I both know that when we catch this creep, Karma may have something to say about it," chided Kurt as he continued walking.

Then before he disappeared around the corner, he turned and let out a laugh and said, "And you know Karma, right," he said. "She can be a real 'Bitch' sometimes, when given some encouragement!"

"Hey!!" exclaimed Abbey to Kurt as he disappeared. "As officers of the law we're not supposed to think like that!" she said.

"At least not out loud we aren't," she softly murmured to herself as she turned and made her way through the double doors of the 'Bull Pen' and headed for her desk.

"We can only hope that Karma does have this creep in her sights," she thought to herself as she walked toward her desk. "But I'm not depending on Karma. I can't wait that long," she thought. "We're going to catch this killer with good ole' fashion police work. And when we do, he'll be put away for so long, he'll never see the light of day for as long as he lives."

He needed to pay for the atrocities he had committed on the young girls that had been found so far. And no one knew how many more there would be. But she knew that her and her team had to catch this killer, or the 'Penance Killer' as he had been aptly named, and soon.

They needed to catch him before any more innocent lives were lost.

Not only were the residents of LA getting antsy with this serial killer on the loose, but the brass upstairs were getting impatient. They wanted results and they wanted them yesterday.

As she looked down at the stacks of paperwork covering her desk, all of which pertained to the serial killer they were after, she took in a deep breath.

"It was as if he always seemed to be able to stay one step ahead of them. And always just out of reach," she mused to herself.

Almost as if he himself was orchestrating his every move in unison with the Police, as if in a calculated way. And what pissed her off more than anything else, was it seemed as if he was mocking them at the same time.

Daring the police to catch him before he struck again.

They had analyzed him as being a psychopathic killer of young girls who had 'mommy' issues, and a penchant of leaning toward being a religious fanatic of sorts. He also hated women. He would kidnap young girls, five so far, who were between the ages of thirteen and eighteen. And then he would hold them for up to a week. During this time they would be repeatedly raped and tortured, and then when they were of no further use to the killer, he would kill them and dump their bodies at locations in the surrounding LA area.

And all of the locations in one way or another had some sort of religious significance to them.

At least that was all that had been released to the public about the murders and the victims.

There was specific information that hadn't been released to the public. Information such as the fact that each of the young girls all had long hair that went to at least the middle of their backs, and that he didn't just dump the bodies.

Both of the bodies that had been found so far had been 'staged' as if they were in the middle of a silent prayer.

They were both on their knees with their heads bowed over their hands that had been secured in front of them with a thin, sharp edged wire that slit into their wrists. And attached to their backs with huge, oversized pins, was a blood soaked piece of paper that simply read:

'God forgive me, for I have sinned. I have used my female body to lure and tempt the righteous for which I must pay penance. I offer that of myself to you which is sinful. Forgive me!'

Finding the young girls in that fashion was bad enough.

But what the killer had done to them was unthinkable, as the officers who found the first body discovered.

When the Police had arrived and found the first body, they secured the area and called it in. While waiting for the coroner, they noticed that the girl had been propped up to where she was kneeling in what appeared to be a pool of her own blood. They couldn't see any wounds other than the piercing of the oversized pins on her back, which they determined would not have caused such a loss of blood.

Then one of the officers noticed that the blood seemed to be coming from the front part of the body that was hidden by the long hair of the victim. Her long hair seemed to have been intentionally draped over each side of her bowed head, hiding her face, hands and the front part of her body. They didn't think anything of it until one of the officers had knelt down in front of the body and partially lifted up one side of the victims' hair.

The reaction of the officer was immediate as he fell back and screamed. It was so intense that it caught the other officers off guard.

"OH MY GGGOD!!!" wailed the officer as he fell back with his hands over his mouth and immediately turned and threw up.

"What the Hell!!!" "What is it Joe? What's under there?" called out the other officers as they ran up to their partners' side trying to comfort him.

But it was to no avail as he threw up again and again and kept screaming, "Ohhh God! Ohhh God! Ohh God!"

When the other officers on site asked him what he had seen, all Joe could do was to shakily point with his right hand at the front part of the girls' body and turn as he continued to vomit again.

"What do you think is under there?" asked one of the officers, not really anxious to look for himself.

"I don't know what's under there," answered the other officer. "And to tell you the truth, I don't wanna know," he said with a shaky voice. "I've seen so much in this job I don't need to add anything else to it. We got some sick people out here and I want to be able to at least lay my head down at night and close my eyes and not have to relive everything that I come across."

"Yeah! Maybe you're right," agreed the other officer. "I don't need to see it either!"

Turning to their friend and partner, they leaned over and helped him stand up and walked him away from the kneeling body. As far as they were concerned, they would wait and let the detectives handle the crime scene when they arrived.

They had done what they were supposed to do. Now they would secure the area and let the ones who were in charge of cases like this take over. And they were happy to let them have it.

⁓

Abbey knew that disclosing all of the information about the crime scene and the exact state of how the bodies were found would do more harm than good. It wouldn't give the residents of LA any more of a secure feeling than they already had.

Especially, after the discovery the officers made after they had secured the area where the first body was found.

The officers noticed that on top of the offering table sitting in front of the first body, was a blood soaked white table cloth. And on top of the table were three items. Actually, the items were three body parts that appeared to have been cut off of the victim while she was alive. Two of the items looked like deflated pieces of flesh that had been gingerly placed onto the table. It wasn't until the officers looked closer that they saw what looked like two nipples on each of the items. They were the right and left breasts of the young girl, as they sat crumpled and squished on the right side of the table.

The third item was also part of the victim's body that had been carved out of her, but for the life of the officers, they couldn't make out what it was. It wasn't until later that the Morgue confirmed that along with the victims' breasts being cut off, the kidnapper had also cut out her vagina and had placed it on the table with the other items.

Abbey knew that by keeping certain facts about the case under wraps was a way to 'weed' out all of the 'sickos' who would gladly step forward to try and seek as much media attention as they could by trying to take credit for the crime.

"And God knows there were too many 'sickos' out there to count," sighed Abbey as she sat down at her desk trying to clear her head and figure out where to start next.

Before she could begin to wrap her head around the paperwork in front of her, she heard the Lieutenant call out her name from his office.

"Anyone!! Has Abbey made it in yet?"

"Comin' Lieutenant!" answered Abbey quickly as she put everything else aside for the moment and rose from her desk and headed toward the Lieutenant's office.

She knew he was going to ask if there were any new leads that would bring her and her team any closer to catching this lunatic. She also knew that he was going to have to ride her just like the brass upstairs was riding him for the capture of the killer and closure of this case. But that was to be expected. The brass upstairs didn't want excuses, they only wanted results.

"You wanted to see me Lieutenant?" asked Abbey as she stepped into the doorway of her superiors' office.

"Yeah! Com'on in," said the Lieutenant as he looked up and motioned for her to come in and close the door behind her.

He always liked Abbey. She carried herself like a lady. But if and when the situation called for it, she could switch into that tough talking, 'Bitch' of a police officer whenever needed.

"She was one of his best," thought the Lieutenant to himself, and he knew it.

That's why he was going to have a hard time figuring out a way to tell her about the new assignment she was being given. She had been heading up the her team from the beginning, investigating the worst serial killer case the city had seen, and had made some real headway. She was not going to be happy being pulled off of the case in the middle of the investigation.

But he had his orders, and they came from the top. He had no choice in the matter, even though he literally begged to keep her in the precinct and on the case. And now he had to break the news to her, and he respected her way too much to try and 'sugar coat' it to make her feel better about the change.

"This was not going to be easy!" he thought to himself. "Not by a long shot."

And then he got a good look at her as she stepped into his office and closed the door.

"You look like Hell worn over, Abbey! Did you get 'any' sleep last night?" he asked in a concerned voice.

"Not really, Lieutenant! Maybe an hour or two," she answered already feeling weary. "Not enough to do any good, but I'll be okay. What's up?"

Seeing the strained expression on his face as he sat down and the way he kept scratching his right eyebrow, told Abbey that something big was up.

"Lieutenant, is everything alright?" she asked.

She could always tell when he fidgeted with his right eyebrow that something was bothering him. As if he was about to do something that he didn't want to do.

"Abbey, how long have you known me?" he asked. "What's it been, six, seven years now?"

"Yeah, something like that, Sir. Why?"

"I just need you to know that if I could have had anything to say about this, we wouldn't be here right now having this conversation."

"I'm sorry Lieutenant, I'm not following you. If you had anything to say about what?" inquired Abbey as she began to get an uneasy feeling in her gut.

"All I know is that there's some sort of big investigation that's brewing from Washington D.C. that apparently has international implications. I don't understand the whole thing, Abbey. It's a little out of my league. And they weren't in what you'd call a 'sharing' mood, if you get my drift. But last night there was an incident that happened right here in our jurisdiction that seems to tie into their investigation. And the brass upstairs has been asked that one of our best people be assigned to the team as point. They asked for you."

Abbey was stunned.

There were dozens of detectives in the precinct who had more experience and years on the force than she did. Why would she be the one that they would ask for? It didn't make any sense.

"I'm honored, Lieutenant, really!" said Abbey as she sat forward in the chair. "But I'm in the middle of one of our biggest cases ever, and I'm close, Lieutenant! I can feel it! We are about to break this case wide open...!" she exclaimed.

"Abbey!" interrupted the Lieutenant. "Abbey, I don't think you understand," he said solemnly as he eyed her intently. "They didn't just ask for you. They went over my head and have already reassigned you," he stated. "You report this afternoon to meet the investigator you'll be working with. I understand she's flying in from Washington. And get this, Abbey," said the Lieutenant as he lowered his voice and leaned in as if someone else might be listening. "It's some French woman who I understand is from the Vatican. Can you believe that? The Vatican! Whatever this investigation is, it's a big one!"

Before Abbey had realized it, she had stood up and was leaning across the Lieutenant's desk with both of her hands firmly planted in front of her.

"This is crazy, Lieutenant!!" yelled Abbey at the top of her voice. "Why me??!! Why not put one of their political flunkies on this assignment? They love the media! This way they can 'brown nose' it with the brass upstairs for the whole world to see. Let them have the assignment!!"

In no way did she want to disrespect the Lieutenant. She knew he had nothing to do with the reassignment. But this couldn't have come a worst time. Not only were they taking her case away from her, but it was her team she would be leaving, too.

It wasn't fair!!

"This case has literally caused the entire city to come to a standstill," exclaimed Abbey. "Some fanatic is out there kidnapping, raping and torturing young girls. And when he's done with them, Lieutenant, he mutilates them in the most unthinkable ways possible while they are still alive! And then he desecrates our churches by dumping the bodies on the front steps, or, or in the chapels for everyone to see what he's done! He's using the victims as his calling card, Lieutenant!"

Abbey pulled herself away from the Lieutenant's desk and came to an upright position. She could feel her emotions coming to a head as her blood pressure rose and her head started to swim.

"Lieutenant," said Abbey in a low voice. "I'm so close! We're so close! And now they want to pull me off! I don't get!!" exclaimed Abbey as she started to pace back and forth in front of her boss' desk. "Am I not working hard enough on this case for them? What…..what is it?"

The Lieutenant let her blow off steam, knowing that he had only delivered half of the bad news to her.

"You know I tried everything I could to keep you, just short of getting myself fired, Abbey," said the Lieutenant quietly. "They didn't want to hear anything I had to say. For some reason the bigwigs in Washington want you. They have their mind set on you being on the team, and there's no getting around it."

"And my case?" asked Abbey. "What happens to my case? And what about my team? What do I tell them?"

Before the Lieutenant could answer, his door opened and in walked another one of his detectives. Actually, it was one of the political flunkies Abbey had just mentioned.

"Montgomery!!" bellowed the Lieutenant. "What the hell are you doing in here? I didn't call for you?"

"I know, Sir," said the Detective as he smiled broadly and then glanced over at Abbey." I just saw Abbey in here with you and I figured you'd want to make the passing of the torch official."

"Wha…..!!!! What are you talking about?" exclaimed Abbey as she glared at Montgomery, one officer she truly disliked.

And then turning to the Lieutenant she asked, "What is he talking about? Passing the torch…..!"

And then it hit her.

When the realization of what Montgomery had said sunk in, it hit her like a ton of bricks.

"Oh my God…no!!" exclaimed Abbey as she backed up. "Lieutenant, how could they give him 'my' case?"

"Abbey, I….." stumbled the Lieutenant.

This was not the way he had wanted her to find out who her case and her team had been assigned to. He had wanted to tell her in his own way. Not like this.

"Hey Abbey, it's no big deal," said Montgomery with a snide look on his face. "Maybe they just needed a new set of eyes on the case, you know? No hard feelings, Kiddo. You've had your shot, now maybe I'll be able to find something you missed. By the way, what ah, what new assignment did they put you on, huh? I'm sure it's something you'll be able to handle!"

"Montgomery, shut the fuck up!!!" shouted the Lieutenant as he rose out of his chair and came around the desk.

If he knew anything, it was that Abbey just might floor this 'douche bag' before he could step in between them and stop it.

"You know, Montgomery," said Abbey as she stepped in close and got in his face. "You wouldn't be able to find your asshole if someone ripped it off and put it right under your nose, you 'Motha fuckin', titty suckin', two ball Bitch!!"

"Hey, hey, hey!! Don't bite 'my' head off!" exclaimed the detective as he backed away from Abbey realizing that she was more than pissed. "I was just told about the reassignment this morning."

"Yeah! Like you had nothing to do with this!" said Abbey as she stood her ground.

She knew that Montgomery was notorious for using his political connections to be placed on high profile cases after other hard working officers had done all of the ground work. He would come in and close out the case and take the credit from those who really deserved it.

"Alright you two, cut it out!!" shouted the Lieutenant as he came in between them. "This came from up top and it is what it is! Montgomery!" he said as he turned to the other detective. "Get the hell out of my office. Now!! I'll call you when I need you."

"Yeah, sure, Lieutenant," said Montgomery as he kept a close eye on Abbey as he opened the door and quickly stepped out of the Lieutenant's office.

But before he could close the door, the Lieutenant called after him.

"Oh, and Montgomery. Next time, don't you ever walk into my office like that without knocking, do you understand? I don't like you that much and I never did. Now get out!"

Abbey couldn't help trying to stifle the smirk that had spread across her face as Montgomery quickly turned on his heel and slinked out of the office. Moments after the door had closed the Lieutenant spoke to Abbey.

"Abbey, I…..I don't know what to say," said the Lieutenant softly. "I didn't want you to find out about Montgomery being given your case and your team like this. You gotta believe me! I was trying to find a way to tell you. I would never….."

"It's alright, Lieutenant. I knew you were trying to tell me something," said Abbey. "I just didn't think it was this."

She tried to suck it up and smile, but she couldn't make it convincing, and the Lieutenant saw right through it.

"Com'on, Abbey. Let's take a walk," said the Lieutenant as he led her out of his office and out of a side entrance of the 'Bull Pen' that led to the hallway.

"Where are we going?" she asked.

"I thought that maybe we'd grab a cup of coffee. Let this whole thing kinda sink in," said the Lieutenant as he walked with her. "And then I told your team to meet us in one of the conference rooms upstairs. I figured you'd want to be the one to tell them about the change."

"Ah…..yeah," said Abbey as she fought to come out of the daze she found herself in. "Thanks Lieutenant. You're right. I, ah, I would like to be the one to tell them. Yeahh! I think that would be best."

"Good. Then let's go and get a cup of what is and probably always will be one of the crappiest cups of coffee the world has ever seen," joked the Lieutenant as he and Abbey made their way down the hall to the elevator. "For the life of me I can never understand why none of these pricks here at the precinct can make a decent pot of coffee," said the Lieutenant trying to make conversation. "You know my granddaughter, now there's someone who can make a great pot of coffee. And hell, she's only thirteen," said the Lieutenant as he laughed uneasily.

Abbey knew he was trying to lighten the situation the best he could, and she appreciated it. But she knew that for now the sting of what she had just been dealt was a little too deep to be so easily swept away. And for now she was pissed at the brass upstairs and wanted to hold on to that feeling for a little while longer.

"Just a little while longer," she mused to herself as she tried to quell her anger at the bosses upstairs and at Montgomery.

"Oh, and ahh, by the way," said the Lieutenant as he and Abbey stepped into the elevator and the doors began to shut. "That thing you called Montgomery, what, a two ball Bitch!" he said. "Wow!!! Did not see that coming. And by the look on his face, neither did Montgomery!!" laughed the Lieutenant out loud.

"Sorry Lieutenant. Just something I heard once," said Abbey. "I thought the situation was appropriate for it."

"You're dammed right it was appropriate," said the Lieutenant. "I'm going to have to remember that one! Motha' fuckin', titty......wait a minute! What was the rest of it, now?" asked her boss.

All Abbey could do was to crack a smile at her boss' fascination of the phrase she had thrown at Montgomery.

As the doors closed and the elevator made its' way up two floors, Abbey thought to herself, "He had done it. He had brought her out of her funk, for now. Damn you, Lieutenant!!" mused Abbey to herself as they rode up. "Damn you, you're good!"

⌐⌐⌐

After a quick cup of coffee, the Lieutenant had given her the name of the woman she was to meet later that afternoon and which conference room had been set aside for them. Twenty minutes later, Abbey found herself breaking the news to her team that she had been reassigned to another case, and that Montgomery would be their new lead. And as was expected, their reaction was exactly what both Abbey and the Lieutenant had thought it would be.

What the Lieutenant had done was enough to help Abbey focus when she spoke to her team in the conference room. But she still had to fight back the tears and the raw anger she felt as she stood in front her them and told them of her reassignment.

"What!!!! You got to be kiddin'!" "Fuck this!! I'd rather transfer to the traffic division than report to Montgomery!" "You got that right!" "Lieutenant! How can you let this happen? What's really going on here?" "Yeah!!!" "Yeah!!!"

"Hey, calm down!" bellowed the Lieutenant loudly. "I said calm down!!"

When the team had quieted down, the Lieutenant spoke again.

"It's like Abbey said. I was informed this morning by the Brass upstairs that this was how it was going to be," said the Lieutenant as he looked around the small conference room. "No ifs, ands or buts. They've made up their minds about this and there was nothing I could do to make them change it. I figured that Abbey should be the one to break it to you guys. Now this is hard enough on her as it is. And God knows I'm spittin' bullets. But give her a break here! She's going to need all of you to support her and help her to move on to this new assignment."

As the Lieutenant spoke, the members of Abbey's team shuffled uneasily where they stood and mumbled among themselves. They all knew that at a moment's notice any of them could be reassigned. That's just the way it was.

After a few moments of silence that seemed like long agonizing minutes, the only other female member of her team members spoke.

"Hey!" she called out. "This new assignment you got. You suppose there's an opening for a sharp, hardworking Detective with a knack for attention to detail?" she said.

"Yeah! How about two openings?" called out another member of the team. "I know I could use a change of scenery."

Abbey smiled. She couldn't help it.

She knew she had their support and they would all follow her if they could. And if it were possible, she would let them. But unfortunately, that wasn't an option.

That's the kind of bond the members of the team had developed among themselves. And Abbey knew that she would finish up this new assignment and try and come back to the team that she knew would always have her back, no matter what.

And that was a promise she had made to them. And God willing, she was going to be able to keep it.

As each member of the team gave her a long lingering hug and made their way out of the conference room, Abbey held back the tears. No matter what, she couldn't let the team or any of the other officers in the precinct see her break.

And the Lieutenant knew that.

He waited until the last team member had left and then he turned to Abbey.

"Abbey, I'm not good at saying 'good bye', you know that. So I won't," said the Lieutenant solemnly. "But if you don't mind, I'd like to give you one last piece of advice."

"Lieutenant, you know I welcome any advice you give me," said Abbey truthfully.

The Lieutenant had been like a surrogate father to her since she had never known her own Father. He had basically taken her under his wings when she first arrived at the precinct and had guided her whenever she needed it. So anything he had to say to her, she would take to heart.

"Abbey, I don't know much about this new assignment they've given you," he said. "But from what I do know about it, I'm getting a 'gut' feeling that it's right for you."

"But Lieutenant.....!" exclaimed Abbey, ready to disagree.

"Wait Abbey," interrupted her boss. "Let me finish. I don't know why, but something about this assignment is telling me it was meant for you and for you alone. Now call me crazy, but when I was sitting upstairs while they were telling me what little bit about this big investigation they were willing to, I kept getting this feeling, you know."

"Lieutenant, you know that you get those 'gut' feelings all the time," said Abbey.

"That's just it, Abbey," said the Lieutenant. "It wasn't just a 'gut' feeling I was getting. And I'll tell you this and you alone," said the Lieutenant as he moved in close to her. "And if anyone asks me about it, I'll deny it til the day I die."

Abbey wasn't sure if it was the way the Lieutenant said it, or if it was the scared look she saw in his eyes when he spoke to her. But whatever it was, at that moment she felt a cold chill creep down her back, and it unsettled her.

"But Abbey, something inside my head is saying, 'Let her go! Help her to move on. It's meant to be.....'"

And Abbey noticed that the Lieutenant stopped short of finishing his sentence and had dropped his head as if he was embarrassed to finish.

"Lieutenant.....?"

"Ahhh, it's nothin', Abbey," said the Lieutenant as he stepped back and tried to shake off the feeling of the moment. "It's nothin'."

"Lieutenant, what were you going to say," insisted Abbey as she looked at her boss intently.

For some reason, she had the feeling as if she needed him to finish what he was going to say to her.

"Oh, it was just somethin' that kept bouncing around in my head, is all," he said. "You know, while I was upstairs with the Brass. I don't even know where it came from," said the Lieutenant as he tried to laugh it off.

"What kept bouncing around in your head, Lieutenant?" asked Abbey again.

"Well, you know I'm not an overly religious kind of guy," he said admittedly. "At least I didn't think I was. I mean, I believe in God and all that, but for the life of me, I can't figure out why this verse keeps popping into my head."

"A verse? What kind of verse?" asked Abbey. "You mean like a verse out of the bible?"

"Hey, your guess is as good as mine," answered the Lieutenant as he shrugged his shoulders, not sure what he meant. "I guess it could be from the bible. I don't know. All I know is while I was being briefed on the reassignment, this voice inside my head keeps saying the same thing over and over again. It said somethin' like, 'There be Prophets among you.....and she is the one to seek them out.' Crazy, huh?" said the Lieutenant as he tried to laugh it off without success.

It really seemed to kind of bothered him.

He had never had that kind of feeling before. Especially a feeling that had a voice that went with it, spouting biblical sayings. It just kind of freaked him out a bit.

"Well, that doesn't make any sense at all, Lieutenant," admitted Abbey as she studied her boss intently.

"Hey! You're preaching to the choir here!" said the Lieutenant indicating that he agreed with her. "But Abbey, I can't shake the feeling that this is just the beginning for you. That something big is gonna come from this and it's just for you, and no one else."

"Okaaay.....Lieutenant! I know better than to dismiss your 'gut' feelings," she said. "I'll keep my head low and my eyes open, like you've taught me. But understand this. I intend on coming back here to the precinct and to my team when this investigation is over. Got it?"

"Got it!" exclaimed the Lieutenant as he smiled and let one of his best detectives give him a hug before she walked out of the door.

As she left out of the small conference room and made her way to the elevator, another feeling swept over the Lieutenant. This time it was different kind of feeling. This time it was the feeling of…..peace. It was as if a feeling of utmost 'peace' seemed to flow over him. And at that moment he knew it was because of Abbey and the investigation she was about to be involved in.

"Now, that was odd," thought the Lieutenant to himself. "Very odd."

CHAPTER SIX

Saturday – 3pm

Abbey had just under an hour to get her desk into some semblance of order before Montgomery took over, and then be at the conference room upstairs by 3pm. The whole thing still irked her to no end. Her team, her case, all gone because some unknown group of political bigwigs in Washington D.C. had gotten together with the Brass of her precinct and decided that she was the one who would work point on an international investigation with some French woman from the Vatican.

She was beginning to feel like the Lieutenant did.

What kind of case here in LA would be important enough for the political movers and shakers in Washington D.C. to request a person from their precinct to be placed as point to work on an international, clandestine investigation?

And with someone from the Vatican of all places!

"The Vatican!!" exclaimed Abbey to herself. "What the Hell was going on?" she thought as she sat in the conference room waiting for her contact to arrive.

She adjusted her body position in the chair as she waited.

"This had better be good!" she thought to herself. "Real good!"

After looking at the clock for the umpteen time, three o' clock had come and gone.

Abbey had always heard that when you watch a pot waiting for it to boil, it could take forever. But by three twenty-five, she was done.

"I have a lot of work to do," she thought absentmindedly as she rose from the table.

Then it hit her.

Not only had her case been taken from her and reassigned to the 'biggest douche bag' in the precinct, but so had her team. And in reality, she didn't have a case to work on or anything else to do but to wait.

"Dammit!!" exclaimed the Detective as she slowly sat back down at the table.

She didn't like this at all. She didn't like this one 'frickin' bit!

Before her anger could slowly rise to a boil again, the door to the conference room quickly swung open. In rushed an attractive woman of slender build and height with her honey blond hair pulled back into a single ponytail. As she entered the room, she placed the briefcase she was carrying onto the table between them.

"Je suis de'sole'!! Je suis de'sole', pardonnez-moi s'il vous plait!!"

Abbey was stunned. Was she speaking French to her?

By the look that spread across Abbey's face, the woman realized that she had spoken in her native tongue of French.

"Ahh, I'm sorry! I'm sorry!" exclaimed the woman in English as she closed the door behind her. "Please forgive me!"

"Ahh!" she exclaimed in English with a very heavy French accent. "I am so sorry!" she said apologetically. "When I am rushed, I tend to think only in French and so I speak in French. Oui? I am so sorry. The plane, it was…..late! And then with all of the traffic. My most sincere apologies!"

Abbey took note that she was wearing a very stylish black trench coat that was the kind of a designer piece you only find in Europe or at one of the outrageously expensive stores that were here in LA. Who could miss the designer details on the shoulders and on the front of the coat, the way it was cut. And the material!

"Oh, yeah!" thought Abbey to herself. "Nice coat! Real nice!!"

It was the kind of piece that was way out of reach of her paycheck, that was for sure.

"I am Fransquie Fabianne 'al Benne," she said as she extended her hand to Abbey. "I am the Inspector that has been dispatched from the Vatican. I take it that you are Abigail, yes?"

"Ahh, yes, yes I am," said the Detective as she stood up and shook hands with the woman. "But, please call me Abbey. Everyone does."

"Ahh, oui! I mean, yes of course," she exclaimed. "If that is what you wish, yes. I will call you, L'Abbaye," she said in her French accent. "And if you do not mind, please call me Fabianne, oui?"

Although she didn't actually pronounce her name quite correctly, Abbey liked the way Fabianne's French accent made her name sound. It was very French like. And even though Abbey didn't know anything about this woman she was supposed to work with, she liked her. Even in her harried state, she had a professional air about her that was paired with a sort of casual chic. And she liked her accent.

Yeah, Abbey had a gut feeling that was going to be interesting.

"Please, please. Sit, L'Abbaye, sit," said the Inspector as she took off her coat and draped it across one of the other chairs at the table.

Looking up, she sighed and gave Abbey a slight smile.

"I know, L'Abbaye, that you have not been told anything about this assignment. And for that, I must apologize. But you will understand when I have finished," stated Fabianne as she looked at Abbey intently. "But time is of the essence. So after I brief you here, we must quickly make our way to another location that is here in the Los Angeles area. And I know that as a detective it is in your nature to want to ask questions that will get you to the answers you desire. And I know it will be very hard for you, but if I may ask," said the woman. "Please allow me to brief you on what we have so far without any questions. After that we must leave. And then while we are on the way to our next destination, any questions you have I will be more than happy to answer for you. Agreed?"

Abbey couldn't help it. She had opened her mouth to ask one of the zillion questions she had, and then she caught herself.

After a momentary pause, she simply said, "Agreed."

"Good, L'Abbaye! Good!" said the woman as she sat down and looked across the table at the detective.

Then she asked her a question.

"L'Abbaye, have you ever heard of the 'Manoscritto di sei eventi?"

"Again, with the foreign languages," thought Abbey to herself.

But if she was right, this time the woman she had just met was speaking what sounded like Italian.

"What is that, Italian?" asked Abbey not quite sure.

"Oui," answered Fabianne in a somewhat surprised tone. "It is Italian. Do you speak it?" she asked quickly.

"Ah, no, no!" said Abbey quickly. "I don't speak Italian. It just sounded like that's what it was."

The last thing she wanted was for this Vatican Inspector to think that she understood any language other than English.

"Ah, oui, oui! I understand," apologized the woman as she opened her briefcase and proceeded to pull out several documents and spread them out on the table in front of her. "Well, the 'Manoscritto di sei eventi' is an ancient manuscript that was discovered in Egypt approximately, Two Thousand years ago".

"According to records, a holy man of this time had a vision of..... what was to come," stated the Inspector as she paused for a moment. "In this vision, he was told to write down what he saw and to share it with the world. When he tried to share it with others, especially those in power, it did not go so well for him. Unfortunately, his vision made no sense to anyone. As far as they were concerned it was..... gibberish. He spoke of places in the world that did not exist. At least they did not exist as far as the people of that time had knowledge of. It was considered blasphemy. He left his village and went out into the desert and was never heard from again," said the Inspector as she paused again.

"Now you are probably asking yourself, 'What happened to his manuscript, oui?' The one he had written down everything he had seen in his vision."

"Actually," interrupted Abbey as she sat forward in her chair. "That's not what I'm asking myself right now," she said carefully trying not to offend the Inspector.

"Now, I know I said that I wouldn't ask any questions until you were finished, and I'm really trying here. Really I am," insisted Abbey. "But what does this ancient manuscript have to do with anything? I'm sorry Inspector, but I just need some current facts that will tie into what all of this has to do with whatever case it is that's going on here in LA, and 'why' you're here talking to me about it."

Abbey had tried to sit and listen for as long as she could. But she found it more than difficult to just sit there and get a historical lesson about an ancient manuscript from Egypt that a Holy man had written Two Thousand years ago.

"Of course, Detective," said the woman. "I understand that me being here speaking to you about this manuscript may seem to have no connection to anything that you know of, so far. But if you will bear with me for a few moments more, you will understand. Oui?"

Taking in a deep breath, Abbey simply nodded her head and sat back in her chair, allowing the Inspector to continue. She didn't have any place else she needed to be at the moment. Her superiors had made sure of that.

The Inspector continued.

"Somehow, one of the other Holy men of the sect was able to hide the manuscript before it could be destroyed. He was able to pass it on over the years to others who believed in what the first Holy man had witnessed. They didn't know why, but according to the records, they felt it was an important foretelling of events that were yet to come that would let Man know that he was to prepare."

"Prepare?" asked Abbey. "Prepare for what?"

"That is just it. They did not know what Man was to prepare for," answered the woman. "But whatever it was, they felt it was an important message to pass on, and that it needed to be preserved. And as the centuries passed, the manuscript found its' way to the church. Now," said the woman as she eyed the Detective intently. "What is not known is that the church had been trying to procure this particular manuscript from the very beginning when they had first heard about it, and what it apparently foretold."

Before continuing, the Inspector took a group of photographs out of the folders that were in front of her and pushed them across the table toward Abbey.

"The Manoscritto di sei eventi," said the Inspector as she eyed Abbey as she reached for the photographs. "These are pictures of the actual manuscript that is currently being kept and preserved in the Vatican vaults beneath the Vatican City in Rome. As far as I know, no one outside of the Vatican has laid eyes upon its image for almost Five Hundred years. Right now, you and I are one of the few who have actually seen it within these last few centuries."

Looking at the pictures, all Abbey saw was images of a very old piece of parchment with what appeared to be ancient writing scrawled on it. And along the sides and across the top were numbers of some sort that were also written in the same ancient writing.

"And what does this manuscript say?" asked Abbey as she looked up at the Inspector.

"Very simply it says, 'In the future of Man they will be witness to six events. Five of those events will be miracles of such magnitude that they will be indisputable and cannot be denied'."

"And the sixth event?" asked Abbey unable to contain her curiosity as the Inspector paused.

"Oui. Well now, the sixth event is a mystery that even the Vatican scholars have been debating over for centuries," said the Inspector. "It says that the sixth event would be of such magnitude, that it will cause Man to reaffirm his faith, and the world will be changed forever. And the last line is the one that has caused most of the debate among Vatican scholars. It says, 'And true to his word, he will return. The Son'," said the Inspector.

And then it dawned on her what the Inspector was referring to. Indisputable miracles all happening before an event that would be a reaffirmation of faith that would change the world.

"Wait a minute!" exclaimed Abbey still somewhat skeptical, but now understanding what the woman sitting across from her was referring to. "That's some kind of heavy religious stuff you're talking about," she said as she sat up in her chair and gave the Inspector an incredulous look. "You aren't saying that this manuscript possibly speaks to…..to the 'second coming' of Jesus Christ, are you?" asked Abbey,

The Inspector tilted her head to one side and smiled slightly.

"So we have come believe," she said simply. "But what is interesting is, here we have a manuscript that could possibly speak to the 'second coming' of Jesus Christ. But it was written before Christ was even born. So you can see why the Vatican scholars were perplexed. How can you speak to the second coming of the Son of God, when he had not even been born yet to make his mark on the world, much less to predict his own return to his followers?" she said. "But as I said, the translation of the sixth event has been up for debate by those who are in a position to do so. That is not my job."

"Then I have to ask, Fabianne," said Abbey. "What exactly 'is' your job, and why am 'I' here?"

"As a Vatican Inspector, I am one of many who investigate events that could possibly be deemed, 'a miracle'," said Fabianne. "I and the other Inspectors do what we do, because the faithful depend on the church to be able to determine which of the many events that happen around the world are actual miracles, and which ones are not. You see L'Abbaye," explained Fabianne. "The church has always been asked to verify such events. Especially those that meet certain criteria that the church has deemed would qualify it as a possible miracle. And my job is to attempt to verify the event or to disqualify it in the eyes of the church. And the incident that happened here last night in your city, meets the church's criteria as a possible miracle. That is why 'I' am here."

"Last night?? Wait a minute," exclaimed Abbey now realizing that must have been what everyone at the precinct had been talking about earlier. "What incident?"

"You did not hear of the accident that happened last night?"

"No! No, I didn't," said Abbey. "I was pulling an all-nighter with my team. We were trying to follow up on some leads for a case we've been working on."

"Oui, so we were informed," stated Fabianne as she stood up and gathered the pictures together and put them back into her briefcase. "Now L'Abbaye, I will explain why I am here talking to you."

"Okay," said the Detective as she leaned forward anxious to hear what the Inspector had to say. "Why me?"

As Abbey waited for a response, she thought to herself, "This has got to be a dozy!"

"Come. I will explain to you while we walk, oui?" said the Inspector as she slung her 'fabulous' European trench coat casually over her arm and picked up her briefcase. "Time is of the essence, and we must get to our next destination as quickly as we can."

Watching the Inspector as she headed for the door, Abbey realized that their meeting here at the precinct was over and that she was apparently supposed to follow her.

"Wait a minute! Where are we going?" asked Abbey.

"We are going to the site where the incident happened last night," answered the Inspector. "Luckily it is not far from here. I have a car waiting for us downstairs. Come."

One thing Abbey realized at that moment was that she didn't like not being in control. But she had been reassigned by her superiors to assist this Inspector, and she knew that she was going to have to 'bite her tongue' for now, if she wanted to keep her job.

Rising up from the table, Abbey followed the Inspector out of the room as she headed for the elevator.

On the ride down to the first floor, the Inspector explained to Abbey that the church had in its possession numerous documents that predicted the occurrence of events that could be deemed as miracles. The 'Manoscritto di sei eventi' was just one of them. And the event that happened last night, because of its nature, caught their attention. And she had been dispatched to investigate, and needed someone within the local Police department to take point and assist her.

"Interesting," mused Abbey to herself as she listened to the Inspector in silence. "If there are numerous documents like this in the Vatican's possession, why does this particular manuscript play such an important part in this investigation?"

Abbey realized that was pertinent information that the Inspector from the Vatican was not giving to her, and that it was a question she would have to ask later.

"When we work with the local authorities, we try to keep a low profile whenever we can," said the Inspector. "It helps not attract too much undue attention when we are conducting an investigation such as this. Especially, from the local churches and Dioceses."

"Really?"

"Oui," said Fabianne as the two exited the elevator and headed toward the front entrance of the building. "We asked for a Detective within the precinct that could assist us in handling a case such as this. We needed someone that could work with total discretion and professionalism," continued Fabianne. "And when we asked for the best they had, your name was presented to us."

"Please, don't get me wrong, Inspector," said Abbey as she walked alongside the woman she had just been assigned to work with. "I'm honored that my bosses upstairs feel that I have what it takes to be put on a case like this. Really I am! But I'm not qualified to investigate miracles for the church!"

"Actually, L'Abbaye," said the woman as she headed for the black Towne car that was waiting outside of the precinct building. "You may be more qualified than you think. And please, call me Fabianne, oui."

As they reached the waiting Towne car, Fabianne handed her briefcase to the driver who opened the door for them.

She then turned to Abbey and said, "Have you ever wondered whether there was something more you could be doing? That perhaps there was a higher calling for you?"

"That was an odd statement for someone I've just met to make," thought Abbey to herself as she eyed the woman.

"No! No I haven't", she responded confidently. "Actually, I'm right where I've always wanted to be. All my life, this is what I've wanted. Trust me, Fabianne. I'm not looking for a new calling, if that's what you mean."

"Forgive me, L'Abbaye," apologized the woman. "I did not mean to offend you in any way. You of course, know what it is that you want. Please. Let us go, oui?"

As Fabianne turned and stepped into the back seat of the Towne car, Abbey reluctantly followed suit.

"This was not the way I had expected my day to go," thought Abbey as she settled in the seat next to her new partner. "Not at all!"

But she knew she was going to have to make the best of the situation even if she really didn't want to be there. Her mind kept going back to her case and her team that was now in the hands of Montgomery. Probably the most incompetent detective there was in the precinct.

And that was being kind.

As the car pulled away from the precinct building, Abbey turned to her new partner.

"The accident that happened last night. Where was it?" she asked.

"Ah, oui," exclaimed Fabianne as she reached inside her briefcase that had been placed in the seat across from her.

She pulled out a manila folder and handed it to Abbey.

"Here is all of the information we have so far" she said. "Basically, early last night a semi collided with a stalled car that was in the middle of the road in a local residential area. It was foggy, and the driver said that he did not see the car until the very last moment. Unfortunately, he was not able to stop, and his semi hit the car demolishing it. Now, what makes this incident interesting is that the woman inside of the car says she was pulled out at the last minute by a man she had never seen before. He, without any effort, ripped the door off of its hinges and pulled her out of the car."

"I'm sorry," interrupted Abbey as she casually looked up at the Inspector. "But it sounds like what you have is a case of a very heroic man pulling a woman from her car and saving her from a horrific accident," said the Detective. "That's great, but I still don't see this as being something that would warrant the 'Vatican' to investigate as a miracle," she said. "It sounds like they both survived the impact. But personally, I think it 'was' a miracle that he was even able to pull her out in time."

"The question is, 'did' he in fact get her out in time?" asked Fabianne.

"What do you mean?" asked the Detective. "You just said....."

"Oui, I know," said Fabianne coyly. "But from the account of the truck driver, when his semi hit the car, he also hit the two people he saw crouching on the road beside it. And from his statement, he undoubtedly was going way too fast for the conditions at the time. And he said he did not just hit them. He ran right through them at seventy to seventy five miles an hour!"

As Fabianne spoke, Abbey gave the Inspector a look.

She knew that anyone who was thrown after being hit by a vehicle going sixty miles an hour would be hard pressed to survive without some injuries. But a person being hit by a semi going seventy five miles an hour, now that was something else altogether.

"But it gets more interesting, Detective," said Fabianne. "That same man who pulled the woman out of her car. Before the accident had even occurred, he was driving in the opposite direction on the same road. That was when he said that a disembodied voice told him to stop his car, get out, and walk back to where the accident, was 'suppose' to happen."

As Abbey listened, she caught the slight change in the inflection of the Inspector's voice when she said that the man was told to go back to where the accident was, 'suppose' to happen, as in future tense.

"Once there he was told…..to wait," continued Fabianne. "When he saw the women's car coming down the road in the fog, it began to stall and then it stopped right in front of where he was standing. He then walked out into the road, up to the car, pulled the door on the driver's side off of its hinges and dragged the woman out just as the eighteen wheeler slammed into them and the car. According to the woman, all they had time to do was to crouch on the ground and pray."

Fabianne paused for a moment as she studied the look that came across the Detective's face.

"And now to answer your question as to 'why' the Vatican is so interested in this event?" said the Inspector. "Look on the last page. Read the last part of the truck driver's statement, if you will."

As Abbey flipped to the last page, she quickly scanned the last part of the statement that the truck driver had given to the authorities on the scene.

After a few moments, Abbey looked up.

"Is this even possible?" Abbey asked, not believing what she had just read.

"Your guess is as good as mine, Detective," answered Fabianne. "All we know is that is the statement he gave to the authorities on the scene. And he was adamant about it when questioned."

The Detective found herself getting a little light headed as she tried to absorb everything that had happened so far.

"Here she was sitting with a Vatican Inspector from Rome investigating a possible….go ahead and say it," she said to herself reluctantly. "Investigating a possible miracle that may have been predicted in an ancient manuscript that was two thousand years old. A manuscript that predicted five miracles and one event that was to be of monumental proportions. Great!" she exclaimed to herself. "How much better can this day get?" she asked herself sarcastically.

"Do you mind if I read the entire report," she asked as any investigator worth their 'spit' would've asked.

"Please, be my guest," answered the Inspector. "It would help if you are up to speed on everything that we have. Because, L'Abbaye, I guarantee you that this case, will get even more intriguing."

As the driver made his way through the late afternoon traffic of the surface streets of LA, Abbey settled herself into the plush seats of the Towne car and read the entire report, including the statement the truck driver had given.

As she began to read the report, she read what the First Responders found at the scene when they arrived. There were several statements about the actual scene of the accident, what was found and how far the debris from the collision was spread. Then she read how they found the truck driver in the middle of the road where the initial impact between the semi and the car had taken place.

According to the report, when the response crew approached the truck driver, he was on his knees crying like a baby while another man stood in front him. And according to one responder, it appeared that the man standing in front of the driver was speaking to him, although they couldn't confirm that. And then she read the truck driver's statement.

'It was foggy, and as far as I could see with my headlights, I didn't see anything in the road in front of me. Then all of a sudden through the fog, I saw the shadow of a stalled car as it appeared in my headlights right in front of me. And then I saw them. There were two people crouched on the ground right next to the car, looking right up at me. The guy was covering the woman with his body like he was trying to shield her. I tried to brake, but I knew it was too

late. But I knew it wouldn't have helped. Before I knew it, my truck just ran right into them and the car. And all I saw was pieces of the car as it exploded in every direction.

'I was able to bring my truck to a stop up the road there, and then I came back to see if there was anything I could do, you know? I don't know why, but I just had to see for myself. And when I got closer, through the fog I could see two bodies in the middle of the road. Man, I gotta tell you, my legs were so wobbly I almost couldn't keep myself standing up.

'And as God is my witness, I saw one of the bodies move! So I called out to the Firemen to come quick! I couldn't believe it, but it looked like someone was alive.

'And then he just stood up like, like nothin' happened. The guy just stood up and looked around like he was in some sort of daze. And then behind him, the other body moved, and she stood up too! And neither of them had nary a scratch on 'em. God is my witness!

'All I remember is dropping to my knees and bawling like a baby. I couldn't believe it. I couldn't! You know they shouldn't be alive, right? My rig ran right through 'em at seventy five miles an hour. I saw it! I saw it!'

When Abbey finished, she tried to focus her attention on the slow moving traffic just outside of her window as she thought about what she had just read in the police report. She didn't know what to make of what the driver had said in his statement.

"Could he have been wrong?" asked the Detective after a few moments. "I mean, in the confusion of everything that was happening, could he have maybe swerved at the last minute and maybe missed them altogether?"

"Highly unlikely," stated Fabianne. "Both the man and the woman gave the exact same statement of what happened. The man literally tore the door off of the car, pulled the woman out, and by the time they both looked up, they could see the metal grill of the truck as it came upon them. As they both stated, they barely had time to duck their heads before the truck hit them."

"But that's.....that's impossible!" exclaimed Abbey. "A big rig going seventy five miles an hour hits them and they don't have a scratch on them. They both probably should have died right then and there."

"Agreed," said Fabianne. "But yet they are both quite alive and well."

"Well, I can see why you would want to investigate this and figure out what really happened," said Abbey. "It does make one stop and wonder what forces are at work here, doesn't it? But I have to ask, Fabianne. What does this accident have to do with the manuscript you spoke of earlier? The manuscript you mentioned back at the precinct foretold about five miracles, this is just one incident.....right?"

Abbey paused as she looked at the woman sitting across from her. In that moment, the Inspector quickly looked down as if to avoid direct eye contact.

"This isn't the only one that's happened, is it?" she asked.

"You are very astute, L'Abbaye," said the Inspector as she looked up and smiled slightly. "There have been two other events that have happened, and the church has already deemed them as viable 'miracles'."

"What??"

"Oui!" confirmed Fabianne. "This is the third event within a week."

"The third!" exclaimed the Detective. "Wait a minute! If there's already been two other events and this is the third, then you believe that the other events eluded to in that manuscript are going to happen too, don't you?" exclaimed Abbey as she sat forward in her seat and a cold chill rushed down her back. "And if that's true, that would mean according to the manuscript, so is the sixth event." Abbey found she couldn't even finish her sentence, it sounded so surreal. "Get outta' here!!"

"Oui," said Fabianne softly. "So it would seem. And that is of course, if this event qualifies as a miracle and there are two more events after this that are also deemed as miracles. Then oui. The church feels there is significant reason to believe that the manuscript's prediction could be real."

Abbey felt her head start to swim as she tried to make sense of what had just been confided to her. All her life she went to church and was taught that if you believed and lived a Christian life you would be rewarded. And that at one point in Man's existence, although no one knew when, Jesus Christ, the Son of God would make good on his promise and return to the faithful. What person on Earth didn't know the story?

"Even those who were of a different religion and believed in a deity with a different name and had the same similar beliefs knew of the story of Jesus Christ," thought Abbey to herself.

But to have to come to grips with the knowledge that it might actually be happening, right now!

"Really!" exclaimed Abbey as she covered her mouth with her hand and leaned back into the seat of the car as she tried to think. She felt as if her head was about to explode from the inside out as the revelation hit home.

"Now do you understand why we do not advertise what we are doing?" asked Fabianne. "Especially, in this case. With the possible interpretation of the sixth event, can you imagine the panic, the upheaval in everyday life that would be caused worldwide if this got out? And what if we are wrong?" she said carefully. "Can you imagine how the church would be viewed if it predicted such a thing, and it did not come to pass?" she asked. "Oui, we must be diligent and investigate anything that could possible shed light on when the Son of God may return. But we must also be responsible how we handle the knowledge we gain."

All the Detective could do was to nod her head that she understood.

"Here, L'Abbaye," said Fabianne as she opened a bottle of water and handed it to the detective. "Drink this, it will make you feel better, oui?"

Thankful for the gesture, Abbey didn't realize that she was thirsty until she had gulped down the water in almost one swig. And even after drinking the water, she found herself still trying to understand what Fabianne was saying.

"I, I just can't believe that this might be happening in my lifetime," said Abbey as she tried to wrap her mind around it.

"L'Abbaye! Detective!!" exclaimed Fabianne as she looked at Abbey intently. "I need to know that you are going to be able to handle this situation with discretion and extreme confidentiality. No one outside of the two of us and the church must know what we are working on, do you understand? No one can know!"

Composing herself, Abbey tried to calm herself down the best she could. She never really thought about how she would react if someone told her that the Son of God was coming back soon.

"Is there any chance that maybe, just maybe you're wrong?" asked Abbey as she got control of herself. "I mean, what if this incident that just happened isn't a miracle? What if there are no more incidents after this?" asked Abbey. "Then what?"

"Then these are not the events that are described in the 'Manoscritto di sei eventi," said Fabianne simply. "But…..additional information we have gathered from the other two events says differently."

But before Abbey could ask about the additional information the Vatican had obtained, the driver opened up the sliding glass window between the passenger and the front compartment and announced that they had arrived at their destination.

CHAPTER SEVEN

The Inspector understood that Abbey would have more questions, especially after what she had just revealed to her. But she also knew that the questions would have to wait. At the moment, there was more pressing business to attend to.

As the Inspector quickly exited the car, she turned to her companion.

"L'Abbaye!" exclaimed Fabianne. "I know that you have many more unanswered questions," she said. "But we must interview the man who lives at this residence. And we must do it quickly, Detective. Time is of the essence. From this point on, I must follow your lead. You are an officer of the law who has jurisdiction here, I am not."

She knew that although Fabianne was a Vatican Inspector from Rome, she could not officially conduct an investigation on a case that occurred on U.S. soil. Nor could she approach any American citizen for questioning unless she was accompanied by someone who was an officer of the law, and had jurisdiction. She was in fact, a guest in the United States with no real official authority.

"Okay, Fabianne," said Abbey as she exited the car.

"But after we do this, if I'm going to continue to work with you on this case, I need all of my questions answered, understood?"

"Understood, Detective," agreed Fabianne.

"Alright then," said Abbey as she got a good look at where they were. "Whose residence is this, and why are we here?" asked Abbey as they made her way up a flagstone walkway that stretched across a well, manicured lawn and led to a two story Tudor home.

"This is where the man who pulled the woman from the car resides," answered Fabianne. "I must interview him to get a better picture of what actually happened last night. There are some very important questions that I must ask him. And then we must speak to the truck driver," said the Inspector.

"And the woman," added the Detective.

"As far as interviewing the woman, that may be.....a bit more difficult, Detective," said Fabianne as she stopped.

"I don't understand, why?" asked Abbey. "Getting both her and the truck driver's statements first hand could prove to be very valuable."

"Oui, but you see, the woman, although physically untouched from the accident, is currently in at one of the local hospitals. According to the doctors, her mind apparently shut down because she could not accept what happened. Detective, she does not remember anything from the time just before the accident happened, up to when the authorities found her in the middle of the road. She remembers nothing at all."

"I see," relented Abbey. "But we will still need to talk to her. Who knows, she may be able to remember something. And the truck driver?" asked Abbey as she continued up the walkway. "I assume you know where he is being held?"

"Ah, oui, the truck driver," said Fabianne. "He is currently being held at the Police station on a 24 hour hold. He was cited for traveling at an unsafe speed for the conditions that were present at the time. And of course, for causing the accident. And as far as the damage to the vehicles, the authorities have already been in touch with the trucking firm and the insurance company representing them. But what I do not understand Detective, is why they would only hold him for 24 hours and then release him. I do not completely understand your laws, but this is an ongoing investigation, is it not?"

"Well, let me see how to explain this to you, Inspector," said Abbey. "Your investigation is ongoing. As far as the authorities here are concerned, this one isn't. There were no injuries to any of the parties to speak of. And if the insurance companies have already been contacted as far as any damages that occurred because of the accident, it sounds like to me, that they're about to close this case and try forget that it ever happened."

"I do not understand. Why?" exclaimed Fabianne. "He is a witness and they are about to release him. We must speak to him tonight also, before that happens, Detective."

"Agreed," said Abbey. "But you can understand why practical thinking people, when faced with something like what happened last night, would to prefer to simply make it go away as quickly as possible. Especially, when you can't come up with a plausible answer for what happened. They really don't want to know why it happened," stated Abbey. "And I don't think they want to go looking for answers that they can't explain. But when we finish up here, we can go and speak to the driver before he's released," stated the Detective as she walked up to the front door of the house. "We'll see what he has to say."

It was easy to tell that they were in a very well-to-do, upscale neighborhood of Los Angeles proper. The houses were part of a well- established development with price tags that started in the low millions and went up from there.

"Very nice neighborhood, oui?" commented Fabianne as she looked around.

"I'll say!" exclaimed Abbey with a little bit of envy. "Not many of us are able to live like this."

"Je suis d'accord, d'accord," said Fabianne in French. "I agree!" repeated Fabianne in English. "Even in France, you must be very, very fortunate to live like this," she said. "Very fortunate, indeed."

"Let's do this," said Abbey as she reached out and rang the doorbell.

Just as she did, their driver was jogging up the walkway toward them.

"Inspector! Inspector," called out the driver. "You have a call. It is the Vatican," he announced.

"L'Abbaye!" said Fabianne. "I must take this. It is my superiors. I will join you as soon as I am finished, oui? You will be alright?"

"Ah, I think I can handle this until you get back," said the Detective, slightly miffed.

"Good. I will return shortly," said Fabianne as she headed back toward the car to take the call.

"Like I've never done a case interview before," mumbled Abbey to herself as she turned toward the door somewhat insulted. "Please!"

After a few minutes had passed and there was no answer at the door, Abbey stepped back and took a look at the front of the house.

"The lights are on," she said to herself as she stepped back up to the door and rang the doorbell again.

"LAPD!" called out the Detective as she pulled out her badge. "I'd like to speak to Benjamin Warren about the accident last night. Is anyone home?"

After a few more moments had passed, the door opened and a middle aged, well-dressed woman stood in the doorway. Abbey noticed that she seemed somewhat flustered.

"I'm Mrs. Warren. May I help you?"

"Yes, I'm Detective Abigail Wells with the LAPD, Madam," said Abbey as she flashed her badge. "I'm here with my partner, and we wanted to know if it was possible to speak with your husband? He was involved in a car accident the other night not too far from here and we'd like to ask him a few more questions."

"Yes. Yes, he was," she said. "But I'm afraid that he's resting now. Can't this wait until tomorrow?" she asked with a slight hint of irritation in her voice. "He's been questioned several times already and he, he needs his rest."

As the woman spoke, Abbey noticed that she seemed uncomfortable and kept glancing back over her shoulder up toward the second floor.

"Is everything alright, Madam?" she asked.

"No, Detective, it's not!" she answered sternly as she caught Abbey off guard. "Everything is 'not' alright. My husband, by the grace of God, has just survived an accident that by all accounts, he should not have survived! And everyone keeps asking him the same questions over and over again. He doesn't know what happened! Alright?" she exclaimed. "I'm afraid that I'm going to have to ask that you come back another time. The doctor doesn't want him to be disturbed anymore tonight."

As she spoke, the woman went to close the door.

"Madam! This will only take a few minutes. Please!" urged Abbey.

As Abbey spoke to the woman, she noticed that she became more agitated at her insistence to speak to her husband. So Abbey went to her back-up plan.

"If Mr. Warren is resting and we can't speak to him," said the Detective. "Then I'd like to ask you a few questions, Mrs. Warren. If you don't mind?"

"Me!!??" exclaimed the woman. "Why, why would you need to ask me any questions? I wasn't involved in the accident!"

"Yes. I know," said Abbey. "But perhaps you could answer some questions for us, and then maybe we wouldn't have to speak to your husband again. May I come in, please," said Abbey as she stepped up to the door showing the woman that she was insistent on speaking to someone tonight. "This will only take a few moments of your time."

"I have to keep a close eye on my husband," the woman said as she glanced upstairs again. "I can't, I….."

"Mrs. Warren. Is there any reason why you can't answer a few questions for me?" asked Abbey pushing her point. "This will only take a few minutes, alright?"

Realizing that she didn't have a reason to give the detective as to why she couldn't answer some of her questions, the woman relented.

"Yes. Yes, of course, Detective," she said. "Please come in."

The woman closed the door and ushered Abbey into a round entry hall that had twelve foot ceilings and was beautifully decorated. There was an oval table sitting in the middle of the hall that had an oversized vase sitting on it that was overflowing with various types of flowers mixed with delicate Baby Breaths. And to the right, there was a curved staircase that went up to the second floor of the home. The design in the inside of the house was typical Tudor style with a few modern touches added to personalize it.

"You have a beautiful home, Mrs. Warren," said Abbey as she took it all in.

"Yes, thank you," she said softly. "It is beautiful isn't it? Bennie, my husband…..he, he works very hard to provide for us. Please, we can talk in here," said Mrs. Warren as she showed the Detective into the living room.

This room, like the entry hall, was decorated with a very modern Tuscan style décor that had warm Autumn colors of Gold, soft Browns and touches of cool Greens. There were also large throw pillows on the floor and along the front of the fireplace. Abbey could tell that the house was not one that was decorated for display only. Rather this house was decorated with the intent that a family was to live in it and enjoy it.

It felt warm and inviting like a home should feel.

The two oversized couches in the living room were facing each other and sat in front of the fireplace. The Detective could see that magazines were strewn about on the top of the large coffee table sitting in front of the couches, and there were a pair of tennis shoes casually left in front of the table.

"I'm sorry," said Mrs. Warren as she tried to straighten up the table. "We have teenagers and they don't always leave the room straight. Please, sit down."

"It's fine, Mrs. Warren," said Abbey as she sat on one of the couches. "Really, your home is beautiful!"

"Thank you!" she said. "It's, it's our home."

Abbey could tell by the demeanor of the woman sitting across from her, that the events of the other night had taken a toll on the family of the man who had unselfishly risked his life to save that of another. She could appreciate the fact that although this woman's husband had saved another person's life, the realization that he could have been killed along with her, was overwhelming.

After a few moments of silence, Mrs. Warren spoke.

"Are you married Detective?" she asked quietly.

"Ahh, no. No I'm not married," answered Abbey somewhat caught off guard by her question. "I guess I'm one of those people who are married to their jobs," she answered truthfully. "There's just not enough time to do everything," she said as she gave a little laugh.

"Well, some would think that Bennie, my husband," she said smiling slightly. "Some would think that he was married to his job, too," she said. "But he's a good man who works hard and takes care of his family, Detective," she stated. "Every waking minute that he's not at work, he's doing something with me and the kids. It's just like him, always trying to be there for someone. I just don't know what I'd do if I lost him." She said in an emotional voice as she lowered her head and began to cry. "I just don't know what I'd do…..!"

Abbey, again caught off guard by the woman's emotional outburst, slowly rose from her seat and approached the woman.

"Mrs. Warren, it's going to be alright," said Abbey as she tried to console the distraught woman. "Your husband put his life in danger to save another person. And it sounds like that's the kind of person he is. And by whatever powers that be, they both are alright. That's something that you should embrace and be thankful for."

"I'm sorry, Detective. Don't misunderstand me. I am thankful. Very thankful," she said as she looked up. "I ahh…..I'm sorry. I didn't mean to fall apart like this, "she said through her tears. "I'm usually stronger than this. It's just that…..I realize sometimes we get complacent in our lives. That God has to pull our coattails to give us a wakeup call to appreciate the here and now. Because, Detective, nothing is guaranteed to stay as it is. Nothing. Everything changes whether we're ready or not."

"Well, then," said Abbey as she knelt in front of the woman. "I guess we just need to pray that we're ready for whatever is to come, don't we?"

As Abbey heard herself speak to the woman, she got an odd feeling that what she was saying had more meaning than she realized.

"Yes," agreed the woman. "And as you said, Detective. We should embrace the blessing that we've been given. Thank you for your kind words," she said. "And I apologize for my behavior earlier. I just kind of found myself spinning out of control with the thought of 'what could have happened'. I have to remember that the worst didn't happen."

"You're welcome, Mrs. Warren. It was my pleasure," said Abbey.

"You said that you had some questions for me, Detective," said the woman composing herself. "I don't know what information I can give you, but I'll do my best to help you in any way that I can."

"That's all that I ask, Mrs. Warren," said Abbey. "I won't take up too much of your time, I promise."

Then as the woman looked around, she asked Abbey a question.

"I'm sorry, Detective. Did you say that you had a partner with you?" asked the woman.

Abbey looked up and realized that Fabianne still hadn't come back from taking her call. But before she could respond to the woman's question there was a knock on the door.

"That must be her now," said Abbey as she got up and went toward the door.

"I'm sorry, Mrs. Warren," she asked before she opened the door. "Do you mind if I get that?"

"Oh no, please," answered the woman. "I don't mind."

As Abbey opened the door, Fabianne was standing in the doorway with an apologetic look on her face.

"I am so sorry," she said as she entered the house. "It was my superiors in Rome. They were checking up on my progress, and they informed me that they have dispatched another Inspector to assist us."

"Another Inspector?" asked Abbey quietly. "Why?"

"Usually, they only dispatch one Inspector for each investigation,"' explained Fabianne. "But as you may have guessed, in this case, they feel that it would be prudent to have another working with us. From my understanding, he will be here sometime tomorrow morning."

"Are you okay, with that?" asked Abbey, knowing that sometimes having your superiors assign another person to your investigation could cause problems.

"Oui, actually, I am okay with that," answered Fabianne. "L'Abbaye, I have a feeling that we may need all of the help that we can get," she said as she cast the Detective a sidelong glance.

For a quick moment, Abbey paused at her partner's response.

"Was there something else that she wasn't telling me?" Abbey asked herself.

Before Abbey could ponder the question further, Fabianne had walked toward Mrs. Warren and proceeded to introduce herself.

"Madame Warren, I am Inspector Fransquie Fabianne 'al Benne. How are you this evening?"

"I'm, fine. Fine."

By the look on Mrs. Warren's face, Abbey could tell that the woman was as taken back by Fabianne as she had been the first time she met her.

"What was a French Inspector doing here investigating a traffic accident involving my husband?" thought the woman to herself.

Abbey decided to intervene before both she and Fabianne were caught in a situation where they were going to have to do some serious explanations.

"Mrs. Warren," interrupted the detective. "The Inspector here is working on a special assignment with the LAPD. She's working with us to get a better understanding of how the Police in the US handles different types of cases."

"Ah, oui! Oui!" exclaimed Fabianne seeing what Abbey was doing. "I am, how do you say? On loan."

"Oh, you mean like an exchange program?" asked the woman.

"Yes, yes!" "Oui!! Oui!!" exclaimed both Abbey and Fabianne in unison as they exchanged looks with each other.

"I didn't know that the Police Department did that," said the woman.

"Oh, oui," said Fabianne. "It is done more often than you may think."

"Well, it's nice to meet you, Inspector. Please come in, sit down," said the woman. "My husband is resting, but the Detective was just about to ask me some questions," she said.

Then, without realizing it, she nervously glanced up again toward the second floor as if she were concerned about something.

"Mrs. Warren, is everything alright?" asked Abbey again. "That's the third time you've looked upstairs since I've been here. Are you sure everything is okay?"

"Actually, I had just left his room and was on my way downstairs when you first rang the doorbell," she said. "I thought I heard….."

"Heard what, Mrs. Warren?" asked Abbey.

"Oh, I'm sure it's nothing," she answered quickly. "I probably just need to get some rest. These last twenty four hours have been very hectic for me and my family."

"Madame Warren, I don't mean to pry," said Fabianne. "But what is it that you thought you heard?" repeated Fabianne, sensing that the woman was hesitant to answer the question.

"It's silly, really," she said. "But as I was coming down the stairs, I thought that I heard my husband speaking to someone."

"Perhaps it was one of your children who was in with him," said the Detective.

"No, that's impossible," said the woman quickly. "The children are all over to my Sister's house. We felt it would be better if they weren't here when all of the Police and the newspaper reporters were swarming around. There's no one in the house but my husband and I."

"Are you sure, Mrs. Warren?" asked the Detective.

"Yes! I'm positive," she said. "The odd thing is, I was sure that I heard someone answer him back. I had just headed back up the stairs to check when I heard you ring the doorbell again."

Instantly, Abbey got a bad feeling in her gut. The kind of feeling that her experience had taught her to not to ignore.

"Mrs. Warren, you're sure there's no else here?" asked the Detective as she slowly walked back into the entry hall and looked toward the second floor landing.

"Yes, I'm sure, Detective," insisted the woman wondering what has happening. "Why? I don't understand! What's going on?"

Quickly glancing at Fabianne, Abbey gave her a slight tilt of her head indicating that she should move Mrs. Warren further into the living room.

Taking the Detective's cue, Fabianne reached for Mrs. Warren's arm and directed her to the far side of the room.

"Please Madame Warren, if you do not mind. We would appreciate it if you do not move from this spot, oui?" said Fabianne as she turned and joined Abbey on the stairs.

"But what's going on?" asked the woman quite concerned. "Do you think someone is up there with my husband? Is he in danger?"

"We don't know, Mrs. Warren," said Abbey as she reached for her weapon and started to head up the stairs. "But you're sure you heard another person?" she asked again.

"I'm positive."

"Is there any other way to get down here from the second floor?" asked Fabianne. "A back staircase, perhaps?"

"No! No, this is the only way up or down," answered the woman as she stood by the fireplace, fearful that someone had broken into their home.

Abbey felt better knowing there was only one way to get off of the second floor. And if there was someone upstairs that shouldn't be, they would be hard pressed to get out of the house without getting past them. Other than jumping out of a window.

As Abbey and Fabianne slowly made their way up the stairs, they spied a set of double doors just to the left of the landing indicating that was where the Master Bedroom was. The right side of the double door was slightly opened revealing a set of bay windows along the left wall. Abbey could see a comfortable lounging chair and a table sitting next to the window, but not much more.

"Mr. Warren! LAPD!" called out Abbey. "Are you alright, Sir? Your wife said that she thought she heard someone up here with you!"

No response.

After a few seconds had passed, Fabianne looked at Abbey and indicated that she was going to make her way to the left side of the door. Nodding that she understood, Abbey waited until Fabianne had made her way across the hall and was in position.

Then the Detective called out again.

"Sir, we're coming in! If there is anyone in the room with you, we need them to 'stand down', now!"

No response.

Abbey's first thought was that Mrs. Warren's husband was in fact asleep and that she had only imagined she heard another voice in the room. But the Detective quickly dismissed that thought. For some reason her radar was ticking off telling her that 'something' wasn't right.

As a matter of fact, her gut was telling her that something was terribly wrong here.

Getting Fabiannes' attention, Abbey indicated that she was going to open the right side of the door all the way and for her to be ready. Fabianne nodded her head that she understood. That was when Abbey noticed that Fabianne had a weapon of her own that she had also drawn.

"Well, I guess it's better to have 'real' back-up when you need it," thought Abbey to herself.

But one thing was for sure.

When this was over, she was going to have ask Fabianne where she got the weapon from. Because as far as she knew, French Police didn't carry weapons.

Abbey decided to slowly open the door all the way so they could see the interior of entire bedroom from the hallway. She didn't want to go barging into the room with her weapon drawn and give the woman's husband an additional scare on top of what he had already gone through, especially if there was nothing wrong.

As she slowly swung the door to the bedroom open, both she and Fabianne held their positions in the hallway until they were sure of what they were walking into.

"Mr. Warren! LAPD!" called out Abbey. "We're coming in!"

And almost as if by instinct, Abbey went in standing up with her gun ready, and Fabianne went in low with her weapon poised.

"Clear on this side!" called out Abbey as she scoped the right side of the bedroom and entered.

"It is clear on this side, also!" answered Fabianne as she got to her feet and entered.

Before they knew it, Mrs. Warren had rushed into the bedroom and let out a curdling scream.

"Ahhhhh!!!" she screamed. "Bennie! Bennie where are you? Are you alright?"

Seeing that the king sized bed was empty except for the crumbled covers, Mrs. Warren ran past the two investigators and into the master bathroom where she let out another curdling scream.

"Ahhhhh!!! Bennie! Bennie, sweetheart, where are you?"

Following behind the woman, both Abbey and Fabianne realized that Mrs. Warren's husband was nowhere to be found, either in the bedroom or in the master bathroom. They even checked the large walk in closets to no avail.

Mr. Benjamin Warren was not there.

"What, what happened? Where is he?" asked his wife as she looked around the room frantically.

"Fabianne," said the Detective. "Check the other rooms on that side. I'll check the ones down the hall."

Within minutes, the entire second floor of the house had been checked and double checked by the two investigators. They even checked all of the windows on the second floor.

Mr. Benjamin Warren was nowhere to be found.

When Abbey came back into the room she had holstered her weapon and looked directly at the woman.

"What happened, Mrs. Warren? Where did he go?" asked the Detective.

"I don't know!!" she exclaimed. "He was here! He was right here when I left to go downstairs! She exclaimed loudly. "He said he wanted to lie down, so I helped him undress and I put him to bed. Then I went downstairs," said Mrs. Warren as she stood at the foot of the empty bed with a frantic look on her face.

"I, I intentionally left one of the doors open so If he called for me, I could hear him from downstairs," she said as she looked at the Detective.

"And when you were on the way downstairs, that's when you thought you heard him speaking to someone?" asked Fabianne.

"Yes! Yes!" exclaimed the woman.

"Mrs. Warren, exactly 'what' did you hear?" asked Abbey intently.

No response.

The woman just stood at the foot of the bed staring at the empty bed as tears rolled down her face.

"Madame Warren," said Fabianne softly in her French accent. "We need you to answer our questions so that we can help. Do you understand?"

Both investigators could tell that for some reason the woman was hesitant to answer.

After a few more moments of silence, the woman answered.

"I know this is going to sound crazy…..," she whispered under her breath as she looked down.

"Mrs. Warren," said Abbey. "Let us decide how crazy it may or may not sound, alright? Please tell us what you heard."

After taking a few moments to compose herself, the woman answered.

"I was halfway down the stairs when I thought.....I thought I heard voices. I knew that there's no one else in the house, so I thought that he was calling for me. So I turned back around and came back up the stairs. When I got to the head of the stairs, I could swear that I heard two distinct voices speaking softly."

"You actually could hear two voices?" asked the Detective.

The woman quickly nodded her head.

"One I recognized as my husband's voice," she said. "The other voice I couldn't hear clearly. It was muffled and I couldn't make out what they were saying. So I started to walk toward the bedroom door. And just as I got there, the door slowly closed on me. So I reached for the doorknob and tried to open it, but the door wouldn't open! I even pushed against it," she exclaimed with a little nervous laugh. "It was as if it had been locked from the inside."

"Why would your husband lock the door?" asked the Detective.

"That's just it! He wouldn't," she said. "So I called out to him to open up the door, but he didn't answer."

Abbey and Fabianne exchanged concerned but somewhat skeptical looks with each other, trying to figure out if the man's wife was telling the truth or not.

"But on the other hand," thought Abbey to herself. "Why would she lie about this?"

"How is this possible, Detective?" asked the woman as she stood before the two investigators. "Tell me how my husband could have gotten out of this room without going past me? Without me seeing him? And 'who' was he talking to?"

"Mrs. Warren!" exclaimed Abbey. "Mrs. Warren! We will do everything we can to find out where your husband is. I promise you."

Then the Detective looked over to Fabianne.

"I'm going to call this in," she said as she pulled out her phone and walked back downstairs. "Something's not right here."

"Oui! I agree," said Fabianne as she gingerly put an arm around the woman and walked her to the nearest chair in the room and sat her down.

"Madame Warren," said Fabianne as she knelt in front of the man's wife. "We will find out where your husband is, do you understand?"

As the Inspector spoke to the woman, she absentmindedly nodded her head and then looked up.

"Inspector," she exclaimed. "What do I tell the children?" she asked. "How do I explain this to them?"

"Madame, it will be alright. It will be alright," said Fabianne as she tried to comfort her. "We will make sure that there is someone here who can help you with that, yes?"

"I don't know what's happening," she exclaimed softly under her breath. "It's like the whole world is slowly being turned head over heels where nothing makes sense anymore."

"Oui, Madame!" said Fabianne sympathetically. "Oui! But I believe it will all make sense very soon."

Half listening to the Inspector, the woman looked up.

"Inspector," she said. "I just remembered something. When I was heading back upstairs, at one point I did hear some of what was being said inside of the room."

"Can you tell me what it was that you heard, Madame," asked Fabianne softly as she leaned in close.

"I could have sworn that I heard the other voice say something like, 'It's time to go. Are you ready?'" stated Mrs. Warren. "At that point I didn't know what to think. But by the time that I headed for the door, it had closed on me."

"Madame," said Fabianne. "Hopefully, everything will make sense soon. I promise you, it will be alright," she said. "But I am going to ask you to do something for me, oui? Do not repeat to anyone what you have just told me. I believe that for now, that may be something that we may need to look into further. And if too many people know of what it was that you heard, they may get the wrong idea about your husband."

"What about the detective?" asked Mrs. Warren.

"I will inform her. But it would help if you did not mention this to anyone else, please."

"Of course, Inspector. I won't say anything."

"Thank you, Madame for your cooperation," said Fabianne.

Then helping her stand, Fabianne led the woman out of the bedroom and back downstairs. Abbey was in the entry hall and had just finished her call when she saw the two women coming down the stairs.

"I thought perhaps it was better that she not be in the room alone until we have a better understanding of what is going on, oui?" said Fabianne as she walked past Abbey and went into the living room.

"Yeah, I think that's a good idea," agreed Abbey. "They're sending a team over to take our statements and to try and figure out what's going on. While we wait I'm going to go outside. I want to check and see if there's any sign of someone trying to enter the house through one of the first floor windows," said Abbey.

Her thoughts were to also check and see if perhaps there was any indication that Mr. Warren had somehow slipped out of the house through one of the second floor windows without his wife realizing it. Abbey couldn't figure out why he would do such a thing. It didn't make any sense.

"But right now, anything is possible," thought Abbey as she turned and made her way toward the front door.

"I'll be right back….." said the Detective as she called back over her shoulder and reached for the doorknob.

But before she could even finish her sentence, she abruptly stopped.

She didn't know 'why', but for some reason her gut told her to turn around. As she quickly turned toward the kitchen door at the end of the hallway behind her, a shadow passed by the door.

"Mr. Warren??" called out Abbey as she slowly turned away from the door and started to walk past the staircase. "Mr. Warren, we're LAPD. We're here to see if you could answer a few more questions for us, Sir."

No response.

Immediately, Abbey turned to Fabianne.

She knew she had seen someone pass by the doorway.

And the weird thing was it wasn't as if they were trying to hide. The shadow, for lack of a better way to describe it, seemed to slowly 'glide' past the doorway.

The Detective indicated to Fabianne that she was to stay with Mrs. Warren and not let her move from where she was. She then drew her weapon again and slowly walked down the hall toward the door that led to the kitchen.

"Bennie!" called out Mrs. Warren from the living room. "Is that Bennie?"

"Please Madame!" exclaimed Fabianne as she stood in front of the woman. "Let us see if it is in fact your husband, oui?" said the Inspector as she directed Mrs. Warren toward the fireplace.

As Abbey made her way down the hall, without any warning, she suddenly got a feeling in her stomach that caused her to abruptly pause. It was a feeling like she had never felt before. Almost a combined feeling of extreme fear and repulsion at the same time.

"What the Hell!!??" she exclaimed to herself as she froze and quickly put one arm out against the wall to steady herself.

She had confronted victims and assailants before in various kinds of situations and would get that nervous 'butterfly' feeling before each confrontation.

"Who didn't!" she thought to herself.

But this, this was something different altogether. It was such a weird feeling that was coursing through her body she almost thought she was going to throw up right then and there. Catching herself, Abbey took in a deep breath and with everything she had, fought back the urge she was feeling. She didn't understand what was happening, but she knew that she had to fight through whatever it was.

She raised her head and pushed herself away from the wall.

"LAPD!" she called out loudly as she shook off the feeling that was churning inside of her, and forced herself to move further down the hall. "Mr. Warren! Is that you?"

As the Detective passed several doorways that lined the hallway, she quickly checked each opening before she went any further. One thing she didn't want was for someone to get the drop on her from behind.

"LAPD! Whoever you are, I'm armed. Come out and show your hands!" called out Abbey as she approached the door to the kitchen.

"Show yourself! Reinforcements are on the way! This doesn't have to get ugly!"

No response.

Pausing just outside of the door that led into the kitchen, Abbey took another deep breath to try and clear her head. That feeling she had felt earlier was getting stronger the closer she got to the kitchen. She didn't know what to expect once she stepped into the kitchen, but Abbey entered with her gun held in position.

Fabianne had slowly walked toward the entry hall with her gun also drawn. She could hear Abbey as she called out to whoever was in the kitchen, but she didn't hear a response.

"Detective!" called out Fabianne. "I have the front door and the stairs covered," she said as she positioned herself in the archway between the living room and the entry hall.

Acknowledging that the front part of the house was covered, Abbey stepped into the kitchen. There were enough lights on to where she could see the entire kitchen and eating area. First she checked the area directly to her right and then made her way past the island that went down the middle of the entire kitchen, careful to look on both sides of the counter before going any further.

Once she had cleared the rest of the main kitchen area, she checked the breakfast nook and the pantry as well as the French doors that led into the backyard. Everything was locked and secured.

"But I know what I saw," said Abbey to herself as she continued to keep her eyes and ears alert for anything out of the ordinary.

There was no mistaking what she had seen. And that feeling that almost brought her to her knees was not imagined. This she knew for a fact because she still had an odd taste in the back of her mouth from it.

After a few moments of double checking the room, Abbey walked back to the door of the kitchen that led to the entry hall and stood in the entrance. She was not one to imagine things, and this she did not imagine.

Looking down the hall to where Fabianne was waiting, Abbey shook her head that it must've been a false alarm and it was all clear. And although she still could feel remnants of that feeling in her gut, she had to relinquish to the fact that there was nothing there.

Fabianne, seeing that Abbey was alright, turned and lowered her gun, and went back to where Mrs. Warren was still sitting by the fireplace, afraid to even breathe.

"Was it Bennie?" she asked as she stood up. "Was it my husband?"

"No, Madame," said Fabianne softly. "I'm afraid it was not. But we will find him," she said.

Taking one more look around the kitchen before she left, Abbey holstered her gun. Just as she turned her back, a shadow crossed the entrance of the door again, and that feeling that she had felt before, returned.

Quickly turning around, Abbey jerked slightly as she saw someone standing on the other side of the island looking out of the kitchen windows with their back turned to her. It startled Abbey to the core because this person was not there moments before. There was no one in the kitchen, and this she knew for a fact. And now what she saw was an old woman with white hair, wearing a flowered housedress. She was standing there casually looking out of the window into the back yard, as if she had been there all along.

Abbey was so taken aback she couldn't find her voice for a few seconds.

Then catching herself, she went to open her mouth to call out to Fabianne. But before Abbey could even get the words mentally formed to speak them, the old woman had slowly turned her head toward the Detective and eyed her. The woman had a weird smirk on her face that sent a chill down Abbey's spine as her body involuntarily shuttered. And it was then that Abbey realized that the old woman's head had not just turned to look at her over her shoulder.

"Oh, my God!!" exclaimed Abbey out loud as she realized that the old woman's head had turned a full 360 degrees around while the rest of her body was still facing the windows.

And her eyes!

"Oh my God!" exclaimed Abbey out loud as she gasped.

Her eyes were now a milky white color with no pupils whatsoever.

Abbey was stunned!

And then the rest of the woman's body turned toward the Detective in quick jerky movements, until she was facing Abbey full on.

The Detective stumbled backwards a few steps as her mind tried to make sense of what she had just seen.

"What..the..Hell..is going on?" Abbey exclaimed softly under her breath as she backed up.

She had never seen anything like that before.

Her heart felt as if it were going to jump right out of her chest as she felt the pounding exploding inside of her body. What she had just witnessed was impossible outside of a horror movie. And as that thought seared into her brain, she took another step back.

"Oh shit!!!" she exclaimed out loud as crazy ideas of what could be happening ran through her mind.

And if that hadn't been enough of a shock for the Detective, before she knew it, the old woman had somehow moved herself from the other side of the island with weird jerky movements and was now standing directly in front of her, without going around the island. And that gut wrenching feeling she had experienced before became so overwhelming it almost caused her to double over.

Abbey looked up at the old woman standing in front of her and realized that she was the source of the sick, repulsive feelings she was experiencing.

"Who the 'Hell' are you?" she asked as she tried to stand. "Where is Mr. Warren?"

The old woman smiled a dirty, toothless smile at Abbey, and bent down so she could lean in toward her face. Immediately, the repulsive feeling became so powerful, Abbey thought she was going to faint. There was no doubt that the source of what she was experiencing was coming from this woman, whoever she was.

"You will not win!!" she exclaimed in a raspy, course voice. "They may have taken the others, but the rest are ours!!"

And then the old woman snickered at the Detective as if she were mocking her.

"Enough of this!!!" thought Abbey as she mustered everything she could and let out a scream.

"Ahhhhh!!!" screamed Abbey.

Hearing the Detective scream, Fabianne and Mrs. Warren both leapt off of the couch and rushed into the hallway.

"L'Abbaye! L'Abbaye!" shouted the Inspector as she reached the Detective's side and bent down to help her stand. "What is it? What has happened?"

"A woman….." exclaimed Abbey under her breath as she looked up at the Inspector. "There was an old woman here….."

Quickly looking around, Fabianne found no evidence of anyone being in the room with Abbey. Turning to Mrs. Warren, the Inspector looked at her intently.

"I thought you said there was no one else in the house with you, Madame!" exclaimed Fabianne angrily, not happy that someone must have attacked her partner.

"But there isn't, Inspector," said the woman defensively. "Only my husband and I are here."

"I saw her, spoke to her," whispered Abbey to Fabianne, not wanting Mrs. Warren to overhear her.

The feeling had now all but dissipated and Abbey was able to stand on her own.

"It was an old woman, Fabianne. I don't know where she came from, but she was standing over there by the windows," whispered Abbey.

"An old woman!" exclaimed Fabianne as she instinctively looked over toward the windows. "There is no old woman here, L'Abbaye."

Just then the doorbell rang, followed by a secession of loud knocks on the door.

"Police! Detectives, you called about a possible disappearance!"

Turning to Mrs. Warren, Fabianne spoke.

"Please, Madame Warren. Would you mind letting the officers in while I see to my partner, oui?"

"Fine!" exclaimed the woman as she turned on her heel and walked down the hall to the front door. "Maybe they can give me some answers as to where my husband is."

Turning to her partner, Fabianne once again inquired if she was alright.

"I saw her, Fabianne!" insisted the Detective as she looked at the Inspector intently. "I saw her!"

Nodding her head that she believed her, Fabianne spoke to Abbey in a low voice.

"I believe you, L'Abbaye," said Fabianne as she looked toward the police officers who had just entered the residence and were now making their way toward them. "But for now do not speak of the woman or of what you just experienced to anyone until we can talk, Oui? Trust me, L'Abbaye, please! They cannot know of this."

"What!!!??" exclaimed Abbey, not believing what Fabianne had just asked her to do.

Before Abbey could contest any further, Fabianne had moved away from her side and walked toward the officers who were making their way down the hall towards them.

She was still trying to get over the fact that Fabianne had asked her to withhold information on a possible suspect that she had had contact with. But then she also knew that there was a whole lot more to this case than what Fabianne was telling her. And if she was going to be asked to withhold information, then she was going to need some real answers for doing that.

"Abbey! Abbey, did you call this in?" called out the officer as he and another officer approached her. "We got a call about a possible kidnapping. You want to tell us what's going on?" he said as he looked at Abbey and then at Fabianne.

When Abbey looked up, she saw it was Kurt. She had just spoken to him earlier before her whole professional career found its way into the crapper and she was assigned to this case.

"Kurt. It's good to see you," she said as she avoided looking at Fabianne.

"Would you have one of your men get Mrs. Warren's statement for me," she said. "It would seem that her husband has disappeared from the upstairs master bedroom. We need to find out how they got in and out, and 'why' they took him. And we need to have someone take a look outside to see if there was any evidence of possible forced entry from any of the doors or windows."

"Sure thing," said Kurt as he directed the officer with him to get a statement from Mrs. Warren.

Then he directed part of his team to check the perimeter of the property and the neighboring houses, and to report back when they were finished. He also dispatched two of his men upstairs to canvass the room where the victim had disappeared from.

When he had finished, he turned back to the Detective.

"You okay, Abbey?" he asked when he turned back to look at her. "You look kinda flushed."

Glancing quickly over to Fabianne, the Detective nodded her head.

"I'm fine, Kurt," she said. "Thanks for asking. I…..ahmm. I thought that maybe I had seen someone else in the house, but I must've been wrong."

"Alright, well…..I'll head upstairs then. I'll talk to you two when we finish, okay," said the Detective as he turned on his heel and headed up the stairs.

After the Detective had left, Abbey quickly looked toward Fabianne.

"Now what was that all about, Fabianne?" she asked briskly. "I feel like I'm working this case without knowing all of the rules. Why did you ask me not to divulge what I saw?"

"Because, L'Abbaye, if you told him what you saw, he would not have believed you," she stated. "What if you did say that you saw an old woman here. Who would believe that such a person would be able to have taken Mr. Warren? And what do you think they would say if you told them that old woman's very presence made you nauseous to the point that it almost doubled you over and incapacitated you? How do you think that would sound?" asked Fabianne.

"Fabainne," said Abbey quietly. "I never told you that her presence made me nauseous. How did you know that?"

"Because, L'Abbaye, I know 'what' it was that you saw here this night," said the Inspector simply as she looked directly at Abbey. "And trust me, when I tell you 'what' it was, you will have a hard time believing it yourself."

"What I saw??" exclaimed the Detective in a low voice. "I know 'what' I saw! It was an old woman in a flowered dress who, who obviously was

97

in need of some personal hygiene tips," said Abbey. "The stench that came off of her was.....was....."

"It was pure evil, L'Abbaye, trust me," stated Fabianne without any hesitancy in her voice. "What you saw was evil incarnate in a form that was meant to lure you into trusting it. To let your guard down so that it could defeat you."

The look on Abbey's face said it all.

"Evil incarnate!" exclaimed Abbey. "Defeat me??" asked Abbey as she looked at the Inspector. "Defeat me how?"

And then Abbey remembered something. It was what the old woman had said to her just before she screamed and Fabianne had rushed to her side.

Seeing the look that had spread across the Detective's face, Fabianne stepped in close.

"L'Abbaye, did it say something to you?" she asked.

After a few moments, Abbey nodded her head and acknowledged that the woman did in fact say something to her.

"I almost forgot!" said Abbey apologetically. "I mean, everything happen so fast, I....."

"What did it say, L'Abbaye?" insisted Fabianne. "Detective!"

"It didn't make any sense," answered Abbey.

"Tell me, Detective. What of anything that has happened this day has made any sense to you?" said Fabianne as she stated the obvious. "What it say to you?"

Not ready to relinquish the fact that 'what' she had seen was not an old woman, Abbey answered.

"She said something like 'You will not win!' and then she kinda snickered and said, 'They may have the others but the rest are ours!' or something like that," said Abbey. "What did she mean, the others are ours? What others?" asked Abbey. "Are there others, Fabianne?"

Fabianne breathed in deep and turned toward Abbey and nodded.

"Yes, there are others," stated the Inspector slowly as she looked at Abbey. "Like Mr. Warren, the persons who were involved with the first and the second miracles have also disappeared without a trace."

Abbey found herself at a loss for words. Again!

"Disappeared?" exclaimed the Detective, not believing that Fabianne had not told her this before. "And just when were you going to tell me this?" she threw out at the Inspector.

"The call I got just before you entered this residence informed me of the second disappearance," said Fabianne. "At first they thought that the Father of the young girl in France had taken her someplace away from the media. But we now know that was not the case. She has disappeared like the first Prophet in Mexico. You asked why they were dispatching another Inspector. That is why, L'Abbaye. We now have three missing people in three different parts of the world. And each of the events that have happened so far, coincide with what was predicted in the Manuscript of the Six Events. In the exact order as penned over two thousand years ago."

"So…..what you're saying is…," started Abbey.

"What I am saying is that the Vatican is getting very concerned," said Fabianne.

"You mean that someone might be kidnapping these people?" asked Abbey. "Why would someone do that?"

"They do not know," said Fabianne. "But you can see that it is too much of a coincidence, oui? And if the events of the manuscript are in fact coming to fruition, how do they deal with it."

"I don't understand," said Abbey. "Isn't this what Christians all over the world have been waiting for?"

"Yes, you are right, L'Abbaye," agreed Fabianne. "But the question is, if everything the manuscript predicts comes to pass, how do you go about telling the world what is about to happen?"

As the silence hung in the air between them, Abbey pondered Fabianne's question.

"If you will excuse me, Detective," said Fabianne as she moved away from the rest of the officers in the hall and pulled out her cellphone. "I must make a phone call."

Vatican City

2:30am

As the Father rushed down the elaborately decorated halls of the Eminence's residence, the soft rustle of his robes and muffled sounds of his shoes was the only sound that could be heard in the early hours of the morning. When he reached the door leading to the Eminence's private rooms, he paused to catch his breath for a few moments. He nodded to the two guards standing on either side of the door and then knocked softly.

"Your Eminence!" he called out through the heavy wooden door. "I'm sorry to disturb you. But you asked to be informed if there was any news!"

After a few minutes of silence, the Father heard movement from inside of the room. And then as the door slowly swung opened, the Father quickly bowed as the Eminence appeared in the doorway.

"Yes, Father!" asked the Eminence. "Do you have word?"

"We do!" exclaimed the Father softly as he gripped his hands in front of him. "We just got a call, your Eminence. It has happened again for a third time!"

The face of the Eminence had turned almost ashen as he steadied himself against the door.

"Have you already dispatched another Inspector?" he asked.

"Yes, your Eminence. Per your direction, another Inspector is already on his way."

"Who have you dispatched?" asked the Eminence.

"Michael, your Eminence," answered the Father. "He was the closest. He's been recovering in Seattle, Washington at St. Augustine's Cathedral."

"Good, Father, good. Now come in!" said the Eminence as he stepped aside. "I have further instructions for you. We must prepare just in case the other two events come to pass."

As the Father stepped inside of the room, the Eminence closed the door. He quickly spoke to the Father in a hushed voice and then opened the door and dismissed him to follow his instructions.

"And Father Girabaldi," said the Eminence. "I want you to make sure the messages are delivered to the Heads of State post haste. No one else is to handle this information, do you understand?"

"Yes, your Eminence," said the Father as he bowed again. "I understand."

And then he quickly turned on his heel and rushed back down the hall to do as he had been instructed.

CHAPTER EIGHT

After almost an hour had passed and the Police had checked the entire perimeter of the house as well as speaking to the neighbors on the street, there still was no evidence that anyone had tried to break in to the Warren's residence. As a matter of fact, there wasn't any evidence that explained how Mr. Warren or anyone else could have gotten out of the house without going through the front door.

"Abbey," said Kurt as he approached the Detective. "So far we're coming up with 'nada'," he said as he spread his hands indicating there seemed to be nothing to find. "The house is locked up tight as a drum. If anyone got out of the house, they went through that front door."

"Thanks Kurt," said Abbey hoping to hear something altogether different. "The problem is, one of us has been down here the entire time. No one could've gotten by us. No one."

"I don't know what to tell you kid," said Kurt as he stood with Abbey and the Inspector in the entry hall. "We'll bag and tag what we've got, write up the report and get it to you sometime tomorrow. At this point I can't write it up as a kidnapping. There's no evidence," he said apologetically. "I'm going to have to write it up as I see for now, and that's a missing person's report. I've already put out an APB on him with a full description that I got from his wife."

"But what about Mrs. Warren? What's she supposed to do?" asked Abbey concerned about a woman who had already gone through one traumatic situation with her husband, and now her husband was missing.

"Kurt, her husband is missing from the upstairs bedroom. There's got to be more that we can do for her!"

"Like I said kid, there's not a whole lot to go on. We've already contacted her family, and they're on the way over. When we finish up here, I'll leave an officer with her until they arrive. But by all accounts, it looks like he somehow got up and just…...left. Now how he got out, that's got us all stumped."

And then he turned and looked over to where Mrs. Warren was standing with another officer. He paused for a moment and then continued.

"That is of course, unless his wife isn't telling us everything," he said with a suspicious tone to his voice. "It just seems kinda odd you know," he said.

And then as an afterthought he turned back to Abbey and the Inspector.

"You both said that he was here when you entered the residence, right?" he asked. "Did either of you actually see him or speak to him?"

It only took a second for both Abbey and Fabianne to realize that they only had Mrs. Warren's word that her husband was in fact upstairs in the bedroom when they came in. Neither of them had actually seen him.

"No!" said the two in unison.

"Neither of us saw him, Kurt," stated Abbey understanding how it was beginning to look.

She wanted to tell him about the old woman that she had seen standing by the kitchen window, but stopped herself just short of blurting it out. There did seem to be a whole lot more to this case just as Fabianne had said there was. So she caught herself and figured she would give the Inspector the time she needed for now.

"Thanks for what you've done, Kurt. I appreciate it," said Abbey as she realized there was nothing else she could do.

"Sure thing, kid. I'll talk to you sometime tomorrow, okay," said Kurt as he turned and joined his men as they prepared to pack up and clear out.

"L'Abbaye. We should go also," said Fabianne. "There is nothing more we can do here. We must speak to the driver before they release him from custody, oui?"

"Ahh, yeah!" exclaimed Abbey almost forgetting about the driver. "We do need to question him," she said as she turned to follow Fabianne to the front door.

And then just before she got to the door, she stopped.

"Fabianne. You go ahead to the car," she said. "I need to speak to Mrs. Warren before I leave. I'll be right behind you."

"Oui! I will wait for you in the car, Detective," said Fabianne as she turned and left the house.

Not really knowing what she could say that would give any comfort to Mrs. Warren in a situation like this, Abbey still needed to let her know that the pain she was going through was acknowledged and not being dismissed.

"Officer, I'd like to speak to Mrs. Warren for a minute," said Abbey as she approached the woman as she stood at the foot of the stairs.

As the officer left the two alone, Abbey turned to the woman.

"Mrs. Warren, I just want you to know that the Police will do everything in their power to find your husband."

"I know what they think, Detective," said Mrs. Warren as she looked around and her eyes began to water again. "They think he's going crazy because of what happened the other night, don't they? That maybe his mind has just snapped. But they're wrong, Detective!" exclaimed the woman.

"Maybe he 'was' having trouble dealing with what happened and you weren't aware....." said Abbey.

Before she could even finish her sentence, Mrs. Warren interrupted her.

"No, Detective, you don't understand!" she exclaimed in a soft voice. "Bennie wasn't confused about what happened last night. He told me that he understood 'why' it had happened. He said that he was 'told' that he was the third of five, whatever that means."

"The third of five," repeated Abbey.

As Abbey realized what the woman's husband was referring to, she became lightheaded..

"Trust me, I have no idea what he meant," said Mrs. Warren. "But I can't tell them that!" she exclaimed. "Then they'll really think that he's crazy. And he's not, Detective," lamented the woman. "My Bennie, he's not....."

Abbey just nodded her head blindly, trying not to let Mrs. Warren know that she knew what her husband meant. But the realization of what she had said sent a chill through her.

"Could this really be happening?" her mind screamed.

She actually felt like she was in the middle of one of those blockbuster movies where the reveal was just around the corner.

"But I'm not sure I'm ready for this!" exclaimed the voice in her head. "I, I don't know if I'm ready."

"Detective, are you alright?" asked Mrs. Warren as she caught the look that had come across Abbey's face.

"I'm.....fine! Fine!" said Abbey as she lied to the woman.

She now understood what Fabianne meant when she said if everything on the 'Manuscript of the Six Events' came to pass, how would you tell the world what was coming? And how would the world react to such a revelation, when she herself was having a problem dealing with it?

The thought was mind blowing.

"Mrs. Warren, I'm sure we'll find your husband," she said. "Everything will be alright," said Abbey as she touched the woman's arm and then turned and walked out, not knowing what else to do.

She couldn't get outside quick enough so she could get some air and clear her head. As she walked to the waiting car her mind was spinning as she tried to make sense of everything that had happened. As Abbey got into the sedan and closed the door, the car pulled away from the residence. As Fabianne sat across from Abbey, she could see that she was deep in thought.

"Are you alright, L'Abbaye?" asked the Inspector, realizing that everything that she had now been made privy to was a lot for anyone to take in.

"Mrs. Warren said her husband told her that he knew 'why' what happened last night had happened. And he said that he was 'told' that he was the 'third of five'," repeated Abby as she blankly stared out of the window.

"He said this, L'Abbaye?" exclaimed Fabianne as she leaned forward. "He said that he was the 'third of five'?" repeated the Inspector trying to confirm what she was hearing.

All Abbey could do was to nod her head, which by now was beginning to throb terribly.

"We must hurry so I can speak to the driver," said Fabianne quickly. "I must ask him certain questions in order to confirm or to deny if this event is what I think it is."

"And if it is what we both are thinking it is," started Abbey. "What's next, Fabianne? Do we just sit around and wait to see if something else happens? What if something does happen, do we just go traipsing off to investigate it? And what if it's in another country like the first two?"

"I do not know, L'Abbaye. But that is a possibility," answered Fabianne honestly. "That is why I need to inquire of you if your passport is current?"

"My.....my passport??!!" exclaimed Abbey not expecting that response. "Are you serious?"

"I am quite serious, Detective," said Fabianne. "If another event does occur, we must be ready to leave at a moment's notice to wherever it may be. You do have a passport, oui?"

"Yes, of course I do, but I don't know.....!" exclaimed Abbey as her head began to throb even more than it had been before. "I mean, are you serious about this?"

"Oui, Detective," said Fabianne. "Your superiors with the approval of your government, has assigned you to work with me. I am sure that after everything that has happened so far, you understand the scope of what we are dealing with. That means wherever the case takes me, it takes you."

Just the thought that at a moment's notice she could be whisking off to another country investigating a miracle with a Vatican Inspector was beyond belief.

"Who would have ever thought that my day would come to this," though Abbey as she leaned back into the seat of the car as it made its way through the streets of LA to the Police station where the truck driver was being held. "Not me that's for sure," she thought.

As the car made its way through the now busy streets of the city, Abbey was content to just sit and stare out of the window. For the moment she didn't want to talk about anything. Not about what had happened at the Warren's house or what Mrs. Warren had said to her about her husband knowing what was happening and that he was the 'third of five'.

Abbey just wanted to be as quiet as she could, and try to think about nothing. Nothing at all!

Fabianne, appreciating the situation that the reluctant Detective had been thrust into, gave her the space that she obviously needed as the car made its way to the Police station.

The traffic was more congested coming back than it had been when they had first went to Warren's residence. But within a half an hour the black sedan had finally pulled up to the precinct station letting Abbey and the Inspector out at the front entrance.

Once inside, Abbey made her way to the prisoner holding area, with Fabianne following close behind. She knew most of the officers who worked in the area and hoped that she didn't have to deal with too many unnecessary questions in order to speak to the truck driver.

As she and Fabianne exited the elevator on the bottom floor, they made their way to where officers were manning the glass enclosed counter area where the holding cells were. When Abbey looked up, she was glad to see someone she knew on duty.

"Hey, Abbey!!" exclaimed the officer at the desk behind the glass enclosure. "What are you doing slumming down here?"

"Hey, Donny!" called out Abbey as she stopped at the counter. "You know I gotta come down here and check on my boys every once in a while, right?"

"Hey, you know you're welcome any time," said the officer as a big grin spread across his face. "We need to see a pretty face down here every once in a while," he said. "You how many 'dog faced' officers we got working at this precinct?"

"Donny! Cut it out!" Abbey exclaimed quietly. "Someone might hear you!" she said as she looked around. "Especially some of the ones you've actually dated!" she said softly.

"Hey!" exclaimed Donny. "I'm very selective," he said as he got defensive.

"Sure you are, Donny. Ah huh!"

But Abbey didn't know why she was surprise by his remark. It was coming from an officer who by all accounts wasn't that attractive himself, but was known throughout the entire precinct as being a 'dog' by most of the single female officers.

"And as I understand, a couple of married ones, too!" exclaimed Abbey to herself as she just smiled at her friend.

Abbey didn't know what Donny was working with, but it had to be something to have gotten with as many women as he had.

And then as if by cue, Donny leaned to one side and looked beyond Abbey so he could get a better look at the woman following behind her.

"And 'who' is this?" exclaimed the officer as he cast a sexy smile toward Fabianne.

"She is a French Inspector from the Vatican in Rome, officer," said Abbey trying to be as professional as she could. "She's on loan to us for a few days, and I know that you'll be on your best behavior while she's with us. Won't you, Donny?"

Abbey could see that Donny was totally taken in by Fabianne's slender frame, her fair skin and her Honey Blond hair. And her almost Azure Blue eyes only added to the full package.

"Officer!" said Abbey as she got Donny's attention. "I need to speak to the truck driver that you're holding from the accident that happened last night. Donny?"

"Yeah! Yeah!" exclaimed Donny as he continued to smile at the Inspector. He reached down and buzzed them into the secure area without taking his eyes off of Fabianne. "Sure thing!"

"Thanks Donny, we'll only be a few minutes," said Abbey as she and Fabianne went through the scanning door that led into the holding cell area.

After signing them both in, Abbey looked up.

"Donny, which way?"

"He's in cell number 24," said officer as he continued to eye Fabianne. "Straight ahead and then to the right. He's in the last cell on the left hand side. Hey Pete!" called out Donny to another officer on duty with him. "Will you escort these two 'lovely' ladies to holding cell #24 for me?"

"Thanks Donny," said Abbey as she and Fabianne followed the other officer.

"Oh, and ah, ladies," called out Donny as he leaned against the counter. "If there is anything, and I mean anything that I can do for you, I'm at your disposal," he said. "Especially, for the beautiful French pastry that's visiting us."

"Ah, Donny!! Show a little class will you," exclaimed Abbey as she gave Fabianne an apologetic look. "She's a visitor, for God's sake! I don't want her to think that all Police Officers in the United States are 'dogs'!"

To Abbey's surprise, Fabianne turned to her and just smiled at her as if to say, 'It's alright, Abbey. I've got this.' And then Fabianne looked back at Donny as she slowly walked over to where the officer was leaning against the counter.

What had Abbey worried was that it wasn't just a smile that Fabianne had on her face. It was more of a mischievous smirk. And that caused her to worry about Donny and what Fabianne had in mind. But she didn't have long to wait.

As Fabianne approached the officer, she stopped just in front of where he was leaning against the counter. Then she tilted her head slightly to the right and started to speak to him in French.

Donny pushed himself off of the counter so he could look at the Inspector as she spoke to him. And although he didn't understand a single word of what she was saying, he was enthralled by her accent and the way she looked at him.

He was in seventh heaven.

And then Fabianne, still smiling, reached out with her right hand as if she were going to caress his left cheek. And without any warning she quickly popped his cheek with her open hand making a loud slapping sound.

"Oww!!" exclaimed the officer as his whole body jerked to attention as the stinging feeling swept through his body. "What the…..! Hey!" he exclaimed. "You can't hit an officer!"

And then she spit out something else in French and turned on her heel and walked away from the officer. As she left, she continued to make gestures with both of her hands while still exclaiming something in French.

Abbey and the other officers could only stand there and watch as their mouths dropped.

And then as Fabianne walked away, Abbey turned to the officer.

"Well, Donny," said Abbey after a few seconds had passed. "I don't have any idea what she just said to you, but I don't think that she wants whatever it is your offering," stated Abbey as she tried to stifle a grin.

Still trying not to openly laugh at the events that had just occurred, Abbey turned to follow Fabianne out of the reception area and down the hall to the right. As she left, she could hear Donny telling the rest of the officers in the room, 'that the show was over and they needed to get back to work.'

As Abbey turned the corner, she caught up with Fabianne.

"What all did you say to him?" she asked.

"I just told him that he was a 'man dog', and that there was nothing he had that I would ever have the slightest interest in," said Fabianne in a low voice so that the officer they were following wouldn't hear. "And then I told him to go and lick himself," she said as she smiled and gave Abbey a quick glance. "I said that was probably the only way that he could get any kind of 'hard on'."

"You did not!" exclaimed Abbey softly, surprised at Fabianne's admission, but amused at her spunk.

"Oui, I did," admitted the Inspector. "Of course, I knew he did not understand a word of what I said…..but it felt good for me to say it anyway. We French women are very direct," said Fabianne. "Besides, he deserved it!"

"That he did, Fabianne, that he did," agreed Abbey as she found that she couldn't contain her grin.

They had walked past about ten cells, most of them empty for now, but Abbey knew that it was Saturday and that would change before the night was over.

When they had reached the last cell at the end of the hall on the left, the Officer stopped. In front of them was a ten by ten glass holding cell where a slightly disheveled, middle aged man was sitting on a bench that sat across from a rumpled bed.

When they stopped in front of the cell, the man inside looked up.

"His name is Frank Crowly," stated the officer as he reached for the clipboard that was hanging on the right of the door. "I suppose you know that he was the driver of the semi that crashed into that car on the South side last night?"

"Yeah, we do," said Abbey as she observed the nondescript man inside of the cell.

"Hell of an accident, too," the officer said as he looked at the man and then back at Abbey. "Any idea of what really happened?" he asked. "I mean, there's gotta be a logical explanation, right?"

"That's what we're trying to figure out, officer," answered the Detective. "Can my partner and I speak to him alone?"

"Sure. He's just about to be released," said the officer as he punched in a code on the keypad to the left of the door and stepped aside.

As the door slide open, the officer said, "When you're finished, just let me or one of the other officers know, we'll open the door for you."

"We'll do that, officer, thank you," said Abbey as she and Fabianne entered the cell and the door closed behind them.

"Mr. Crowly, I'm Detective….."

Before Abbey could finish her sentence, the man looked at both of them and exclaimed, "I don't know what else to tell you guys!" he said. "How many times can I say it? I know what I saw and I still don't believe it! End of story!"

"Mr. Crowly," said Abbey trying not to push too hard. "My partner would like to ask you a couple more questions. Please, if you don't mind."

"I'm done answering questions," said the man obviously irritated. "My company's lawyers said that I was not to say anything else about the accident, so yeah! I do mind!"

Then Fabianne stepped forward.

"Monsieur Crowley. I am an Inspector from France. I am on loan to the United States for a short period of time," said Fabianne. "I do not wish to ask you anything about the accident. But if I may ask, did Monsieur Warren, the man who pulled the woman from the car, say anything to you? Did he say anything at all?"

Like everyone else, the man sitting in the cell was surprised to see a French Officer working a case in LA. It just wasn't something that you heard of.

"You're from France?" asked the man somewhat surprised. "Huh!!"

"Oui, Monsieur," said Fabinne as she smiled as sweetly as she could.

She knew that old saying that honey gets you a whole lot further that vinegar did was in fact very true. So in order to get the answers that she needed from this man, she was going to use whatever female whiles she had to. And since time was of the essence and she didn't have a whole lot of it to waste.

"Please, did he say anything to you at all?" asked Fabianne as she stepped in closer to the man. "Something perhaps, that did not make any sense to you at the time. Something that you may not have thought was important."

The man looked down for a moment and then looked back up at Fabianne. She could sense that there was something he wasn't saying.

"Monsieur, please," she said. "Did he say anything at all?"

Abbey could tell that Fabianne was looking to hear something in particular from this man, but she didn't know what it was. But she knew it was something specific that was related to the case.

"Well, he did recite something that sounded like a bible verse to me when I saw him get up off the ground," said the man. "I mean, that's what it sounded like to me," he said. "Hey, I was in shock when I saw him get up, so.....I'm not sure."

And then the man looked around and whispered softly as if someone else was listening in on their conversation.

"All I know is that I started to bawl like a baby when he got up," admitted the man. "Not a scratch on him. It just wasn't possible, you know?"

"You said he recited what sounded like a biblical verse," asked Abbey. "What verse?"

"Hey, I'm not the most religious man around, you know," said the man as he shrugged his shoulders. "So I don't know if it was a verse from the bible or not. All I know is that he said something like, ahh.....'Blessed are those who believe in him, you are loved.' And then he said what sounded like, 'Watch for him, or for his return. He is coming, the Son.' I'm not sure," said the man. "Do you know what he meant?" he asked.

"No," replied Fabianne simply. "I am sorry. I do not know what that means. But thank you anyway for your time, Monsieur."

Turning to Abbey, Fabianne said, "Detective, I am done. I'm afraid I did not find what I thought I would," she said. "We can go now."

Calling for the officer to open the door, Abbey gave Fabianne a side-long glance as they exited the cell. She could tell by Fabianne's reaction to what the truck driver had said, that it meant more than she was letting on. But she also knew that this was not the time, nor the place to question Fabianne about it.

It could wait until they were someplace where they could talk.

As they exited the precinct building, Abbey stopped in the middle of the steps.

"Okay, Fabianne," she said. "I know that what the truck driver said in there meant something to you. I just don't know what. But from the look that came across your face, I'd say you've heard that phrase before, haven't you?"

"Oui, L'Abbaye, I have," said the Inspector. "But before I discuss it with you, I need to call my supervisors in Rome. They will let me know how they wish me to proceed," she said. "Shall we call it a night for now and meet in the morning, Detective? I believe we have done all that we can for today."

"Okay," agreed Abby. "Sounds like a plan to me."

She was more than ready to go home. She had seen and heard more than enough for one day as far as this case was concerned. And since she had already had very little sleep from the night before, she was seriously looking forward to getting some rest.

"If you don't mind, Detective, can you meet me at my hotel tomorrow morning at about nine thirty?" asked Fabianne. "I will treat you to breakfast, oui?"

"Now that sounds like a really good plan," exclaimed Abbey.

"Good!" said Fabianne.

The Inspector handed Abbey a card with the name of the hotel she was staying in, and then continued down the stairs to her car.

"Bon soir, bonne soiree, L'Abbaye," said Fabianne. "Get some rest. Until tomorrow. Oh, and I believe that the second Inspector they dispatched should have arrived by then. He will be there also. I will introduce you."

Although Abbey wasn't exactly sure 'what' Fabianne had said, she was pretty confident it was something along the lines of, 'Good Night, Good Evening', or something like that. Whatever it was she said, Abbey had decided that she liked the way that the French spoke.

When Fabianne handed Abbey the card with her hotel name and address on it, the Detective quickly took note of where the Inspector was staying. And when she saw where the Inspector was staying, she would have expected nothing less for someone working for the Vatican.

CHAPTER NINE

Sunday, 9:15 am

A s Abbey drove to the exclusive hotel in downtown LA, she mused to herself.

"The best, I had expected, but this. This was beyond the best. This hotel was one of the top five star hotels in the entire LA area. And expensive, too!" she thought.

"I guess it really does pay to work for the Vatican," she thought as she pulled into the driveway leading up to the hotel. "Private cars with drivers, five star hotels. Nice! Real nice!"

As she got out of the car and handed her keys to the Valet, she made her way into the hotel lobby where she went directly to the front desk.

"I'm Detective Abigail Wells," said Abbey as she pulled out her badge and showed it to the clerk. "I'm here to see Inspector, ahh, wait minute," she said as she reached for the card that Fabianne had given her and showed it to the desk clerk.

She knew that if she had tried any attempt to pronounce Fabianne's full name, she would have surely slaughtered it.

Typing in the name indicated on the card into the computer, the clerk looked up and indicated which of the house phones Abbey could go to.

"I'll connect you to our guest, Detective," she said.

"Thank you," said Abbey as she made her way over to the group of house phones that were lined up in the hallway just off of the main lobby.

Picking up the first phone, Abbey waited.

"Bonjour!" answered Fabianne.

"Fabianne, it's Detective Wells. I'm in the lobby downstairs."

"Oh, oui, L'Abbaye. Oui," said Fabianane. "Please come up to the room. I am in Suite 3535. I will see you when you get here."

"Suite!" thought Abbey to herself as she hung up. "Now that's what I'm talking about!"

Crossing the hall to the elevators, Abbey stepped into the one that went to the upper floors of the hotel. Pushing the button for the thirty-fifth floor, Abbey contemplated what it would be like to live like this.

"I don't know if I could get used to this," thought Abbey to herself as the elevator made its silent run up to the thirty-fifth floor. "But I would sure try."

As the elevator stopped and the doors silently slid open they revealed an even more elaborately decorated hallway than the lobby downstairs. Plush pile rugs, mahogany credenzas with beautiful vases sitting on top them filled with flowers of every variety.

"It even smells rich," thought Abbey as she stepped out of the elevator and went to the right.

Within moments she came to two double doors at the end of the hall with 'Suite 3535' embellished across the top. Reaching out, she rang the bell and waited.

As the door swung open, Fabianne greeted the Detective.

"Ah, L'Abbaye!" exclaimed the Inspector. "Bonjour!"

She was dressed casually in a pair of straight legged jeans topped off with an off white loose sweater and was wearing a pair of slouchy socks.

"It is so good to see you," she said. "How are you? Please, come in. You are right on time. They will be bringing breakfast up any moment now."

"Thank you, Fabianne," said the Detective as she entered into the entry hall of the suite. "You know, you didn't have to do this. We could have met at the precinct," she said as she got her first look at what an exclusive suite in a five plus star hotel looked like.

"Although, I'm glad that you did," admitted Abbey.

"You will see why I wanted to meet here instead of at the precinct, L'Abbaye," said Fabianne as she closed the door and showed the Detective into the living room.

Stretched out in front of her were floor to ceiling windows framing the skyline of Los Angeles. Just to the right of the living room was the dining room with a large dining table sitting in the middle. Spread out over the entire surface of the table, were pictures and pages of notes. Some were hand written while others had been printed. The wall behind the table was being used as a board where there were charts and more pages of notes tacked to the wall.

"What's all this?" asked Abbey as she slowly walked into the dining area.

"This, L'Abbaye is everything that we have on the events that have happened so far, as they pertain to the 'Manuscript of the Six Events'," she said. "They are all in chronological order. You see, it would have been very difficult to utilize space at the precinct and not to raise questions from the other Officers. It would have been very hard to keep what we have uncovered so far, under wraps. Do you not agree?"

"Yeah, you're right about that," agreed Abbey knowing there were as many leaks within the precinct as there were Officers.

As she walked around the table covered with neatly stacked piles, she noticed there were pictures of several people included among the stacks.

"And these pictures?" asked Abbey as she looked at various glossy prints of three people. "Who are they?"

"These are all of the people who have been involved with the three miracles that have happened so far," said Fabianne. "We call them Prophets."

"Prophets?" asked the Detective.

"Yes," said the Inspector. "Whenever a person is a part of a miracle, or an extraordinary event that shows evidence of the manifestation of divine intervention in human affairs, the Vatican calls them Prophets."

"I see. And now you have three miracles!" exclaimed Abbey as she gave Fabianne a surprised look. "You've declared the accident that happened on Thursday night, as a miracle?" she asked."

"Oui. I have already given my report to my superiors in Rome," stated Fabianne. "They agree with me that there are too many coincidences that have happened in each of the cases to dismiss."

"Coincidences? Like what?" asked Abbey.

"Here, L'Abbaye, is where you get all of the answers to the questions that you have been wanting to ask," said Fabianne as she too approached the table and leaned against it with both arms extended. "Everything and anything that you want or need to know about what has happened so far, is now at your disposal, Detective."

"Finally!" exclaimed the voice in Abbey's head.

But before Abbey could respond, the doorbell rang.

"But after we have breakfast, oui?" said Fabianne as she rushed to the door and opened it.

As the bell boy rolled in his cart of food and left it beside the couch table, Abbey realized that she was in fact very hungry. She had gone home and went straight to bed where she collapsed. She didn't wake up until two hours before she was to meet Fabianne, which left her no time for anything except to shower, brush her teeth and put her hair up.

Fabianne had ordered scrambled eggs with cheese and green onions, little three inch, hot mini croissants with soft garlic butter, crispy bacon, fresh fruit and hot tea, coffee and orange juice.

"I hope that you are hungry, L'Abbaye," said Fabianne as she picked up a plate and started to fill it with a little bit of everything. "I tried to order an American breakfast. I love American food," she said excitedly. "It is so satisfying, you know?"

"Yeah, I know what you mean," said Abbey as she too picked up a plate and began to fill it. "I think it's all of the fat that we use in everything we cook. But I gotta say, it may not always be good for you, but it sure as heck tastes good!"

"Oui, I agree!" exclaimed Fabianne as she walked around to the couch and plopped down with her plate firmly in hand as she stuffed one of the mini croissants into her mouth. "Hmm, so good!" she exclaimed as she chewed her food.

At that moment, Abbey realized that possibly under different circumstances and closer geography, she and Fabianne could have been friends. She seemed so down to earth.

"Sit, L'Abbaye, sit!" said Fabianne as she tucked her feet underneath her and continued to eat. "There are so few times that one can actually relax and enjoy food such as this and with company that you enjoy."

As Abbey sat down on the couch to eat, she noticed that Fabianne was indeed enjoying the breakfast she had ordered for them. Then as she ate a forkful of the scrambled eggs laced with cheddar cheese and green onions, she knew exactly what Fabianne meant.

"Hmmm! These eggs are great!" exclaimed Abbey as she took another forkful.

She didn't know how they had prepared them, but she'd swear that they were the best scrambled eggs she had ever tasted.

"Well, if this is the quality of the food that they serve in five-plus star hotels, I may have to make a point to come here more often," thought Abbey to herself. "Even if it is only to eat."

But before Abbey could raise another forkful of the scrambled eggs to her mouth, the doorbell rang again.

"Ah!" exclaimed Fabianne as she popped up and made her way to the door. "That must be the other Inspector sent by the Vatican."

Abbey wasn't sure what she had expected the other Inspector to be like, but she was hoping that it wasn't some uptight, old guy that the Vatican had decided to dump on them. She was rather enjoying the relationship that she and Fabianne had started to develop between themselves.

"You know, two Femme la Fatales, one American and the other French, investigating possibly one of the greatest mysteries in the history of Man," thought Abbey as she watched Fabianne answer the door.

Who would have ever thought?

As Fabianne opened the door, Abbey was able to get a look at the new Inspector the Vatican had sent as he stood in the doorway.

"Holy crap!!" exclaimed Abbey as she swallowed quickly and put her plate down onto the table in front of the couch.

"This can't be who the Vatican dispatched," she thought as she stood up and quickly wiped any remnants of food from her mouth. "I thought they only had weathered old men and a couple of middle aged misfits working at the Vatican. Of course, not counting Fabianne. But not someone like…..this!"

Standing in the doorway, being greeted by Fabianne, was the best looking, six foot two or maybe three inch tall, latte hunk of a man Abbey had ever remember seeing. And the fact that she had reached all the way back to her old days in the 'hood' when she and her girlfriends would use such slang to describe good looking white boys, didn't bother her one bit.

He looked to be about in his mid to late thirties, and you would have sworn that he had just stepped out of a Men's cologne advertisement in one of those fancy magazines.

"Damm!!" the voice in her head exclaimed as she tried not to stare. "It didn't matter what ethnicity he was, he was gorgeous!"

And she found it hard not to stare as he strode into the room and walked toward her. All Abbey could see was the deep vertical dimples that appeared as he flashed his sexy smile at her.

"L'Abbaye," said Fabianne as she went to introduce him. "This is Michael Givant," she said. "He has been dispatched from the Vatican to work with us. He just arrived late last night. Michael, this is L'Abbaye Wells. She's a Detective with the LA Police Department working on the investigation with us."

"Yes, I've been briefed," said the Inspector as he reached out and shook Abbey's hand and held it for a moment.

He seemed to hold eye contact with her a little longer that one would have normally done. And then he gave her a slow but lingering up and down glance as he continued to hold her hand.

"It's a pleasure to meet you, Abbey," as he looked at her intently.

"Aw, double damm!!" exclaimed the voice in her head again as she tried to smile nonchalantly.

Right off, Abbey could tell that there was certainly some kind of an attraction between the two of them. His hand had gently wrapped around hers and was slightly warm to the touch.

"And they felt good!" purred the voice inside of her head. "Real good!"

It was a feeling that actually caused her to emit a girlish giggle until she caught herself. Even Fabianne cast her a look when she heard Abbey giggle slightly.

"I'm sorry, yes, it is…..a pleasure," she said as she continued to shake his hand.

Then she caught herself.

"To meet you," she said as she released his hand. "It's a pleasure….. to meet you!"

"Damm, it should be a crime for someone to be walking around and look that good," screamed the voice in Abbey's head.

"And that smile," thought Abbey. "He had that killer smile that would do anyone in."

Glancing over to Fabianne, Abbey noticed that she too, was taking it all in.

She actually caught Fabianne's quick up and down glance as she took in his physique and how he looked in the Black leather jacket and the Black crew neck shirt he wore over slightly worn jeans. And then she almost choked when she saw Fabianne lean her head slightly to the right to take a quick look to see how his jeans fit from behind.

And then as if he knew what was happening all along, he smiled even broader.

"Ladies, do you mind if I join you?" he asked. "I got in late last night and was lucky to be able to get a room down the hall from you."

"Ahh! What room did they put you in?" inquired Fabianne.

"I'm in room #3540," said the Inspector as he smiled again. "Hey, I see you've already ordered breakfast! Do you mind if I join you?" he asked. "I'm famished."

"Of course not!" exclaimed Fabianne as she eyed him carefully and handed him a plate. "We would not be self-respecting women if we declined an offer from…..such a Man as you?" said Fabianne as all of the French charm in her came out.

"And what was that look that she gave him?" thought Abbey as she sat back down. "Leave it to the French women to be able to say so much with so few words. And so subtle, too! It was as if she was flirting with him with her eyes," she thought. "But in a, I don't know, French way," lamented Abbey as she tried to pretend she was interested in what was on her plate and tried to continue to eat. "I'm going to have to ask her how she does that. You know, for future reference," she thought to herself.

When the newly arrived Inspector had finished fixing his plate, he walked over to one of the side chairs, put his plate down and took off his leather jacket.

Abbey was just about to ask herself, 'When did people who worked for the Vatican go around wearing Black leather jackets?' when she found herself not being able to even finish the thought.

At the same time, Fabianne had turned to her and gave her a look with one raised eyebrow as if to say, 'Now that's what I'm talking about!'

And Abbey understood why.

The Vatican Inspector introduced as Michael Givant, had taken off his jacket and had casually tossed it across the back of the chair and sat down. He was six foot two with well-toned upper body muscles that easily showed through the slight fitting, short sleeved, Black t-shirt he was wearing.

"And, Oh my God, he's got a tattoo!" exclaimed Abbey to herself as she took note of an intricate ink pattern that could be seen on his right bicep as it peeked out from underneath the sleeve of his t-shirt. "Well, that just added to his sexiness," she thought. "He's definitely not what I would have expected the Vatican to send. But I'm so happy that they did!" she thought. "It just made this case even more interesting."

Abbey and Fabianne literally ate the rest of their meal in silence as they cleaned their plates and watched Michael do the same. After about ten minutes had passed, Fabianne spoke.

"That was very good!" she exclaimed as she looked over at Abbey. "Did I say how much I love American breakfast food?"

"Yeah, you did." said Abbey as she laughed a little. "But I have to agree with you, Fabianne. I never knew that eggs could taste so great! And that was the best coffee I think I've ever had."

"This hotel is well known for the chefs they have on staff, and how they make the simple foods you love, taste a hundred times better," said

Michael as he joined in on their conversation. "It's their signature. You won't find all of that fancy food that you can't even pronounce the name of here. Their entire menu is built around making the simple foods, sublime."

"I take it you have frequented this hotel before, Michael?" asked Fabianne.

"Yes, a couple of times when I've been on an investigation for the Vatican," answered Michael as he flashed his killer smile again.

"I'm sorry," said Abbey as she took note of something she had sensed earlier. "I thought that the two of you knew each other. I mean, being from the Vatican and all."

"Ahh, no, L'Abbaye! This is the first time that I have met Michael, also," said Fabianne. "You see, the Vatican has many, many Inspectors working for them that are assigned all over the world."

"She's right!" confirmed Michael. "I just happened to be in Washington State, ah….. finishing up some business for the Vatican when I got the call to report here. They felt that I might be needed considering the situation. And besides, it gives me the chance to work with the great Fransquie Fabianne al Benne," stated Michael. "You do know that in the Rome, she is legendary in her own right?"

"No, I didn't know that," admitted Abbey as she looked over at Fabianne with a surprised look on her face.

"Thank you for that, Michael," said Fabianne, truly honored by his accolades. "But like all Inspectors, I just do my job."

"Obviously, you do it very well to be thought of so highly by your superiors and your fellow Inspectors," said Abbey as she saw the true respect that Michael had for her.

"I just want to take this opportunity to say it's great to finally meet you and to get a chance to work with you," stated Michael.

"And I with you, Michael," said Fabianne. "Your reputation in Rome as a 'Guerriero' is also well known."

"I'm sorry, Fabianne. What, what did you call him?" asked Abbey, Fabianne smiled coyly and looked over at Michael.

"Michael and others like him are called, 'Guerrieros,' L'Abbaye," said Fabianne. "The Vatican sometimes has need of their 'special skills' in situations such as this."

"Others like him? I thought that he was an Inspector like you?" asked Abbey.

"He is," answered Fabianne. "But there are times when the Vatican needs Inspectors with 'special skills,'" she said. "That is when he and the others are dispatched and charged with a different mission," said Fabianne. "And with that, I will defer any further explanations as to what his exact expertise is to him while I get dressed. Oui? Then we can bring Michael up to speed and go over what we have so far. Please, if you will excuse me," said Fabianne as she left out of the room and headed for the bedroom leaving Abbey and Michael alone.

"Well, I guess the great Fabianne has spoken," said Michael as he stood up and reached for his plate. "Please," he said as he walked over to where Abbey was sitting and retrieved her plate as well. "Can I get you anything else?" he asked.

"Oh, no! Thank you! I'm full," exclaimed Abbey as she reveled in his attention like a teenaged girl.

"But she couldn't help it. He was so hot!!" she exclaimed to herself.

And she didn't know why she was acting like such a 'girl'! She never fell over herself for a Man before.

"Yes, he was extremely handsome," she noted to herself. "Not a pretty boy, but a man who had serious smoldering sex appeal about him. Even the way he moved! It was with such purpose," she thought.

And his eyes! They were a rich, Brown, almost see through, tortoise shell color. They seemed to almost catch you off guard for a moment when you looked directly at him. Of course, that was after his general presence floored you.

Alright, maybe she hadn't felt this kind of 'wow!' since she was fifteen years old, and had a crush on a high school boy named Thomas back in the neighborhood. She actually dated Thomas for the last part of her Sophomore year until a girl in the Junior class ended up getting pregnant by him.

"Well, that ended that!! The lying, cheating, 'whore' dog!!" lamented Abbey to herself.

Then she realized that after all of this time, she was still 'miffed' at him for breaking her heart. And as usual, she was the last one to find out, which for a teenager, was even more embarrassing. Since then she had dated a few guys here and there throughout college, but nothing very serious. She found more gratification in pursuing her career goals than anything else. And having achieved them gave her the greatest gratification of all.

Well, almost.

There was one thing that did give her a bit more gratification.

She did happen to see Thomas a couple of years back in the 'hood'. He was hustling on the streets and hadn't done much to get away from the negative elements of their old haunt. She also found out that he now had six kids from four different women.

"Whew!! Dodged a bullet there," thought Abbey to herself as she smiled to herself.

Sometimes you don't know why things happen the way they do, but in the end, it seems to always work out for the best.

Abbey had been so deep in thought, that she hadn't noticed that Michael was watching her all of this time.

"A penny for your thoughts," he said as he leaned forward onto the back of the couch.

"What?? I'm sorry!" exclaimed Abbey as she looked up. "What did you say?"

She also hadn't noticed that he had moved so close to her.

"I said, 'A penny for your thoughts'," repeated Michael as he looked down at her smiling slightly. "You looked like you were thinking of something pretty serious, there for a minute," he said. "And then at the end this satisfying look kind of came across your face," he said. "I hope it was something good?"

As he spoke to her, he gave her this closed mouth smile that made his dimples just jump out at you so much that it caused her to sit straight up and clear her throat.

"Now, maybe it was the way he said that last part to her that made her feel as if he was referring to something else altogether," thought Abbey to herself.

She don't know, but she was feeling slightly uncomfortable right about now.

"Maybe, I'm just freakin' horny and with him looking the way he looks has got me all hot and bothered. And dammit, I think he knows it!!" lamented Abbey not liking the idea of being manipulated like that.

Even if it was by someone who looked as smoldering hot as he did.

"Stop it!" yelled the voice in her head. "Girl, get a grip on yourself!!"

This was when Abbey would have appreciated it if Fabianne had come back into the room easing the sexual tension she was obviously feeling at the moment. After realizing that wasn't going to happen, Abbey quickly put herself into her Detective mode and took control of the situation by changing the subject.

"Actually, I have to apologize. What I was thinking about was personal," said Abbey as she stood up and took in a deep breath as walked over to the table in the dining room. "I try to never mix personal and professional business. It just helps to keep me on track, you know?"

"No, I understand what you mean," agreed Michael as he joined her at the dining room table.

As he stood a little too close for comfort to her as she looked over the various stacks of paperwork strewn across the table, she found herself getting a little flushed.

"For me, distractions can prove to be fatal if I'm not careful," said Michael.

Wondering what he meant by that last statement, Abbey decided to press the issue.

"Okay, when I started out investigating this case, I never would have expected some of the things that have happened, to happen," she said. "But they did. Weird things I might add. Now you show up. And you gotta admit. You're not exactly the type of person one would have expected the Vatican to dispatch."

"Really?" said Michael as he turned and looked directly at her.

"Really. Fabianne called you a 'Guerriero'," stated Abbey. "What does that mean? I'm curious just how dangerous can investigating miracles for the Vatican get?"

"Well, as you already experienced last night, sometimes these investigations can turn to the 'dark side'," stated Michael. "When they do, that's when I get involved."

"Are you referring to the old woman I saw last night?" asked Abbey.

"I'm sure Fabianne has already explained to you, that you saw last night was not an old woman," said Michael. "Although that's what it wanted you to think."

"Ahh, wait a minute!" said Abbey now slightly irritated as she turned to face him. "I was the one who saw her. Neither you nor Fabianne were there. But it seems that you both have an opinion of what really happened, so, be my guess," exclaimed Abbey as she waved her hand as if giving him the floor. "Why don't you enlighten 'me' to what it was that really I saw, then."

Michael smiled as he heard the sarcasm in her voice as she spoke.

"I know that we just met and don't know each other very well. And I'm not trying to imply that what you did or did not see last night didn't look like an old woman," said Michael. "I'm just trying to make sure you truly understand what 'it' was you faced down, and what it is we may to have to face every step of the way from this point forward."

"Then why don't you enlighten me, Inspector!" exclaimed Abbey as she crossed her arms firmly in front of her indicating that his explanation had better be a good one. "I'm all ears!"

"All right!" said Michael as he turned to face her. "I work for the Vatican as an Inspector like Fabianne does, yes. But I am also what's known as a 'Guerriero'. An Inspector who's expertise is in battling supernatural entities that have been dispatched from Hell. We call them 'L'arginatos', or 'The Dammed', or 'Demons'. Whatever word you chose to use."

"Say what??" exclaimed Abbey as she laughed a little, not believing what he had just disclosed to her. "Are you trying to tell me that the old woman that I saw last night was a.....a Demon.....from Hell!!"

"That's right," confirmed Michael as he carefully watched her facial expressions.

"And what is it that you do, Inspector?" asked Abbey sarcastically. "Pull out your sword and fight them back until the sun can rise on another day?" chided the Detective. "Come on!! Give me a break here, okay?"

As Abbey spoke, she noticed that Michael flashed her a look that spoke volumes. He didn't like the way she had depicted what he did for the Vatican as if he were a comic book character.

"L'Abbaye."

Hearing someone call her name from behind her, Abbey quickly turned to find that Fabianne had reentered the room. She was now dressed in a pair of dressy slacks and a loose blouse, and had pulled her hair up into a single ponytail, ready to go to work.

"It may seem difficult to believe right now, but what Michael speaks of is in fact true," she said. "He and the others like him are called 'Guerrieros', or Warriors. Or more precisely, 'Holy Warriors against the Darkness'. They are blessed by the Vatican and are called upon when creatures of the supernatural try to interfere with the Vatican's investigations, or with those who have been a part of events that the Vatican has declared as miracles. Like the woman you saw last night."

"And just so the record is straight, Detective," said Michael as he put extra emphasis on the last word. "Yes, in a way, that's exactly what 'I' do. Except I use a wide dagger that has ancient markings on the blade to fight back the very same Demons you seem to find humorous. And with the skills that I've been trained in, I fight until only one of us is left standing. And for your information, I do it very well."

"And believe it or not, this is not a game we're playing here," he continued. "When we tell you something that may seem hard to believe at first, or even impossible, I think you need to take some time to pause and think about it for a minute."

Yep, there was no denying it.

She could tell that she had really insulted him, and there were going to be no 'do overs' here. Abbey could tell by the tone of his voice and the look on his face that she had truly insulted him and what it was that he was charged to do in the name of the Vatican. And as he continued, she now felt that her usual cynicism and smart comeback remarks weren't playing to her strong suit as they usually did in other situations.

"One thing you need to realize is that not everything in the world is as it seems. Not by a long shot, trust me!" continued Michael. "Up until yesterday, everyone, including you, has gone about living their lives without a clue as to what may be about to happen," he said. "And now, by being involved in this case, Detective, you are one of the few people who've been made privy to the truth!" said Michael as she stood in front of her.

"Ahh, there it was again," thought Abbey as she listened. "The insulting way that he said, 'Detective' as if he were talking down to her while he gave her a tongue lashing.

And she really didn't think that she liked the way that he said it, either. Although, he did still look smoldering hot while doing it.

"But in all honesty, I was the first one to insult him and what he did," she thought to herself as she just listened.

"So what is the truth?" asked Abbey quietly, trying to reset things back to where they had been before her unfiltered remark had been made.

"The truth is that there's been an ongoing battle being fought between good and evil since the beginning of time," answered Michel. "And I am not just talking about the spiritual battle the Priests, Ministers and Fathers speak of in church on Sunday morning to their parishioners," said Michael. "I'm talking about the real, unseen battle that's continually being fought underground and in the shadows around the world by 'Guerrieros' like me.

"We're Holy Warriors blessed by the Church to engage these demons, like the one you saw last night. Demons who are the spawns of Hell sent to strip away anything that might give Man any sign of hope or faith. To mislead them into losing their belief and their faith in their God," said Michael as his voice became emotional. "This is a real war that we're engaged in where some of us have actually given their lives to keep them at bay," stated Michael as he thought about Thomas losing his battle in Michigan. "And it shouldn't be mocked because you don't understand it."

"Oui, I agree," said Fabianne to Abbey as she concurred with Michael.

And then she turned to Michael and spoke.

"But Michael, we must give L'Abbaye time," she said. "This is a war that we have been fighting for as long as we can remember. We must understand that this is only her second day, oui?"

Realizing that he was expecting more understanding from Abbey than he should have, he backed down.

"You're right. I'm sorry, Abbey," said Michael apologetically. "Sometimes I tend to get a little passionate about what I do. I tend to forget that not everyone is as invested as we are."

"No it's alright," started Abbey. "I have to apologize, too! I sometimes forget that I need a filter for my mouth when I'm not working around the guys in the precinct," she said. "And trust me, I don't diminish or dismiss anything that the two of you do for the Vatican. It's just going to take me a little time to process everything that's happened, is all."

"Understood," said Fabianne, seeing that the tension in the room had been eased considerably.

She was glad to see that they now had a better respect for each other and where each of them were coming from.

As she walked to the other side of the dining room table she continued.

"Now that we are back on track, let us go over what we have, shall we?" said Fabianne. "Until we hear that there is a fourth event and where it has occurred, all we can do is wait."

"Agreed," said Michael as he walked back over to the table and leaned against it with both arms outstretched.

"Detective, I'd like to think that we can both be on the same team, but agree to disagree," said Michael. "If you're willing to give it a try, I sure as hell am," he said as he looked over at Abbey and smiled.

He found that he was very attracted to her despite her disbelief in what it was that he did. He knew that being in the type of profession he was in, any kind of relationship including the casual ones were hard to maintain. And not that he was being presumptuous that anything personal might happen between the two of them, but he didn't want any unnecessary 'bad blood' to get between them either. Especially, since they were going to have to depend on each other if they were going to see this situation through to the end.

"It takes a lot more than a disagreement of opinions to hurt my feelings, Inspector," said Abbey as she walked over to the table and stood next to him. "And if you don't mind, call me Abbey," she said.

"Deal," said Michael as he gave her his killer smile again. "But only if you call me Michael."

"You've got a deal, Michael," said Abbey as she smiled back and quickly looked down.

As Fabianne looked on, she could see the mutual attraction that the two of them had for each other.

"Nice," she said to herself. "Very nice!"

As Michael turned to look over the pictures and papers that were spread out over the table, he noticed that in the middle was the enlarged, glossy photograph of the actual manuscript that the Vatican had stored in the underground vaults in Rome.

"Is this the manuscript?" he asked as he picked up the picture and looked at it.

He had heard of the manuscript before, as many of the elite 'Guerrieros' had, and what it could mean for Mankind. But he had never been privy to be able to lay eyes on it.

"Yes, it is," answered Fabianne. "And as you can see, here are the six events listed in the order they are to happen," she said as she pointed at the picture.

"The Manuscript speaks of six events," stated Michael. "Five of the events are depicted to be miracles, and the sixth event is thought to possibly refer to the second coming of Jesus Christ, if everything else comes to pass, correct?"

"Oui!" confirmed Fabianne again.

"I don't mind telling you that this feels like Déjà vu for me," said Michael as he reminisced about the experience he had while recovering at St. Augustine's Cathedral in Seattle a week before.

"What was it that happened, Michael?" asked Fabianne, curious as to what he was referring to.

Feeling somewhat uncomfortable about repeating what had happened, Michael went ahead and relayed to Abbey and Fabianne what he and the Father had experienced. When he finished there was an odd silence in the room.

After a few moments had passed, Fabianne spoke.

"Michael, do you think what the 'L'arginato' was referring to was this manuscript and what it predicts?"

"In all honesty, based on what's been happening around the world these last couple of days, yes I do!" stated the Inspector. "Somehow they are aware of this manuscript and its' predictions. And they've been try-ing everything to keep the miracles from happening, and if that doesn't work, to take possession of the Prophets that participate in the miracles themselves. And me and the other 'Holy Warriors' are the only thing standing in their way. I think that's why they've been targeting and trying to eliminate as many of us that they can."

"But what is it about the three miracles that have already happened that make you think that they are the ones described in the manuscript?" asked Abbey as she joined in on the conversation.

"At first we were not sure," stated Fabianne honestly. "We proceeded to investigate the first event that occurred in Mexico last Friday as we normally would. But on Monday, three days later, a second miracle occurred in France. Now, what made it interesting was that when the second miracle occurred in France on Monday, the young boy involved in the first miracle in Mexico, disappeared sometime during that same day without a trace. Pouf!! He was gone," exclaimed Fabianne as she made gestures with her hands as if she were performing a magic trick.

"Coincidence?" asked Michael as he looked at Fabianne.

"Perhaps," said Fabianne. "But not so much so when three days later, on the same day that the third miracle happened here in LA, the young teenager involved in the second miracle in France, also disappeared."

"So…..let me get this straight," started Michael as he was analyzing everything in his head. "It sounds like the events are occurring approxi-mately two to three days apart. And at some time during the third day, when the next event happens, the people involved in the previous event disappear."

"Oui!" confirmed Fabianne. "Our superiors in Rome got very anx-ious when the young girl in France disappeared," explained Fabianne. "And now the third person, Mr. Warren, has also disappeared here in LA, three days after the second miracle took place. There are now too many coincidences to ignore," said Fabianne. "So I am sure that you can appreciate why our superiors in Rome are more anxious now than they were before."

"But I don't understand," said Abbey as the analytical side of her came out. "What ties these three miracles to this manuscript?" she asked. "There obviously has to be something that you and your superiors feels connects them to the manuscript other than just being declared as miracles by the Vatican."

"Oui, L'Abbaye," said the Inspector as she walked around to the other side of the table where the two of them were standing. "Do you see here," she said as she pointed to the picture of the manuscript that Michael was holding. "These are the first five events. The scholars at the Vatican have translated them to read, that the first event will be, 'a foretelling of the future'. The second will be a 'taking' that will not be fulfilled."

"I'm sorry. A 'taking that will not be fulfilled?" inquired Abbey. "What does that mean?"

"You will understand in a moment," stated Fabianne as she continued.

"The third event speaks of an act of 'self-sacrifice', and the fourth, an act of heroism. The fifth event speaks of 'a return from the death of disease to live again.'. And then there is the sixth event that says, following these five events, Man will witness an occurrence that will, and I quote," said Fabianne as she paused for a moment. "Will be a reaffirmation of faith that no Man can deny. And as the manuscript states, they are all to happen in the order that they are written."

"Can you give us a breakdown of the first three miracles that have happened?" asked Michael. "I've already read the files on the interviews with the families and the Prophets who were part of the first two miracles. But it may help to give Abbey and me a better handle on what has already happened and how they relate to the manuscript and to each other."

"Oui," said Fabianne as she walked over to the wall where there was a chronological display of all of the events that had happened so far.

"Last Friday, near the southern tip of the Central Plateau region of Mexico, just North of Guadalupe, there is a small town called 'Ciudad del Cano'n'. The City of the Canyons. It is a small, rural town. A school bus loaded with students was returning from an outing, when a young boy on the bus said that he knew that the bridge that went over a dry ravine was out. He said that another young boy, whom no one had ever seen before, told him that is was so. And that if he did not warn the teacher and the driver, that the bus would go over the side of the cliff. And if that had happened, surely all of the children on board would have been killed," explained Fabianne.

"I take it that they believed the boy?" asked Michael.

"Oui!" exclaimed Fabianne. "They pulled over to the side of the dirt road, but just barely in time. That was the first miracle that happened last Friday around 2:30 in the afternoon. A 'foretelling of the future'," stated Fabianne.

Before she could continue, Michael interrupted her.

"I'm sorry, Fabianne. What time did that happen as last Friday?" he asked as he got an uncomfortable feeling in his gut.

"It was around 2:30 in the afternoon, Michael. Why?" asked Fabianne as she eyed her counterpart.

"It's just that right before that, oh, maybe around 2:25 that same afternoon, that's when the Father and I had that weird experience I just told you about inside of the St Augustine Cathedral. It felt as if time just stopped for a minute and then resumed. And we both had the feeling that something was about to happen. I wonder if that wasn't God's way of stopping everything to prepare for the first miracle?" he asked to no one in particular.

"Okay, this case just got weirder," exclaimed Abbey as she shifted her weight.

"Well, we may never know, oui?" said Fabianne as she returned her attention back to the table. "Now, three days later," continued Fabianne. "The teenage daughter of a very wealthy French businessman was kidnapped sometime during the weekend. They demanded an enormous amount of money or they threatened to kill the girl," said Fabianne. "The money was to be exchanged at one of the most public and well known places in Paris. The Eiffel Tower."

"And of course there was to be no Police," added Fabianne. "Unfortunately, an off duty French Officer happened to be there with his family, and tried to intervene. When he identified himself as a Police Officer, the kidnappers made good on their threat."

"What happened?" asked Abbey as she listened.

"The kidnappers threw the young girl off of the Eiffel Tower in front of her father and vacationing tourists," said Fabianne. "They must have pried loose one of the security panels ahead of time that were meant to prevent anything like this from happening."

"Oh my God!" exclaimed Abbey. "How could they?"

"As it turns out, they were not interested in the money at all," explained Fabianne. "They were home grown terrorists with their own agenda of trying to make a political statement about the French government and its' stance on foreign policies with other countries. They were extremists and were ready to die for what they believed in, and didn't care who they took with them to make their point."

"Oh my God!!" exclaimed Michael as his head just dropped onto his chest.

"I don't understand," asked Abbey saddened by what she had just heard. "How can that qualify as a miracle? I'd say it was more of a terrible tragedy than anything else."

"A tragedy, oui," said Fabianne. "But the young girl that was thrown off of the Eiffel tower, survived the fall," said Fabianne as she watched for Abbey and Michael's reaction.

And she got exactly the response from both of them that she thought she would.

"What!!" exclaimed Michael not believing what he had just heard.

"Are you telling us that the young girl who was thrown from the Eiffel Tower, survived?" exclaimed Abbey not able to believe it either.

"Oui. She not only survived," said Fabianne. "There was not a single scratch on her. Anyhere! She got up and was walking around as if nothing had happened. That was the second miracle. 'A taking that was not fulfilled'. Of course, something like that would be very difficult to explain with so many witnesses, but I understand that they were able to give the tourists a good story to tell," said Fabianne. "I believe they said that it was a special trick that was being practiced by a Master Magician for an upcoming show or something like that."

"And they believed that?" asked Abbey not understanding how any-one could accept an explanation such as that.

"Of course they believed it," said Michael. "The public has believed far more unexplainable stories before. Besides, I don't think that they were ready to hear that what they had just witnessed was possibly an event that might be a prelude to the 'Second Coming of the Son of God.' I don't think that the world is quite ready to hear that yet."

"And then we have the third miracle that happened here in LA," continued Fabianne as she moved along the wall. "I'm sure, Michael that you have heard what has been on the news about this."

"Yes, I have," said Michael. "But just like the incident in Paris, the public has been given an explanation that would satisfy them. I under-stand that they are saying that the truck driver did hit the car, but by some kind of 'miracle', missed the two people," he stated. "And despite what the driver is saying, everyone is of the belief that had to be what happened. How else could the two people have survived?"

"Oui, so there you have it," said Fabianne. "The first three events that have already happened, and that have been verified by the Vatican as being miracles. The foretelling of the future, 'a taking that was not to be fulfilled', and then an act of self-sacrifice. They all coincide with what is written in the manuscript. But to answer your question, L'Abbaye," said Fabianne. "That is not the only thing that ties these three miracles to the manuscript. Look here, at the bottom of the picture," said the Inspector as she pointed to the ancient writing that was scrawled across the bottom of the parchment.

As both Abbey and Michael leaned in to get a look at the writing, Michael spoke first.

"I'm afraid I'm not familiar with this language," said Michael as he strained to read the inscription. "Perhaps it's the dialect it's written in that I don't understand. What does it say?" he asked.

"It has been interpreted to read, and I quote," said Fabianne as she paused. "Blessed are those who believe in him. You are loved. Watch for his return, for he is coming.....soon."

"Fabianne, isn't that kind of what the truck driver said that Mr. Warren recited to him right after the accident," exclaimed Abbey as she turned to look at the Inspector.

"Oui, you are correct, L'Abbaye," said Fabianne. "It is the same statement. As a matter of fact, it is the exact statement that the student said to his teacher in Mexico, just after the driver was able to stop his school bus full of students from careening off of the hillside. And it is the exact statement that the young teenage girl who was kidnapped in France said to her Mother just before she, too disappeared."

"Wait a minute! Are you saying that the people involved in the first three miracles said the exact same thing that's written on the bottom of a two thousand year old manuscript, before they disappeared?" questioned Abbey.

"Oui. That was the missing piece that made the difference of whether or not to declare the event that happened here in LA as one of the miracles referred to in the manuscript," said Fabianne. "That, and of course the fact that now Mr. Warren has also disappeared without a trace like the other two Prophets have. And as far as the Vatican is concerned, the events that have happened so far are no longer being viewed as coincidences."

"I would agree," said Michael as even he shuddered a bit. "And from what we know so far, the fourth event should be happening sometime today, right?"

Fabianne nodded her head.

"The Vatican has everyone on alert, as are all of the Inspectors that are in the field," said Fabianne. "If anything happens we will hear of it. And when we do get word of the fourth event and the fifth, we must be ready to leave immediately," she said. "We have to get to the two remaining Prophets before they disappear, too."

Then Michael turned to Abbey.

"Abbey, are you up to answering a couple of questions about what happened last night and your encounter with the 'L'arginato' at the Warren's home right after the husband disappeared?" asked Michael.

"Sure," answered Abbey as she shuddered slightly at the thought of what she had experienced.

She really didn't want to relive what happened at all if she didn't have to. But she knew that if Michael was as good as he said he was at fighting these Demons from Hell, then he was going to need any and all information he could obtain about what had happened.

Michael took note of Abbey's body as it tensed up, and he promised himself that he wouldn't be too rough on her. He could see from her body language that the experience was still having an effect on her.

"What is it you want to know?" asked Abbey.

"Why don't you just talk me through what transpired when you and Fabianne went to Mr. Warren's home," said Michael. "I don't want this to be like an inquisition or anything like that," he said. "If you don't mind, I'll be taking notes and then asking you some questions. That way I won't disrupt your train of thought, alright?"

Nodding that she understood, Abbey related to Michael everything that happened from the time that she and Fabianne had arrived at the Warren's home up to when she had encountered the 'L'arginato' in the kitchen. When she finished, he had made notes about everything. He must have had his own version of shorthand because he had kept up with her all the way until she had finished.

Taking time to peruse over his notes, Michael quietly read what he had written down. Both Abbey and Fabianne sat quietly as they watched him. A couple of times they noticed that he furrowed his brow and frowned, and then his face would go blank as he concentrated.

After about ten minutes, Michael broke the silence.

"Abbey. you said that Mrs. Warren was positive that she heard two distinct voices coming from the upstairs bedroom before the door closed on her, right?"

"Right! She was adamant that she heard two voices coming from the bedroom," answered Abbey. "She recognized one of the voices as being her husband's, but didn't recognize the other one."

"And did she say if she heard any of 'what' they were talking about?" asked Michael. "Anything at all?"

"No, not to me she didn't," said Abbey.

"At that point I went back downstairs and called in Mr. Warren's disappearance to the precinct."

"How about to you, Fabianne?" inquired Michael as he turned to the Inspector. "Did Mrs. Warren say anything to you about hearing any of the conversation that was going on in the bedroom before the door closed?"

Fabianne could not divulge to Michael or to Abbey that Mr. Warren's wife had indeed told her what she had briefly heard.

"It was not something that they needed to know at this time," she thought to herself."

So, without any hesitation, or change in the fluctuation in her voice, Fabianne answered.

"No, Michael. She said that she did not hear anything of what was being said inside of the room," stated Fabianne. "Do you think it was one of the 'L'arginatos' that was in Mr. Warren's bedroom with him? Do you think they have taken him along with the others?"

"No, I don't!" exclaimed Michael quietly as he appeared to be deep in thought. "And that's what's got me stumped. From what Abbey said, the old woman in the kitchen told her, 'You will not win! They may have taken the others, but the rest are ours!' They may have taken the others….." repeated Michael as he mulled over and over again what the old woman had told Abbey.

"What is it, Michael?" asked Fabianne.

"Why would the old woman say, 'They may have taken the others, but the rest are ours', if they already had the three Prophets that have disappeared?" asked Michael as he thought out loud to himself.

"She wouldn't," said Abbey as she saw where Michael was going with his train of thought. "And if the 'L'arginatos' don't have them, then that means that someone else does."

"Yes it does!" exclaimed Michael as he quickly got up and strode to the dining room table again. "Someone else is taking the Prophets before we or the 'L'arginatos' can get to them."

"But who?" asked Abbey and Fabianne in unison.

"I don't know!" exclaimed Michael as he just stared at the various pictures and pieces of paper that were spread out over the table, hoping that the missing piece would jump out at him. "That's the sixty four thousand dollar question! But there is one thing that I do know, ladies," said Michael as he looked over at Abbey and Fabiane.

"Someone, and I don't know who, has been one step ahead of the Vatican's investigation since the very beginning," stated Michael. "And if there are other players that are involved, whoever it is, they're getting to the Prophets before anyone else can. And we have no clue as to 'who' they are, and for that matter, 'why' they're taking them. And to add fuel to the fire, that means that we still have the 'L'arginatos' to deal with."

"I must let my superiors know what is happening," said Fabianne as she reached for her phone and began dialing.

As Fabianne walked out of the room waiting for her call to be connected, Abbey looked over at Michael.

"So what do we do, now?" she asked.

"Well, until the Vatican can figure out who's been taking the Prophets and why, I guess all we can do is wait until we hear if the fourth event happens," said Michael. "And if it does, where? Then wherever it is, we need to 'hightail it' there, and hopefully get to the Prophet before the 'L'arginatos' do, and whoever else we in a race with."

"Well, I have to honestly say, when I went into the precinct yesterday afternoon, I never would have had thought I would have one of the most interesting and unexpected twenty four hours of my life," admitted Abbey. "I mean look at me. I'm working on an investigation with Inspectors from the Vatican in Rome concerning a two thousand year old manuscript that's predicting miracles all over the place. And then there are the disappearances and my favorite, Demons from Hell," said Abbey with a humorous tone. "And oh, yeah, not to mention the possibility that the end product of all of this could be the 'second coming of Jesus Christ'," admitted Abbey as she paused for a moment.

"Kind of blows you mind doesn't it?" said Michael as he looked over at her.

"Mind blowing doesn't even come close," said Abbey as she smiled slightly. "And then there's you. A full-fledged, and sexy I might add, 'Guerriero'," said Abbey as she did her own version of flirting." Who would have guessed that I'd be standing here next to a Holy Warrior that has been blessed by the Vatican to battle Demons in today's modern world. Not me, that's for sure."

"Abbey," started Michael as he stepped in close enough to her to make sure there was no mistaking what his intentions were. "I hope that what I do doesn't make you frightened of me," he said quietly. "Because I'm seriously attracted to you. I think you know that. And more than anything, I wouldn't want what I do to be something that will cause you a problem."

Seeing that he was putting himself out there to let her know that he was interested, Abbey decided to let her guard down and let this Man know that the feeling was mutual. With her pursuing her career fulltime, it had left little time for anything else. It had been a long time since she had let herself relax and 'just go with it'. And she had been attracted to him from the time that he walked through the door.

"And Boy, was she attracted to him!" she exclaimed to herself as she began to feel a little giddy at the prospect of being with him.

And now she knew that the attraction was mutual.

"Yep!" she thought to herself. "Did not see that coming."

"So you suppose that maybe we can have a drink later after we finish up here?" he asked.

"That would be nice," said Abbey. "But I think I'm going to need a couple of drinks after today."

Without any warning, Michael broke out into laughter and gave her a full smile with his dimples thrown in for good measure.

"Good!" he exclaimed. "Then it's a date."

Then moving himself away from the table, Michael passed by Abbey and then stopped. She could feel the energy of his body as he intentionally stood close to her. His scent was nothing but sensual and intoxicating as she inhaled it in.

"Oh, God!" exclaimed the voice in her head as she exhaled shallowly. "I can tell I'm in deep trouble, here!"

But the excitement of what kind of trouble it could mean for her, turned her on. And she was determined not to back out of this. Not this time. She was as horny as hell, and he was a 'hellava' sexy, Holy Warrior from the Vatican who fought Demons.

Enough said!

"Until later!" said Michael as he brushed past her and walked to the door. "I need to shower and put some clean clothes on," he said as he looked coyly back at her over his shoulder. "Is around four o'clock alright?"

"Ah, yeah! That's good,!" exclaimed Abbey as she watched him slowly strode across the floor to the door, open it, and then leave out of the room.

"Boy does he know how to make an exit," she said softly under her breath as the door closed slowly behind him. "Then again," she said out loud. "Right now I'm so turned on that anything that he did would seem 'hot'!"

Trying to shake the excited feeling that had unexpectedly spread throughout her entire body, Abbey turned to the table and began to peruse over the information there. Michael had truly thrown her an unexpected curve and she needed to focus and get back on track.

She looked at the pictures of the three people who had disappeared so far.

One was a picture of a cute young Hispanic boy who looked to be about nine or ten years old. The picture must have been a school photograph because he had on a crisp white shirt with a red tie, and his hair was combed and smoothed to the side. And he had that strained, fake smile that kids sometime give when they are forced to sit down and take a picture.

The second picture was of a pretty teenage girl with dark shoulder length hair, blue eyes and full lips. And from just looking at the picture you could tell that she was going to grow up to be a real looker when she got older.

And then the third picture was of Benjamin Warren.

"Bennie," mused Abbey as she remembered how Mrs. Warren fondly spoke of him.

He was an average looking middle aged man with a receding hairline and a jovial kind of smile. And even though she was just looking at a picture of him, he had the type of infectious smile that if you saw him walking toward you and he smiled, you would immediately have to smile back.

Abbey looked back over her shoulder to see if Fabianne had returned from making her phone call to the Vatican.

"Nope, still just me!" exclaimed the Detective as she returned her attention back to the table.

Actually, this was great! It gave her some private time to look over all of the information that had been collected about the case so far without anyone else interfering.

Then Abbey reached over and picked up the picture of the manuscript that started it all.

As she put the picture down in front of her, she ran the tips of her fingers over its' glossy surface. She wondered what it would have been like for a Priest over two thousand years ago, to have been shown a vision of a series of events to come, that he himself couldn't even comprehend.

Mulling over the picture, Abbey took note of the ancient numbers that were written along both sides of the picture. Two separate sets of numbers were along the right side as well as along the left side. And then across the top of the manuscript was another set of numbers.

"What do you refer to," said Abbey out loud to herself.

Going back to her training and the personal insight that she had gotten from her Lieutenant, she knew that it had to mean something or it wouldn't have been scrawled onto the manuscript. Lying next to the picture was a folder that had the translations of the inscriptions of the manuscript. The first page was in French, and the second was in Italian. The third page in the folder was the English translation.

Looking over the page, Abbey read what the scholars at the Vatican had translated the ancient language to read. It was everything that Fabianne had said it was. It spoke of the six events, and how five of the events would be 'objects of such wonder, that it would manifest the presence of divine intervention in human affairs.'

Namely, it would be a miracle.

And then she read the translation of the writing that was written across the bottom of the manuscript. 'Blessed are those who believe in him. You are loved. Watch for his return, for he is coming.....soon!'

"Yep!" exclaimed Abbey to herself. "It was what each of the Prophets had said word for word before they disappeared."

And that left only the numbers along the border of the manuscript. There weren't any notes of any kind from the scholars pertaining to what the numbers meant which coincided with what Fabianne had said.

The scholars were stumped as to their meaning. They could pertain to something that only the Priest was aware of at the time. And if that was true, then there was no way that any of them were going to be able to determine what he meant.

At least not without some sort of key.

Then it hit Abbey.

"A key! Maybe there's a key somewhere on the manuscript that would help decipher the numbers," thought Abbey to herself.

So picking up the magnifying glass that was sitting on the table, Abbey bent over the table and carefully went over every inch of the picture of the manuscript. After a few minutes of holding her breath, she straightened herself up and exhaled.

Nothing.

Of course it wasn't as if she thought that a lowly Detective from the LAPD, would be able to find something that the Vatican scholars in Rome couldn't find, but.....she gave it her best shot. But as she looked at the manuscript in the picture, she couldn't shake the feeling that the numbers meant something.

They had to.

She did notice that while looking at the manuscript through the magnifying glass, she could see crudely sketched drawings that were intermingled between the numbers along the sides of the parchment. They had almost faded away with time, but a few of them could still be seen etched into the manuscript.

From what she could make out, they were simple drawings of stars of various sizes. Some were four simple lines crossing each other, and some were made up of one continuous line that had been drawn to form what looked like a crude Star of David. There couldn't have been any more than maybe a total of four or five of them altogether.

"Maybe the Priest was adding his own touch of artistry to the document," thought Abbey as she continued to ponder it.

But for some reason, the more she thought about it, the more something was tugging at her gut telling her that there was something else there. Something that everyone had missed, including the scholars at the Vatican.

And if it was one thing that Abbey had learned to do, it was to follow her gut. It had never let her down before, and she didn't think that it would now.

"But what was her gut trying to tell her now?" she thought.

As she pushed away from the table, she was getting frustrated.

"Stars, ah…..the sky," exclaimed Abbey as she walked around the room trying to power through the puzzle the best she could. "Ah…..the stars mean what? To follow the stars, the stars point the way. What are they trying to say?" lamented Abbey. "The answer is in the sky, in the stars! Wait a minute!" exclaimed Abbey out loud as she stopped dead in her tracks.

"The stars point the way," she said softly. "But what does that mean? What are the stars trying to tell us?' she asked herself.

And then she paused.

"Wait a minute," she said. "First, I have to ask, 'What is the question? And the question we've been stumped with is, 'Where will the next event happen?' Where is the next event going to happen?" repeated Abbey as she bit her lower lip as she concentrated. "We already know 'when'! That's sometime today! But where will it happen?"

Then she stopped pacing the room when it hit her. But she couldn't believe it.

"No!!" she exclaimed loudly as she went over to the table and picked up the sheet with the English translation. "It can't be!"

Going over to the computer that was sitting on the desk, Abbey sat down with the paper in her hand. She was relieved that Fabianne had left it on. It would save her some time from trying to hack into her password.

"Yes, she did have other skills," she thought to herself.

As a matter of fact, she had serious skills with computers. Everyone had always said that she should have gone into IT and became a computer programmer with the skills that seemed to come naturally to her. But she had other plans for her future.

Quickly bringing up the internet, she typed in three words and waited while the screen flashed a couple of times and then took her to the site she was looking for.

"Got it!" exclaimed Abbey as she picked up the paper that had the translated numbers on it that were listed on the side of the manuscript.

She entered the first set of numbers into the computer, and then second set and so on until she had entered all five sets of the numbers. As the screen flashed with each entry that she put in and gave her the information that she was looking for, she wrote it down onto another piece of paper and went on to the next set of numbers.

She didn't recognize the information from the first two entries that she had put in. But by the time she had gotten to the third set of numbers, she felt a chill creep down her spine that she couldn't shake.

"It can't be!" she exclaimed to herself as the light from the computer screen reflected off of her face. "Oh, my God! It can't be!"

When she had finished gathering the information for all five numbers, she sat back in her chair and breathed for the first time since she had sat down.

Then the sense of urgency hit her as she jumped up from the chair and rushed over to the bedroom door where Fabianne had disappeared to. She knocked twice but got no answer.

"Maybe she was still on the phone with the Vatican and didn't want to be disturbed," thought Abbey as she looked frantically around.

She had to tell someone what she had discovered, and she had to tell them now! Before it was too late!

"Michael!" she exclaimed out loud. "I've got to tell him what I've found out!"

Abbey rushed over to the door of the hotel room, and made her way out into the hallway.

"What room did he say he was in?" said Abbey to herself as she half way jogged down the hall looking for Michael's room number.

Within moments she had turned the corner and passed several doors until she came to room #3540.

"Michael!" exclaimed Abbey as she knocked on the door. "Michael, I've got to talk to you right away!"

No answer.

Knocking even harder, Abbey found herself pounding on the door. She only hoped that no one would report to security that they saw a woman pounding on one of the hotel room doors calling out for someone named Michael.

That would be the last thing she needed.

When there was no answer after she had knocked a third time, she realized that he was probably in the shower and couldn't hear her. Just as she started to turn and go back to Fabianne's room, she got a familiar but unpleasant feeling again.

Then it hit her when she had felt that feeling before.

It was last night at the Warren's house when she had the run in with the 'Demon'. And the fact that she was experiencing the same feeling again, here at the hotel, made one thing clear to her.

"It was here in the hotel with them, somewhere in close proximity. And it was getting stronger."

Quickly looking down the hallway toward Fabianne's room, Abbey didn't see anything. Turning to look behind her she gasped as she spotted the same old woman she had seen in the Warren's kitchen last night. She was just standing at the far end of the hallway as if she was waiting for something. And she had on the same flowered housedress that she had on the other night.

"Oh, Hell!! Not you again!" exclaimed Abbey out loud.

Abbey wasted no time as she turned and began to pound on Michael's door.

"If anyone could handle this 'Bitch' it was him!" she exclaimed to herself as she kept knocking on the door while keeping one eye on the old woman.

She was ready to draw her gun if she had to. But being that this was a Demon from Hell, she figured firing on the 'bitch' wouldn't have done any good. And how would she explain firing a weapon inside of a five star hotel without good reason But one thing was for sure, and that was that she wasn't going to turn her back on a Demon if she had anything to say about it.

Just as she was about to lay her fist onto Michael's door again, it swung open.

"Abbey! What's going on?" exclaimed Michael as he stood in the doorway with only a towel wrapped around his waist and a concerned look on his face.

Wasting no time, Abbey took a quick look up and down of Michael's physique as he stood in the doorway with only a towel around him, not missing the bulge that was protruding from the front. Then she side-stepped him and rushed into his room.

"Quick, close the door!" she yelled as she moved further into his room. "It's back! The, the 'Demon'," she exclaimed. "The old woman! I saw her down the hall just a minute ago."

"Which way?" asked Michael as he strode over to the bed and quickly discarded the towel revealing the sweetest looking 'tight end' it had ever been Abbey's pleasure to witness.

"Damm!!" exclaimed the voice in her head as she caught herself just staring at his rear end.

He had picked up his jeans and slipped into them, and then reached for something from the under the pillow of the bed. It was then that she noticed the injury on his left side that he had sustained in Seattle.

"Oh God," she exclaimed to herself.

Although it had healed, it looked like it he had been hurt really bad!

"Which direction did you see her?" he asked again as he opened the door.

"To the right, down the hall!" answered Abbey. "Wait, I'm coming with you!" said the Detective as she went to reach for her gun.

"No, Abbey!" exclaimed Michael as he blocked her from leaving the room. "This is something I need to do without having to worry about watching out for someone else," he said as he looked at her intently. "Please, do me this favor and stay here. I need you to call Fabianne on the house phone and warn her what's happening," he said. "I'll be right back. Stay here and close the door, do you understand me?"

And then without another word, Michael rushed out of the room and made his way down the hall to the right in search of the old woman. It was then that Abbey got a look at what it was that he had grabbed out from under the pillow.

It was a knife that was about twelve inches long and had an odd shape to it. It looked wider than most knifes and had one edge that was slightly curved with a smooth cut to it. And the other side it had irregular ridges along its' edges. And on the flat side of the blade, Abbey could see markings that had been cut into the metal itself.

"So he wasn't kidding when he had said that he used a blade that had been blessed by the Church to fight the Demons that he had encountered," said Abbey to herself.

"How sexy was that?" she thought as she quickly closed the door.

Going over to the bed, she picked up the phone and dialed the operator.

"Yes, could you connect me with room #3535 please. And hurry, please!"

On the second ring, Fabianne picked up the phone and answered.

"Oui! Bonjour! May I help you?"

"Fabianne, this is Abbey. I'm in Michael's room down the hall."

"Ahh, so the two of you are, shall I say, 'Ooh la la', eh?"

"No we are not, 'Ooh la la'ing', Fabianne," exclaimed Abbey. "At least not yet we aren't!"

"Ooh!! Not yet, eh!" smiled Fabianne.

"Fabianne, it's back! The 'Demon' from the Warren's house," she said. "The old woman. Michael is out checking the floor to see if he can find her, but he wanted me to warn you."

Silence.

"Fabianne! Fabianne, are you there?" asked Abbey again.

As Fabianne held the phone to her ear, she had turned and was looking over toward the middle of the living room. She thought she had felt something disturbing when she had come out of the bedroom.

And she was right.

Standing in front of her by the couch, was the source of that feeling.

The 'Demon' stood directly opposite her as it rocked back and forth from side to side as it watched her.

The old woman's hair was disheveled and her eyes were the same milky white color that Abbey had described. And as she rocked from side to side, her arms hung listlessly by her side as she made a low gurgling sound. As she stood her ground and eyed Fabianne intently, drool fell from the corner of her mouth and began to pool onto the floor.

"L'Abbaye!" said Fabianne after a few moments had passed. "I will have to talk to you later. 'It' is here with me now!" she said quietly.

"What!!" exclaimed Abbey quickly. "I'm on my way, Fabianne! I'm on my way!" yelled Abbey as she went to hang up the phone.

"No, L'Abbaye!" insisted the Inspector in a calm voice. "Listen to me. Stay where you are! You will be safe there. I will deal with this."

Hanging up the phone, Fabianne turned to face the 'Demon'.

"So, we finally meet, eh?" said Fabianne as she slowly moved herself toward the intruder.

As the 'Demon' continued to sway back and forth ever so slightly, she lifted her head and spoke to Fabianne.

"You may have taken the others, but the rest will be ours!" exclaimed the 'Demon' in a raspy, harsh voice. "And my Master will be more than pleased when I bring 'your' soul to him!" it exclaimed as it tried to laugh.

"Ah, ma tres chere" said Fabianne as she continued to slowly move toward the 'Demon' as it stood in the middle of the room. "Ah, my dearest. That will not happen," she said. "Not only will I not be going with you, but you will not be returning either."

And almost instantaneously, the smile slowly disappeared from the 'Demons' face as its eyes became as large as saucers as it understood what Fabianne meant. And before it could react, Fabianne was upon the 'Demon' before it knew what had happened.

As Fabianne rushed toward the 'Demon', she slapped an opened palm onto its forehead and instantaneously a pure yellow light poured out from its eyes and its gaping mouth as it threw its head back and shrieked.

Standing over the 'L'arginato' as it fell to the floor and disintegrated, Fabianne exclaimed, "You will never harm a child of God again, 'Demon'! Never!" she said.

⌒

Hearing the other end of the phone go dead, Abbey was stunned.

She couldn't believe it!

That was the second time in the last five minutes that she had been directed to 'stay where she was and not to get involved'.

"Then why am I here if I can't be of some help?" questioned Abbey as she quickly hung up the phone and headed for the door. "Stay here, my ass!" she exclaimed as she flung open the door and headed for Fabianne's room.

Just as she swung open the door, she found Michael standing there with only his jeans on and no shirt.

"I thought I told you to stay put!" he said when he saw that she was trying to leave.

"Yeah, you did, but no can do!" exclaimed Abbey as she pushed by him and ran into the hall. "We've got to hurry. The 'Demon' is in Fabianne's room!"

"What??" exclaimed Michael as he rushed down the hall catching up with Abbey.

Just as they turned the corner and were about to approach the door to Fabianne's suite, they heard the most horrific shrieking sound that caused them to stop dead in their tracks. The sound lasted only a couple of seconds. And then they saw a bright flash of light come from underneath the door while at the same time they heard a kind of sizzling sound that lasted only a couple of seconds. And then within moments, there was silence.

"What the 'hell' was that?" exclaimed Abbey as she looked at Michael with a terrified look on her face.

"I think I know," answered Michael as he rushed to the double door of the suite and started to pound on it.

In the middle of his pounding, the door opened.

"Fabianne! Are you alright?" asked Michael as he moved into the room ready for a fight. "The 'Demon', where is it?" he asked quickly.

"It is gone!" said Fabianne nonchalantly as she moved back into the room. "And thank you for the warning, L'Abbaye," she said. "I barely had time to deal with it."

"Sure, sure," said Abbey as she cautiously looked around the room also, and then back at Fabianne somewhat confused. "That was weird," thought Abbey.

Fabianne was acting as if nothing out of the ordinary had happened.

"What happened, Fabianne?" asked Michael insistently as he too canvassed the room. "Where is it? Are you alright?"

"No, I am quite well, Michael," said the Inspector. "Trust me. It gave me the same warning that it had given you last night, L'Abbaye."

"So, it would seem that they don't care that we're on to them, wouldn't it?" stated Michael as he watched Fabianne carefully. "It's almost as if they're 'taunting' us to try and stop them."

"So it would seem, Michael," answered Fabianne. "But it does not matter. It will take much more than that to stop us from doing what we must, oui?"

"I recognize that scream," he said as he continued to watch her. "It was the scream of a 'Demon' being vanquished. I didn't know that you were able to vanquish a 'Demon' Fabianne?" he asked.

"Oui. There are many things that you would be surprised to learn about me, Michael," said Fabianne as she smiled.

"But the flash of light. That was new! What was it?" asked Michael carefully. "I've never seen that before when a 'Demon has been vanquished."

"Oui. We Inspectors each have our own weapon of choice, do we not," said Fabianne. "You have yours, Michael, and I have mine. You see, I am not the Warrior that you are, so I must resort to other means to defeat 'Demons'."

"So.....what did you do?" asked Abbey.

"I recited a verse from a very old book that was used to vanquish 'Demons' centuries ago. I was not sure that it would work," stated the Inspector. "But I am glad that it did!"

"You'll have to teach that on to me some time, Fabianne," said Michael as he let his guard down for the first time since entering into Fabianne's room.

And then Fabianne changed the subject altogether.

"So. We are getting to know each other better, oui?" said Fabianne as she smiled at both Abbey and Michael. "Ooh la la, L'Abbaye, eh! Very good!"

That was when Abbey noticed the smile that crossed Fabianne's face when she saw the two of them standing together, and that Michael had no shirt on and his hair was slightly disheveled.

"No!" exclaimed Abbey as she looked over at a shirtless Michael and then back at Fabianne. "No, no, no! Nothing happened, Fabianne!" lamented Abbey. "I, I went to Michael's room to tell him what I found because you were still on the call to the Vatican. That's when I had the same feeling that I had last night at the Warren's house and I realized that the old woman in the housedress was back. I tried to warn Michael but he, he was in the shower and didn't hear me knocking on the door. When he finally did open the door, I, I told him what I saw, and he went down the hall to look for the, ah, the old woman. And, and he told me to call and warn you. That's it! Yep, that's, ah, that's what happened alright. That's, 'all' that happened."

And then looking over at Michael, Abbey said, "Tell her that's what happened, Michael!"

Abbey hadn't felt like this since she and her ex, Thomas had almost been caught by her parents in her bedroom one night when no one was supposed to be home. It was not a pleasant situation.

"And besides," thought Abbey to herself as she wondered why she was trying to explain herself. "I'm not in high school anymore. I'm a grown woman!"

Just as she was regaining her confidence as an independent woman, able to do what she wanted, with whomever she chose, Michael burst her bubble.

"Well, that's not all that happened, Abbey," said Michael as he tried not to give it away.

"What, what are you talking about?" exclaimed Abbey.

"Well, when you came into the room, I did have on only a towel after getting out of the shower," stated Michael as he tried not to break into laughter. "I had to drop the towel and put on my jeans before I ran into the hall after the old woman," he said. "And by the way, I'm sorry you had to see that."

"Ooh la la, L'Abbaye," said Fabianne as she smiled even more. "So, the goose got to see what the fox has been hiding, eh! That is always very good!"

Realizing that both Fabianne and Michael were milking the situation to the max as they broke into laughter, Abbey relinquished.

"Okay, Fabianne, Michael. I get it!" she said. "Go ahead get it out of your systems. Go on! I'll wait!"

"I am so sorry, L'Abbaye," apologized Fabianne. "I could not help myself. You looked like, ah, how do you say? A deer caught in the headlights, oui. Besides, what can I say! I am French. We French think about sex all of the time."

"And I'm sorry, too, Abbey," said Michael. "You just kept trying to explain, and the more that you talked, the deeper you dug yourself into a hole."

"Very funny," said Abbey as she walked over to the computer and sat down.

She was not amused.

"Oh, and by the way, when the two of you are done, I have something to show you. But take your time, okay. It's not important. I mean, it's only something that the 'scholars' at the Vatican couldn't figure out, but I did."

"What??" "What are you talking about??"

Both Fabianne and Michael were all ears as they joined her at the computer.

"What is it that you have found, L'Abbaye?" asked Fabianne.

"Well, you know the numbers that were inscribed along the sides of the manuscript? There were two sets of numbers on each side and one set of numbers along the top," explained Abbey. "My gut was telling me that they had to mean something, they had to have some kind of significance as it pertained to the manuscript. And then I took a closer look at the picture of the manuscript and saw the drawings of stars mixed in between the numbers."

"Oui!" said Fabianne. "But according to the scholars, they were just simple drawings that the Priest must have decorated the parchment with."

"That's what I thought at first when I saw them, too," said Abbey. "But that was until I asked myself, 'why' would the Priest who wrote the manuscript put anything on it that didn't have some kind of significance as to the message he was trying to leave? Right?"

"Then I realized that everything on the manuscript was telling us something. And that meant that the stars that were drawn on the manuscript were maybe trying to tell us something too," said Abbey. "Then it hit me. You know the phrases, 'Follow the stars,' or 'the stars point the way?' What if by using the numbers on the manuscript it would allow us to use the stars so they could indicate 'where' something was going to happen. And that the numbers are the key."

"I don't understand," said Michael as he leaned in closer. "A key to what?"

"A key to 'where' the events were going to happen, of course," said Abbey simply as she turned toward him.

"You've gotta be kiddin' me!" exclaimed Michael. "How?"

"What if the numbers on the manuscript were for longitude and latitude?" stated Abbey. "I went ahead and put in the locations for the three miracles that have already happened. And look what I came up with."

As Abbey showed them the piece of paper where she had written down some numbers, the silence in the room became stifling. Written on the paper were the longitude and latitudes for the cities where the first three miracles had already happened. The general area in Mexico where the City of the Canyons was located, Paris, France, and Los Angeles California.

"And these locations listed on the bottom?" asked Michael.

"Those are the names of the areas that coincide with the remaining two sets of numbers on the manuscript," explained Abbey. "Afghanistan and Montreal Canada."

"Oh mon dieu!!" "Oh my, God!" exclaimed Fabianne as she grabbed Abbey by the shoulders and hugged her. "L'Abbaye! You have done it! Now that we know where the next two events are going to happen we can be ready."

"I am impressed," said Michael as he looked over at her. "You are good!"

"Hey, I'm just trying to do my part to help out the team, that's all," beamed Abbey.

She did feel good about the breakthrough she had discovered. It could make all of the difference for the investigation if they could get to the last two Prophets before they were taken like the others.

"I will alert the Vatican about the two new locations," announced Fabianne as she dialed her phone and walked into the dining room. "At least now we have narrowed the field down most considerably, I'd say, oui! Thank you, again L'Abbaye!" said Fabianne. "I am not sure how we are to get into Afghanistan, but we will let the Vatican work on that, oui?"

As Fabianne walked over to the window with her phone up to her ear, Abbey noticed that Michael was eying her intently. And it was the look of mistrust that spread across his face that made her pause.

"Is something wrong, Michael?" asked Abbey.

Shaking his head 'no', he gave her a forced smile.

"Hey, you know something?" he said as he tore his eyes away from Fabianne and looked at her. "I think that maybe I just might be ready for that drink right about now, rather than later. How about you?" asked Michael.

"You get an 'amen' from me on that," agreed Abbey as she cut off the computer and stood up. "As a matter of fact, I think I'm ready for a couple of drinks," said Abbey. "But you know you might want to…..ah," said Abbey as she nodded her head toward Michael's bare chest. "I don't know, maybe put on a shirt or something."

"Oh, yeah! I almost forgot!" said Michael as he looked down. "I'll be back and pick you up in ten."

"I'll be waiting," said Abbey as she smiled broadly

As Michael walked to the door he turned around.

"And if you can, Abbey, please try and stay out of trouble until I get back, okay?"

"I can't promise anything, but I'll try."

"I guess that'll have to be good enough," chided Michael as he left the room looking forward to spending some private time with Abbey.

But in the back of his mind something was still nagging at him and wouldn't let go. He hadn't quite figured it out yet, but it had to do with the first three miracles and some similarities he found in the statements from the family members of the three Prophets just before they had disappeared. With his many years of professional experience as an Inspector investigating these kinds of cases, something just wasn't adding up. But until he had more information to go on, he would set his concerns aside for the time being and concentrate on something much more pleasant.

Like getting to know Abbey better.

Ten minutes later, at around one thirty, Michael was ringing the doorbell to Fabianne's suite. He had changed into a more comfortable pair of slacks, slip in loafers and lightweight, cream colored linen sweater that really brought out his eyes.

As Abbey opened the door, needless to say, she was more than pleased.

"Wow!" she exclaimed. "You clean up good!" she said as she stepped aside and let him in.

"I try," he said as he smiled and walked past her. "Where's Fabianne?" he asked as he noticed she wasn't in the front room.

"Oh, she decided to take a nap for a couple of hours," said Abbey. "The Vatican is working on trying to get clearance for us to enter Afghanistan," she said. "Besides, I think she's trying to give us some space. But if you want, I can ask her to join us?"

"No, I ah, I think I'd like the two of us to spend some time alone, if you don't mind?"

"Mind?" said Abbey as she walked back to the door. "Michael, I don't mind one bit. I'm all yours."

"You know Abbey, you might want to rephrase that," said Michael as he watched her walk past him.

"Oh, really!" asked Abbey playfully as she turned around to face him. "Why?"

"Because," said Michael as he followed her and then stood as close to her as he possibly could without touching her. "You don't make an offer like that to someone who is as attracted to you as I am. 'That' can get you into a lot of trouble."

"Michael," said Abbey as she picked up her jacket and walked around him without taking her eyes off of him. "I'm counting on it."

She then opened the door and stepped into the hall and waited for him. "You see, it's been one of those days, and I think I need to release some serious pent up stress," she said. "Do you think that you can help me with that, Inspector?" she asked as she smiled slightly.

Following her out into the hallway and closing the door behind him, Michael paused for a moment as she stood in front of her.

"As a matter of fact, I think I can," answered Michael quietly as he put his hand to the small of Abbey's back and directed her down the hall toward the elevator.

Abbey wasn't sure if she should mix business with pleasure or not. And especially, with Michael. But at that moment she didn't care. And besides, the little sexual innuendos they had been bantering back and forth between the two of them were intoxicating and as sensual as 'hell'. She hadn't felt turned on like this for a long time, and she was going to cast caution to the wind tonight.

But instead of stopping at the elevator so they could go downstairs to the bar, Michael walked right past it. And with his hand still in the small her back, he gently directed her beyond the elevator, around the corner and stopped in front of his room.

"We're not going to have a drink?" asked Abbey as she eyed him. "Michael, I 'need' a drink!"

"Might I recommend we take care of that stress you spoke about first," said Michael as he opened his door and stepped aside so she could enter. "I think we need to do something about that stress now."

"Hmm," purred Abbey under her breath as she walked past him and into his room. "Like I said, Michael. I'm all yours."

Following Abbey into the room, Michael let the door close behind him as he reached over and grabbed his sweater and had pulled it off before Abbey had turned around. And then before the door could even close good, he had already reached for Abbey's top and pulled it up over her head and had pushed her up against the wall while he pressed himself against her. His mouth had found hers as he kissed her deep and hard.

And as the door to Michael's room slowly closed and the lock clicked, the only sound that could be heard was the sounds of two people getting to know each other better.

Much better.

CHAPTER TEN

Monday 9:34 am

The 4th Miracle

When Fabianne got up the next morning, she relished at the wonderful sleep she had gotten. She hadn't realized that she was as tired as she was. As she made her way out of the bedroom and into the living room, she wasn't concerned about where Abbey and Michael were. She could see the mutual attraction the two of them had for each other last night and felt that Abbey would be foolish not to 'tap' that at least once for good measure.

"And why not," she thought to herself.

If she were in a position to do so, it may have crossed her mind, too. But she was not.

She knew that when this was over and all of the miracles predicted in the manuscript had come to pass, her assignment here would be over and she would have to return home. But in the meantime, she would enjoy all of the sensory delights that this assignment had to offer.

But she was happy for Abbey and Michael.

She smiled as she thought of the attraction that seemed to have developed between the two of them. She prayed when all was said and done and the sixth event came to pass, they would find happiness. It would be a gracious reward for them.

Since she hadn't received a call from her superiors in Rome during the night that the fourth event had happened or not, for now all they could do was to wait. And good thing there was no news during the night. It would have interrupted Abbey and Michael during their evening together.

Taking the time to move about the hotel room by herself and enjoy the morning, Fabianne ordered breakfast for one. The bell boy brought up her breakfast at about ten thirty, and set it up for her. Thanking him, when he left, Fabianne jumped in and enjoyed her meal. She relished in the tastes and the smells of the food and enjoyed every morsel there was. And then she relaxed on the couch in a food stupor and slept the rest of the morning.

When she awoke at about one in the afternoon, she still hadn't had any messages from the Vatican about the fourth event, or how they were going to get them into Afghanistan. But she knew that Rome was aware that time was of the essence. And since she hadn't heard from Abbey or Michael either, she decided to take a long, hot bath and enjoy the afternoon in solitude.

At just after two thirty in the afternoon, her cellphone rang.

Fabianne answered her phone and just listened. After a few moments she spoke.

"Yes, your Eminence I understand," said Fabianne as she listened carefully. "We will leave immediately. Yes!"

She quickly she slipped into a pair of comfortable slacks and put on a light sweater. As she set about throwing what few items she had into her bag, she dialed Michael's number.

After a couple of rings, Michael picked up.

"Fabianne, what is it?" he asked quickly.

"Michael," she said. "The fourth event has happened," said Fabianne. "Actually, the fourth event happened sometime yesterday in Afghanistan when it was supposed to."

"What!!??" exclaimed Michael as he swept his legs out from under the covers and sat on the side of the bed. "Why weren't we notified?"

"I'll explain it to you later," said Fabianne.

She knew that now time was of the essence. They had to get to the fourth Prophet as soon as possible.

"We need to leave as soon as we can," she explained. "The Vatican is making our flight reservations as we speak. Please tell L'Abbaye to be ready."

"So we're headed to Afghanistan?" inquired Michael.

"No, not Afghanistan, Michael," said Fabianne. "We're going to Bowling Green, Virginia to the military base there. I will meet you in my room as soon as you can get here."

Without waiting for a response, Fabianne hung up the phone and finished getting ready.

As Michael sat on the side of the bed, Abbey leaned forward onto her elbows and just looked at him.

"Did Fabianne say that you're going to Afghanistan?" she asked.

"No," answered Michael simply. "Not Afghanistan. We're headed to a military base in Virginia. And you're coming with," he said.

"What! Wait a minute!" exclaimed Abbey as she sat all the way up in the bed and leaned her back against the headboard. "First of all, what's in Virginia? And second, why am I going with you? I don't have any jurisdiction in another state."

And then as an afterthought she asked, "And 'what' time is it, anyway?"

"I can't answer your first question, because Fabianne didn't give me an explanation yet," explained Michael. "But as far as your second question, until this investigation is over, you're on the team. And wherever we go, you go. And the time is now approximately, two forty in the afternoon."

Abbey was stunned when Michael told her what time it was. That wasn't possible.

"No, Michael, that can't be!" exclaimed Abbey not ready to believe that she had just spent the better of yesterday afternoon and today in bed having hot, passionate sex with an Inspector who was also a Holy Warrior for the Vatican.

"That just wasn't possible!" the voice in her head keep saying over and over again.

Yeah, of course they slept several times in between when they found that they couldn't go any further and were totally spent. But still!

"Were they both that aroused with each other?" she asked herself.

"That had to be a record for anyone," she thought to herself realizing that as she tried to swing her legs out of the bed that she was sore in places she didn't even know that she had as the events of the evening started to slowly come back to her.

"Oh, God!" exclaimed Abbey as she leaned over the side of the bed and cradled her head in her hands. "What did we do last night, Michael?" she asked. "And all this morning and this afternoon."

Pausing a moment before he answered her, Michael just turned toward her and smiled.

"I'm not trying to be cliché or anything like that, but, what didn't we do, Abbey," he said as he smiled quite satisfied with himself. "And to be honest, everything that we did do, we did several times."

"Oh, God!" exclaimed Abbey again. "I'm going to Hell. I know it. I'm.....going to Hell! Here I am corrupting someone from the Vatican. Oh, God, Michael! You're not a priest or anything like that are you?" lamented Abbey as her voice went up a couple of octaves. "Or, or a priest in training?"

"Don't worry, Abbey," said Michael as he walked over to the side of the bed where she was sitting and knelt down in front of her. "You haven't corrupted anyone," he said. "And no, I'm not a priest or anything like that," he said. "I'm just a man, that's all."

As he quietly spoke to her, he placed both of his hands on either side of her face and gently lifted it to his.

"And you have just given me one of the most sensual and satisfying experiences I have truly ever had. And trust me," he said. "That's saying a lot."

Abbey knew right then and there how it was that she had lost all sense of time when she was with him. When he touched her, she just wanted to melt into his arms and let him hold her, love her. Whatever he wanted to do, she would let him and she would welcome it.

He leaned in and gently kissed her. She could feel his lips as they pressed softly against hers. And then she could feel his tongue as it slid past her lips and playfully sought her out. Then as he opened his mouth wider she could feel him gently suck on her tongue as if it were the entry to her soul as he sought to possess it and everything she had to give.

She heard herself moan as he pressed her back onto the bed and laid on top of her as he gathered her into his arms. She could feel him as he thrust his hips against her with a slow riding kind of motion. And as he became erect and hard, her body instinctively responded to him.

She wrapped her arms around his head, as his lips began to trace along her neck and down to her chest. As he began to fondle her breasts, she could see for the first time the extent of the tattoo that he had, and she realized that what she and Fabianne had seen earlier was only a small part of his tattoo.

It covered his entire back where parts of it even overlapped onto his shoulders. It was intricate as it depicted a shield of some sort with a sword going through it, and above the shield across his shoulder blades were what looked like ancient symbols.

It was the mark of the Vatican's 'Holy Warrior' that he bore.

But Abbey found that she couldn't focus on Michael's tattoos. She had become so aroused by Michael fondling her breasts that she heard herself call out to him.

"Michael! Please!! Please!!"

And even though her breasts were tender from the night before, as his tongue played with them, she couldn't help reveling in the delight and the pain he was giving her as she moaned louder.

She couldn't believe it. She wanted him, again! And he knew it.

And he obliged her by making love to her again.

As he spread her legs wide and lifted her hips up off of the bed, he pressed his swollen member into her, but only part of the way. And then he would pull himself partially out, and then he repeated the motion again. But each time he would ease himself a little further into her and a little harder until he could go no further. And then he would start all over again adding to her arousal as he slowly sought to bring her to her breaking point of sexual release.

Even though Michael found that he loved the sensual 'itch' that the slow motion gave him, he knew that he wasn't going to be able to hold back for much longer. He felt his member as it started to throb involuntarily, and he found that he had started to thrust harder. He wanted to go as far and as deep into Abbey as he could.

Each time that she felt Michael hit her spot it would cause her to jerk uncontrollably. Abbey found her body had started to tremble as she could feel him pull away and then come back to her. Each time that he did, it caused her body to arch up to meet him. She needed him to burrow himself into her and drain her of everything she had.

And then reaching his breaking point, Michael did just that as she felt a scream rise to her throat as he pulled her to him and she felt him release everything that he had.

An hour later, Michael and Abbey were at Fabianne's door, not as bright eyed as they could have been, but ready to go.

Without any mention of the fact that they had been MIA for twenty four hours, Fabianne opened the door and stepped out into the hallway.

"We have a flight to Virginia that leaves at five thirty five," she said as she headed for the elevator with them following close behind her. "There will be a car waiting for us downstairs. Oh, and L'Abbaye, you did bring your passport, did you not?"

"Ah, yes, I have it" answered Abbey as she glanced over at Michael.

"Good!" said Fabianne. "Because once we leave Virginia we will be heading up to Montreal, Canada where the fifth and final event is supposed to happen."

"But why are we going to Virginia?" asked Abbey.

"Because that is where they have taken the soldier who is currently the center of a military investigation concerning an incident that happened in Afghanistan on Sunday."

"What happened?" asked Michael.

"All I know is that they were doing military maneuvers for a highly secret mission, and a land mine was triggered. One of the soldiers threw himself onto the mine in an effort to save the rest of the men in his platoon. The bomb went off, and after all of the sand had settled, the soldier was found to be unharmed. Not a scratch on him."

"So why are we just now hearing about this?" asked Michael as they rode down to the lobby of the hotel. "If that happened on Sunday, then we've lost almost a day and a half!"

"Oui, I agree," said Fabianne. "But it would seem that because of the sensitive nature of the mission the soldiers were on, the military kept a tight lid on everything until they could get him and the others debriefed and back on American soil. The Vatican only got notified of what happened this afternoon, just before I called you and L'Abbaye."

As the elevator doors opened onto the lobby, the trio of investigators made their way to the front of the hotel and the waiting car.

Without wasting any time, the car sped away from the front of the hotel and made its' way to the airport. Their flight was leaving out of LA at five thirty five and would arrive in Virginia at approximately ten thirty that evening. With luck they would just make it to the base before eleven o'clock that night.

As they rode to the airport in silence, Abbey didn't know what to say.

She felt kind of guilty for letting her professional guard down. She never liked mixing business with her personal life. It was a rule she had always fought to abide by. But she couldn't explain what happened. It was as if she was drawn to Michael for some reason, and it felt as if there was more than just the sexual attraction that they both felt for each other. And she knew that Fabianne was aware that she and Michael had spent the night together.

"And okay," she exclaimed to herself. " All of the morning, and yes the first part of the afternoon up until about fifteen minutes before they showed up at Fabianne's door. But I couldn't help it!" she lamented to herself. "I just had never felt such intensity like that with anyone I had been with before," she admitted.

"Boy, I need to clear my head for a minute," thought Abbey as she let the window down on her side and gave Michael a quick glance.

It was then that she realized that Michael had been watching her intently as she tried to regain some composure.

"Are you alright, L'Abbaye?" asked Fabianne as she noticed that she was beginning to get flustered.

"Yes, I'm fine," said Abbey. "I, ah, just needed a little air is all. Thanks for asking,"

"I know that everything is happening very quickly and that perhaps it is a little overwhelming for you," said Fabianne. "But just take it slowly and do not forget to breathe, oui!"

Nodding her head that she understood, Abbey tried to concentrate on the fresh, cool air as it brushed her face as the car made its' way through the traffic.

Luckily the hotel wasn't that far from the airport, and twenty minutes later the car pulled up to the curb and let them out. Since everything that Fabianne and Michael had could be carried on the plane with them, they quickly checked in, got their boarding passes and headed for the departure gate. As for Abbey, she was traveling light with nothing to have to carry on whatsoever. But she knew she was going to have to pick up a few items before too long.

Because of Fabianne and Michael's special credentials, they all were quickly ushered through the security check point after their weapons were checked and everything cleared. Then they were directed to the Elite lounge until their flight was ready to board. At five o' five, the call came over the speaker that their fight was beginning to board, and that all priority passengers were to report to their gate.

It was then that Abbey realized that she, Fabianne and Michael were flying First Class.

It was kind of nice to be ushered to the front of the plane to be seated before anyone else, and then to be offered any kind of drink that her heart desired. And the seats! They were extra wide and plush, and they even reclined all the way back!

"Nice!" exclaimed Abbey as she relaxed into the folds of her seat by the window. "I could get used to living like this," she said to Michael as he slid into the seat next to her. "This isn't how all Vatican employees travel, is it? Because if it is, where 'do' I sign up?"

"Maybe not all, but most do," said Michael as he settled into his seat. "The Vatican takes care of their Inspectors and always has," he said.

"Where's Fabianne seated?" asked Abbey as she looked around the cabin.

"She's up a couple of rows on the other side," answered Michael as he took note of where she was.

And then he asked her a question that had been on his mind since the ride over from the hotel.

"Are you sure that you're alright, Abbey?" he asked with concern in his voice. "You did look a little flushed in the car coming over."

"Oh, I'm fine," said Abbey. "I was just thinking about, you know. What happened last night between us. And this morning, and this afternoon!"

Then out of the corner of her eye, she saw him drop his head onto his chest as he tried to stifle a laugh.

"Oh! So it's funny to you, now?" she exclaimed under her breath. "Michael, I'm feeling, I don't know, confused."

"Abbey. I'm not laughing about anything that happened between us last night, this morning, or this afternoon," stated Michael. "What happened between us was.....I can't even begin to explain it, or what I'm feeling right now. All I can say is that, being with you has made me feel something I've never felt before. And that's kind of scary for me."

"Oh, so, why were you snickering, then?"

"Because you seem to find it difficult to believe that you could have that kind of effect on a Man," explained Michael as he looked at her affectionately. "You don't seem to realize that you are a vibrant, sexual woman who is attractive as hell! And sporting that badge and your gun just adds to your sex appeal."

"Oh!" exclaimed Abbey as she turned her head to look out of the window so he couldn't see that she was getting embarrassed. "I, ah, I never thought of myself like that."

"Well, Detective, you should," said Michael as he put emphasis on the way he said, Detective.

But unlike before, she liked the way he said it this time. Kind of sexy like. So much so, that she was smiling to herself even as the plane backed out and took flight as they headed for Virginia.

CHAPTER ELEVEN

After the flight got underway, the passengers in First Class were served their dinner meal and a wonderful desert afterwards. After finishing her meal, Abbey was inclined to get as much rest as she could since she and Michael didn't get much the night before.

As she reclined her seat all the way back, she pulled the blanket up over her that was provided, and thought to herself, that going First Class wasn't such a bad thing.

"She could definitely get used to traveling like this," she thought.

She had halfway turned toward Michael and before she knew it, he had slipped his hand under her blanket and rested it onto the inside of her right thigh and lightly squeezed it.

"Oh, God!" screamed the voice in her head. "Please don't do anything here, Michael. Please!"

She thought that she was going to jump right out of her skin as she felt his hand slide up her thigh a little further and then stop. As he started to gently massage her thigh she could feel the heat of his hand through the thickness of her jeans as he continued to let his hand rest on her leg.

As Michael looked over at Abbey, he could see the terror in her eyes as his hand crept up her leg.

"Don't worry," he whispered to her under his breath as he continued to rest his hand on her leg. "I wouldn't do anything to embarrass you," he said. "I just wanted to feel close to you. Do you mind?"

Shaking her head that she didn't mind, Abbey smiled back at him.

And then, before she knew it, she had closed her eyes and had quickly fallen asleep. It wasn't until she felt the jolt of the plane landing on the runway that she was shaken out of her sound sleep for what seemed like only an hour. But as she sat up, she realized that except for dinner, she had slept through the entire trip.

And as she sat up, she felt Michael's hand as it still rested on her leg. As he rolled his head over to look at her he smiled.

"Did you rest okay?" he asked.

"Oh God yes! It felt great," she said as she stretched.

She noted to herself that she didn't mind having him touch her like that at all. It actually made her feel safe in a way, and she liked that.

It took the plane another fifteen minutes to taxi to the 'Hub', and then they let the passengers disembark. Once they had cleared the secure area of the airport, they headed for the taxi area where a military car was waiting for them.

Within minutes they had loaded into the car, and it pulled away from the airport heading for the military base of Fort A.P. Hill in Bowling Green, Virginia.

It was now eleven o'clock PM.

The driver of the car introduced himself as Sargent Lawrence, and that he was to brief them on the situation before they arrived at the base.

Fabianne introduced herself, Abbey and then Michael.

"Nice to meet ya'll," said the Lieutenant in a slow, southern drawl. "Our commanding officer instructed me to inform you that he doesn't agree with letting you interview any of the soldiers that were involved in the incident that occurred on Sunday. But because he got direct orders from Washington, he was going to allow you to speak to Private Paulson. But he was only going to allow one of you to speak to him."

"Is that the name of the soldier who was involved in the land mine incident?" asked Michael.

"I believe it is, Sir, yes," said the Lieutenant.

"Is there anything else you can tell us about what happened, Lieutenant?" asked Fabianne.

"No, I'm sorry there isn't."

Fabianne and Michael both understood that because the incident happened to an American soldier on foreign soil while participating in a highly classified operation, any information they were going to get was going to be limited if that. They also knew that the United States military operated under a totally different set of rules than the rest of the world did. And that could hamper their investigation.

And if it did, they were going to have to wait and see to what degree.

As the military car pulled up to the security gate of the base, the Lieutenant passed the ID's of Fabianne, Abbey and Michael through the window to the guard on duty. After a few minutes, they were cleared to come onto the base.

Within minutes they had pulled up to the administration building that was surrounded by bright flood lights and guards. Fabianne and the others exited the car and were ushered into one of the side entrances of the building and asked to wait in a small room with only a table, a couch and several chairs in it.

It was eleven thirty two PM.

Almost ten minutes had passed since they were placed in the room, and still no one had come in to speak to them.

"So, do you think that they forgot that we're here?" asked Michael, sarcastically as he paced around the small room.

"No," answered Fabianne. "I just think that they are getting all of their 'ducks' in order, if you will. They want to make sure that we speak to only who we are to speak to and to no one else. I do not think that they even want anyone to know that we are here, or why. And I think that may have a lot to do with the Vatican's request."

Abbey just sat on the couch and remained quiet and just observed from the sidelines. She still wasn't quite sure exactly 'why' she was there.

"But hey," she said to herself. "I got to fly First Class for the first time in my life, and that in itself, was awesome!"

Finding it impossible to wait any longer, Fabianne got up and walked over to the door and knocked.

"Is someone there?" she called out. "I need to use the facilities!"

Turning to Abbey and Michael, she simply shrugged her shoulders.

"That usually works in the movies, oui!" she said.

And before she had barely finished her sentenced, they heard the door unlock from the other side and open up.

"Is there something I can help you with?" asked the soldier as he stood in the doorway.

"Oui!" exclaimed Fabianne as she used all of the French charm she had. "I must go to the ladies room, if you do not mind?" she said as she smiled sweetly at the soldier.

"Sure, Miss. Right this way," said the soldier.

As he stepped aside and let Fabianne exit the room, he quickly closed the door back and secured it from the other side.

"Are you beginning to get the feeling that we're being held prisoner?" asked Michael not liking the idea of being kept locked up in a small room for any period of time.

Especially, against his will.

"Michael. What happens if we're too late?" asked Abbey as she watched Michael pace the room like a caged animal biting at his bit. "What if the soldier disappears like the others? What will they do?"

"One thing is for sure," said Michael. "If one of their soldiers disappears from here, and from right under their own noses, there will be 'hell' to pay, I can guarantee you that. And I wouldn't want to be in any of these 'grunts' shoes when that happens."

It was eleven forty five.

Ten minutes had passed and Fabianne hadn't returned.

It was eleven fifty five PM.

Then all of a sudden they heard the door unlock from the other side.

"Okay, they're ready for you," said the soldier as he swung the door opened.

Then he noticed that Fabianne wasn't in the room.

"Where's the other woman who was with you?" he asked.

"She went to the restroom a few minutes ago," answered Abbey. "One of your men opened the door for her and they were going to show her the way."

Turning to the other soldiers with him, he barked orders that they were to be taken to an interview room while he looked for Fabianne. And then he took off halfway jogging down the hall with several other soldiers while Abbey and Michael were ushered in the other direction. When they reached a well lit room with frosted windows, the guard opened the door and directed them to stay inside until someone came to speak to them.

Just as Abbey and Michael entered the room, an overhead alarm went off as the halls filled with armed guards rushing in all directions.

"What's going on?" asked Michael. "What's the alarm for?"

Ignoring his questions, the guard quickly went to close the door, but not before Michael had shoved his foot into the opening to keep from being locked in yet another room again.

"Hey!!" yelled Michael as he went to push his way out of the room.

"Michael!" screamed Abbey, not sure what was happening.

But when two of the guards lifted their weapons and pointed them at Michael, he realized that not only was he outnumbered, but also out gunned.

"Step back, Sir, please!" shouted the first guard.

"Michael, step back!" exclaimed Abbey frantically. "Step back!"

"Okay! Okay!" said Michael as he raised his hands and obliged the soldier's request by backing off. "Let's not get carried away guys, okay! I'm moving back."

Before the soldier could reach over and try to close the door again, a higher ranking Officer appeared in the doorway. The other soldiers stepped aside and snapped to attention as he entered the room. As he did, he glared at Michael barked out a question.

"Where's the other woman who was with you earlier?" he demanded.

"What are you talking about? We don't know where she is!" yelled Michael back.

And then he realized that's why the alarm went off. The soldier must have disappeared like the other three Prophets had.

Michael then directed a question to the soldier standing in front of him.

"What, don't tell me? Did your 'miracle boy' do a disappearing act right from under your noses?" he asked. "And let me guess, you guys don't know how he did it?" he said sarcastically.

And that did it!

The Officer in charge strode straight up to Michael and stood in his face with his nostrils flaring. As he stood even to Michael's six foot two height he bellowed at him.

"Mister, I can guarantee you one thing right now!" he yelled. "I will have you drawn and quartered from here to anywhere I dammed well please! And no one will ever know what happened to you! Do you understand me?"

Abbey wasn't sure how this was going to end, but one thing she knew for sure, was that if it came down to a fight between the two of them, she'd have to bet on Michael. Especially understanding what he did for the Vatican and what his training was, it didn't matter how loud the soldier bellowed. Michael could have taken him in probably two, maybe three moves.

But Michael surprised her.

She saw him exhale slightly and then take a couple of steps away from the soldier as he backed down. He knew that he couldn't afford to get into a brawl with the military. He was there to help with the investigation and if necessary, to provide protection for the others against any 'Demons' if necessary. Not to fight with the soldiers who were just doing their job.

Right then, she had more respect for him and what he stood for than she had before.

"Now! I'm going to ask you again!" shouted the soldier as he watched Michael back down. "Where is the other woman who was with you when you came onto this base?"

Before Michael could answer, a voice from in the hallway with a very distinct accent spoke.

"Are you looking for me, Officer?"

It was Fabianne as she strode into the room as if nothing out of the ordinary had happened. "I am sorry," she said. "I must have gotten lost when I came out of the ladies room. Why are the alarms going off?" she asked. "What has happened?"

"One guess," said Michael as he gave Fabianne an odd look.

Abbey wasn't sure, but there was something going on with Michael and Fabianne. And for some reason it seemed as if he no longer trusted her, or for that matter, anything that she said.

"Enough of this!" yelled the Officer in charge. "Bring all of them!"

As the Officer in charge turned and left the room, Fabianne, Abbey and Michael were ushered out behind him. As they made their way through the maze of hallways, they entered an area that was obviously where the upper brass had their offices. And even though it was well after normal operating hours even for a military base, the place was buzzing with activity.

"And no wonder," thought Michael to himself as he assessed the area they had been taken to. "They have a situation that's landed in their laps, that none of them could even begin to explain it."

First, they have the incident where one of their soldiers throws himself onto a landmine in Afghanistan to save the other members of his troop. And then he gets up and doesn't even have a scratch on him. And second, after being brought back to the states for debriefing, he ends up disappearing from right under the noses of a military base that was one of the most secure military bases in the country.

"Yep!" thought Michael to himself. "It looks like it's going to be a long night for them."

Stopping in front of one of the main offices, the Officer in charge knocked on the door and waited. No sooner had the Officer finished knocking did they heard a voice answer from inside.

"Come!"

Swinging the door open, the soldier snapped at attention and saluted the man sitting behind the desk.

"Sir, the Inspectors from the Vatican."

"Thank you Lieutenant. That will be all," said the man without looking up.

After a few moments of silence, the man addressed them.

"Please, come in."

Taking the lead, Fabianne walked into the office followed by Abbey and Michael. Only after the door closed, and the remaining soldiers took up their positions outside of the office on either side of the door, did the man look up.

"Miss 'al Benne, I'm Commander James," said the man as he stood and introduced himself. "And I take it that these are the two Inspectors who came with you?"

"Oui, Commander, they are," said Fabianne. "May I ask what has happened, and why have we not been allowed to interview the soldier in question as we were promised?"

"Well, Miss 'al Benne," he said as he tried to pronounce her name. "There's been a situation that frankly, has us stumped," stated the man as he eyed the trio. "It would seem that one of our soldiers has disappeared from a secure location within this facility. And I'll be dammed if we can figure out how in the 'hell' that happened!"

"Disappeared? Who's disappeared?" asked Michael again with a sarcastic tone. "Oh wait a minute. You think that we had something to do with it?"

"That's just it, Son. I don't know! And when I don't know what happens on my base, I am not a happy camper," said the man as he raised his voice. "And when I'm not a happy camper, I can guarantee you that 'no one' on this base is going to be happy until I get some answers."

"I do not know what to tell you, Commander James," said Fabianne. "I came here with my colleagues to speak to the soldier in question who was involved in the incident that took place in Afghanistan. And as of yet, I have not been able to do so."

"Well, Miss 'al Benne. I'm afraid that's not going to happen."

"And why not?" exclaimed Fabianne. "We understood that Washington had directed you to….."

Before Fabianne could finish her sentence, the Commander interrupted her.

"It doesn't mean a dammed thing what Washington says to do, if I can't comply, Miss al' Benne!" said the Commander.

And then dialing his tone back, he continued.

"It would seem that the soldier that has disappeared is the same young man that you came to see," explained the Commander. "Now, for some reason I have the feeling that you and your, 'colleagues' here, aren't surprised by this turn of events. And you know what? I don't give a 'flying fuck!!' All I know is that one of my boys is missing and if you can't, or won't give me what information I need to find him, I think it's time that you all left. I'm having the entire base searched now. When we locate him, I'll let you know. Please leave a number with one of the gentlemen outside where you can be contacted. Now if you'll excuse me."

Fabianne and the others knew full well what had happened. They were too late! The fourth Prophet was gone.

But it was obvious that Washington hadn't informed the Commander of the base the exact nature of the investigation that Fabianne and the others were working on for the Vatican, or why they wanted to talk to the soldier. And he was truly a soldier who didn't question his orders when given, he just followed them.

And Fabianne and the others could only hope that by knowing where the fifth event was going to happen, they could possibly get ahead in this investigation for once. The only problem was, if the fifth event did occur in Montreal as predicted, there was no guarantee that the Prophet wouldn't disappear at any time right after the event happened, since it 'was' the last one.

They may not have had two days before the Prophet disappeared as in the other cases. There was no guarantee of what kind of timeline they were working with once the fifth miracle happened. They just didn't know.

"Well, Commander. Thank you anyway," said Fabianne as she stood up. "But before I leave, I would like to have a transcript of the entire interview your people did with the soldier before he disappeared, oui!" stated Fabianne. "And I am sure that if you have a problem with this request, I can contact Washington if necessary. But I would rather not have to do that, Commander. You do understand, oui! We will be waiting outside while someone gets the transcripts for us."

Then without another word, Fabianne turned to leave out of the office until the Commander stopped her.

"You know, Lady," he said. "You must have a real powerful ally up in Washington to come in here on 'my' base, and demand that I give you confidential military information. And you must have a pair of 'big' ones to boot to be that gutsy! I like that!" said the Commander as he half way smiled. "If you will wait outside, one of my men will get that information for you. Good night, Miss 'al Benne. It's been a pleasure to make your acquaintance."

"Thank you, Commander. It has been my pleasure, also."

As Abbey and Michael followed Fabianne out of the Commander's office, they were slightly confused at what had just happened. Once outside and away from the rest of the guards, Michael had to ask.

"Okay, what just happened in there?" he exclaimed. "I understand that somehow the fourth Prophet has disappeared, which means, we need to get to Montreal and fast," said Michael. "But what was that thing that was going on between you and the Commander?"

"It is called, understanding who holds the bigger stick, Michael," said Fabianne as she smiled at him. "Nothing more, I can assure you. But he did say that he liked my 'big ones', did he not?" stated Fabianne as she smiled and walked over to where there were several seats.

"That he did," said Abbey amused by what had just happened.

"Well, my motto is, by whatever means it takes to get what we need, oui!" said Fabianne.

"Works for me!" exclaimed Abbey as she smiled at the way that Fabianane handled the Commander to get the transcripts. "Com'on Michael," encouraged Abbey. "At least we're going to be able to get the transcripts of the debriefing so we'll have a better idea of what happened in Afghanistan, right?"

Abbbey noticed that he still seemed to be bothered by something.

"What's the matter Michael?" she asked. "It's all good!" she exclaimed.

Without answering her, Michael continued to watch Fabianne intently, and then he asked her a question.

"Where were you when the alarm went off, Fabianne?" he asked as he approached her.

"Like I told the Officer, Michael," she said. "After I came out of the Ladies room, I must have gotten turned around in this maze of hallways they have. It is most disorienting."

And then trying to understand why Michael was acting so distrustful, Fabianne asked him a question.

"Is there something wrong, Michael?" she asked. "I have noticed that you have been in quite a mood lately. Is there something that you wish to ask me?" she said as she matched his stare.

"I just did."

"And I answered you," said Fabianne tightly. "End of discussion, oui?"

Fabianne turned and sat down on one of the couches that were in the open aired lobby, while Abbey and Michael sat on another one.

"What's going on with you, Michael?" asked Abbey quietly as she looked over at Fabianne.

At that moment, she felt torn not knowing exactly what was going on between the two of them. And she didn't know how to fix it either.

After about twenty minutes had passed, one of the soldiers appeared with a binder containing not only the interview with the soldier that they had originally come to speak with, but also the interviews with the other members of his troop and what they had witnessed.

"Nothing like pulling a little weight," thought Abbey as they all left the Administration Building.

As they were being escorted off the base and back to the airport, the tension in the air between Fabianne and Michael was so thick it could be sliced with a knife. Once at the airport they only had to wait a couple of hours before their flight to Montreal, Canada was to board. The flight was uneventful, and by the time they had arrived in Montreal it was mid-morning. After their arrival, they were driven to a five star hotel in the downtown district of Montreal where they each retreated to their own rooms and waited.

Fabianne didn't relish having to tell her superiors at the Vatican that she wasn't able to get a chance to speak to the fourth Prophet before he too, had disappeared. But she was able to report that she had obtained the transcripts of the soldiers' debriefing, and that gave her enough insight as to what had happened.

Especially since within those transcripts she found statements from some of the soldiers who verified what the soldier in question had said to them after the incident. According to two of his fellow soldiers, when he first got up after the land mine exploded, they were stunned to find that he wasn't injured in any way. Then they stated that he just looked at them like he was in a daze and recited the phrase, 'Blessed are those who believe in him. You are loved. Watch for his return, for he is coming, soon'.

They thought he was in shock and was just spouting a biblical phrase because of what he had just experienced. Especially after he realized that he had survived something that no one should have.

"And who wouldn't be in shock!" thought Fabianne to herself.

But aside from the actual event itself, it was all she needed to recommend to the Vatican that what took place in Afghanistan was indeed one of the miracles spoken of in the manuscript.

After relaying her findings to her superiors at the Vatican, Fabianne was able to finally stretch out across her hotel bed and close her eyes and try and catch up on some well-deserved sleep. There wasn't anything they could do now but to wait for news that the fifth and final event had happened. And then they had to try and get to the fifth Prophet before they too disappeared.

CHAPTER TWELVE

Montreal, Canada

'A Man Will Rise From the Death of Disease and Live Again'

Tuesday -7:55 pm

The 5th Miracle

Fabianne wasn't sure if she was dreaming or not.

She kept hearing a low ringing in the back of her head as she turned over and tried to dismiss it. When that didn't work, she sat straight up in the bed and realized it was her cellphone that was ringing. Sliding herself off of the bed, she picked up the phone and answered it.

"Oui," she said as she listened carefully.

After a few moments, she had been fully briefed by her superiors in Rome.

She said, "I understand! Right away, your Eminence!"

Wasting no time, she quickly hung up and dialed Michael's room.

"Hello."

"Michael, the fifth event has happened," exclaimed Fabianne. "I need you and L'Abbaye over here immediately. We must hurry!"

"Got it!" answered Michael as he hung up and rolled over to nudge Abbey.

"It's showtime!" he said affectionately as he kissed her shoulder lightly. "It's happened."

"The fifth event?" asked Abbey as she sat up and shuddered slightly.

"Yep!" he answered. "We're supposed to meet Fabianne over at her room.

Abbey knew that if this event was indeed the last one spoken of in the manuscript, and it was declared a miracle by the Vatican, she wondered what was next. Trying not to think about it, she slid out of the bed quickly washed up and got dressed.

Twenty minutes later she and Michael met up with Fabianne in the hallway and made their way to the lobby of the hotel. The waiting car took them to a midtown hospital where the Vatican had been informed that nothing short of a 'miracle' had just occurred.

It seemed that for now, the tension that had occurred between Fabianne and Michael had been set aside for. For now, all that was important was trying to get to the fifth Prophet before they disappeared like the others had.

"So what are we walking into, Fabianne?" asked Michael as they rode to the hospital. "What's the event?"

"It would seem that there was a patient who had an incurable and very aggressive Cancer that had spread to over ninety percent of his vital organs in a matter of three weeks," said Fabianne. "They said it was one of the most aggressive Cancers they had ever seen to date. I understand that he was being treated at the hospital that we are now heading for. There was very little hope that he could survive the treatments that were supposed to help him, because the Cancer had spread too far and too fast. As I understand it, they had given him his last rites and his family was called in."

Fabianne paused for a moment trying not to become immune to what had happened.

"He died around four thirty this afternoon while his family was standing vigil over him," continued Fabianne. "After a couple of hours, around six thirty, they cleared the room so that the nurses could prepare the body for removal to the morgue. One of the nurses was standing over the body when someone reached out and grabbed her arm. It was the patient who had died more than two hours earlier from the advanced, aggressive moving Cancer."

"He came back from the dead, didn't he?" said Michael. "It's the fifth and final event. So what is it you need to have to confirm it as one of the miracles that's quoted in the manuscript?"

"The statement that each of the other four Prophets has given," answered Fabianne. "That will confirm it as the fifth miracle."

"But how do you plan to go about finding out if he made the statement to anyone," asked Abbey.

"Talk to the family members, the nursing staff," said Fabianne. "Anyone who may have come in contact with him after his resurrection."

"You know that may be easier said than done, being that it's a hospital," said Abbey. "They have pretty strict rules about who can get in to talk to the patients. Especially, patients who've died and come back to life."

"And not to mention it's probably going to be a media circus around the hospital when word of what happened gets out," stated Michael.

"Ah, oui, that is true," agreed Fabianne. "But it's something that just might work to our advantage. We will just have to wait and see what we are up against."

For the rest of the ride to the hospital, there was a heavy silence in the car as each of them were immersed in their own private thoughts of what the verification of this event would mean. To them as individuals, and to the rest of the world.

They all understood what kind of global affect could be expected if the existence of the manuscript and the five miracles were made public. How would people react? Would there be panic in the streets? Would the faithful flock to their places of worship to reaffirm their faith and their place in the afterlife?

And what about those who didn't believe?

What fate awaited them once the sixth event happened?

There was no way for anyone to know the answers to these or the multitude of other questions that were going to be asked once everything was revealed. There was no way for anyone to know what would actually happen, until it did.

As the car got closer to the hospital, they quickly realized that what Michael had said about the media finding out, had already happened. No one knew who had leaked information to the media and the public about the miraculous recovery of a patient, who after being dead for over two hours, had come back to life.

But it was obvious that someone had.

The streets surrounding the hospital for at least two city blocks had been blocked off and no one was being allowed in unless they had official business at the hospital. And even then, they had to be cleared by the Hospital Administrator.

Everyone was startled when Fabianne's cellphone rang. It broke the stifling silence inside of the car as Fabianne answered.

"Oui, your Eminence," said Fabianne as she listened.

Then she said, "I think that is exactly what we need to get to the patient, Father. Oui. Thank you."

After hanging up, Fabianne turned to Abbey and Michael.

"The patient and his entire family are devout, practicing Catholics," she said. "And the Church has already spoken to several of the family members and informed them that the Vatican has dispatched someone to comfort them in their moment of crisis. They are expecting us."

"But isn't it sacrilegious to prey on people during a time like this when they need someone to give them comfort and guidance?" asked Abbey. "I mean it feels deceitful to me for us to infringe on them during this time."

"L'Abbaye, you are right," said Fabianne. "But we are not going to represent ourselves as something we are not. They are expecting three Investigators who work for the Vatican, who just happen to have been in the area. All of that is true," stated Fabianne. "We will try to answer their questions as best we can as to 'why' this has happened, and hopefully in the process, get as much information that we can to help us conclude our own investigation. Trust me, no one will be deceived or misled."

Leaning forward, Fabianne gave directions to the driver which as to which direction he should go to get to a passable street near the hospital. Within a few minutes they had arrived at a closed off street blocked by Police barriers. After the Police had confirmed that they were expected, they were being waved past the barriers that had been set up to keep the curious onlookers and the religious fanatics at bay.

But as the car made its' way through the throngs of media trucks and reporters that were already there, it wasn't hard to see that this was just the beginning of what was to be expected. It all depended on whether or not the Church leaders and the Heads of State from around the world decided to make the existence of the manuscript and what it predicted public or not.

Especially, if this event 'was' verified as the fifth and last miracle. Then the only thing that was left to come to pass was the sixth event.

It took the driver some time to slowly make his way to the underground driveway. From there they were to take the North Tower elevator up to the tenth floor where the patient in question and his family were. No other new patients or visitors were being allowed on the floor until the current situation could be contained.

As Fabianne and the others exited the elevator onto the tenth floor, they were met by one of the Hospital Administrators and her Assistant.

"Miss. 'al Benne?" said a very pleasant, woman dressed in a dark two piece suit who looked to be in her mid-forties. "I'm Gretchen Langley, the Hospital Administrator for the hospital," she said as she extended her hand and shook each of the Inspectors hands. "We were informed by the family that the Vatican was going to send someone over. We are so glad that they have allowed this. I have to tell you that this situation has the entire hospital staff stumped. We've, we've never seen anything like this happen before," she exclaimed as her voice failed to cover up the fact that she too, was unnerved by what had transpired.

"Thank you, Miss. Langley," said Fabianne politely. "We will try and do whatever we can. The Vatican understands that this is a time when everyone involved will need some comforting. May I introduce my colleagues," she said as she stepped aside and introduced Abbey and Michael.

"They will be assisting me, oui! May I ask that while my two colleagues speak to the family members, I would like to speak to anyone in the hospital who may have had contact with the patient in question after the incident happened."

"Of course, Inspector. I'll arrange that for you," she said. "You can interview them in the office down the hall here. I'll show you. It's out of the way and no one will disturb you. My Assistant will show your colleagues where we have the family sequestered. They are extremely shaken by what's happened. We all are."

"Thank you, Miss. Langley," said Fabianne.

"Miss. Langley, may I ask you a question?" asked Michael before he and Abbey followed the Assistant. "We understand that the patient died at around four thirty this afternoon and then at around six thirty this evening he was....." Michael paused for a moment.

He didn't want to use the word 'resurrected', although that's what appeared to have happened. So he chose to use another phrase to describe what had happened and had all of the staff at the hospital stumped.

"I don't know how else to say it," he said apologetically. "But the patient was somehow 'revived' after being pronounced dead after more than two hours. I'm curious as to how the media found out about what happened so quickly?"

"We don't know," admitted the Administrator. "All employees at the hospital are all bound by a nondisclosure agreement of not discussing patient care or anything pertaining to their condition. Information is only disclosed to immediate family members and no one else," she said. "But as I'm sure you took note of the media circus that has surrounded the hospital, someone has given information out that shouldn't have. And I guarantee you that we will find out exactly 'who' it was and they will be disciplined accordingly. And please understand Inspector, this is not the way our facility operates."

Nodding his head slowly, Michael acknowledged that he understood how a breach in confidentiality such as this was something that no hospital would want to have to deal with.

But just as he and Abbey turned to follow the Assistant, the Hospital Administrator spoke again as she stepped in close.

"And so that you understand our position here, Inspectors," she stated. "The patient wasn't 'revived' by any of our staff members," she said. "The staff present in the room at the time of the patient's....."

Even she was having a hard time putting an appropriate word to describe what had happened. And being the professional that she was, she used an acceptable term that best described it.

"At the time of the patient's 'recovery', everything that had been used to keep him alive at the time had been disconnected two hours before," explained the Administrator. "All of his vital organs had shut down completely and had been of no use for days. He was brain dead, and it was the machines that kept him alive. His major organs had been reduced to, for lack of a better description, mush, Inspector. And now he's been sitting up and speaking with his family who've declared his recovery as nothing short of being a miracle from God. And I don't mind admitting to you that I agree with them."

"Well, we'll do what we can to help the family through this," said Michael. "Is there anything else we should know before we speak to the family?"

"I would just caution you on trying to give a rational explanation to what's happened, other than it was a miracle."

"Ah, pardon', Miss. Langley," interjected Fabianne surprised by the woman's statement. "As of yet, the Vatican has not declared this as a miracle. I would like to wait until that can be confirmed, oui!"

"Oh, I understand, Miss. 'al Benne. Believe me, I do," she said. "But this is a Catholic hospital, and we are stout believers in miracles. But you try and explain to the family or to anyone here at the hospital how the patient in question has now been given a complete, clean bill of health. All of his organs are healthy and functioning perfectly. There is no indication that there was ever a Cancer of any kind in his body, whatsoever," she said. "Oh, and you're gonna love this," she added. "According to our examination of him that was just completed less than an hour ago, he now has a new functioning appendix and tonsils! Both of which were taken out years ago," she said. "I'm sorry to say that aside from his recovery, if that doesn't fall into the category of a miracle, I don't know what would."

"Thank you for explaining everything to us, Miss. Langley," said Fabianne."It is most appreciated."

Then turning to Michael, Fabianne spoke directly to him.

"Father, if you do not mind," she said. "I trust that you and Miss. Wells will be able to console the family while I speak to the other staff members of the hospital, oui?"

Michael nodded his head slightly and turned to follow the Assistant as she ushered them down the hall to one of the quiet rooms where the family was.

But Abbey found that she couldn't move herself from the spot she was standing in to follow them. She couldn't. Because she couldn't believe what she had just heard.

"What did Fabianne just call Michael?" screamed the voice in her head. "Father?? Father!! But, but Michael said he wasn't a man of the cloth. He said that he wasn't a Priest! He lied to me!" she exclaimed to herself trying not to let anyone around her know how what she had just heard had affected her.

But she couldn't help it. As her head started to spin, she tried to compose herself.

"She had slept with a Priest from the Vatican! A Priest!!" the voice in her head kept screaming. "I'm going to Hell! Oh, my God, I'm going to Hell!"

"L'Abbaye!" exclaimed Fabianne as she noticed the look that had spread across Abbey's face. "Are you alright?"

"I'll be fine," she said as she looked up at Michael and then quickly turned away. "Just a little tired, that's all."

As Michael moved to her side with a concerned look on his face, Abbey quickly strode by him. She couldn't look at him right now.

"I'm fine!" she exclaimed as the Assistant led her down the hall to where the family was located.

With Fabianne and Michael looking after her, Fabianane paused.

"Michael, you need to explain to her, now!" exclaimed Fabianne quickly.

Nodding his head that he understood, Michael quickly caught up with Abbey and took her by the arm.

Then turning to the Administrator, Fabianne announced that she was ready to be shown to the office where she could conduct her interviews with the hospital staff members.

Quickly catching up with Abbey, Michael took her by the arm and turned her around to face him. Then before Abbey could object, he turned to the Assistant.

"Would you give us a minute here, please," he said as he moved Abbey into one of the enclaves along the side of the hallway where they were standing.

The Assistant who couldn't have been any older than in her mid-twenties, not understanding what was going on, quickly nodded her head and just stood in the middle of the hall and waited. She didn't know what was going on between the Father and the other Inspector, but it seemed pretty intense to her.

And then her thoughts started to wander.

"When did Priests get to be so good looking and sexy?" she thought to herself.

She definitely didn't remember any of the Priests in her church being so easy on the eyes.

"And that body!" she exclaimed to herself. "I mean, he was tall, had an awesome body, and those dimples!" she mused to herself as she smiled a 'wickedly' sexy smile. "God, I would let him do whatever he wanted to do to me, that was for sure,"

Then she nervously looked around to see if anyone had been watching her and might have known what it was that she was thinking about. And then she caught herself when she realized that she was thinking about a man of the cloth.

"Oh my God!" she exclaimed to herself under her breath as she quickly looked around again.

She was embarrassed at what she had been thinking and hoped that no one had noticed that her face had become totally flushed. At that point she was good to wait in the hall until the two Inspectors had resolved whatever issues it was that they had going on between them.

And while she waited, she said a silent prayer asking for forgiveness.

As Michael pulled Abbey into one of the vacant waiting rooms in the hallway, he shut the door behind them.

"Let go of me!" exclaimed Abbey under her breath as Michael forced her into the room. She tried to break his hold on her arm, but it was no use.

"Abbey! Abbey listen to me!" he exclaimed softly in her ear as he pressed against her pinning her between him and the wall on the far side of the room.

Michael not only towered over her, but his grip was steadfast. As he reached over and grabbed her other arm, he pulled her to him. She could feel the strength in his body as he pushed her up against the wall. And as he leaned into her, she could feel him as he pressed his hips into her.

As he restrained her, she could feel the muscles of his body as they tensed up. It was a good thing that the room they were in didn't have any windows in it. The interaction they were having with each other would have been difficult to explain if anyone had been watching.

"Oh God, no!" she exclaimed softly to him as her body reacted and pushed back in response to what he was doing to her. "You're a Priest! You're a Priest, Michael!" she kept saying over and over. "And you lied to me, Dammit! You lied to me!" she exclaimed.

She cursed herself because of the way her body was reacting to him. The way he was so close to her and touching her. It wasn't right for her to feel the way that she did.

But he was intent on making sure that she didn't go anywhere until he said what he needed to say.

"Abbey, listen to me!" he exclaimed softly in her ear as he continued to move against her. "I'm not a Priest!" he said. "I'm not a Priest! Not anymore! I gave up the Priesthood for a higher calling. That's why I became a 'Guerriero' for the Vatican," he said as he softly whispered in her ear.

She could feel the slight roughness of his intentional 'five o'clock' stubble as he leaned in close and brushed her face lightly. She didn't know why, but it seemed to make him even more irresistible. She could feel his breath on her neck as he breathed hard trying to keep her contained. And even though she knew it was wrong, it made her want him even more as her nipples got hard and she could feel the wetness between her legs as her body seemed to have a mind of its own as it answered him.

"No Michael! Please!" she pleaded as she tried to try her head away from him. "Please don't! Don't!"

Abbey didn't know what to think as she felt herself losing the strength to resist him as she felt her body stop struggling and she breathed a sigh of relief as she let him gather her into his arms and just hold her.

"Fabianne felt that because I used to be a Priest it would help when we talk to the family," he said as he held onto her. "That's all," he said. "I'm sorry! I didn't think how you would react when she said it. I just didn't think!"

As he wrapped his arms completely around her and held her, he buried his head into her neck and kissed her softly. He had become so aroused that he couldn't help dropping his right hand below her waist and pulling her to him as he pushed into her letting her feel him. Letting her know what it was that she did to him when they were in such close proximity with each other.

She didn't know if it was just the way they reacted toward each other, or if it was the tussle they had just engaged in that added to the intensity of their sexual attraction. But whatever it was, she could feel that Michael was now fully erect and then some.

And at that moment, she didn't care where they were or who may have come in. All she wanted was for him to lift her up against the wall, spread her legs as wide as they would go, and take her as hard as he could. Then she wanted him to turn her over and force her onto her knees and take her from behind until she screamed for him to stop. She wanted him anyway she could have him.

She couldn't remember when she had been so aroused before, and it scared her. He scared her.

Abbey moaned softly as she felt him pressed back against her indicating that he felt the same way. She could feel the heat from inside rush up into her chest and spread across her neck and face as his lips found hers and he kissed her deep and hard. As she suckled on his tongue, he thrust it deeper and deeper into her mouth demanding everything she had. She wanted to feel him inside of her now more than she ever had before. She wanted his hard, throbbing member to push through her clothes and claim her, all of her.

And it was then that she realized.....she was about to have an orgasm.

As she grabbed a hold of Michael, she bit into his arm to stifle her scream as her body shook uncontrollably. It couldn't be helped it as she felt herself come and her body quivered as the wetness between her legs began to escape from the confines of her underwear.

Then she could feel Michael's body as it tensed up and his breath became labored. As she felt him push harder against her, she could tell that he too, was about to lose control. She heard him moan softly as he slammed his left hand against the wall above her, and rolled his hips against her harder and harder. And then with one final push, his body shook with sexual release as he moaned softly into her ear.

As her head fell forward and rested onto his chest, she felt herself relax in his arms as he continued to hold her up against the wall. They both were breathing hard and their clothes were damp from their impromptu sexual experience.

"Good thing he had on a loose shirt that wasn't tucked in," thought Abbey as she let him continue to move his hips against her as he leaned into her. She knew it could have been embarrassing for the both of them if the after effects of what had just happened were visible.

She wished they were alone someplace where they could roll over onto each other and Michael could make hard, passionate love to her, over and over again. She wanted him to claim her as his, just like he had done the night before. That was all that she wanted.

After a few minutes, they could feel the cool temperature of the hospital room as it began to chill their skin as the intensity of their passion began to subside, and the temperature of their bodies had begun to return to normal.

Out in the hallway, about ten minutes had passed before the Assistant decided to knock on the door.

As she leaned close to the door to listen, she couldn't hear anything coming from inside of the room. She only hoped that whatever issues the Father and the Inspector had with each other, it had been resolved.

"Father?" she called out as she knocked on the door. "Is everything alright?" she said. "I think that the family is waiting for you."

After a few moments of silence from inside of the room, the Assistant heard Michael answered her. As he spoke, he tried to steady his voice so she wouldn't be any more suspicious than she probably already was.

"Give us a few more minutes, please," he said as he tried to sound as aloof and professional as he could. "Go on ahead and we'll catch up with you. We have a few more things to discuss in private," he said as he tried to control his breathing.

"Ah, well, Father. I, I was directed to take you to the family," said the Assistant as she started to object to just leaving them.

She didn't want her Administrator to be angry with her for not doing as she had been instructed.

"Don't worry," said Michael from in an authoritative voice. "I'll let your Administrator know that I insisted. Now, please if you don't mind."

"Ah, sure! Okay!" said the Assistant. "I, I'll be down at the nurse's station at the other end of the hall waiting for you, Father. Okay?"

"We'll meet you there. Thank you."

"Okay! Okay!" said the Assistant as she backed away from the door and stood in the middle of the deserted hallway for a minute, unsure of what to do next.

Then taking in a deep breath, she turned and made her way down to the other end of the hall to the nurse's station where all she could do was to wait.

After another fifteen minutes had passed, the young Assistant looked up and spied Michael coming toward her.

"Father!" she exclaimed as she approached him. "I didn't mean to interrupt you," she said apologetically. "I just….."

Before she could go into an explanation, Michael stopped her.

"It's quite alright," he said as he flashed his signature smile at her, making sure that his dimples were in full view. "The Inspector and I had a slight disagreement between us that we had to resolve first," he said.

"Where 'is' the Inspector?" she asked as she looked down the hall behind him. "She's not coming?"

"Oh she came alright!" thought Michael to himself as he had to look down to camouflage what he was privately thinking, and to avoid looking directly at the young Assistant. "As a matter of fact," he mused to himself. "She came twice."

And for a moment. For just one moment, he flashed back to being in the room with Abbey, and how he had made her come once without actually being inside of her. But for Michael that wasn't enough for him.

He wanted more and he knew it was a risk, but it was a risk he was willing to take it.

Right after he and Abbey had both come the first time, he took a few minutes to catch his breath while he still had Abbey up against the wall. He was still hard, but he wasn't finished. He needed to be inside of her and feel the warm and wetness of her body as it wrapped around his swollen member, and forced him to claim everything that she had. And he wasn't going to let her go before he got everything that he wanted. He had reached down, undid her pants and let them slide down to her ankles, and then he did the same to his pants.

And with the determination of a Man who knew what he wanted and was going to go after it no matter what, Michael put both of his hands behind Abbeys knees and slid her up the wall as he lifted her up off of the floor. And then feeling his desire to claim her coming to a head once again, he thrust himself roughly into her and pinned her against the wall so hard, she thought she was going to lose her breath.

Michael rode her like there was no tomorrow.

He thrust his himself up and into her again and again as he rolled his hips in one direction and then in the other. He had grabbed her buttocks and squeezed them so hard that his fingers had left imprints on her skin as he went as deep as he could. All Abbey could do was to roll her head back and moan deeply as Michael's body shook uncontrollably as he found what he was looking for.

Bringing himself back to the present while standing at the nurses' station, Michael found himself almost getting aroused again just thinking about the sexual encounter that he and Abbey had had, just engaged in only a few feet from where the Assistant and the nurses manning the station were standing.

"Yes, she's…..she's coming," he said. "She'll be along in a few minutes. Why don't we go on ahead and speak to the family," he said as he placed his hand on the Assistant's arm and turned her around.

The Assistant found herself embarrassed as she felt herself tremble slightly at Michael's touch.

"Oh, okay!" she said weakly as she let him direct her away from the nurse's station.

"Where exactly are the family members right now?"

"Ah, down this hall, Father," she said. "Right this way!"

As the Assistant moved away from the Nurse's desk with Michael, the two RN's manning the desk couldn't help themselves. They had stepped out from behind the counter and watched Michael as he walked down the hall with the young woman.

When they were far enough down the hall and out of hearing range, the first Nurse turned to her co-worker.

"Damm, it's been a long time since I've seen eye candy that looked that good," she said as she took in a deep breath. "Too bad he's a man of the cloth."

"I don't care!" said the other Nurse as she stretched herself onto one foot trying to watch him for as long as she could before he and the Assistant turned the corner. "Given the chance, I'd snap that thick piece of candy in two and lick it until it was all gone!" she said with a laugh.

"Gladys!" exclaimed the first Nurse as she turned to look at her co-worker. She was surprised at her response. "He's a Priest!"

"Oh I know. But are you telling me that given the chance, you won't jump all over that if you could?" she said. "I'm just saying!"

After Michael and the Assistant had disappeared around the corner, a few moments of silence had passed between the two Nurses. Then the first Nurse spoke again.

"Yeah, you're right!" she finally admitted to her co-worker. "I'd hit it so hard he won't know what happened! Huh! And then I'd go back for seconds!" she said as she smiled with the thought of what it might be like.

And then she added, "I am so horny!"

"Tell me about it," agreed the first Nurse as they both returned to their places behind the desk and took their seats and just stared down the empty hallway.

After being aroused like they had been, it was going to prove to be a long night for the two of them. Both of them were thinking ahead to when their shift was over and they were heading home to their husbands.

Neither of who had a clue of what to expect when their wives' shift was over, and they came home, hot and horny.

Michael and the Assistant had just turned the corner and headed for the 'quiet room' where the family was sequestered. When they got to the room and Michael opened the door, they found that the room was empty.

"Where are they?" asked Michael as he looked around the room.

"I, I don't know," admitted the Assistant as she stepped in and looked in at the empty room. "They were right here!" she exclaimed.

And then from behind them, they heard a commotion as a couple of Doctors and Nurses rushed past them and headed down the other hallway in the direction where the ICU unit was.

"What's going on? What's happened?" called out the Assistant as she and Michael stepped into the middle of the hallway.

"We're not sure," said one of the Nurses as she rushed past them. "I think it has something to do with the patient who had the miraculous recovery, earlier!"

Taking his cue Michael quickly followed behind the Nurses, leaving the Assistant standing alone in the hall.

"Father!" she called out. "Father, where are you going?"

When he didn't respond but continued on down the hall, she realized that he had left her.

Rushing down the hall after him, she called out, "Wait for me, Father! I'm coming, too!"

By the time Assistant had caught up with Michael and the other Nurses and Doctors, they had stopped outside of the ICU doors. Everyone was milling about talking in hushed voices asking all kinds of questions.

"Did something else happen?" "I don't know, but I heard over the intercom that security is searching for the patient now." "What??" "Yeah, they think he's disappeared!" "What??"

Peering through the window of the ICU doors, Michael could see a group of people who were not part of the medical staff, standing in the middle of the hall inside of the ICU unit. Some appeared to be crying and hugging each other while others were up in the Doctor's faces demanding answers. And standing with them was Miss. Langley, the Hospital Administrator and a Priest.

Just as Michael turned to the Assistant to tell her he needed to get inside the ICU unit, he saw Abbey as she sprinted down the hall toward them. She was able to compose herself so she could join Michael when he talked to the family without looking too disheveled.

"Abbey, are you alright?" he asked as he looked at her intently.

As Abbey nodded her head that she was okay, she glanced nervously at Michael.

Although she was embarrassed that he had taken with her in a public place, much less in a hospital waiting room, she still couldn't help being aroused by it. But for now, she had to try and put that and everything that had happened aside and deal with the situation that was before them.

The Assistant paused as she looked back and for the between Abbey and Michael, not understanding what was going on. She only hoped that they didn't have another one of their 'blowouts' like what had happened earlier. She wasn't sure, but she knew there was more to what had happened between the two of them inside of the waiting room than they were letting on.

And to tell the truth, she kind of had an idea of what may have happened seeing the way Abbey was flushed in the face and that her clothes were somewhat disheveled. Even the Father's clothes seemed slightly rumpled. And to tell the truth, she herself had had her share of 'kinky' sexual encounters before.

"But never with a Priest!" she thought to herself. "And definitely not with a Priest who was a hunk of smoldering hot, sex appeal like this Father was."

Turning to the young Assistant, Michael brought her back from her intimate thoughts.

"We need to get inside to speak to the family!" said Michael as he broke the Assistant's train of thought. "Now!"

"Yes, okay, Father!" she said as she pushed her way through the medical staff that had gathered outside of the ICU unit and quickly pushed in her code.

Once the doors had unlocked, the Assistant swung the door open and ushered Michael and Abbey into the unit, closing the door behind them. Just as Abbey and Michael stepped through the ICU doors with the Assistant, they were stunned as they looked beyond the group that was gathered in the middle of the hall.

Who did they see none other than Fabianne as she rounded the corner and came toward them from the other end of the ICU unit.

"Is that Fabianne?" asked Abbey as she watched the Inspector head towards them. "But.....I thought that she was interviewing the hospital staff. How'd she get here so fast?" asked Abbey as she turned to Michael looking for an answer.

That was when she noticed the look that was his face as he also watched Fabianne approach them.

"What's going on, Michael?" asked Abbey. "I've noticed that you and Fabianne have had some issues between the two of you lately?"

"Actually, I'm not sure what 'is' going on, Abbey," he said as he turned to her. "Something's not adding up and I can't quite put my finger on it," he said. "But whatever it is, I intend to find out," he exclaimed as they waited for Fabianne to reach them.

When Fabianne reached them, Michael immediately questioned her.

"We thought that you were interviewing the hospital staff that had contact with the patient right after his recovery?" he asked the Inspector with a questioning tone.

"Oui, I was," she said. "But after speaking to the Nurse who was the first one to witness the patient's recovery, I found out that he did cite the same statement to her as did the other four Prophets before they disappeared," she said. "But then I heard that something had happened, and I rushed over right away. I take it that our patient has somehow disappeared, also," she said in a hushed voice not wanting others to overhear.

Although what Fabianne had said made sense to Abbey, for some reason, Michael seemed to distrust her explanation. And Abbey wasn't quite sure why.

"Fabianne," said Michael. "It's interesting how at each of the last two events, you've always somehow managed to be MIA just before the Prophets have disappeared," he stated. "And then right afterwards, you show up with some kind of explanation of why you weren't around. Why is that?"

As Michael waited for an answer, he stared intently at Fabianne wondering what kind of explanation she'd give this time.

"Michael," said Fabianne as she watched his demeanor change. "It would seem as if you have some doubts about me, oui?"

"So it would seem," said Michael as he answered her back without taking his eyes off of her.

All Abbey could do was to just stand by and look on wondering what the 'hell' was happening.

Before they knew it, the group standing in the hall of the ICU unit had become loud and demanding.

The group that was standing in the middle of the hall of the ICU unit, were apparently family members of the patient they had come to interview, and they were not happy.

"But where is he?" exclaimed one member of the family as they got into the Doctor's face.

"Are you trying to tell us that my Father just got up and walked out of your hospital, and no one knows where he is?" exclaimed another member. "Especially after what he's been through?"

"Please, everyone, quiet!" exclaimed the Hospital Administrator as she tried to control the irate group. "We are standing in the middle of the ICU unit and we have other patients here who are in critical condition and need to recuperate," she said. "Can we please move this outside?"

"Oh, so you care about the other patients here, but didn't care enough to keep track of our Father!" exclaimed another one of the family members.

"He was suffering from a rare and aggressive Cancer and just made a miraculous recovery from it!" said another. "And now you're telling us that you don't know where he's at! What kind of hospital are you running here?"

"Please, can we move this outside," asked one of the Doctors, trying to support the Hospital Administrator.

But the family wasn't going to have it until the family Priest intervened.

He spoke quietly to the family members as he tried to console them. He was trying to get them to understand that this was not the way to go about finding their family member, and that they should remove themselves to another part of the hospital as asked, so that the Doctors could do their job.

As Abbey and Michael stood inside of the ICU unit, they couldn't help feel for the family of the patient. He had been in one of the rooms, only moments before, and against all odds, had made a miraculous recovery from an illness that he couldn't have survived unless it was by 'divine intervention'. And now, with no explanation, he had disappeared from his room inside of the ICU unit without a trace, leaving more questions for the family and for the hospital.

Abbey didn't understand why any of this was happening. Why would God allow such a miraculous recover to occur, and then take the happiness and elation that the family was feeling, and just yank it away like that?

It didn't make any sense to her, whatsoever.

By the time the family members had quieted down, hospital security had arrived to move them to another area of the hospital floor to avoid any more disruptions. As they escorted everyone out of the ICU Unit, Fabianne, Abbey and Michael stood back as the rest of the group made their way down the hall to another designated area where the family could regroup.

And then before either Abbey or Fabianne could say anything, Michael got a call on his cellphone. He knew that using phones in certain areas of the hospital were prohibited, but when he saw who it was calling, he knew that this was a call that he had to take.

"Excuse me, I have to take this," he said as he moved himself away from Abbey and Fabianne and further down the hall away from the ICU unit and any of the other patient areas.

"My Son," said the voice on the other end of the line. "This is your Eminence. Are you somewhere where you can speak in private?" he asked quickly.

"Ah, yes I am your Eminence," said Michael as he looked around, curious as to why the Eminence was calling him directly and would ask such a question.

"Good! Where is Fabianne and the Detective?" he asked with a somewhat anxious tone to his voice.

"Fabianne and Detective Wells are here at the hospital with me," answered Michael. "Your Eminence, I'm sorry to report that the fifth Prophet has disappeared like the others. I'm afraid that we didn't get here in time to try and prevent it, Sir."

"I understand, Michael," said the Eminence. "Somehow, we here in Rome felt that no matter what we did, we weren't going to be able to prevent any of the Prophets from disappearing, although you and the others did your best," he said. "But my Son, that is not the reason for my call. Is there any way that you can get to a fax machine?" he asked.

"I'm sorry, your Eminence. Did you say a fax machine?" repeated Michael.

"Yes, my Son. My Assistant will be faxing you something as soon as you can find a machine," he said. "And under no circumstances are you to inform Fabianne or the Detective what it is that you receive. Do you understand?" the Eminence insisted. "No one else other than you is to be privy to what is being sent."

"I don't understand, your Eminence," said Michael. "Fabianne is the lead Inspector on this investigation. Am I not to share this information with her?"

Michael didn't understand why what his Eminence was sending was so secretive that it had to be kept from Fabianne and Abbey. They were all on the investigation as a team.

"With no one Michael!" repeated the Eminence. "I will have my Assistant hold on to the line until you get a fax number. And Michael, do not hang up until you confirm that you have received the document we are sending. And I will need you to confirm what is on the document with my Assistant," he said. "You will understand why the contents of this fax must not be revealed to anyone when you receive it. We must know 'who' it is that we are dealing with. But then you will also understand what needs to be done."

When the Eminence spoke those last words, Michael knew that his superior was referring to him possibly having to use his skills as a Holy Warrior to get the information that they needed.

"But from who?" he asked himself. "Who among them was it that the Vatican thought was a possible 'L'arginato'? Was it possible that the concerns that he had earlier were now coming to fruition?"

This was something that he truly did not want to think about. Not now.

Not wasting any time on pondering the question any further, Michael's adrenaline began to pump as he headed back down the hall past where Fabianne and Abbey were standing, and in the direction that the family had gone.

"I need to ask the Hospital Administrator something," said Michael as he passed by them without another word.

"Michael, what's going on?" called out Abbey as she watched him leave.

"There's something that I need to do," he called back over his shoulder. "I'll meet you later. Don't worry, I'll find you," he said as he disappeared down the hall leaving Abbey and Fabianne as they just looked after him.

"L'Abbaye, do you know what seems to be bothering Michael?" asked Fabianne. "He seems to be, I do not know, very distrustful towards me lately. Have I done something wrong?"

"I don't know, Fabianne," answered Abbey as she shrugged her shoulders. "Whatever is going on, he's not talking to me about it either," she said. "But you're right. Something's been bothering him ever since we left the hotel in LA."

"Really," exclaimed Fabianne as she watched Michael catch up with the Hospital Administrator and ask her a question as they moved down the hall away from the ICU Unit.

Then Fabianne quickly changed the subject.

"L'Abbaye," she said. "I have what I need to recommend to the Vatican to declare this event not only as a miracle, but as one of the miracles described in the manuscript. If you will excuse me. I will meet you and Michael downstairs in the hospital lobby, oui?"

"What do you think that the Vatican is going to do, Fabianne," asked Abbey. "Do you think that they'll go public with the manuscript and what it predicts? Especially, now that you're declaring the fifth event as a miracle?" she said.

"I do not know, L'Abbaye" said Fabianne. "The manuscript spoke of five miracles of significance that would come to pass," she said. "And so they have."

"So what happens now? I mean, is that it?" she asked needing answers. "Do we just pack up and go home and close the investigation? We still have five people who are missing. Two of them are American citizens. One of them is even from your own country," she stated. "Do we just stop looking for them now that the Vatican has its' five miracles as predicted by the manuscript?"

"Yes, L'Abbaye, that is what we do," said Fabianne simply.

"Well, I disagree!" exclaimed Abbey as she involuntarily stepped away from Fabianne and turned to look back at her. "I'm a Detective, this is what I do! I can't just dismiss the families of these people as if their loved ones didn't matter. Because they do, Fabianne! They do matter!" exclaimed Abbey. "At least they do to me, even if they don't seem matter to you."

Abbey couldn't believe what she was hearing from Fabianne.

"And Fabianne, I thought that you of all people would understand!" she said as she continued. "I thought that you being from the Vatican meant that you cared about the faithful, the people who depend on you and the Vatican to give them the answers they're looking for. But I guess I was wrong, wasn't I?" said Abbey as she turned to walk away from Fabianne.

"No, L'Abbaye, you are wrong! I do care!" called out Fabianne. "But as Inspectors, it is not our job to look for the Prophets," she said. "We let the authorities who have jurisdiction in each of the countries where the Prophets have disappeared from, take over from here," exclaimed Fabianne. "There is nothing more that 'we' can do. But you are right. They do matter," said Fabianne. "But the five that have disappeared will never be found by you or anyone else. It is what it is," she said simply. "They will not be found until it is time for them to come forth with the others. And that is not until the sixth event comes to pass," she said.

"How can you say that, Fabianne?" exclaimed Abbey as she looked at her.

And then before either of them could say another word, from behind them, they were both startled by a disembodied voice as it interrupted them.

"She's right, my Child," said the voice. "You should listen to the Inspector."

As they both turned around, they were surprised to find that the same Priest who was in the ICU unit with the family earlier, was standing right behind them.

"Father," said Fabianne softly with respect and reverence as she turned to face him. "Forgive me I did not see you standing there. But if I may ask. What is it that you know of the events that have happened here tonight?"

"Ah, Sister," said the Priest politely as he spoke to Fabianne. "We of the Diocese know a little something about the Manuscript of the Six Events, and what it predicts, despite the Vatican trying to keep it a secret," he said. "We don't know a great deal about it, but we know more than the Vatican thinks we do. They think they are protecting Man, when in fact they are depriving us from God's word."

"What do you mean, Father?" asked Abbey.

"There are some of us who believe that God, in all of his wisdom, meant for the 'Manuscript of the Six Events' to be shared," continued the Priest. "But perhaps in their attempt to protect Man, those at the Vatican have put themselves above what God wanted. They have put themselves in the position to decide which 'words of God' should be shared with Man and which should not. And for whatever reason, that which they feel should not be shared is hidden away in the vaults underneath the Vatican in Rome, like this manuscript has been. They have been keeping God's words from his children," he said. God's words, as given to his Prophets here on Earth, are kept from those for whom they were written for," said the Priest.

"So Father," said Fabianne. "What is it that you know about the five Prophets?" she asked, curious as to just how much he really knew.

"Only that you are right. The five Prophets who were part of the miracles that were described in the manuscript and have already happened, are no longer of this world," he said. "Some of us believe that once the Prophets have fulfilled their 'calling' here, they are shown the way home."

"Wait, wait a minute!" exclaimed Abbey as she stepped in close to the Priest. "What do you mean by that, Father? Are you saying that they, that they were what, called back to Heaven?"

"Is that so hard for you to believe that God would send one of his Angels to escort the Prophets home, my Child?" asked the Priest as he looked at Abbey intently. "You do believe, do you not?"

"Right now I don't know what to believe, Father," admitted Abbey as she tried to comprehend everything that had happened so far. "Actually, I thought that I had it all figured out. Now, I just don't know."

"I believe that the Inspector understands what I speak of" he said as he looked back at Fabianne. "Am I not correct, Sister?"

Fabianne just stared at the Priest and smiled, indicating that she in fact understood what he was speaking of. And it seemed that this Priest and others like him, men ordained in the service of God, knew a great deal more about the events surrounding the manuscript than the Vatican gave them credit for.

"And may I ask something of you, Inspector?" said the Priest.

"Of course, Father," answered Fabianne.

"Tell me, what is your purpose here?" he asked as he watched her intently.

"To do the will of God, Father, of course," answered Fabianne simply.

"Interesting," thought Fabianne to herself as she stared back at the Priest. "It would also seem that he was also trying as hard as he could to 'read' her. As if he was trying to figure her out.

And then bringing an end to the conversation altogether, Fabianne turned to Abbey.

"I will meet you and Michael downstairs in the main lobby of the hospital, oui?"

And then as she passed the Priest, she said, "Goodbye, Father, if you will excuse me."

"I'll find Michael and meet you at the front entrance," said Abbey as she smiled and nodded to the Priest and then also turned to leave.

Before she could take a step away from the Priest, he spoke to her again.

"Sometimes, God works in mysterious ways, my Child," he said to her. "The Inspector is here for a specific reason. But for whatever reason he has placed you here at this moment, it is for a purpose that only you can fulfill. I'm sure that it will all be made clear to you when you need it most," he said. "Just have faith and trust in him," he said.

Then as silently as he had appeared, he turned and strode back down the hall to give whatever comfort he could the family of the fifth Prophet. As he left Abbey staring after him, she couldn't help to think about what he had said.

"He placed me here at this moment for a purpose that only I can fulfill," she repeated under her breath.

"Hmmm, now what could that purpose possibly be?" she mused to herself as she turned on her heel and went in search of Michael.

◡⟶

As Michael caught up with the Hospital Administrator, he quickly asked her a question.

"Excuse me, Miss. Langley," he said as he caught her by the arm. "I understand that you have a situation to deal with here, but I'd like to ask a favor if I may," he said.

Once the Administrator directed him to an empty office off of the main hallway and told him that he could use the fax that was on one of the desks, she quickly excused herself. She still had a huge situation to deal with concerning the patient and his family. Not only did she have to alert the governing board of the hospital of what had transpired, but the authorities as well. They had a missing patient to report.

She knew this was going to be one of the longest nights of her career, if not the last one. She just didn't know how this evening was going to end for anyone at this point.

Within minutes after Michael had relayed the fax number to the Eminence's Assistant who was holding on the line, he heard the fax machine began to buzz and come alive as its lights flashed. Seconds later a single sheet of paper rolled out of the machine and landed into the tray.

Reaching for it, Michael picked it up and looked at it for a minute. He couldn't help it as a blank stare came across his face and he heard himself murmur under his breath.

"No, this can't be!" he exclaimed to himself as he read what was typed across the bottom of the page. "It can't be!"

"Michael! Michael!" called out the disembodied voice of the Assistant from the other end of the phone. "Did you receive it?" he asked.

"Yes, I got it. But this can't be right!" stammered Michael, still not believing what he was seeing. "Are you trying to tell me that…..?"

Before Michael could finish his sentence, the Assistant interrupted him.

"Michael, the Eminence needs a confirmation from you," stated the Assistant abruptly.

Michael now understood why he had been asked not to divulge to anyone what he had received.

"No!" stated Michael simply as he stared at the single sheet of paper he had taken off of the fax machine.

"No?" repeated the Eminence's Assistant.

"No!" repeated Michael. "This is not who is with us," he said.

"The Eminence wants me to tell you what we know so far, Michael. After I finish, he said that you know what must be done. We need to know 'who', or 'what' it is that we are dealing with. And you are the only one who is in a position to find out. When you do find out, you are to inform us immediately," said the Assistant.

Michael then listened closely as the Eminence's Assistant gave him all of the information that they had.

Moments later, when he had finished, the Eminence's Assistant simply said, "May God be with you, Michael."

Michael quickly hung up his phone as he folded the fax several times and shoved it into his pocket and then headed out of the office. He needed to get some air before he spoke to Abbey and Fabianne.

CHAPTER THIRTEEN

As Abbey went from one end of the deserted hallway to the other, she was unable to find Michael anywhere. As a matter of fact, the entire floor they were on had been shut down. All non-essential staff who had nothing to do with the care of the patients who were still on the tenth floor had been vacated because of the situation the hospital was currently trying to deal with.

And that gave the floor a deserted, eerie feel to it. And that was something that Abbey did not like.

The one fear Abbey had was of hospitals, not to mention having to be a patient in one. It was just the thought of getting lost inside of the maze of hallways that all hospitals seemed to have.

She was sure that it had to do with all of the horror movies she and her friends used to watch when they were kids. In the movies they would watch as the actors would inadvertently end up in a deserted hospital while being chased, and for some reason they could never find their way out. And by the end of the movie, most of them would've been killed by whoever was chasing them. And they usually were killed in the most horrible ways!

"Uggh!!" shuddered Abbey as a cold chill swept down her back.

She was really trying not to think about it!

After about twenty minutes of searching, Abbey was done. She decided to go downstairs to the main lobby of the hospital on the first floor and wait for Fabianne and Michael there.

"Besides," she thought to herself. "There were other people there along with some of the hospital staff who were still milling around in the lobby. And that felt a bit more comfortable to her than searching the deserted hallways on tenth floor for Michael by herself."

When she got off the elevator on the first floor, she could see the hospital parking lot through the floor to ceiling windows surrounding the front part of the hospital lobby. And it was no surprise to her when she saw that the parking lot had turned into more of a media circus than it was when they had first arrived.

There were reporters with their microphones ready and their cameramen in tow, hovering just outside of the doors of the hospital. They were all waiting for anyone to exit so they could get the jump on possibly the biggest scope of the day, perhaps of the century before anyone else got it.

Abbey looked around and didn't see any signs of Michael, but she did spot Fabianne standing over by the registration desk speaking to one of the receptionists. When Fabianne turned and saw her, she waved Abbey over.

"L'Abbaye, where is Michael?" she called out. "I have the car being brought around to the side of the hospital, and then we can leave for the hotel."

"I don't know," she answered. "I looked but I couldn't find him on the floor upstairs, so I decided to come down here. He's got to be around here somewhere," she said as she looked around.

Fabianne knew that Abbey was not happy about concluding the investigation and leaving before she felt all of the loose ends had been accounted for. Mainly, the five missing Prophets. But Fabianne knew it was something that had to be done.

Their part of the investigation was done.

"I have tried to reach him on his cell but he is not answering," stated Fabianne as a concerned look came across her face.

Even though Fabianne hadn't known Michael for long, she was always confident that whenever she called him, he would answer. She now had the feeling that something was amiss.

And then Abbey looked up, and saw Michael through the sliding doors of the lobby as he came towards them from the outside parking lot.

"There he is, Fabianne," exclaimed Abbey somewhat relieved as she moved away from the reception desk toward him. "What's he doing outside?" she asked out loud. "I thought that he was up on the tenth floor where we were?" she asked.

"Oui, L'Abbaye. There is your Michael," said Fabianne with an odd tone to her voice. "If you will excuse me, I need to speak to the Hospital Administrator for a moment."

But Abbey wasn't listening as she moved across the lobby toward the front doors of the hospital to meet Michael.

As Michael approached the double doors to the hospital, she noticed that he had an odd but determined look on his face. His body movements spoke volumes as he moved with tense, ridged motions as if he was on a mission and that no one should try and stop him from completing. And Abbey could tell by the expression on Michael's face, that at that moment, it was probably best if the guards didn't try and confront him. It was the same look he had when they were in his the hotel room in LA and he had to deal the 'Demon'.

But the security guards stationed at the doors were about to do just that.

They had been directed to stop all of the media from entering the hospital lobby until further notice. And they assumed that Michael was with the news people who had been camped out in the parking lot all evening. As they moved to keep him from entering the facility, Abbey quickly rushed over to them. She informed them that he was an Inspector from the Vatican and was with her, and that they were both there at the request of the Hospital Administrator, Miss Langley.

After verifying at Michaels' identification with the Hospital Administrator's Assistant, the guards allowed Michael into the lobby. As he passed through the double doors, Abbey had a gut feeling that something else had happened since the last time that she had seen him.

But before Abbey could say anything, Michael spoke first.

"Where's Fabianne??" he said in a demanding tone.

Abbey could tell by the tone of his voice that he was bothered by something.

"Michael, what's wrong?" she asked.

Without answering her, he asked the question again but with a more forceful, angry tone.

"WHERE IS Fabianne?" he asked almost yelling at her.

His demeanor was so abrupt that Abbey found herself actually taken aback by it.

Not wanting to get into an argument with him in the middle of the lobby about yelling at her for no particular reason, she backed off.

"Not cool, Michael!" she exclaimed. "Not cool at all!!"

"She's over there," said Abbey with a curt tone as she pointed over toward the hospital registration desk where she had left Fabianne only moments before.

At the same time, she 'cut' him a serious look that told him that was not something that she was going to just let slide. Abbey made a mental note that she was going to call him on how he had so rudely yelled at her. She didn't deserve that, and like anyone else, she didn't like being yelled at in a public place much less at all.

Realizing that he had overstepped his bounds, especially with some-one like Abbey, Michael toned back his tense demeanor with her as far as he could without losing sight of 'why' he was so agitated in the first place. He knew that she didn't know why he was acting the way he had, and he couldn't blame her for getting an attitude with him.

"Abbey.....!" he said trying to apologize. "I'm sorry!" he exclaimed in a low voice as he tried to lean in to her. "I didn't mean....."

Not in the mood to accept an apology, Abbey threw both of her hands up to the side and took a step away from him. As she moved back she glared at him.

She was angry and hurt, and it pissed her off that she cared about him as much as she did.

She knew this was only a temporary, sexual encounter that they had ventured into, and it couldn't go any further than it had. But he still had no reason to treat her the way that he had. And more than anything, she was angry at herself for letting her feelings get involved while she was on an investigation.

Michael quickly reached into his pocket and pulled out the folded fax that had been sent to him from the Vatican in Rome. He understood why the Eminence had said not to show it to anyone, but Michael felt that Abbey needed to know.

"Abbey! I'm sorry!" he exclaimed. "But you need to see this!"

Unfolding the fax and thrusting it toward her, as she took it, he waited for her reaction. It only took a couple of seconds for Abbey to realize what it was that Michael had given her

"But….." was the only thing that Abbey could murmur as her brain tried to comprehend what she was reading.

As she looked up at Michael, she didn't know what to think.

Looking back at her, printed across the page of the fax that had been sent to Michael was a picture of an attractive woman in her late thirties to early forties. She had dark shoulder length Auburn hair that fell loosely to either side of her face. She had a somewhat stern look about herself and although it was only a 'head shot', Abbey could tell that she was also somewhat overweight.

And printed across the bottom of the page in Italian were the words, 'Fabianne 'al Benne – Inspettore assegnato al Viticano.

Not waiting for Abbey to try and struggle to read the Italian script on the bottom of the page, Michael translated it for her.

"It says Fabianne 'al Benne, Inspector for the Vatican," he said as Abbey just looked at him. "Abbey, it's a picture of Fabianne 'al Benne, the Inspector from France who works with the Vatican and was dispatched to work on this investigation," he said. "They wanted me to confirm that the woman who is in that picture is the same person who has been working with us."

Abbey felt as if someone had just taken all of the air out of her lungs and she had been left totally depleted. At one point she even thought that her she felt slightly lightheaded.

Then Abbey's brain tried to form the question that was trying to break free.

"But, but if this is Fabianne 'al Benne," she stammered. Then, then who is….."

As Abbey spoke, she turned herself halfway around as if she had expected to see Fabianne standing over at the hospital desk where she had left her.

215

But she wasn't there.

As a matter of fact, Fabianne.....or the woman they had thought to be Fabianne, and who they had been working with since the beginning of the investigation, was nowhere in sight. As Michael also scanned the lobby for the woman who had been posing as Fabianne, Abbey could see the tension to his face return.

"Michael, I don't understand," exclaimed Abbey as she continued to stare at the picture. "If this is Fabianne, then 'who' have we been working with all of this time?" she asked.

"I don't know!" answered Michael as he continued to scan the lobby. "But the Vatican wants me to find out," he said.

"But how can a thing like this happen, Michael?" asked Abbey still confused by what Michael had just shared with her. "How could the Vatican not have known that the real Fabianne 'al Benne wasn't who had been calling in and giving them updates on the investigation? And what about the real Fabianne?" she asked. "Where has she been all of this time? I mean, I would have thought that she would have realized that someone was impersonating her and come forward at one point and said something like, 'Hey, here I am! Right here! That's not me running around all over the world, and calling in to the Vatican!"

Michael smiled slightly as he listened to Abbey. It was good that she could still find humor even in this type of situation.

"From what the Assistant to the Eminence told me, it would seem that at one point, the real Fabianne 'al Benne apparently disappeared right after she was dispatched to investigate the first miracle in Mexico," said Michael as he continued to scan for the woman. "The Vatican didn't even know it wasn't her calling in until tonight when they got a phone call from a remote part of South America. Some church volunteers who were doing work with some of the local tribes there, found the real Fabianne unconscious in the jungle. They had no idea how she got there or how long she was there before they found her."

"What!!" exclaimed Abbey, as she forgot all about being pissed at Michael for the way that he had acted toward her.

This turn of events was truly something that would explain why he had been so distrusting of her.

"She apparently just regained consciousness a couple of hours ago and was able to get a message out to the Vatican that she was alright," explained Michael as continued to walk around the lobby area. "That's when they called me and wanted to verify who was actually with us."

And then it finally dawned on Abbey as she gasped.

"Oh no, Michael!" she exclaimed as she grabbed his arm. "Do you suppose she's a…..'Demon' like the old woman I saw at the Warren's house?" she asked. "Has she been hunting the Prophets all along, and we led her to each of them?" she exclaimed.

"I don't know, Abbey. But that could be why they were always one step ahead of us all of this time," said Michael. "She was right there with us all along, and we just handed her the Prophets on a silver platter," he said.

Abbey was stunned. How could it have been that neither she nor Michael didn't see the signs before?

"Abbey…..I don't know what to think right now," he said as he checked for his weapon. "All I do know is that my superiors want me to find this woman, if she's even that, and get her to tell me who she's working for."

"Well, I'm coming with you!" she said as she fell in step beside him determined to see this through to the end.

"No, Abbey! I need you to stay here!" he said as he turned to her. "When I catch her, I'm going to do what it is that I do best," he said. "And if anyone sees what I'm about to do and I get caught by the authorities, the Vatican will have a hard enough time explaining why one of their people has seemingly tortured an Inspector who is supposedly working for them. I'm sure they would rather not have to explain to the same authorities why you're involved," he stated. "And if you're caught, it would destroy any career you have or may have ever wanted to have. Trust me on this"

Quickly turning on her heel, Abbey spun around to face Michael.

"Oh, I trust you, Michael. But have you 'met' me before?" she said sarcastically. "I mean really! I know that we haven't known each other that long, but you should know me well enough by now to know I'm not staying out of this! That, that imposter has not only misled you and the Vatican, but she lied to me too. I'm a part of this investigation, even if it's taken some weird turns along the way. And above everything else, I'm not leaving my partner to finish this case alone. That's just not the way I work!"

Turning and walking away from him, Abbey called back over her shoulder.

"Are you coming, Inspector?"

All Michael could do was to catch up with her and pray that the two of them would get out of this without being locked up by the authorities. But inside, he had found a more profound respect for Abbey than he had ever had before.

But after about thirty minutes, they both had searched the entire first floor including the cafeteria, and came up with nothing. The stairwells leading to and from the lobby had been secured and all of the elevators had been shut down except for one. And that one elevator had a security guard posted in front of it to make sure that it was used by hospital staff only.

After checking with the security guards, no one had seen where the woman posing as Fabianne 'al Benne had gone. She didn't leave the lobby by going up the stairwell or out one of the other exits. For all accounts, she had just disappeared.

As they regrouped with each other in the lobby area, Abbey had to ask Michael something she had been wanting to ask him for some time now.

"Michael, you thought something wasn't quite right with Fabianne for some time now, didn't you?" she asked, remembering how he had reacted to Fabianne after she had the confrontation with the 'Demon' inside of her hotel room. "I didn't see anything that would've raised any flags," she said. "So what was it that made you suspicious of her?"

"Actually," said Michael as he continued to keep an eye out for the imposter they had been looking for. "When the Vatican dispatched me to LA to work on the investigation with you, they also sent me the entire file of what had transpired before the third miracle happened in LA," he said. "On the flight down to LA, I was able to read the transcripts from the witnesses and what they had observed before and after the first two miracles had happened, and before the two Prophets disappeared," stated Michael. "I noticed there was a recurring observation in the witnesses' statements," he said. "And it had more to do with what they noticed about the Inspector than anything else."

"What do you mean?" asked Abbey as she watched Michael intently.

"It was interesting that this woman posing as Fabianne was always MIA just before the Prophets disappeared," explained Michael. "Several of the witnesses stated that she wasn't where she was supposed to be, and when they tried to locate her, she was nowhere to be found. And then after the Prophet disappeared, she'd showed up. And she always had some kind of explanation for where she had been, but no one really thought anything of it. They just noted that it was odd."

"Wait a minute!" exclaimed Abbey remembering what had happened in LA. "That's what she did when we were at the Warren's house!" she exclaimed. "She had to take a call just before I went in to interview Mrs. Warren, and then right after that Mr. Warren was gone. And then she did the same thing at the base last night?" said Abbey as she stared to recount all of the familiarities that had occurred in each of the situations that they had investigated.

The same thing had happened in each case.

"Exactly!" confirmed Michael. "And just like she did today in the ICU unit upstairs, remember?" he added. "Each time just before a Prophet disappears, she was always missing for some reason. And then she'd show up after they were gone. And then when we were in LA and I saw the way she simply dismissed her encounter with the 'Demon' that was in her room. She had such a cavalier attitude about it," said Michael. "That in itself didn't make any sense, because that was not the way I understand that the real Fabianne would have dealt with the situation."

"And you couldn't have mention this to me before, Michael?" asked Abbey feeling somewhat left out.

"Abbey, I only had bits and pieces of doubt," admitted Michael. "And without any real proof, I had to take a step back and observe the situation until I was sure. But somewhere deep in my gut, I knew there were too many coincidences that weren't adding up."

"But if she's not a Demon like the old woman is, then 'who' is she?" asked Abbey. "Who else are we up against here?"

"I don't know, Abbey! But whoever she's working with, she set us up from the beginning to get access to the Prophets!" exclaimed Michael, which got Abbey even more pissed off than she already had been.

She never did like being a scapegoat for someone else's agenda, and this situation was no different.

"Abbey, I've not only lost the Demon and the woman posing as Fabianne," he said. "But I've lost the last two Prophets as well," stated Michael as he became frustrated with himself.

This was not how he liked his investigations to go. And he wasn't looking forward to having to report everything that had happened to his Eminence.

And Abbey felt helpless seeing the way that Michael was putting the burden of the outcome of the investigation on his shoulders alone.

Pulling out his cellphone, he said to Abbey, "I guess I'd better report to the Vatican so they know what's happened."

"Michael, you did everything that was humanly possible. None of what happened is your fault," said Abbey as she tried to reassure him. "They have to realize that there were extenuating circumstances in this case that you had no control over. They need to know there were other factors involved here," exclaimed Abbey. "Like them not knowing that one of their Inspectors has missing all of this time!"

But Michael wasn't listening. He had already dialed the Vatican and was being put through to the Eminence.

Abbey knew that tracking Demons and eliminating them was what he did for the Vatican, and that he was one of the best they had. But she also knew that having to report that the Demon who had replaced one of their most revered Inspectors on such an important investigation as this, had by some kind of fluke, continued to impersonate her for almost a week without being discovered. And in the end, culminated in losing not only the last two Prophets, but the woman, whether she be Demon or not, who was impersonating one of their Inspectors.

She knew the supervisors that they eventually all had to report to, didn't always care about what happened in the field. They were only interested in the results and nothing more.

And for some reason, she felt that Michael's supervisors at the Vatican would be no different.

After Michael had been on the phone for almost fifteen minutes with the Vatican, Abbey could tell by his body language that his Eminence did not take his report well. She saw him at one point try and explain something, but was apparently cut off by the person on the other end of the phone. After a few more minutes of listening, she saw him simply nod his head and then he hung up.

As he walked back to where Abbey was waiting for him, she could see there was tension in his brow as he gave her a strained smile. She could tell that the call didn't go well.

"What happened, Michael?" asked Abbey, afraid to hear the answer.

"As you may have guessed, they are not happy," he said as he just looked down at her. "I've been recalled back to Rome where I have to give them a full report of what happened here," he said. "I'll have to do it in front of the Eminence himself and the Investigation Committee for the Vatican," he added. "And I'm supposed to leave as soon as possible."

And that was something Abbey wasn't prepared to hear.

"But Michael, you're putting the full responsibility of how this investigation turned out onto your shoulders alone, and the Vatican is acting as if they had no part in it," exclaimed Abbey.

"Abbey, they understand that there obviously was a breakdown in the process somewhere along the line during this investigation. They're trying to figure out how they didn't know until tonight, that Fabianne had been missing all along, and they're looking into it," explained Michael. "But you have to understand that this wasn't just another investigation. This could be 'The' most important investigation the Vatican has had to handle in the history of Man," he said. "The implication of what's possibly coming next is.....huge!" he said. "It's something that can affect the whole world and how it functions from this point forward. The Vatican, religious leaders from around the world and the Heads of State from all over the globe are going to have to decide what their next step is going to be. Abbey, this wasn't an investigation that I needed to drop the ball on," he said solemnly. "Not with so much riding on it."

"And what if the sixth event doesn't happen?" exclaimed Abbey as she tried to find some solace in having to let Michael go. "What if, what if nothing happens after this and everything goes on as it has? What then?"

"I guess we'll just have to wait and see, wont' we," he said.

"I know I'm going to kick myself for asking this, but, what about us?"" she asked quickly. "I'm not saying that we had any kind of commitment between us, or anything like that. I just wanted to know if you go back to Rome, will I ever see you again?"

Michael dropped his head trying to conceal his smile.

It felt good to know that she wanted to be with him as much as he wanted to be with her. Somewhere during his time working with the Vatican as a 'Guerriero', he had lost all hope of possibly finding someone like Abbey. Someone that he felt good about, and who had even allowed himself to think that there could possibly be something more between them. Especially considering what it was that he did, he knew it was a long shot. She was so full of guts and independence, and was as sexy as Hell!

"A great all around package!" he thought to himself as he continued to smile.

Seeing him smile at that moment, made Abbey think that he obviously thought that what she had said to him was funny. So she asked.

"I'm sorry, Michael, did I say something that was funny," she asked. "Because if I did, please tell me!"

"No! No, Abbey!" he exclaimed quickly before she got an attitude. "It's not that, really," he said still smiling. "It's just that I was thinking the same thing about you. I'm not ready to let go of what we've got, either. But I may not have a choice in the matter."

"So, when do you have to leave?" she asked.

"I'm supposed to be on the next flight out of Montreal," he said. "And I'm supposed to put you on the next flight to LA," he said.

"Okay!" said Abbey as a mischievous smile spread across her face. "But you know, it's really too bad that you're not going to able to get a flight out of here until, oh I don't know. Tomorrow afternoon."

"Tomorrow afternoon?" repeated Michael as he couldn't help to smile, seeing where Abbey was going with her train of thought.

"Well yeah! You know those flights to Rome are really hard to come by at the last minute," she said. "I mean, for God's sake Michael, we're in Canada!"

"Abbey, you do know that Canada is not off of the beaten path, right?" said Michael.

"Yeah, I know. But what can they do to you from the other side of the Atlantic, right?" she said as she eyed him. "Com'on big boy! What else can they do?" she asked

After a few moments Michael responded.

"My thoughts exactly, Abbey," he said. "The car's parked on the side of the building," he said. "I'll meet you there after I let Miss. Langley know I don't think that there's much more we can do here."

As Michael turned to make his way back over to the reception desk to leave a message, Abbey called out to him.

"And Michael, it's going to be alright!" she said to him.

"I know," he said as he looked back over his shoulder and smiled at her, and then continued on to the desk.

As Abbey walked across the lobby in the opposite direction that Michael had gone, she nodded to the Security guards at the front entrance as she exited the hospital. She wasn't sure if she was glad that the investigation was over for her or not. Sure she could go back to her life as it was before all of this.

"But what about Michael?" she thought to herself as she walked outside into the night air.

She was still worried about what the outcome of the inquiry board would mean for him as an Inspector once he gave his report in Rome. She could only pray that he wouldn't be made the scapegoat for everything that didn't go right with the investigation. It wasn't fair for him to have to take the entire burden for its outcome.

"It wasn't!" she exclaimed to herself as she got a wrenching feeling in her stomach. "It just wasn't right!"

As she exited the hospital lobby, she avoided making any kind of eye contact with the media that was waiting behind the barriers that had been set up by the Police. She looked over to the right where she saw the Black Towne car that had brought them to the hospital. It was waiting as it sat parked along the right side of the building. Making her way over to the waiting car, she was deep in thought about everything that had happened and didn't notice that two men standing on the other side of the parking lot to the left of the front entrance were observing her intently.

As the two men watched her get into the car and close the rear passenger door, the taller of the two glanced over to the other one and just nodded his head once. Then when they saw Michael walk across the inside lobby of the hospital and head for the front doors, they both moved forward to intercept him when he came out.

They were two fellow Inspectors that the Vatican had dispatched because of the turn of events that had taken place during this investigation. And although they were well aware of Michael's reputation as an Inspector and of his fighting skills, they weren't there to test either of those. And they had hoped that being the Inspector that he was, he knew that.

They were there under direct orders from the Vatican to make sure that he and Fabianne were on the next flight out of Montreal and returned to Rome immediately. And the next flight was leaving within the next two and a half hours. There were many unanswered questions that had to be sorted through before the Vatican met with the religious leaders of the world as well as the heads of state. They all knew that there was much more at stake here than simply concluding the investigation just because the five miracles from the manuscript had occurred.

What was equally if not more important, was the implication of what was predicted to happen following the five miracles. That was what was on everyone's mind. And how the world would respond if what was predicted on the manuscript were made public?

After waiting in the car for about ten minutes and Michael still hadn't showed up, Abbey started to get worried. Then she heard someone's cellphone ring, and saw that it was the Driver's phone. As the Driver answered the call, Abbey turned around in her seat to scan the parking lot to see if she could lay eyes on Michael.

"It shouldn't have taken Michael this long just to leave a message for the Hospital Administrator," thought Abbey as she turned in her seat to see where he might have gone.

Just as she turned, she saw Michael standing beside a car on the other side of the parking lot with a man she had never seen before. As she watched, she could tell Michael was upset as he spoke with the man.

"What the hell's going on?" exclaimed Abbey to herself as she opened the car door and got back out of the car.

Before she could close the door of the car and make her way across to where Michael was standing, another man she had never seen before stepped in front of her and cut her off.

"Detective Wells," said the man as he blocked Abbey. "The driver has been instructed to take you back to the hotel," he said. "You've been booked on a flight out of Montreal going to LA tomorrow at eleven thirty in the morning. The car will pick you up at the hotel at eight o'clock in the morning outside of the hotel lobby," he said. "And I'm to inform you that the Vatican thanks you for your assistance with the investigation. A full report will be sent to your supervisors at the LA Police Department."

"Who the hell are you?" exclaimed Abbey as she tried to go around the man. "Get out of my way! I want to speak to Michael!"

"Detective Wells," said the man in a firm tone. "I'm sorry, but Inspector Givant will not be going back to the hotel with you," he said.

"What do you mean?" asked Abbey as she turned and tried to see what was happening with Michael.

"We're escorting Inspector Givant to the airport where he will be put on a flight to Rome tonight," answered the man.

"No! That can't be!" exclaimed Abbey as she went to go around the man again. "He wouldn't leave without telling me!"

"Miss Wells," said the man as he continued to block Abbey. "He doesn't have a choice in the matter. Whereas you are no longer a part of the investigation, he is still on Vatican business."

Abbey felt like the breath had been literally sucked out of her as she fell back against the side of the car feeling as if there should have been something else she could have done.

"I should've stayed with him," she lamented to herself. "I, I should've stayed."

Then as she looked over the shoulder of the man standing in front of her, she caught Michael's eye. He simply smiled at her for a few moments as if to say, he was sorry. Then he looked down and got into the back seat of the car.

"Thank you, Detective," said the man as he turned and walked back across the parking lot to the waiting car with Michael in it.

As Abbey watched the man get in on the passenger side, the car pulled away from the curb and slowly made its' way through the throngs of television trucks and media people that were milling around in the parking lot.

Abbey felt helpless.

She didn't realize that tears had already began to cascade down her face as she watched the other car pull away and head in the other direction. And as the taillights turned the corner and disappeared, she quickly wiped away the tears and tried to compose herself.

"Why am I acting like this?" she said to herself as she tried to dismiss what she was feeling as something that would pass in time. "It's not like I love him or anything like that!" she said trying to convince herself there were no feelings between them.

"It's just that, if this is possibly the end of everything that we know," she thought. "Then I'd rather be with him than anyone else."

There, she had finally admitted it to herself.

She had slipped and developed an emotional attachment with someone, and she didn't even realize it until it was too late. Something she had been trying to sidestep for as long as she could remember. But she had finally found someone she wanted to be with whether the end came or not. She didn't have any other family to speak of, and being with Michael just felt right to her.

He was who she wanted to be with.

Then it hit her.

"I don't even have his number!" she exclaimed to herself as she looked in the direction the car had went that had Michael in it.

But it was too late.

She had no way, whatsoever to get in touch with him, and now he was gone. It hadn't occurred to her that she might need to get his number. She had no idea that it would end the way it had, with Michael being whisked off back to Rome, and neither of them being able to say goodbye to each other.

"So, I guess it is back to the old grind," she murmured softly under her breath as she got into the back seat of the car and tried to deal with the sudden feeling of loss she was experiencing. "Dammit!" she said as she chastised herself. "That's what I get for letting my guard down and getting close to someone!" she said to herself. "When am I going to learn my lesson and just concentrate on the sex and leave emotions out of the mix?"

As the car pulled out of the parking lot, Abbey could see the mayhem and pandemonium that was beginning to develop among the reporters and the people who were gathered in the parking lot of the hospital. The leaked report about a manuscript that had been kept hidden for centuries by the Vatican, and that predicted not only the miracle that had happened at this hospital, but four other miracles that had already occurred in different parts of the world, was beginning to have its affect.

People were rushing back and forth, trying to verify if what had been leaked to the media was true, and where had the information come from.

"Is it true? Does such a manuscript really exist?" "How long did the Vatican know about this?" "Why did the public not know about it before now?" "And is it true what the manuscript predicts about the sixth event? Is it really the 'second coming of the Son of God?"

Some of the news people and their cameramen were still trying to report what they had learned, while others had actually left the media circus behind. Some of the people who had been watching from the sidelines, quickly left and went in search of whatever personal solace they could find to help them come to grips with what was supposedly going to happen.

"This can't be happening! It has to be some kind of hoax someone is playing!"

People began to rush around, calling on their cellphones to their loved ones trying to figure out if this revelation was in fact true or not. Some even headed for the nearest church to pray and reaffirm themselves in their faith.

And the word had spread like wildfire around the world in a matter of minutes.

Every media vehicle, whether it be the radio, television, cellphones or the world wide web, had picked up the report and announced it. No one knew how it had been leaked or for that matter, who had leaked it. But one thing was for sure. The world now knew about the Manuscript of the Six Events and what it predicted. And the Vatican and the other religious and world leaders now had a near global panic on their hands.

And it was only the beginning.

Abbey also knew that after tonight, because she was no longer part of the investigation, she wouldn't be privy to any information as to what the Vatican and the leaders of the world were going to do about the manuscript. And she might not ever know what was going to happen to Michael since the Vatican was so secretive about what it did and the people who worked incognito for them.

All she knew was that whatever was going to happen in the world after tonight, it was going to be hard to face without Michael.

And that was something she wasn't looking forward to.

As the driver made his way through the throngs of people rushing about on the streets, he looked into the rearview mirror.

"Are you going to be alright, Miss?" he asked.

Abbey realized that she must have looked pretty distraught after seeing Michael being driven off and escorted to the airport without her even being given the chance to tell him goodbye. But she didn't care how she looked at the moment. There were so many things running through her head she couldn't figure out how to start to sort everything out.

"Miss, are you alright?" asked the driver again.

Looking up, Abbey realized that he was speaking to her.

"Yes! Yes, I'm.....fine." mumbled Abbey. "Thank you."

All she wanted to do was to break down and cry like a baby. She had never felt as alone as she did at that very moment. The only comfort she had was that tomorrow morning she was headed back to LA and the life and the job that she knew and had loved.

But now it all seemed incomplete for some reason.

Then she realized what it was.

After being exposed to a world that existed right under everyone's noses, and that few were even privy to know about, she realized that she wanted to be a part of that world.

"And it wasn't just because of Michael either," she thought to herself. "Although he did make the idea more enticing."

It was because of the excitement and the rush of working on an international investigation that went beyond the normal boundaries of any case she had ever worked on before as a Detective. It was exhilarating to every part of her being, and she wanted more.

But the investigation was over, and there was no possibility of that ever happening now.

Michael was on his way back to Rome to give what could possibly be his last report to his superiors at the Vatican, and she was headed back to LA in the morning. And if the events of the manuscript did in fact come to pass, there was no telling what tomorrow or the days following would bring.

The world was already beginning to spin out of control with the knowledge of the manuscript's existence being leaked and what it predicted. Each person was reacting in their own way to the news, and had set about seeking direction on what to do next.

No one knew what was next, or what to do and it frightened them.

It was as if Chicken Little had sent an email out to the entire world that read, 'The sky is falling! The sky is falling! Run for your life, the sky is falling.'

"But in reality, everyone has known what to do all along," mused Abbey to herself as she watched the people on the streets of Montreal rushing about trying to figure it out. "Most had just become complacent to something they have heard a million times over and over again in the churches and the synagogues they attended. And now that it might be actually happening, they seemed to be lost."

On the ride back to the hotel, Abbey leaned back into the folds of the seats and tried to close her eyes and think about what she herself was going to do when she got back to LA. But as the car rolled through the streets of Montreal, she couldn't help thinking about Michael and what waited for him when he arrived back in Rome and had to go before the Eminence at the Vatican.

After about a twenty minute ride, the driver dropped Abbey off at the hotel entrance and said that he would be back at eight o'clock in the morning to pick her up. Getting out of the car, Abbey slowly walked into the hotel lobby and went directly to the elevator.

She tried to ignore the harried conversations going on in the lobby as groups of people gathered and exchanged what information they had heard about the manuscript. Many of the hotel guests were checking out and trying to get whatever flights out of Montreal that they could, as long as it would get them to their families and loved ones.

Abbey didn't want to think about what tomorrow morning was going to be like. She had had her share of a plethora of emotional ups and downs and totally unexpected situations for one day. She was done. She just wanted to get to her room and fall into bed and sleep.

That was all.

She knew that overnight the word would have spread to the rest of the world that had been asleep when the news was first leaked about the manuscript, and there was no telling what state the world's population would be in by then.

Hysteria was contagious, but she also knew that that was something she had no control over.

Once she got to her room, she closed the door behind her, walked straight to the bed and collapsed. It felt good to just be able to close her eyes and relax. No other responsibilities were on her shoulders for the rest of night, and that was fine with her as she immediately fell into an exhausted, induced sleep.

And sleep she did.

Abbey slept deep and hard oblivious to what was happening in the world outside, until twelve o'clock midnight.

At one minute after twelve midnight, from the deep recesses of her mind, Abbey felt herself being drawn back to consciousness. It was if as if she was gently being coaxed from her sleep and back into an awakened state. As she awoke and opened her eyes, she rolled from her left side onto her back and stretched by bringing her arms up over her head. She had just started to focus her eyes to adjust them to the darkness of the room, when she gasped and bolted straight up into a sitting position.

She nearly choked when she came face to face with the woman who had been posing as Fabianne as she stood over her.

"My gun! Where's my gun?" she asked herself as she attempted to roll her eyes to the right to see just how far she was going to have to reach to get to her weapon.

And Abbey couldn't be sure, but there something different about woman who she had come to know as Fabianne. Her face seemed to be bathed in a veil of soft light. And the light surrounding her had an almost relaxing and soothing effect as Abbey just stared back at her.

Without a word, the woman put her two forefingers in the middle of Abbey's forehead and gently eased her back into a reclining position onto the bed. Abbey tried to resist and struggled to sit back up but she found that she couldn't.

And then Abbey was startled again when the woman spoke to her.

"L'Abbaye," said the woman softly as she leaned over her and smiled. "Do not resist," she said. "Close your eyes and let yourself go. Believe again as you once did, oui? Look upon what it is that you are meant to see."

As Abbey's eyes closed and her body relaxed, she felt herself slide into a semi-dreamlike state. It was as if she were floating in a pool of soft yellow light that bathed and caressed her, as she was freed from all of her burdens and cares. Never in her life had she felt so invigorated, and yet so at peace before, as every fiber of her being came alive.

And then as the soft light that had surrounded her cleared, Abbey found herself standing on a grassy hillside looking off into the distance. As she stood there, she wasn't sure what it was that she was waiting for, but she knew something was coming.

Something she was meant to witness.

As a slight breeze ruffled her clothes, Abbey could see off in the distance the gathering of clouds as they billowed and formed on the horizon.

"Was that a storm coming?" she thought to herself as she watched the cloud bank as it continued to grow as it filled the sky above.

And as the cloud bank moved closer, the air around her begin to change as the breeze suddenly died. And then without warning, everything fell silent. The air became still as Abbey felt a feeling sweep over her. The feeling that what she was waiting for would soon be there.

As the cloud bank rolled forward and moved across the land, Abbey could see from underneath it there were wispy filaments that were too many to count, as they rose up from the ground to meet the rolling cloud bank as it passed over.

And Abbey just stared not believing what she was witnessing.

In the middle of the cloud, riding astride a huge, white horse, was a man dressed in simple white garments as he urged his steed onward. Jesus was coming to gather up his children as he had promised he would.

The Son of God had returned as prophesied!

And all of the faithful who had been patiently sleeping as they waited, were now being called forth to join him as he returned. And then as he passed overhead, the Son of God looked down at Abbey and smiled. And then she heard a voice speak to her that vibrated throughout her entire being.

"Well done, My child!" he said as he continued to smile at her. "Well done!"

Abbey couldn't catch her breath as the tears began to fall.

She thought that she was going to falter and felt as if her heart was going to burst with all of the love she felt for him, and the love that she knew he had for her.

She was his child and he loved her!

And riding on either side of him were his Angels as they spread out across the sky announcing his arrival to all who were watching. It was a sight to behold as Abbey watched from the hillside in awe at the beauty and the exhilaration of it all. Her heart and soul was so overwhelmed with joy she couldn't find the words to describe it.

And then as Abbey watched them pass overhead, she was stunned. One of the Angels riding alongside of the Son of God had also turned toward her and smiled as she nodded her head.

"Oh my God!" gasped Abbey as she stumbled back and looked upon the face of the woman she had known as Fabianne.

"Now you know who I am, L'Abbaye," said a voice inside of her head. "Now you know."

Abbey smiled and just nodded her head in acknowledgement.

"Yes, now I know," she answered back. "Now I know! Thank you! Thank you!"

And then the voice of the Angel spoke to her again.

"I sense a regret within you, L'Abbaye," she said with sincerity. "Why?"

Abbey was startled.

She didn't know how the woman whom she now knew to be one of God's Angels, could have sensed the one regret she had briefly thought about in passing. She had thought about not being able to catch and bring to justice, The 'Penance Killer' back in LA. And she knew that with everything in the world changing as it was going to, it would probably never happen now.

And then the Angel spoke to her again.

"Do not worry, L'Abbaye, she said. "Those who have sinned in the name of our Lord will get their just punishment. Let it go. It will be as it is written."

And although Abbey wasn't quite sure what the Angel meant, immediately the regret she had felt slipped away, and in her heart she knew that everything was going to be alright. Everything was going to come to pass as it was meant to.

"And L'Abbaye," said the Angel. "There is still work for you and Michael to do before the next Holy Day when on that day your vision will come to pass," she said. "Be diligent and faithful. And you both shall be rewarded," she said.

And then before she knew it, someone had stepped up beside her on the hillside and took her hand into his. As she turned to see who it was, she smiled delighted to see that it was Michael as he stood next to her.

"Michael look!" she exclaimed. "It's so beautiful!"

"Yes, Abbey," said Michael as he watched too. "It is beautiful, isn't it? What a blessing it is for you to be able to witness his return," he said as he looked down at her and smiled.

"Yes it is, Michael!" she said. "Yes it is!"

And then as the clock in the hotel room clicked over to read the time as ten minutes after twelve midnight, Abbey awoke with a start as she sat straight up in the bed and looked around. And before she knew it, she began to sob uncontrollably as she reveled in the vision she had been given. Never before in her life had she felt so blessed, as she felt at that very moment. All of the doubts, all of the fear was gone. All she felt was a calm, unburdened peace as it flowed over her.

As she laid back onto the bed, she felt herself fall back into a light, blissful sleep that she didn't wake up from until she heard a phone ringing off in the distance.

As the phone continued to ring, she heard herself ask, "Is that my phone?" as she rolled over and reached for her cellphone.

"Michael! Is that you?" she asked quickly, praying that it was.

And when she heard his voice on the other end of the line, she almost jumped out of her skin.

"Abbey, it's me!" he said trying to contain his relief. "Are you alright?"

"I'm fine, Michael!" she answered as she felt the emotion start to well up inside of her again and she started to cry. "I'm fine, now! You?"

"Abbey, why are you crying?" he said. "Everything is going to be alright," he said softly.

"Michael, I think I just had a vision," she tells him.

"A vision? What kind of vision, Abbey?" he asks quickly. "Can you tell me about it?" he asked.

"Well, I, I was asleep when something woke me. When I turned over, Fabianne, or the woman who was posing as Fabianne, was standing over me. The next thing I know, Michael, she puts two fingers on my forehead and makes me lie back down. I close my eyes and when I open them back up, I'm on a hillside somewhere," she said. "And Michael, I look off in the distance and I saw him!" she exclaimed softly as her voice started to tremble. "I saw the second coming of the Son of God as he rode overhead and gathered up the faithful. Michael, I was there!" she exclaimed quietly. "I was there, and so were you!"

On the other end of the phone, Michael found that he was unable to speak for a few moments as he absorbed what Abbey had just said to him. What she had just said caused him to bow his head and say a silent prayer as he felt emotion rise up inside of him.

When he did find his voice again, he spoke.

"Abbey, I don't know what to say," he said.

"Michael," said Abbey. "The woman who was posing as Fabianne, she was in my vision and she was an Angel riding alongside of the Son of God!" she said as her voice became emotional.

"Now it all makes sense," exclaimed Michael quickly. "That's why the Angel took Fabianne's place. She was sent to escort the Prophets 'home' after each of the miracles took place. And that must be how she dealt with the 'Demon' that was in her hotel room. She was an Angel! All of this time, we've been in the presence of an Angel from God!" exclaimed Michael as he became quiet.

After a few moments, Michael spoke again.

"But I have to ask you something, Abbey," he said. "Did we rise up with the others and join with our Father as he rode overhead?"

The question Michael had asked Abbey caught her off guard for a minute.

She didn't realize it until he asked, but from what she remembered, she and Michael weren't joining the others as they rose up to meet him. Rather, the two of them were watching from below as the others ascended.

"No Michael, we didn't," she said slowly as she paused for a minute and thought about the question. "We didn't. What does that mean?" she asked quietly. "Does that mean that we.....?"

Abbey couldn't bring herself to ask the question that was screaming to get out. She wasn't sure if she even wanted to know the answer.

Finally, after a few more moments of silence, Michael spoke.

"Abbey, what you've been blessed to witness, is something that any of us would have been honored to have been invited to see," stated Michael. "But I believe I have an idea of what you saw in your vision means."

"Tell me, Michael," said Abbey. "Tell me."

"There are several different interpretations of Revelations and what the sequence of events for the Second Coming means. It depends on which branch of Christianity you practice. But basically, those who are believers will rise up to be with him during the Rapture," stated Michael. "Now, there are those who for whatever reason, will not rise up to join him right away. Some believe that for those, God still has work for them to do during the times to come. But when he does return, those who did not rise up during the Rapture, will then join him and the others when he sits upon his throne to cast judgment. At that time he will cast judgment on those who claim to be believers. You see, Abbey. According to the scriptures, in the end when we are judged, we will be judged as either 'sheep', or as 'goats'," said Michael.

"Sheep or goats?" exclaimed Abbey. "I'm not familiar with that reference, Michael. What does it mean?"

"It means that if what is truly in your heart is love for the Lord and his word, and that you are a true believer in him, it will have been evident by the words you spoke and your actions before the time of judgment. If that is the case, and you are judged to be a true believer, you will be referenced as a 'sheep'. On the other hand, for those who have clearly defined themselves as nonbelievers at the time of judgment, and have no faith in him or in his word and their actions show this, they will be referenced as 'goats'. This will also include those people who will voice the words of the faithful, thinking that will save them, but it's not what's really in their hearts."

"Oh," said Abbey as she thought about it for a few moments.

Then she spoke again.

"So, if in my vision both you and I are watching from below as the 'Second Coming' happens, does that mean that God has other plans for us?"

"It could possibly mean that, yes," answered Michael not wanting to leave Abbey with the impression that what he was saying was fact.

"Abbey, interpretation of visions is not something that I do," he said. "Let me talk to one of the scholars from the Vatican that are here with me in Washington. I'll ask them about what you saw in your vision," he said. "Maybe one of them can shed some light on it, okay?"

Then it dawned her where Michael had said he was.

"Michael! I'm sorry, but did you just say that you were in Washington?" asked a stunned Abbey. "As in, Washington D.C.?"

"Yes Abbey, I'm in Washington D. C.," he confirmed. "We never made it to Rome. The Eminence thought that it would be better if I was in Washington to meet with the Heads of State and the religious leaders that were here to discuss the manuscript and what's happened so far, and what to expect. Abbey," said Michael as he leaned in close to the phone. "The whole world is beginning to react to the manuscript and what it's predicting. It's getting crazy out here, and it's going to get worse. You need to be careful," he said.

"I know!" agreed Abbey. "On the way back to the hotel I saw people rushing around in the streets and in the hotel lobby like it was the end of the world. Everyone is scared Michael and they don't know what to do."

And then as the Priest in him came forth, Michael corrected her.

"Actually, Abbey, the faithful knew this was going to happen, they just didn't know when," he said. "It's been something that's been spoken of and anticipated for as long as Christianity has been around. And as the manuscript proves, the return of Jesus Christ was predicted more than two thousand years before his birth," said Michael. "I know it makes it seem so overwhelming and hard to be able to accept, but I just think that people don't know what to do, now that it's actually about to happen. In today's world, the belief in his return has been put on the back burner because we're not ready. Well, we're no longer on our timetable," he said. "We're on his."

"So what's next, Michael?" asked Abbey.

"I need you to go back to LA, and I'll be in touch with you after you get there. And take my number down just in case you need to get in touch with me for anything, understand?" he said to her relief.

It just felt good to have a way to keep in contact with him with everything that was happening.

After another few moments of silence, Michael spoke again.

"Abbey, you're going to be alright," he said. "Until I get back to LA, remember I'm only a phone call away from you."

"Good to know," she said softly, not wanting to let him know that for her, even that was too far.

But she knew it was going to have to do for the time being.

As the silence on the line continued, Michael spoke first.

"Abbey, I.....I want you to know that I....."

Michael found it difficult to say the words that he wanted to say to her. For him, he was in unfamiliar territory, and he didn't know exactly how to say what he wanted to. What he needed to say.

Abbey, sensing that he was having difficulty expressing himself, let him know that she understood.

"I know, Michael," she said. "Me too!"

They were two of a kind, and she didn't know if what they were heading into would go anywhere, but at the moment, she knew there wasn't any time left to play games. It was all or nothing and she wanted it all, and she wanted it with him.

It was as simple as that.

As they said good-bye to each other and hung up, Abbey reluctantly laid back onto the bed and tried to return to sleep until she had to get up and catch her flight back to LA, and return to her job as a Detective.

⌒

After Abbey's flight had landed at LAX, she saw passengers at the ticket desk as they pushed and jostled trying to get flights to wherever it was they needed to be. Students and parents, business people and tourists, were all in line. If there weren't any flights out to wherever it was that they needed to go, they rushed out of the airport in a mad race to get to the nearest bus or train station. The news about the manuscript had now spread throughout this and every country in the world, and the reaction worldwide was slowly beginning to surface.

As she made her way through the airport, the television stations were reporting about the New York Stock Exchange and how the world markets had begun to drop after hearing the news. Stock traders and investors around the world were getting skittish, while banks and other major institutions around the country were calling emergency meetings to determine how they were going to ride out the storm.

Religious groups and churches hailed the revelation of the manuscript as an inevitable process in the evolution of Man that would bring us to the final chapter of our existence.

Not what others wanted to hear.

Abbey tried to ignore everything that was going on around her, and immediately caught the first Airport Shuttle going in the direction of her apartment without even thinking of contacting anyone at the precinct. She'd let them know she was back in town after she had a chance to go home and get settled and get a decent night sleep.

She owed that to herself.

Once the shuttle dropped her off at her apartment, she checked her cellphone for any messages from Michael. Seeing that he hadn't called, she took the opportunity to take a hot shower, put on her favorite nightshirt and crawl into bed.

"Nothing like sleeping in your own bed and being in your own surroundings," she thought to herself as she reveled in the familiarity of her own apartment.

And although she missed Michael and the feeling of being with him, it felt good for her to be home again.

CHAPTER FOURTEEN

Thursday 10 am

As Abbey drove to work through the streets of LA, she couldn't help having mixed feelings about being back. She loved her job as a Detective with the LAPD, and never thought that anything could have ever made her want more.

But she was wrong.

She had had a taste of something that was so exciting and exhilarating that she almost couldn't see herself happy with just being a Detective in LA anymore. But as the Vatican had made it quite clear to her in Montreal, her services were no longer required, and she had been released to return to her former position with the LAPD.

So she was back at her old precinct.

As she pulled into one of the vacant spaces along the side of the building she actually felt somewhat out of place. Before she could turn the ignition off and even get out of the car, she heard someone call out her name from across the parking lot.

"Abbbbeeeey!!! Hey girl! What's up??"

Without even having to turn around to see who it was, Abbey recognized the voice. It was none other than Kurt.

When she turned around and saw him jogging across the lot to meet her, he had the biggest smile on his face. When she saw him, she couldn't help to smile, too. It was good to be back with those she was familiar with. They didn't play games, and she knew where she stood with them right from the 'get go'.

It was the LAPD.

Although she was going to miss all of the traveling, and the intrigue, and not to mention the first class accommodations she had been privy to while working on the investigation for the Vatican, there was still nothing like being home.

As she turned around after closing the car door, Kurt had rushed up to her and literally swept her up in his arms and landed a big one on the side of her cheek.

"Girl, you've been gone 'too' long!!" he exclaimed as Abbey gave him one of her looks.

As Kurt put her down he stepped back. He still had the biggest smile on his face.

"So, are you back?" he asked hoping that it was for good. "Everyone here at the precinct has had their fill of that little 'prick', Montgomery," said Kurt as he looked around to be sure that none of the big brass had overheard him.

Satisfied that there wasn't anyone else in the parking lot with them, Kurt continued.

"Abbey, if something doesn't change soon, he's going to find himself on the wrong end of a blunt stick. I'm not naming names but, you know what I mean, right?"

She could tell that Kurt was really peeved off about Montgomery.

"Com'on, Kurt. It can't be that bad," said Abbey as she walked across the parking lot with him toward the building. "It's only been a couple of days. You're not trying to tell me that Montgomery has screwed things up that badly in a couple of days, are you?"

"Abbey, all I know is that the team working on your case, has gone to the brass upstairs with complaints about him and how he's been trying to 'exploit' the 'Pennace Killer' case," said Kurt. "He's been try-ing to make it all about him, and has had the media following him around like it's some kind of documentary or somethin', and not a serial murder case," complained Kurt. "But you of all people know how complaining to the boys upstairs turns out, right?" said Kurt as he gave Abbey a look.

Yes, Abbey knew what Kurt was referring to when it came to dealing with the big brass of the Police Department. Especially, when it came to one of their 'golden boys'.

As they walked into the precinct building, Abbey listened intently to Kurt as he went on about how Montgomery had stalled the investigation. And all of the time she was listening, she realized that she didn't feel the weight of the case or what was or was not happening with it on her shoulders. It was as if for some reason, she knew that solving the case was no longer a priority for her.

She didn't know why, but for some reason she knew that the case would find its own resolution. Then suddenly she stopped midstride causing Kurt to give her a questioning look.

"Now how would I know that?" she asked herself as she tried to pinpoint the feeling of how she would know something like that.

"You okay, Abbey?" he asked as he looked at her.

"Yeah, something just crossed my mind, is all," she answered nonchalantly, not sure why she would have that feeling.

Shaking it off, she and Kurt continued to the elevators.

Little did she know that across town, a chain of events concerning the 'Penance Killer' case had already been put in motion and was about to come to fruition.

By the time they got off the elevator and arrived at the double doors of the 'Bull Pen', Abbey had heard everything there was to know about how Montgomery had literally sabotaged the entire case and that no one was happy about it.

Especially, the Lieutenant.

As Abbey and Kurt walked through the 'Bull Pen', they headed straight for the Lieutenant's office without stopping. She looked straight ahead trying to avoid looking in the direction of where her desk was and where she had sat for the last couple of years. She really wasn't in the mood of having some kind of nostalgic reaction. And if Montgomery had been sitting there, she thought she might have more than that.

She was still pissed off even though the feeling had subsided.

"Humm," she mused to herself as she realized that she wasn't as mad as she wanted to be. "I never thought I'd just dismiss Montgomery like that, but I have."

But luckily he wasn't there, and she wasn't going to have to test her new found theory.

As she reached the Lieutenant's office, she wasn't quite sure if he would put her back on the 'Penance Killer's' case or give her another assignment. At the moment she didn't care. All she wanted to do was to get back to work so she could think about something else other than the 'End of days.'

Stepping into his doorway, she just stood there for a minute. He had been looking over paperwork that was spread over his desk, and didn't notice her standing there at first. When he did look up, his face said it all.

"Well looka' here!" he exclaimed as he got up from behind his desk and went to hug Abbey. "They always come back home, don't they?" he said as he wrapped his arms around her and gave a hearty laugh.

"Hello, Lieutenant," said Abbey quietly as she hugged him back, lingering just a little longer than she normally would have. "It's good to see you!" she said.

Stepping back, he just smiled down at her like he was seeing an old friend for the first time after a long absence.

"Well, com'on in here!" said the Lieutenant as he ushered Abbey into the office.

And then just as Kurt went to follow Abbey into his office, the Lieutenant reached over and closed the door on him saying, "Yeah, not a chance, Kurt! Get lost!!" he said as he firmly closed the door in his face and turned to Abbey.

"Well, sit down, Lil Lady," he said as he pulled the chair out for her. "Talk to me! How was it?" he asked anxious to know everything that she could tell him.

And then as if he had to ask something before he forgot, he quickly blurted out, "Before you say anything, kid!" he said. "I gotta ask. This assignment they put you on. Did it have anything to do with what's going on now?" he asked.

Without any hesitation, Abbey just nodded her head.

"Get outta here!! Really!!" exclaimed the Lieutenant a little louder than he had intended to as he quickly returned to his chair on the other side of the desk and sat down.

He was like a kid as he sat in his chair and leaned forward with his arms crossed, waiting for the next words to come out of Abbey's mouth.

And although Abbey would have never divulged information to anyone else concerning an active case she had been working on, this was different.

First of all, she was no longer working on the case, and as far as she knew, the case was over and therefore no longer active. The whole world now knew about the manuscript and what it predicted. There wasn't anything that needed to be kept confidential now.

"And besides," she thought to herself. "The Lieutenant was different. If anyone had the right to know what she had been working on, it was him."

So, she relayed to him, everything that had happened from the time that she had met with the Inspector from the Vatican there at the precinct, up until what had happened in Montreal, Canada the other night.

She told the Lieutenant about where they had traveled to including their trip to the military base in Virginia, and about all of the miracles that had happened and how they corresponded to what was written on a manuscript that was over two thousand years old. She talked about the Prophets and how each of them had disappeared. And then when she relayed to him how they found out that the woman, with whom she had originally met with here at the precinct, was not who she had presented herself to be, the Lieutenant's face literally dropped.

"And to think I thought she was kinda attractive," said the Lieutenant as he shook his head slowly from side to side. "That'll teach me!" he murmured to himself under his breath as he leaned back in his chair.

And all the while Abbey was talking, the Lieutenant felt as if he had been listening to excerpts from a novel that had come right off of the shelves of a bookstore.

And then when she told him about Michael being a 'Holy Warrior' for the Vatican, and that his main purpose was to fight 'L'arginatos' or

'Demons' that had been sent from Hell to stall the Vatican's investigation, the Lieutenant nearly fell out of his chair.

"Abbey! Are you fuckin' telling me that, that there are…..'Demons' running around here?" asked the Lieutenant as he looked around himself quickly, not believing what he was hearing.

"Sorry to say, Lieutenant, but yep!" confirmed the Detective as she sat across from him.

"Holy Mother of God!" he exclaimed out loud as he leaned back in his chair.

As far as he was concerned, this was better than a Sunday night movie with freshly popped, buttered popcorn and a beer by his side. And of course Abbey left out telling him about the vision she had the night before returning to LA, and any details of what had happened between her and Michael. They weren't to be shared.

"What happened between them was going to stay just between the two of them," she thought to herself.

After Abbey had finished detailing everything that had happened from the time that she had left up until her last night in Montreal, Canada, a serious look spread across the Lieutenant's face.

"What's wrong, Lieutenant?" she asked.

"Ah! It's nothin'!" he exclaimed as he waved his hand in the air. "I guess it's just that none of us really knows what's going to happen next, do we? And even if this sixth event doesn't happen, there's one good thing that's come from it," he said. "Everybody's treating each other a whole lot nicer than they were before, that's for sure. Even the foreign countries seem to be getting along better with each other," he said. "And have you seen the lines outside of all of the churches around the city? My God, there's not enough room inside for everyone. They're all trying to get baptized and make amends before, well, you know."

"Yeah, I know, Lieutenant," said Abbey. "I know."

"Nothin' like putting a little scare in everyone, is it?" chuckled her boss as he had a private laugh with himself.

And then he turned serious.

"But Abbey, there's something I have to tell you about the 'Penance Killer's' case," said her boss.

"If you're talking about what's been happening with the case, I already heard about it from Kurt, Lieutenant," said Abbey, thinking she knew what he was going to tell her. "He kind of brought me up to speed on how Montgomery's been jeopardizing everything."

"Well, that was what 'had' happening up until this morning," stated the Lieutenant as he became quiet. "Abbey, I'm going to tell you something that no one other me, and the Brass upstairs knows about. And after I finish, I know that you'll keep everything that's been said here in the strictest of confidence."

"You know I will, Lieutenant," confirmed Abbey as she leaned forward, wondering what it was that the Lieutenant had to tell her that so confidential.

"Abbey, the world has been turned upside down with the revelation of this, this manuscript the Vatican has. And with all of the strange things that have been going on, this morning was no different. On the other side of town, out of the blue, three young girls walked into St Joseph's Hospital and said they were the ones everyone's been looking for. They said they had been kidnapped, tortured and raped."

He could hear Abbey as she gasped. And then when she found her voice she spoke.

"Lieutenant," said Abbey in a voice that was just above a whisper. "Are you telling me that the last three victims of the 'Penance Killer', just walked into a hospital on the other side of town?"

"Yeah, Abbey," he said. "And I won't say that they're alright. Hell, who would be alright after going through what they have. But they're safe now."

"What about their families, Lieutenant?" asked the Detective, eager to know everything. "Have they been notified? Do they know where they're at?"

"It's all been taken care of, Abbey," said her boss trying to reassure her and calm her down. "It's all been taken care of."

"How'd they get away?" asked Abbey as she half way rose out of her seat. "And the kidnapper, what about him?" she asked. "Do we have him in custody? Are the girls able to identify him?"

Abbey was on fire as she had a million and one questions that needed answering.

"Well that's the thing, Abbey," said the Lieutenant quickly. "The girls don't know how they got to the hospital. And they're telling the strangest story about what happened just before they suddenly appeared in the hospital parking lot. And Abbey, it wasn't just one man who we've been looking for," he said.

"What??"

"Apparently the 'Penance Killer' wasn't just one person," said the Lieutenant. "It was a Father and his two Sons who lived on a two acre piece of land in a neighborhood not far from the hospital. That's where they were being held all of this time."

Abbey felt sick to her stomach.

She never could wrap her head around the fact that people could do such things to other people, much less to innocent children. It sickened her to the core to think of what the girls who had been kidnapped went through while being held. And what about the girls who didn't make it? The ones who had been tortured and then slaughtered, and then made to look as if they were the ones who needed to be forgiven.

"Where are they, Lieutenant?" asked Abbey as she looked at her boss intently. "Please tell me they're in custody!"

Abbey could feel the anger rise up to her chest and then threaten to fill her throat as she waited for an answer.

"No, they're not in custody, Abbey," said the Lieutenant simply.

"What??!!" exclaimed Abbey.

"And that's where this whole case gets even stranger," stated the Lieutenant. "Abbey, the girls said that they were being held in some kind of root cellar where it was cold and dark and they said it always had a damp feeling to it. And ahh….."

The Lieutenant paused for a moment, not really wanting to hear himself repeat the details of what had happened to the girls. But he knew she would want to know. After he took a few deep breaths, he continued.

"From their statements, at least three times a day, the men would take turns and come down and drag one of the girls off to another part of the cellar. Even though they couldn't see what was going on, the other girls could hear what was happening to each other."

As the Lieutenant spoke, Abbey could feel the tears as they started to fall uncontrollably from her eyes.

"Apparently, the men would take turns with each of the girls, including the Father. And then right afterwards they would beat and torture them. They would yell obscenities at them, and tell them that they were whores, using their female bodies to make men desire them, thus causing the Father and the two Sons to fall out of grace with God. At least that's what the Father had been teaching his Sons all of their lives. And then he told them that God was angry with them for letting their desires get the best of them. So they had to purge themselves of their carnal desires in order to get back into the good graces of God. And also to make the whores suffer for misleading them."

"Whores?" exclaimed Abbey. "They kidnapped, tortured and raped little girls as an excuse so they could get rid of their sick desires, just so God would forgive them? What kind of insane thinking is that?" exclaimed Abbey as she bowed her head. "Lieutenant, the youngest one was only thirteen. Thirteen! And she wasn't even one of the ones who made it, Lieutenant!"

The Lieutenant just listened as Abbey vented and let it out of her system. He knew that this was something that she had needed for a long time.

After she had calmed down a bit, he spoke again.

"Abbey, they're off of their rockers," he said. "You know it, we all know it. These fanatics are out there all over the place. It's just that sometimes these crazy fanatics take what they believe and try and put it onto the unsuspecting public like these guys did. Sometimes there's nothing any of us can do about it except try and stop the bastards."

"But Lieutenant, that's just it!" exclaimed Abbey as she got up and paced the floor. "We haven't caught them, have we? They're still out there somewhere just waiting to set themselves up in a different place so they can start all over again. It isn't right, Lieutenant," she said. "It isn't right that they should even be allowed to live."

"I agree with you Abbey, I do," said the Lieutenant. "But trust me, this is where the case gets even stranger."

Hearing the frightened sound of her boss's voice, Abbey stopped and turned to look at him.

"What is it, Lieutenant?" she asked.

"Remember when I said that really strange things have happening since that manuscript has been found?" said the Lieutenant. "Well, this is one for the books," he said as he motioned for her to sit back down.

Reluctantly taking her seat, Abbey sat down in her chair across from her boss and waited.

"Abbey, the girls said that this morning as usual, the youngest of the Sons came into the root cellar and went to unchain one of the girls and started to drag her across the dirt floor to this little cubby area on the other side of the stairs," said the Lieutenant quietly. "He seemed to have a favorite of all the girls. Anyway, he unchained her and was dragging her across the floor when the girls said that there was this, this bright, white light that flashed inside of the cellar.

"They didn't know where it came from, all they knew is that it was almost blinding. When it was gone and they looked up, there was this, woman standing there in the middle of the cellar. They said she was dressed in all white and there was this soft light that surrounded her. One of the girls immediately thought they were all dead and were going to heaven. She, she thought that it was an Angel. Well, she was half right," said the Lieutenant as he paused.

"Are you telling me that they saw an Angel, Lieutenant?" asked Abbey as a familiar feeling swept over her. "A woman dressed in white with, ah, with white light surrounding her?"

"That's what their statement said," confirmed the Lieutenant. "And of course the boy called out to his Brother and Father to come down there quick. 'That there was some kind of woman there.' It must've scared the little 'fuck' shitless, because he forgot about the girl, dropped her and headed back up the stairs," said her boss. "And here's where it gets real crazy."

Abbey knew why everything that her boss was telling her sounded so, so familiar.

"Could it be?" she asked herself. "Could it be the same Angel who had posed as Fabianne during the investigation, and the same Angel she had seen in her vision who told her that she shouldn't have any regrets? 'That those who had sinned against the Lord by using his name would get their just punishment.' Could it be?"

Abbey didn't know what to think at this point as she continued to listen.

"When the other two men came down the stairs, they had their guns with them," said the Lieutenant. "The girls said that the Angel told them to cover their eyes, and that they weren't to watch. And when they opened their eyes again, they would be someplace safe. So they did."

"What happened, Lieutenant?" asked Abbey as she sat on the edge of her seat. "What happened then?"

"They did as they were told," stated the Lieutenant. "But not before they heard the Father yell at the woman as he came down the steps. He yelled something like, 'You fuckin' whore! You won't deceive us!' And then he tried to fire his gun, but nothin' happened. Even the other Son tried to fire his gun. Nothin'!" exclaimed the Lieutenant. "And then the girls said that the Angel turned to the men and said that they had used God's name in vain, and had sinned upon the innocent. That their souls were to be given to the 'dammed', and that their punishment and pain would be eternal and everlasting."

"Given to the 'dammed'," repeated Abbey under her breath as she remembered that the 'L'arginatos' or the 'Demons' were the 'dammed'. "Could it be that the Angel was referring to the 'Demons' who were the same as the one that she had faced at the Warren's home, and then she and Michael had faced again in the hotel," she asked herself as she returned her attention back to the Lieutenant.

"Then the girls saw the bright light again. They said they closed their eyes like they were told, and the next thing they knew, they were all standing in the parking lot of St. Joseph's Hospital."

"What?? How is that possible, Lieutenant?" asked Abbey. "And what about the man and his two Sons?" asked Abbey quickly. "What, happened to them? They didn't get away, did they?" lamented Abbey. "Please tell me they didn't!"

"Actually, Abbey, I don't think that they did," stated the Lieutenant. "At just about the same time that the girls miraculously appeared in the hospital parking lot, the Police got numerous calls from the same neighborhood where the man and his two Sons lived," stated the Lieutenant. "It seems that the neighbors heard the screams of the man and his two Sons as they came from inside of the garage that was behind the house. And they didn't hear just screams, Abbey," said the Lieutenant as he watched her intently. "The neighbors said they were more like shrieks and howling of the likes they had never heard before. It almost sounded like, like dogs screaming and yelping as if they were in the most excruciating pain.

"People had gathered on the property line, but no one would dare get any closer to the garage. They said that there was this bright light coming from inside of the garage that was almost blinding. They could see the light as it flooded out from in between the planks of the walls and from around the doors and windows. And some even said that they could see the garage walls shake as the men inside kept screaming for mercy!"

"Oh, my god!" exclaimed Abbey as she thought back to when she and Michael were rushing to Fabianne's room in the hotel after she had been warned about the 'Demon'.

They heard same kind of shrieking coming from inside and had seen the same kind of bright light that the Lieutenant was describing as it came from underneath the door of Fabianne's hotel room.

"By the time that the Police and the Fire Department got there, the light had disappeared. When they searched the property including the garage, they found all kinds of evidence that this man and his two Sons were in fact the 'Penance Killers'," said the Lieutenant. "They found articles of clothing that belonged to the girls, some of their school books, blood samples. They even found the chains and shackles they had used to secure the girls in the root cellar underneath the garage floor. And pictures, Abbey. They found pictures of what they did to those girls while they were being held captive."

The Lieutenant fell silent as he tried to compose himself. For sure this was one of the most disturbing cases he had ever had to deal with in his entire career.

"And the man and his two Sons. What happened to them?" asked Abbey wanting to have some kind of closure.

"That's just it!" exclaimed the Lieutenant as he looked up. "There was no sign of them anywhere even though the entire neighborhood heard them inside of the garage only moments before, whaling and screaming for mercy. They did find the two guns and something that looked like, ashes, but that was all."

"You're not going to close the case are you, Lieutenant?" asked Abbey after a few moments.

She knew that even with the remaining girls being found safe, and with no rational explanation for the disappearance of the men who were obviously responsible for the kidnappings and murders of the other girls, they had to be sure the men were gone.

They had to be sure.

"Abbey, the Brass upstairs want this case to go away," he said. "They're going to keep the file open for now, but, I don't know what else they can do. They're saying that it looks like with all of the statements from the neighbors and the ashes that they found, they may have incinerated themselves to keep from being caught. I know it sounds crazy and all, but considering what's been happening lately, it's possible,"

Abbey started to object when in the back of her mind, she heard a voice speak softly to her. At first she thought that she was imagining things until it kept prodding at her.

"L'Abbaye," it said. "Let it go. It is done. God's will is done."

Seeing the look that had spread across her face, the Lieutenant leaned forward and asked Abbey if she was alright.

"Hey! Everything okay?" he asked. "You looked kinda zoned out there for a minute," he said.

Bowing her head for a moment, Abbey took a deep breath and then looked back up and smiled.

"You know, Lieutenant, I think you're right," she said. "I think the 'Penance Killers' have been dealt with."

"So do I, Abbey," agreed the Lieutenant quietly. "Don't tell anyone that I said it, but I think that the big guy upstairs took care of this one himself."

"So do I, Lieutenant. I think it's over," she said as she nodded and gave him a smile, now knowing that the 'Penance Killers' had gotten their just due.

Abbey knew in heart and soul that the Lieutenant was in fact right. She just smiled. She knew that God had indeed dealt with them in his own way.

"Yeah, it's over, kiddo. You done good," said the Lieutenant. "You can let it go now, Abbey. You can move on."

The Lieutenant knew that she had put her heart and soul into this case, and that she was committed to bring as many of the victims home as she could. And he knew that her heart broke for every one of the girls she couldn't bring home safe and sound. But now she could let it all go.

After a few moments had passed, the Lieutenant changed the subject altogether as he reached over and pulled out a white envelope and handed it to her.

"Hey, this was left for you earlier this morning," he said as he watched her intently.

"For me?" she asked as she took it. "Who is it from?"

"Ah, I don't know who he was. He said he was one of the Inspectors that worked with you on the case for the Vatican," stated the Lieutenant. "He said his name was Inspector Givant, or something like that."

"Where is he?" exclaimed Abbey as she almost jumped out of her chair and swung herself around to see if she could lay eyes on whomever it was that had left the envelope. "When did he leave it? Lieutenant, what did he say when he left it?"

"Maybe you'd better read it, Abbey," said the Lieutenant seeing how anxious she got when he had mentioned who had left it. "The guy said to just give it to you and you'd know what it meant."

And then he asked another question that was from left field.

"Abigail, who is this fella that's got you so riled up?" he asked in a Fatherly tone. "It seems like he's someone who's kinda special to you."

Hearing the way that the Lieutenant asked the question and used her given name, Abbey immediately looked at her boss. He had hit the nail on the head and there was not denying it.

"Is it that obvious?" she said somewhat embarrassed as she sat back down.

"Hey, it's been a long time since I've seen you react to anyone like that, kid. I think it's great!" he exclaimed. "Is he a good guy?" he asked.

"Yeah, Lieutenant, he is. He's a really great guy."

"Then that's all that matters," he said. "Now, why don't you open the envelope that he left for you. If I'm not mistaken, you have a decision to make."

Curious as to what he meant, Abbey held the envelope up in one hand. It wasn't the normal type of white envelope that you would usually see. It seemed 'Official'. The paper was thicker than most envelopes were, and it had a very smooth, rich texture to it. And in the upper left hand corner, there was a reddish orange emblem stamped on it. And as she read what it said, she gasped as she looked back at her boss.

"It's from the Vatican!" she said in a surprised tone. "I guess it's a 'Thank You' letter from them for helping out with the investigation," she said as she gave a half smile.

But for some reason, as she opened the envelope, she became nervous about what was inside. She didn't know why she would have anything to be nervous about.

"Or did she?"

As the thought crossed her mind, she hesitated for a moment before sliding the single piece of paper out and holding it in her hand.

"What if it was a letter about what had happened between her and Michael while they were investigating the case for the Vatican? What if the Vatican frowned on any kind of fraternizations between Inspectors while on a case? But then, how would they have known?"

As the questions kept popping into her head she was beginning to get a headache.

"Well, aren't you gonna read it" exclaimed the Lieutenant as he was anxious for her to open it up and read it.

Seeing that he was as excited as she was, Abbey unfolded the rich, textured sheet of paper and saw that it had the same emblem stamped across the top of the page as was stamped on the envelope. As she silently read the letter, after a few minutes had passed, she just looked up with a stunned look on her face.

"Well, kid!" exclaimed the Lieutenant. "What are you going to do?"

"Wait a minute! You knew about this, Lieutenant?" she asked. "But how…..?"

"Ahh, the Inspector was kind enough to let me in on why he was here. And besides," he said. "I am still your boss, right? At least I am until you decide whether or not you're going to take the job offer that they're giving you."

Abbey was beside herself with excitement.

She didn't understand why the Vatican would extend her an offer to become an Inspector. She had only worked on the case for four days. That was it! And then after she thought about it for a few moments, she realized that Michael must have had something to do with this.

"Why else would he deliver it himself?" she thought to herself.

But she didn't care!

At that moment, she was so excited she didn't know what to do.

She had gotten an offer to work with the Vatican in Rome as one of its Inspectors. Nothing could top that except the fact that she might even get the chance to work with Michael.

"You never know!" she exclaimed to herself as she realized she was just about to jump out of her skin.

But it didn't matter. The offer was something that she would have never expected in a million years.

"Well, Abbey!" exclaimed the Lieutenant again as he smiled at her. "Are you gonna except the offer or not?"

"What do you think?" answered Abbey back as she jumped up and reached across the desk and gave her boss a hug.

She knew that she would miss the precinct and all of the guys, but this was an opportunity that came along once in a lifetime. If she didn't take it, she'd regret it for the rest of her life. And she wasn't about to have that regret on her shoulders.

And before she could let go of the Lieutenant, there was a knock on the door.

"Well, speak of the devil," said the Lieutenant as he waved Michael in. "Com'on in, Inspector," he said. "I believe the two of you know each other," he said.

As Michael walked through the door, the Lieutenant couldn't help seeing why Abbey was attracted to him. He was tall, good build, and dammed good looking!

"And hell, that smile would bring any woman, and probably a few men to their knees!" he mused to himself as he observed the chemistry that seemed to exist between the two of them.

"Good morning, Lieutenant. It's good to see you again," said Michael as he extended his hand.

"Same here, Inspector. Same here," acknowledged Abbey's boss.

And then when the Lieutenant turned toward Abbey, she could see the sadness that had filled his eyes.

"Well kiddo! I guess this is good-bye again," he said solemnly. "But somehow I think that this time, it might be for good."

"No way Lieutenant, you're not going to get rid of me that easily," said Abbey as she hugged him again. "As long as I know where you are, I'll always be in touch with you. You can count on that," she said. "You're family."

"Good to know, kiddo," said the Lieutenant as he stepped back.

And then he looked directly at Michael.

"And as I'm sure you know, Inspector," said the Lieutenant as his voice got serious. "This lil' Lady here means the world to me. And I'm betting your pretty 'man balls' that you'll remember that and take good care of her, right?"

Stunned but not surprised by the directness of Abbey's boss, Michael nodded his head.

Michael could tell that Abbey's boss was sincere about her welfare and that she meant a great deal to him, and that the feeling between them was mutual.

"I.....totally will remember that, Sir!" answered Michael respectively as he glanced at Abbey and then back at her boss.

"Good! Then if you two will excuse me," said the Lieutenant as he walked to the door of his office. "I've got to go and make a statement to the rest of the department and then to the press about the 'Penance Killer' case. Bye, Abbey. You take care of yourself, you hear?"

"I will Lieutenant," said Abbey as she watched him quickly turn and leave the office before he got all emotional on them.

As they watched him strode to the middle of the 'Bull Pen', he called all of the officers together so he could make an announcement about the 'Penance Killer' case and what was going to be said to the Press.

Turning to Michael, Abbey just grinned as she looked up at him. She couldn't help herself.

She hadn't seen him since that night in the hospital parking lot in Montreal, Canada when he was being whisked away to the airport. Supposedly they were taking him back to Rome, but in fact he ended up in Washington D.C. It was just good to see that he was okay, and that whatever it was that he had said to the Inquiry board for the Vatican in Washington, everything had turned out to be alright.

"Well, Inspector," said Michael as he looked back at her feeling a little turned on just being close to her again. "Shall we?" he said politely as he showed her the way to the door. "You know that I flew all night to get here, right?" he said. "The car is waiting for us downstairs," he said. "We can stop by your place so you can pick up a few things, and then we have to fly to Rome."

"Rome?" asked Abbey, stunned as she walked next to him.

"You're the newest Inspector the Vatican has indoctrinated into a very elite and clandestine organization," said Michael. "The Eminence wants to meet with you personally, and then you'll begin your training."

"Training??!!" exclaimed Abbey as she came to a dead stop. "What training, Michael?" she asked as she had to catch up with him as he walked out of the office and into the hall outside of the 'Bull Pen'. "I didn't know there was going to be any kind of training. And what exactly did you say to them that caused them to offer me a position as an Inspector?" she asked.

"I told them the truth, Abbey," he said. "I told them the truth about everything that happened including how well you worked the case and how it was you who discovered what the numbers on the side of the manuscript meant. I gotta tell you, they were amazed with that. You deciphered in a few days what all of the scholars at the Vatican haven't been able to do for centuries. Very impressive!" he said. "With all of that, and my recommendation, they wanted me to make you the offer."

And then as an afterthought he said, "And yes, there will be training, Inspector," said Michael as he walked to the elevator and pushed the button. "And I'm going to be your teacher," he said with a slight smile.

"You!!" exclaimed Abbey as she just stared at him.

She wasn't sure if she could handle him teaching her, considering the kind of intimate relationship that they had. She wasn't sure if she would be able to concentrate on any kind of training with him that close all of the time.

"And I can assure you," stated Michael as the elevator doors opened and he stepped inside. I'm going to keep my promise to the Lieutenant."

"Your promise?" asked Abbey as she followed him inside of the elevator. She was confused as to what promise it was that he had made to the Lieutenant

"Yeah, Abbey," said Michael as a mischievous smile spread across his face. "You know the one where I'm going to make sure that my 'man balls' take very good care of you," he said as he looked at her. "You definitely don't have to worry about that," he said as he reached over and pressed the button for the ground floor, still smiling.

"Ah, Michael, that is not what he meant," clarified Abbey as she gave him a side glance.

"No, but that's what I mean," he said as he continued to watch her and was amused at how he had made her squirm most uncomfortably on the ride down.

He had succeeded in pushing the right button to turn her on, and that pleased him to no end.

But Abbey wasn't going to let him get away with having the last word, so she came back at him.

"And to think they let you into the Priesthood with a mouth like that, Michael," exclaimed Abbey trying to get keep up with him as she subdued a smile. "If they only knew."

"Abbey, if they knew where my mouth was thinking of going at this moment, they'd probably kick me out," he said. "And I can guarantee you, my mouth did this long before I went into the Priesthood. And I'm very good at it, as you well know," he said with an even bigger smile on his face.

That was it!

Abbey wasn't going to respond to any more of his remarks. When she did, not only did it encourage him, but it also got her aroused, and he knew it.

So the rest of the ride down in the elevator was quiet as they cast quick glances at each other and nothing more.

As s they exited the elevator and made their way out of the building and down the steps to the waiting Towne car, Abbey had to turn around one more time and pause for a minute. She had to take one more look at the place where she had worked for so long and where all of her friends were, and silently prayed that she was making the right decision.

It wasn't a decision that she had made lightly, and it wasn't just because of Michael. Although having him as part of the package was a bonus in itself.

Then she heard Michael speak to her from where he was standing by the car.

"Abbey," he said to her. "I promise you that you are about to embark on something that will be life changing and more rewarding than any-thing you've ever done before," he said as he stepped up next to her. "And if you ever are unsure about anything, you need to know that I'll always be there for you, no matter what," he said.

"Thanks, Michael. I really needed to hear that right about now," said Abbey as she took a deep breath and then turned around and followed him to the car.

After they both got into the car, Abbey gave the driver the address to her apartment. And then as the car pulled away from the curb, she fell quiet. As she sat next to Michael, she began to fidget as she tried to find a way to tell him something that had been bothering her ever since her last night in Montreal when she had her vision. There was something from her vision that had been bothering her, and she truly didn't know how to tell anyone about it.

Actually, she was afraid to even think about it because she knew what it meant.

And although Michael could sense that there was something bother-ing Abbey, he didn't want to intrude on her private thoughts. He knew that she had just made a major life decision and that she probably had a lot of things that were going through her mind right now. So he was going to give her whatever time she needed to sort everything out.

But Abbey knew that she had to talk to someone about the part of her vision that she hadn't shared with anyone until now. She knew she had to talk to someone.

So she turned to Michael.

"Michael, I have to ask you something," she said. "What happens now that all of the miracles have been confirmed?" she asked quietly. "What will the Vatican and the other church leaders do now?"

"Well, I guess we just have to go on as usual with the time that we have left," he said. "You know, after everything that's happened, I think that God wants us to put what his Son said about returning, back in the forefront of our lives. We've become quite complacent," he said sadly. "And at this point, no one really knows 'when' it will come to pass. Who knows," he said. "I'm not sure that I actually want to think about it," he admitted. "We'll just have to wait until the sixth event actually happens."

Abbey swallowed hard and tried to choose her words carefully before she spoke.

"Actually Michael, we won't have to wait long," she said softly as a chill swept down her spine as she finally heard herself mouth the words that had been haunting her ever since she had left Montreal.

As Michael listened, when it finally dawned on him what she was saying, he sat up and turned toward her with the strangest look on his face.

"I'm sorry, Abbey. What did you just say?" he asked.

"I, I said, we won't have to wait long," she said as she repeated herself.

As Michael heard Abbey repeat what she had said, he could have sworn that he had just had an aneurism. Inside of his head, it felt as if a mini explosion had gone off and now he was just waiting for the end to come. But when it didn't come, he found himself blinking several times trying to comprehend what he had just heard.

"Abbey, what are you saying?" he forced himself to ask.

"Michael," said Abbey under her breath. "Remember when I told you that in my vision when I was standing on the hillside looking up, and the Son of God was passing overhead with his Angels. And how you came to stand next to me and took my hand?"

"I remember," said Michael slowly as he kept watching her.

He couldn't take his eyes off of her. He needed to hear what she was about to say.

"Before I woke up, the Son of God smiled at me and said, 'Well done!'," she said. "And then I heard his Angel speak to me again."

Abbey paused for a minute as she felt tears well in her eyes.

"Michael, she said that there was still work that you and I had to do. And that we had until the next Holy Day before my vision.....came to pass."

"The next Holy Day?" exclaimed Michael softly under his breath as he put his brain to work.

And then it hit him.

"Abbey, are you referring to Easter?" he asked. "Are you saying that the Angel told you that Easter would be when the Son of God was going to return? Is that what you're saying?"

All Abbey could do was to look at him and just nod her head slowly.

And from his calculations, that meant that the sixth event would happen in less than a year since it was already the middle of May.

Michael closed his eyes tightly and bowed his head as he said a silent prayer.

"Why not?" exclaimed Michael under his breath as he just shook his head. "Why not return on the same day that he rose from the dead," said Michael to himself. "It would only be appropriate."

"Michael," said Abbey as she reached out for him. "What do we do now?"

"We do as we have been told," he said as he held her hand in his. "We do what our God has instructed us to do, Abbey."

As she started to tremble, she leaned against Michael and whispered to him.

"I think I'm afraid," she said. "I think I'm afraid for all of those who don't find their way back in time."

"Abbey, God can only pull our coattails to pay attention to his word so many times," he said. "When what he prophesied keeps falling on deaf ears, eventually the time to acknowledge his word will run out. After that, everyone will have to be accountable for themselves."

After a few moments had passed, Michael spoke again.

"You know we'll have to inform the Vatican."

"I know, Michael," whispered Abbey as she sat up and looked mindlessly out of the side window. "I know."

She only hoped that she was going to be able to carry on knowing what she did. But having Michaell beside her was more than a comfort for her. He was also her strength.

As the Towne car made its way through the mid-afternoon traffic, it had stopped at a red signal light as pedestrians crowded into the crosswalk, rushing to wherever it was that they needed to be. Abbey had just looked up when she thought that she recognized someone in the crowd.

"Oh my…..!" she gasped to herself as she sat up. "It can't be!"

And at the same time, Michael had looked over and saw the same thing.

There amid the people crossing the street was a familiar face that they both had recognized. It was the woman they both had come to know as Fabianne as she made her way to the other side of the street with the other pedestrians. She was still wearing her signature trench coat and her Azure Blue eyes were unmistakable as she stopped briefly and looked directly at the two of them as they stared back.

And then from the deep recesses of their minds, they heard the voice of one of God's Angels as she spoke to them.

"L'Abbaye. Michael. Blessed are those who believe. For you are a child of God, and he loves you. Have no fear. He will walk with you until the end."

No sooner had they hear the voice of the Angel, did she disappear within the crowd and was gone.

And immediately, any doubt or fear either of them had about what was going to come to pass had been lifted. All that was left was a feeling of peace within them. And they both knew that whatever was needed of them during the coming days, they would willing go forth and do what was needed to help Man prepare for the return of the Son of God.

Epilogue

The dark clouds that had stretched from one side of the horizon to the other had cleared, leaving behind nothing but Blue skies. And the loud thunder and roar that had accompanied the rolling cloud bank moments earlier had ceased.

It was the Holy Day, and true to his word, the Son of God had returned.

And from around the world, all those who had not risen up during the Rapture came forth, until there were multitudes upon multitudes of people as they gathered on the hill before the King.

All Races, all cultures. All that was left of Mankind came forth.

It was time.

One by one they were called forth before the King and were judged for their deeds. It was the time of judgment for all Men to determine if they were Goats or Sheep.

As Abbey stood among the multitudes of people on the hill, she felt a heaviness in her heart.

"Had she done enough to be granted favor by her King to enter into his kingdom?" she thought to herself. "Was 'she' in fact worthy?"

As the crowd around her moved forward, Abbey found that she was rooted to the spot where she was standing, unable to even look upon the King.

As she felt the emotion rise up within her, she fell to her knees and wept uncontrollably.

"Oh Father, I have tried! Truly I have!" she lamented to herself. "Forgive me if I have fallen short of your will and have not met your

265

expectations of me! I wanted to do good in your name, but I fear I have not."

As she continued to kneel on the ground, she found that she couldn't stop weeping as her body heaved with emotion.

And then from the deep recesses of her mind and from the depths of her heart, she heard a voice speak to her. It was a tender voice that seemed to caress her fears and then dispel them.

"Child. Do you not know that I see all that is in your heart? Do you not know that I have seen all that you have done, and all that you have not. It is your imperfections that make you who you are. That is how I created you. And to see you attempt to rise above those imperfections in my name, only strengthens my love for you. Even in those times that you failed, you continued to strive to do better. And for that, you are loved."

As Abbey listened to the voice, it was then that she realized that 'He' was speaking to her, speaking directly to her heart and soul as if she were the only one before him. That in this time of judgment, with the multitudes of people that were on the hill with her, 'He' had heard her cries of fear and had answered her.

He had answered her.

And then the voice spoke to her again.

"Child. I have watched over you before your time of conception," He said. "Do not fear to look upon my face."

Slowly lifting her head and bringing he eyes up, Abbey froze as she saw the hem of a white robe coming towards her as the multitudes of people surrounding her had all stepped aside. And there, standing in before her was the Son of God in all of his glory and grace.

And as Abbey looked upon his face, He smiled, and she trembled as tears fell from her eyes. But she was not afraid, for his was the face of the love she had known all of her life, in her heart, her mind and her body and soul.

He was her Savior.

"Come, my Child," He said as He extended his hand to her. "It is time."

Taking his hand, Abbey slowly got to her feet and stood next to him, but found it was still hard to look upon him. And then the joyfulness of just being in his presence was too much for Abbey to bear, as she stepped forward and wrapped her arms about her King and wept upon his chest.

"How I love thee, Father!" she exclaimed softly. "How I love thee so much!"

"And I love thee, my Child!" He exclaimed as He hugged her back. "I always have."

Then realizing what she had done, Abbey quickly stepped back and apologized for her overzealous show of emotion. But it was not necessary as the King just smiled and continued to walk with her. As they passed by the others awaiting their turn, they approached the throne 'He' had been sitting upon only moments before.

And then raising his left arm, 'He' directed her to the side of the throne where the ones who had been deemed as Sheep were waiting. Looking into his eyes she felt a calming peace flow over her as 'He' spoke to her again.

"Well done, my Child!" 'He' said. "Well done!"

Abbey couldn't stop crying as she bowed her head and walked forward into the waiting arms that extended out to her. And then her heart leapt with joy as she saw Michael among those who were waiting. As Abbey ran and embraced him, her joy overflowed as she looked into the crowd and saw the faces of the five Prophets as they also stood next to the King's throne. And beside them was the Lieutenant as he stood with the five victims of the 'Penance Killers'. Abbey was so overwhelmed that she couldn't help to weep as they, along with the other Sheep who were standing on the right hand side of the throne of the King, were then engulfed in the warm light that was his everlasting love where they would dwell forever.

Matthew 25:31-46

And it will be the final judgment of all Nations to stand before Christ and be judged as Sheep or Goats.

Made in the USA
Middletown, DE
18 September 2024

60610759R00156